PRAISE FOR THE JANE YELLOWROCK NOVELS

Blood Trade

"Faith Hunter's Jane Yellowrock series is a high-octane urban fantasy that follows its own rules and keeps you guessing until the very end. Heavily character driven, each one is able to hold a story in their own right . . . a well-plotted story line."
—Smexy Books Romance Reviews

"The action is wild and woolly, with aerial and underground operations, and you will learn more about weapons and ammunition than you've ever had reason to know. . . . Not only is there a lot of carnage, but the inner turmoil is raised to a high level. Hunter knows how to twist readers in every direction but loose and still leave them thinking of it as therapeutic massage."
—Kings River Life Magazine

"Jane to the rescue again. She truly is top-notch, kick butt!! Book six in the Jane Yellowrock series does not disappoint."
—Urban Fant_____ ___igations

"*Blood Trade* is a ____ ___ _____ _ystery with a complex an_ ___ _____

"[*Blood Trade*] mo_ ___ _____ _ ___ _apons play, which results __ _____ _____ This urban fantasy has j____ _____ ___ _____guing and enough weapons and _____ ___ _____ action fans. Gun-loving guys, if you thought urban fantasy wasn't for you, then you haven't met Jane Yellowrock."
—Bull Spec

Death's Rival

"Fans of Jane Yellowrock are in for a true treat with *Death's Rival*. . . . Hunter has done it again, delivering a thrilling combination of mystery and romance that will delight her fans."
—SF Site

"A thrilling mystery with epic action scenes and a kick-ass heroine with claws and fangs."
—All Things Urban Fantasy

"Holy moly, this was an amazing read! Jane is the best urban fantasy heroine around. *Death's Rival* catapulted this series to the top of my must-buy list."
—Night Owl Reviews

"A wild, danger-filled adventure. The world building includes a perfect blend of seductive romance, nail-biting action, intriguing characters, and betrayal from all sides."
—RT Book Reviews

continued . . .

Raven Cursed

"Faith Hunter has outdone herself in *Raven Cursed* . . . rife with snarky dialogue, vivid descriptions, and enough hairpin turns to keep a fantastic driver busy. . . . A lot of series seek to emulate Hunter's work, but few come close to capturing the essence of urban fantasy: the perfect blend of intriguing heroine, suspense, [and] fantasy with just enough romance."   —SF Site

"Hunter doesn't disappoint. . . . I say you can't get enough of one of my favorite kick-ass heroines, so if you are new to the series, give yourself the gift of books one through three. You won't regret it."   —Fresh Fiction

"A super thriller. . . . Fast-paced, *Raven Cursed* is an exhilarating paranormal whodunit with several thriller spins."
                                               —Genre Go Round Reviews

Mercy Blade

"Fans of Faith Hunter's Jane Yellowrock novels will gobble down *Mercy Blade* . . . which has all the complexity, twists, and surprises readers have come to expect . . . a thrill ride from start to finish. . . . Hunter has an amazing talent for capturing mood."   —SF Site

"There was something about the Jane Yellowrock series that drew me in from the very beginning. . . . *Mercy Blade* is top-notch, a five-star book!"   —Night Owl Reviews

"I was delighted to have the opportunity to read another Jane Yellowrock adventure. I was not disappointed, but was somewhat overwhelmed by the obvious growth in Faith Hunter's writing skill."   —*San Francisco Book Review*

"A thrilling novel. . . . Fans of suspenseful tales filled with vampires, weres, and more will enjoy this book. Jane is a strong heroine who knows how to take charge of a situation and kick butt if necessary."   —Romance Reviews Today

"Faith Hunter has created one of my favorite characters, ever. Jane Yellowrock is full of contradictions . . . highly recommended."   —Fresh Fiction

Blood Cross

"Readers eager for the next book in Patricia Briggs's Mercy Thompson series may want to give Faith Hunter a try."
                                               —*Library Journal*

"In a genre flooded with strong, sexy females, Jane Yellowrock is unique. . . . Her bold first-person narrative shows that she's one tough cookie, but with a likable vulnerability . . . a pulse-pounding, page-turning adventure."   —*RT Book Reviews*

Also by Faith Hunter

The Jane Yellowrock Novels

Skinwalker
Blood Cross
Mercy Blade
Cat Tales (a short-story compilation)
Raven Cursed
Have Stakes Will Travel (a short-story compilation)
Death's Rival
Blood Trade
Jane Yellowrock World Companion

The Rogue Mage Novels

Bloodring
Seraphs
Host

BLACK ARTS

A Jane Yellowrock Novel

Faith Hunter

A ROC BOOK

ROC
Published by the Penguin Group
Penguin Group (USA) LLC, 375 Hudson Street,
New York, New York 10014

USA | Canada | UK | Ireland | Australia | New Zealand | India | South Africa | China
penguin.com
A Penguin Random House Company

First published by Roc, an imprint of New American Library,
a division of Penguin Group (USA) LLC

First Printing, January 2014

 REGISTERED TRADEMARK — MARCA REGISTRADA

ISBN 978-0-451-46524-5

Printed in the United States of America
10 9 8 7 6 5 4 3 2 1

*To the Hubby for the newly remodeled writing room,
kitchen, floors, windows, and the generous loving spirit
(while I wailed about how long it took . . .).
You truly are my Renaissance Man.*

ACKNOWLEDGMENTS

I want to thank:

Mud for poisons and continuity.

The Beast Claws for being such a fantastic street team. GO, CLAWS!

Lee Williams Watts for being the Claws' primo, and for offering constant encouragement, assistance, and friendship.

A certain gentleman for the name of one of the Bad Guys, Jack Shoffru, and the lizard's name, LongFellow. Excellent names, by the way!

Misty Massey for bits and pieces of pirates. Errr . . . pirate info. Not pirates themselves. That would be very messy.

My new PR team, Mindy and Audrey at Let's Talk! Promotions.

Most importantly—my editors, Jessica Wade and Jesse Feldman.

CHAPTER 1

Insanity's Not the Point

The crash shook the house, sounding as though the front wall had exploded. I whirled as my front door blew in, icy wind gusting with hurricane force. My ears popped. The bed skirt blew flat beneath the bed. My Beast rammed into me, the light going sharp and the colors bleaching into greens. Beast-fast, I grabbed two nine-mils from the bed, off-safetied, and chambered rounds into both. Raced into the foyer.

The door was open, the knob stuck into the wallboard, the hinges bent. The glass of its small window was busted all over the floor. Again.

Gale-force winds rushed through the open door. No one stood there. Icy air whirled through the house with a scream. I heard windows breaking in back. My ears popped again. A table in the living room tumbled over. Daylight patterned the wood floor off the foyer and reflected off broken glass shoved by the wind into the corner. *Not vamps*, I thought. But I'd been a target for blood-servants and scions for months. This wasn't the first such attack, but it was the first that had gotten this far. And then the frigid cold tingled up my arms, blue and golden, flecked with darker sparks of frozen force. It smelled like the air over a glacier, fresh and full of suspended, preserved power. It circled over me, tried to latch onto my skin.

My Beast rose and batted the spell away. *Magic*, she thought. *Air magic. Angry, like storms rising on the horizon. Witches.*

I advanced the few steps from my room to the front door, the frigid squall pushing against me. In my peripheral vision, I saw Eli at the top of the stairs, his hunting rifle in one hand, a blade in the other, a small subgun on a sling over his back. The former Ranger was wearing boxers, his dark skin slick with shower water.

There was no music in the attack, no wind instrument, no whistling, no singing, none of the usual methods air witches used when they attacked. And the wind seemed random, blustery, not the tornado of might from a focused attack. More like wild magic, the kind teenaged witches might toss when their power first fell on them, out of control and turbulent. I danced into the doorway and back, getting a glimpse out. Despair pelted over me, sharp and burning as sleet, as I identified him. Sorcerer Evan Trueblood, my best friend Molly's husband, was standing in the street, attacking my home.

Eli raced halfway down the stairs, his bare feet placed with rooted precision, his wet skin pebbled from the cold.

"No guns," I shouted to Eli.

"Are you insane?" he shouted back.

"Probably, but insanity's not the point. It's Evan."

Understanding dawned in the set of his shoulders and Eli raced back up the stairs. I turned my full attention to the open door. "Whaddaya want, Evan?" I shouted.

The wind receded marginally.

"I don't want to fight you," I called out. "I know I'd lose." *Maybe. Possibly.* Okay, not likely, not with Eli and Beast on my side, but why stir a frozen pot? My big-cat huffed with agreement. "Talk to me, Evan! Please!"

"Tell Molly to come out and I'll leave your house standing."

My eyes went wide. I hadn't seen Evan's wife, Molly, in months, not since I killed her sister. Instantly *I felt my hand on the knife as the blade slid into Evangelina. Hot blood gushed over me.* I blinked away the unexpected tears that the cold wind stimulated and the memory evoked. I had killed her. I'd had no choice.

The police in Asheville had cleared me. There had been a hearing two weeks ago, attended by me, my lawyer, Adelaide Mooney, two local vamps, the PsyLED hand of the law, Rick LaFleur, and lots of press.

Molly hadn't come to my hearing. None of her sisters had come. I'd kept glancing to the back of the courtroom, hoping. But they hadn't come. I had only seen two of the Everhart witches while I was in Asheville, and that was because of vamp business, not friendship. Molly's friendship had died. And why not? I didn't deserve to have a relationship with her.

Despite, or maybe because of, the media coverage of Evangelina's dying, I'd been cleared of any wrongdoing in the same way anyone would have been cleared, anyone who had stopped an armed killer from talking more lives. But the feeling that I'd managed to hide from in the months since I killed Evangelina had roared up like hot flame and taken me over. I couldn't get rid of the feel of her blood, hot and sticky on my hand. Even now, I wiped the back of my hand on my jeans, feeling the cooling blood, long gone, but as real to my flesh and nerves as if it still coated my hand.

I had survived the distance from New Orleans and my accidental binding by Leo Pellissier, Master of the City of New Orleans, but only by hours. I'd flown back on Leo's private jet, the fastest transport available to me. And retched the entire way home, sick as a dog because of my Beast's inadvertent binding to the MOC, one that put a deadline on how long I could be apart from him, and also how far away from him I could go, even for short time periods. Getting my legal problems settled had made me deathly sick, but maybe the nausea was only partly from the binding. Maybe the rest of the sickness had been because Molly hadn't been there. Hadn't returned my fifteen million phone calls to her cell.

"Send her out!" Evan shouted, and a burst of wind hit the house. It creaked under the pressure. Evan wasn't attacking my house on purpose. He was losing control. He was so furious that his magic was operating on its own, ripping free.

"Molly . . ." I stopped as my voice cracked. I took a slow breath, bent, and set the nine-millimeter semiautomatics on the floor in the open doorway where he could see them. The rushing air nearly froze the skin on my hands. I stood and crossed my arms, putting my hands under my armpits to warm them. "Molly's not here. I haven't seen her," I shouted to him. "Why would you think she'd come to see me? If

Molly ever really forgave me, she would have called. Answered my calls. Texted me. *Something.*" I laughed shakily. "She didn't." My voice dropped. "Though why that would surprise me, I have no idea. I haven't been able to forgive myself."

Moments later, the wind slowed to a trickle. Something in my bedroom overbalanced at the change in pressure and shattered to the floor. I glanced back to see the bed skirt dropping down and a lamp on the floor. I shivered in the cold. Over my head on the landing upstairs, I heard a faint click. Eli readying a gun. I looked up and saw the barrel of the rifle angled down from the floor. Eli was lying prone, aiming into the doorway. "Put it away, Eli." When he didn't move, I stepped into the doorway, standing so he'd have to shoot me first, before any attackers. He cursed softly behind me.

I stood in the doorway, the sun's glare hiding Evan from me, except for a silhouette. A huge bear of a silhouette, six-six and more. Squinting, I made out his red hair and beard, fire-bright, his flannel plaid shirt and jeans. Boots laced up.

I put up a hand to shield my eyes from the sun and studied him. His face was drawn and pale, nose red as if from crying. Dark circles puffed beneath his eyes. He stood less than fifteen feet from the freebie house I lived in. Molly's minivan was behind him, sunlight bouncing off the chrome. Evan's rattletrap red truck hadn't made the trip; it had barely made the previous trip to the Deep South, even with an air sorcerer tinkering with it. Which meant that if Molly was traveling, it was by air or rental car. Or maybe bus. Train. Anyway, easy to track, no matter how she'd traveled. My investigational brain kicking in when the emotional one was in turmoil. I tried for something lighter than his unintentional attack on my house. "You coulda called, you know. I'd have told you she wasn't here, saved you a trip."

Big Evan looked bewildered. "Why would you tell me the truth? Where is she?" he whispered. Louder, he said, "Her sisters agreed that she wanted to put things to rights with you. She'd been talking to all of us about you." His body wavered, and he put a hand to the minivan to steady himself. I figured he was drained by the magic, or maybe drained by trying to control his magic, and wondered if my house would still be standing had he really been trying to destroy it. He said, "She forgave you a long time ago. I told you that she forgave you." He raised his head and met my eyes, his cloudy with worry, his leaning, propped body looking unutterably weary. "She even went to your trial, in disguise, so the press wouldn't give her trouble. With the numbers of people, you never caught her scent, did you?"

I opened my mouth, but no words came. I couldn't help the rush of joy that flooded through me. Molly had come? Did that mean she had really, truly forgiven me?

"I've looked everywhere. Her mother hasn't seen her. There's . . . no other place she could have gone. No other place. She just vanished."

And then I realized Molly was *missing*. And the cold from Evan's magic stabbed into my heart. *Where was Molly?*

The van's back door, on the far side, opened, and I tensed, until I heard the scamper of small feet racing toward the house. I took a step out the door as Angie Baby rounded the front of the van and hurled herself at me. I caught her up in my arms and sank to my knees on the front porch. And then settled into a sitting position, Angie on my lap. Her arms tightened on my neck, holding me so close I could feel her heart beating fastfastfast in her chest. She smelled of strawberry shampoo and sunlight and love. A moment later Little Evan joined us, pushing onto my lap. He smelled of baby powder, prepackaged juice, and crayons. I pulled him into the group hug.

Inside me, Beast murmured, *Kits . . . Missed kits.* She huffed and settled her chin to her paws.

I started crying in earnest, my tears falling to Angie Baby's head and trickling into her hair. Little Evan, who had grown three inches since I saw him last, stood on my jeans-clad thighs and grabbed my braid like a rope, saying, "Aunt Jane. Aunt Jane. Aunt Jane," like a chant over and over.

There was no way he could remember me. Not with the memory of a child and the months that separated us. Yet he seemed to know who I was, and that was enough for now. "Yes. Aunt Jane," I said. "Ow. That hurts. Stop that." Which made Little Evan giggle and yank harder, pulling my hair until my scalp protested. "Stop," I said, laughing, wiping my face, pulling them close. I stood, holding them both. Most people couldn't carry a six-year-old—seven-year-old now—and a toddler, but I wasn't just anyone. And since most of the world now knew that I was a skinwalker, I didn't have to hide my stronger-than-human strength. "You coming in?" I asked their father.

Evan scowled. I shrugged and toted his children, Molly's children, inside. I looked up, not seeing the barrel of a rifle, which meant my backup had stood down. "Eli," I called, "can you get the door to close, and cover the broken windows with plywood?"

"On it," he said, clattering down the steps from the second story. He was dressed in jeans, unlaced combat boots, and layered T-shirts, the tees hiding the weapons he never went without. A toolbox was in his left hand, keeping his right free for weapons. "Alex's getting his toys, on the way down to start a search for one Molly Everhart Trueblood." Eli paused in the doorway, studying the big man who still stood on the street, as if he couldn't make up his mind if he wanted to enter my home. "How long has she been gone?" he asked Evan.

"Three days. No. Four now." Evan wiped his face with a hand as if trying to wake up. "Sorry. It's been a long drive."

I felt, more than saw, Big Evan approach the house, blocking off the light at the door for a long space of time as he made up his mind to enter. Standing in the middle of the foyer, his hands hanging loose and empty, he said, "Molly's not here? You haven't seen her? For real?"

"For real," I said. His face looked ravaged, his eyes bleary.

"Details," Eli said, setting the tools on the floor and kicking aside broken glass.

I wanted to make Big Evan talk, with my fists, if necessary, but the children were more important. I moved into the house and sat on the couch, holding my godchildren to me. My partners, Eli and his little brother, the Kid, were a well-oiled team, capable and self-reliant. They had listened to the dialogue between Big Evan and me and were already getting to work, even though it wasn't a for-pay search. Money was important, but not even close to the importance of family. The Truebloods were my family.

"I saw her last on Monday. I kissed her and left for work in town. I have a gig installing lights in a new bar. When I got home that night, her sisters were there." He stepped into the house and stood in the foyer, so tired he was nearly wavering on his feet. "Regan and Amelia. Babysitting. Not unusual. Until they left and I found the note on the bed."

The hurt in his voice made my eyes tear up. "Evan, may I see the note?" He put a hand to his back pocket, but didn't pull anything from it. "Does the note tell you why you thought Molly was coming to New Orleans? Coming to see me?"

Evan handed me the paper. It was oft folded and worn, shaped to a slightly rounded curve, like the way a wallet shapes to the wearer's buttock.

Juggling children, I slowly opened the note and read aloud. "Darlin', I've gone to New Orleans to make things right with Jane, and put some other things to rights too. I can't hide from it anymore. But don't try to contact me. I'll be busy and not able to answer for a while. I love you with all my heart and soul and might. Kiss our babies. Molly." Something about the message sounded so final. As if a good-bye was included in the words, without ever being said. I turned the paper over. Nothing was written on the back. "What can't she hide from anymore?" I asked.

"I don't know. Something about her magic. She was having trouble growing things, making them thrive. The woods behind the house were hit with some kind of blight, beetles or fungus or something, and they were dying and she . . . couldn't make them right."

Put some other things to rights too, she had written, like maybe a hitch in her magic. But what was magical here that could help her? Except the magical implements and gizmos in my possession, which she knew about. Not that Molly would ever use black magic items. So it had to be something else, like the witches here in New Orleans, who might know things she didn't. I hadn't attempted to get to know the witches here. Maybe I should have.

Softly, I said, "You really could have called. I'd have told you she wasn't here. I'd have helped."

"But Mol said she was coming. Why would she say she was coming and then not show up?" He asked again, "You really haven't—"

"No. I haven't seen or heard from her." I started to ask more questions, but the tension in the small bodies in my arms suggested that the children needed a break from their overwrought father and his worry. Folding the note, I repositioned Little Evan and handed it back, to see Big Evan tuck it carefully in his pocket, as if he'd done it hundreds of times in the last few days, maybe rereading it over and over, looking for reasons or information he'd missed on a previous read. Maybe just holding it because Molly had touched it. "Are you hungry?" I asked the children, pulling them closer, feeling them snuggle against me. "I have cheese toast. Ravioli." And steaks and salad and oatmeal and beer. I'd need to shop or send out for food the children would like. I'd make a list and put the Kid on it. He could order online while we did other stuff. If no one wanted to go out, it could be delivered. I pulled a blanket from the back of the couch over the three of us, the new energy-efficient heater unable to keep up with the cold air still moving through the house, by nature now, not magic.

"Do you have her credit card numbers?" Eli asked from the door.

"Yeah. That for starters," the Kid said as he made his way down from the second floor. He handed Eli a broom as he traversed the glass-strewn foyer. "I need her maiden name, DOB, social and all electronic info, starting with cell numbers and credit card numbers."

"Everhart," I said as Evan rattled off her birth date and Social Security number. He pulled out his cell and gave the Kid the other numbers, and sent him three pictures of Molly to use in the search. The security business in the electronic age was so much easier than in the old days.

Before Evan had his phone put away, the Kid said, "Got it. I'm in." He settled to his comfy chair and the small table where he worked. "She rented a car in Asheville the day she disappeared, on her Visa. Like most rental cars, it has GPS. It'll take a bit, but I can access it."

"You can tell that already?" Evan asked, his voice pained and incredulous at once.

"Yeah. You came to the right place, dude. Even if you did huff and puff and try to blow the house down."

"Three little pigs," Little Evan chortled. "Daddy's a wolf-ees!"

"Yes, he is," I said to Little Evan. To Big Evan, I said, "Go help Eli. It's cold in here." His eyes widened, and he acted as though he was gonna balk at taking orders from me, but really, what choice did he have? Whether subconsciously or by deliberation, he had come to me. My turf, which meant my rules. And I needed to set the parameters early because my team needed freedom to search the way we wanted, not under the thumb of a distraught husband.

Big Evan blew out a breath and his shoulders drooped. He called to Eli, "I got a drill in the van. I think I stripped out the screws when I blew the door open like some hormonally charged teenager."

"Yeah, I see that," Eli said, his voice casual, as if he dealt with air witches every day. He knelt at the doorway and fingered the splintered wood. "Better than a battering ram."

"Daddy's a wolf-ees!" Little Evan chortled again. "He huffed and he puffed!" Then he turned in my arms, yanked my braid, and demanded, "I'm hungry. Fruit Loops!"

Big Evan looked up at that. "In the van. I'll bring them."

Eli chuffed slightly, a catlike sound he had picked up from me in the last few months. I detected derision in the tone and knew it had to do with the amount of sugar in the cereal. As well as a former Army Ranger, Eli was a dyed-in-the-wool health nut.

"Fruit Loops it is," I said cheerfully. Eli shrugged slightly without turning his head, his body language so restrained no one else might have detected it. I was still learning what the minuscule changes meant. This one meant *People are idiots. They eat too much sugar and fats and carbs. This is why everybody's gaining weight.*

I carried the kids to the kitchen and grabbed the high chair in the back of the butler's pantry (a tiny, windowed room off the kitchen that the guys and I had started using for a tea and coffee bar) and deposited Little Evan at the table. The Kid, watching from the living area where he worked, chuckled when he saw the high chair. It had been in the way, but I hadn't let anyone put it in the small attic, and hadn't explained why. Now the Kid asked, "Skinwalkers are psychic?"

I grabbed the tall books that Angie sat on so she could be a big girl at meals. I ignored how easy it was getting the children settled in my house. Molly hadn't talked to me in months, and yet I had kept all their things handy. "No, not psychic. Just . . ." *Pitiful?* I settled on "Just hopeful. We used it when Molly visited last summer."

My Beast was hyperaware, alert, and focused on all the people, especially the children, in her den as I opened a can of ravioli for Angelina. *Kits,* she purred, her happiness like a warm blanket.

Yeah, well, we get to keep all the guys too, I thought at her. *We can't have the kits without the grown-ups.*

Pack, Beast spat. I could tell by her tone that she wasn't pleased. As I opened the ravioli and heated it in the microwave, she sent a series of memory pictures to my forebrain, and I understood her disquiet. In the wild, mountain lions were solitary creatures, except when a female had kits. For a while after they were weaned, the female kits stayed in the den with the mother cat, sometimes for several years, hunting together, sleeping together, and even, rarely, mothering another litter together, until wanderlust hit the females and they disappeared. Which I had totally not known. But never, ever were males allowed to stay once they were grown. They were kicked out to fend for themselves as soon as they learned to hunt and kill.

Will be trouble, Beast thought at me. *Too many males.* She sent me a memory of big-cat brothers fighting to the death over a female. They were her kits, these young males, who bit and shredded flesh with teeth and claws. From a high promontory, Beast had watched them fight. The memory was detailed—bloody, vicious, the memory-scent of blood and rage pheromones rising on the wind, the sound of yowling, spitting, screaming. My breath caught in my throat as one male sank his teeth into his brother's belly and ripped. Gore and blood spattered the ground. Beast had watched as the injured male dragged himself off to die.

I shivered, horrified, ravioli scent filling the kitchen, replacing the memory-scents. But from Beast I got nothing, no emotional reaction to the memory at all. I had no idea of her feelings at the time of the fight, or now, when she shared the memory with me. *Trouble,* she thought.

Big Evan has a mate, I thought at her. *Eli has a mate in Natchez. The Kid is too young for a mate.*

Beast growled at me and sent me a memory picture of Rick LaFleur, stretched on my sheets. *Jane had mate. Jane is stupid.* With that pithy thought she prowled into the back of my mind and lay down, her head on her paws.

"Yeah," I whispered to her and to myself. "I am." The microwave dinged, pulling me back to my kitchen. Big Evan entered and set a half-empty grocery bag of food, one of garbage, and a cooler on the kitchen table. "We ate on the road," he said.

"Yeah. I see that," I managed, and poured milk and Fruit Loops into a bowl for Little Evan.

An hour later, the door was closed on new hinges that Eli had bought, just in case, and the back windows were boarded over with plywood he had bought for the same reason. The former Ranger was Mr. Prepared. Or Mr. Paranoid, though I'd never say so aloud.

Evan, when he wasn't helping Eli, had moved in, which felt so weird. I hadn't even had to beg or insist. And since Evan had agreed so readily when I suggested that they stay here, I had spent that hour getting my new guests settled, the children in the bedroom directly over my own, in the twin beds they had stayed in on their one visit, and Big Evan in the room directly behind them. His bed was shoved against the wall, to make room for the workout equipment that had made its way into the house in the last few months, but he didn't seem to mind. I wasn't exactly Betsy Homemaker, but I put sheets on the beds and got towels from the stash in the upstairs linen closet. There were two bathrooms upstairs and Eli had cleaned his out, without being asked, now sharing one with his brother.

It had been a seamless transition from a family of three to a family of six, and when I let myself think of it, that was weirder than weird. The house felt odd and full and not quite right, as if it was shifting to accommodate the bodies, probably more people than it had housed since it had been used as a brothel back in the late eighteen hundreds and early nineteen hundreds.

But while all the situational stuff was good, by the end of that first hour we had lost Molly's trail. The car she rented had been turned in to the rental company in Knoxville, only a few hours' drive from Asheville, and Molly's trail had stopped cold. The Kid had not found a single credit card purchase since, and my idea of easily tracking Molly by train, plane, or bus had proven incorrect. My former best friend had truly disappeared.

I stood over his shoulder, as Alex worked on four electronic tablets simultaneously, smelling the stink of his worry and stress, seeing it in the tightness of his shoulders, hearing it in the pounding of his fingers on the tablets. I took a calming breath and asked, "Thoughts? Ideas?"

The Kid looked around the room. Finding us alone, he said, "I have an untraceable account in India."

I drew a slow breath. Alex was on parole for hacking into the Pentagon to get a look at his brother's military records. Eli had put his younger brother on a short leash in computer terms, denying the Kid the opportunity for any illegalities. Well, except for a short stint in Natchez, and that had been life and death. And very, very big bucks, a hypocrisy that hadn't been lost on any of us.

But Molly was missing. What if someone picked her up out of the parking lot? What if she had met a rogue-vamp who smelled her witch blood and came after her? Okay, that wasn't likely, but . . . *Molly was missing*. Was finding her worth incurring Eli's wrath? Getting the Kid stuck in a parole violation and tossed in jail? I thought about Molly, hurt somewhere, in an accident; off the road, in a gully. Or abused by some kid who had stopped for the lone female on the side of the road and decided to hurt her. *Yes. It was worth it.* "What are we talking about?" I hedged.

"Security cameras in front of the car rental center for starters, to see what happened to Molly immediately after she dropped off the car."

"Dangers?"

"Minimal to none. Except pis— Sorry. Ticking off big brother and hiding from Big Brother."

"Do it," I said. "I'll talk to your brother."

"Better you than me," he said, and opened a black screen with white code on it. He bent his head over this tablet, his fingers moving with nearly balletic precision.

I walked to the back of the house, to the small washroom/mudroom I had never used until I had housemates, where Eli was putting his tools onto the shelves he had built. The house was darker with the windows covered, more intimate, safer, and more claustrophobic. But my big-cat and I could live with the denlike feeling for a while. Until the smell of male got too strong.

Eli glanced up, took in my face and posture, and sighed, reading my body language, or maybe just knowing me too well to miss what would happen next. He stood and angled his body to me, dipping his nearly shaved head, his brown eyes narrowed. We stood within inches of each other, nearly the same height, so the posture looked both uncomfortable and aggressive. "How dangerous?" he growled.

"Minimal to none, he says. For now, just checking the rental car's security cameras to see where she went when she turned in her car."

He thought about that for a while, while I sweated and waited. "We monitor every step along the way."

"Thank you," I said. And dang if my eyes didn't fill with tears. I turned away fast, but Eli caught my shoulder and pulled me back, an action I'd never have allowed anyone else to make.

"We'll find her," he said, one hand on my shoulder, gripping hard.

"I just . . ." Words failed me. I didn't know what I felt. Or thought.

"She's family," he said. "I know what it means when family is in trouble. I cried a few tears when Alex was arrested and they wouldn't let me in to see him for forty-eight hours."

I blinked away my own tears and gave him a disbelieving glare.

"Okay. I busted down a wall in my rental unit. I did shed a few tears digging the splinters out of my knuckles."

I laughed, a small hiccup of sound, which was what he intended, I'm sure.

"Look. It's possible she really intended to come to you for help. It's also possible that she intended that as a distraction for Evan and she went elsewhere, and then it took longer than she expected to get finished with whatever she needed to do. A lot of things are possible, not just her dead in a ravine." He did that little lip-twitch smile at my reaction to his mind reading. "We don't know enough yet to worry. We'll do the best we can to find her." Her patted my shoulder and left me in the cold mudroom, swallowing down more tears, my breath harsh.

"Yeah," I whispered. "She could have called if she had a problem. She could have asked for my help. Instead she's disappeared. And I don't know how to help her."

Eli paused in the short hallway and said over his shoulder, "Help her husband. Keep her kids safe. Let us work. That would be my best guess as to what Molly would want."

And of course, my partner was right. I took a ragged breath and squared my shoulders. "Okay. Yeah. Okay. We can do this."

CHAPTER 2

'Cause Wolf-ees Stinks!

It was nearly dark when the groceries arrived by delivery, and Eli and Evan shared kitchen duties, putting away groceries and making supper. It was peanut butter and jelly for the Trueblood children, steak and potatoes and beer for the adults, cola and pizza for the Kid. We were silent and worried, Alex sitting at one end of the table, his electronic devices in a semicircle around him, running programs I couldn't even guess at. Several times he paused, put down his fork, and punched some keys, mumbling things that sounded like Klingon cusswords and probably were. He had learned he could cuss in my presence if I didn't know what he was saying.

Midmeal my phone rang. I yanked it out of my jeans pocket, hoping it was Molly. The table went silent, hopeful. I grimaced and mouthed, *Katie,* my landlady. I answered, "Yellowrock," and put the phone on speaker.

Troll's gravel-crunching voice said, "Bliss and Rachael are missing. Get your ass over here."

I frowned. I didn't have time for missing *working girls* and Katie's drama

"Go ahead," Eli said, mind-reading again. "We got Molly covered for now."

I said to Troll, "Language. Give me details." I pulled out an old-fashioned spiral pad and pen.

"They went to a party last night and they didn't come home. Missed their ride. Haven't called. Haven't answered their cells. Now, what part of 'get your ass over here' is confusing?"

We had a communication problem. "We have children in the house," I clarified. "Watch your language."

"The Kid is, like, nineteen. When I was nineteen I was living in a whore—"

"Molly's children," I said loudly. The Kid snorted softly, hiding a smile.

"Oh. Why'n't you say so? Get your butt over here." The connection ended.

"I'll be right there," I said to the air, and closed the cell. I stuffed the last bite of steak into my mouth and said, "I don't want to go, but it shouldn't take long and I'm no help here right now. This is the Kid's search for the moment. I'll be back."

"Is this related to Molly?" Evan asked, his eyes on his plate.

I stopped, surprised. *Bliss is a witch.* So . . .

"Statistically improbable," Eli said.

"Yeah. What he said." I stood and went to my room, brushed my teeth, put on my boots, and weaponed up. I had started carrying fewer guns and more blades, worried that someone would get a weapon off me and use it to kill a human. Or worse, that I'd miss a vamp I was aiming at and kill a human. Silver shot would kill humans as easily as vamps. But this time I holstered up with two .308s and grabbed a light jacket to hide the weapons. And considered the rest of my armament. Most of it was locked safely away, but not all. We had children in the house. I laid all my guns on the bed and closed my bedroom door behind me.

To Evan I said, "How 'bout you give the kids a bath?" To Eli I said, "And make sure everything is locked in the safe room."

The guys looked at the kids and then at each other. Eli said, "Message received." He would put all the guns in the hidden room where we kept our armaments, and do it while the children were upstairs and not able to see the secret room.

Without another word, I spun on a heel and took the side door into the dark, heading for Katie's. The chill hit me, a wet, cold slap of air. I had once thought that Louisiana didn't have a winter. I had been wrong. It was just winter

Deep South–style, wet, icy air, a little road ice, the cold spells broken up with long periods of warm springlike air. We had been in the wet icy part for the last three days, and it would be later in the week before the seventies hit us again, a tropical storm front raging in off the coast. We'd have rain, rain, and then maybe a little rain. Some wind. Maybe some lightning. And some more rain. Inches of it. But at least it would be warm.

I jumped to the top of the splintered boulder pile in my backyard, grabbed a jutting brick as a handhold, and leaped, pulling myself over the wall, swinging across and dropping down. It wasn't a move a human could've made. Sometimes being human was overrated.

I knocked on the back door of Katie's Ladies and felt myself being viewed through the dynamic camera anchored overhead—a security upgrade I had installed when I first came to the Big Easy. There was another camera, smaller and better hidden, in the corner. Most people would never look for a hidden camera once they saw a big, obvious one. And most robbers, rapists, kidnappers, and general bad guys wouldn't think about a hidden camera after they had disabled the obvious one. The door opened—a steel door with no windows, a far better security arrangement than the glass door originally installed. Troll looked down at me from his six-feet-plus height and grinned. "Little Janie. Come on in. Katie's waiting for you in her study. You know the way."

"*Little* Janie," I grumbled. But I was getting used to the moniker. I was also called Legs, by some of the security experts in the city. Maybe it was dumb, but nicknames made me feel at home, welcomed, in some obscure way. And helped to alleviate some of the discomfort I always felt in Katie's presence. I had never been comfortable with her, but, to make it worse, she had fed on me not that long ago, and it's hard to excuse that kind of thing, even for me—and I understood a predator's drive to dominate and feed.

I blew out a breath, shook off the memory, and turned left, meandering down the hallway to Katie's office. Katie was the heir to Leo Pellissier, the Master of New Orleans and the Southeastern U.S., except for Florida. She was dominant, strong, and a little scary, with less control than the MOC, less charisma, but, possibly, more raw power. Katie was the first sane vamp I'd ever met, and her office was the first place I had come when I got to New Orleans.

Her office was much as it had been then, though the walls were now painted a cooler, darker seafoam green, and the hardwood floor was covered with a new silk Oriental rug, a burnt persimmon background woven with green waves along the border with a darker green and burnt orange sea serpent crashing through the waves in the center. The rug was modern and luxuriant and probably cost more than I had in the business' checking account, which was a lot. The leather sofa still faced the desk, two leather chairs to either side. The bar and minifridge were on the left wall, and Katie's ancient blackwood, hand-carved desk with the leather center was to the right, lit by a brass lamp in the shape of a swan, its neck arched back to ruffle its half-lifted wings.

Also on the desk tonight, however, and totally unexpected, was a computer monitor. Katie was a Luddite. She didn't understand the modern world. She hated changes. She more than hated the electronic changes. And yet she was sitting behind the desk, her eyes wide and entranced—in the human manner, not vamped-out—studying the wide screen.

"Uhhh. Katie?" Great entrance. Almost as if I'd practiced it.

She looked up and tinkled a laugh. It was delicate and soft and feminine and nothing like my own laugh, which was more of a donkey bray. "This is fascinating," she said. "I have no idea why I feared it for so long." One fragile-looking hand waved me closer. "Come. See. This is marvelous!"

I stuck my hands into my pockets and stepped around the desk. Katie, wearing a dark orange-red sheath dress with her hair coiled up in a chignon, was staring at some sort of financial spreadsheet, one with dollar amounts upward of five figures—not counting the pennies. And the total at the bottom of the page was in the high six figures.

My eyebrows rose all by themselves. "Yeah. Cool." I mean, what else could I say?

"Since I rose again, for the second time, this new world is no longer a fearful place." She whipped her head to me, and her fangs snicked down. "In fact, I fear nothing and no one."

I managed not to take three quick steps back, which was smart because hunting predators chase things that run away. I held my hands up and open in the universal "peace" gesture and tried to control my breathing and heart rate. "Good by me, Katie. No woman should ever have to be afraid."

"Yes. Exactly." Her fangs flipped back into the roof of her mouth with a faint click. She hadn't vamped out—her eyes had remained fully human. It was a demonstration of control I hadn't seen in her before, one worthy of a master. Katie had been injured not long after I arrived in NOLA, and to save her undead life, she had been buried with the blood of all the clans of New Orleans, some of which no longer even existed. She had risen crazy strong. And maybe just crazy, until a couple of months ago when she seemed to be settling in. Sorta.

But I was wasting time. It was nearly seven thirty, the kids' bedtime, and I needed an update on Molly. I wanted to be at home. "Troll tells me you have some missing girls?"

"Bliss and Rachael went to a private party last night at Guilbeau's Restaurant. They called their driver at exactly two twenty-three this morning. When their driver arrived four minutes later, there was no sign of them. Find them. When you discover who took them, kill him. Funds have been placed at your discretion, though I require a detailed expense accounting, of course."

My mouth opened. And closed on the words I was about to say. Calling a vamp insane might not be the wisest course of action, especially when it hadn't been demonstrated that she was fully in control of her predatory instincts. When I opened my mouth again, I said, "I'll find the girls. But I'm not a hired killer."

"Of course you are. Don't be foolish." She turned back to the screen. "We all must accept our natures, and you are a predator." She sniffed the air without looking at me. "You smell of wild places and violence and blood. You will kill. It is your nature and it is what you have been paid to do."

The reality of her statement hit me like an icy fist, right in my midsection. Her words were almost like the ones Beast said to me when she called me a killer. Words I denied. Still wanted to deny. Slowly, carefully, I said, "Unless the person or persons who has them is being violent, refuses to let them go, or tries to do them, my team, or me harm, I won't be killing anyone."

Katie's head inclined, a snakelike movement no human spine could mimic. Her face moved half into shadow, and the other half brightened into creamy gold; the dim bulb shaded her hair into honey with pale highlights. Her eyes met mine, dark in the lamplight and full of compulsion. She held me with her eyes, and a deeply twisted gleam brightened her gaze as she parted her lips, the motion slow and sensual. "This I shall accept: You will find my girls. You will free them. You will return them to me, with the names of the ones who took them. I will take care of the rest."

I knew what she meant. She would take the names I gave her, track them, drain them, and kill them. She would leave their dead bodies where no one would ever find them. And it would be my fault. Totally my fault. As much as if I took their lives myself.

Katie smiled sweetly as the facts found a place in my brain, and returned her attention to the computer screen. "Tom has all the information you will need to locate my employees. You are dismissed."

I didn't know how to reconcile her demands, and though my Beast fought me to challenge her, predator to predator, and fight it out on the desktop, here and now, I shoved Beast down and walked away. Katie was my employer and landlady, the owner of my freebie home. Katie was a vamp no one crossed, and if I wanted to keep my own peace of mind *and* my own blood in my veins, I would need to find a way to deal with Katie wanting to kill the kidnappers—which would totally be my fault, if I gave her the names. But I could worry about that later. Was I a Scarlett O'Hara or what?

Inside me, my Beast—the soul of a mountain lion I had dragged into me during an act of accidental black magic, when I was five years old and fighting for my life—turned her back to me, a predator insult of the worst kind. I held in the frustration the gesture brought on.

Troll, whose real name was Tom, and who was Katie's primo blood-servant, was waiting for me in the hallway, his face like a stone bust, emotionless and cold. He had been listening.

Dumbly, I followed him to the kitchen, where Deon, Katie's

three-star Jamaican chef, was putting a rack of lamb into one of the commercial ovens he supervised. We sat at the kitchen bar, my right foot on the floor, the other on the bar stool footrest. Troll handed me a paper with all the pertinent info about the missing girls written on it in his neat block printing.

"Is she . . ." I stopped, not knowing what to ask.

"Sane?" he said softly. "I don't know, but I'm careful around her, treat her with kid gloves. Her girls are careful. According to Mithran definitions, and within Mithran parameters, she's fine. She's not drained anyone. She's injured no one." He rubbed his bald pate in consternation. Troll wasn't the most communicative man, but even I could tell he wasn't finished. "But she's powerful and strong and different from what she was before the blood-burial."

With palpable relief at the interruption, he accepted a glass of white wine from Deon, looked at it, swirled it, sniffed it, and sipped it. "Buttery and rich," he said. "The best Chardonnay to date. Order up five cases."

He set the glass on the counter and said to me, "I've asked around. The few blood-servants who've heard of a rising after a blood-burial aren't real helpful, except to say that all Mithrans who survive are changed, are different. It takes months for the mixed blood to work its way through a Mithran's system. Sometimes years. And they're always left with extraordinary strength and speed and what George Dumas calls *mental acuity*. What she'll become, I don't know and can't say."

"Ducky." I looked at the paper and said, "I need to talk to the driver who came to pick up the girls. I also need to talk to the others who were at the party. That isn't listed here. No names from the party at all."

"Katie wasn't informed of the party. The girls were out on the town together, not working for her."

I tried to put the two sentences together into something that made sense. And then it hit me why Katie was so predatory. "They were working a side job? One without Katie's approval and one that Katie didn't get a cut of?"

Troll nodded, then shook his shiny bald head. "I didn't think so at the time, but with them disappearing, I'm startin' to reconsider. I was the pickup driver, and I know the girls were there one minute and gone the next, 'cause I talked with one of the waiters. They wouldn't have gotten into a car with people they didn't know, so either they left with someone they knew or they were taken." He ran a hand across his scalp, thinking. "They know better than to stiff Katie, so . . . I don't know."

I chuckled at the double entendre and Troll managed a smile. "Unintentional," he said.

"Sure. Send me photos of the girls. I'll check it out and see what I can find. On another note, my friend Molly is missing. Her husband thought she might be coming to New Orleans to see me, but she didn't." I tapped the paper on the bar top, thinking. "She didn't see me, that is. I don't know if she actually came to New Orleans. We're looking into that. So, if you hear anything about witches, call?"

Troll nodded. "Will do."

"Now tell me about picking up the girls."

"Nothing to say. They called for a ride home from Guilbeau's, per orders of Katie." I looked my question at him and he said, "For their safety, they call after dark, even on their nights off. When I got there, they were gone."

I sighed. "It's never easy."

"That's why you get paid the big bucks, Legs."

Back at the house, I checked in with Alex. He was hunched over his tablets in the living room, working. The TV was on, the big screen divided into four sections, MSNBC, FOX, a March madness college basketball game, and a black-and-white rerun of an old *I Love Lucy* show. Counting the four tablet screens, he was watching eight screens, all silent except for the Lucy show, with the laugh track turned up high. Evan sat on the couch with his kids, one snuggled into either arm, watching the show, holding the children as if they'd vanish if he let go. Eli was nowhere in sight, but it was after dark, and time for his nightly chat with his sweetie, Sylvia Turpin, the sheriff of Natchez, so it might be an hour before I saw him again. The front door window and the back windows were boarded over, and oddly, the door had strips of silver duct tape running in horizontal bands across it. I didn't want to know why.

I bent over Alex's chair, my weight on one arm on the chair back, and asked softly, "How's it going?"

"Same thing I'm telling him." He pointed a finger at Evan. "So far, nothing. Leave me alone."

"Yeah. No." I swatted him on the back of the head for the rudeness. "My friend, his wife, we'll ask as much as we want."

"Whatever," he grumbled, sounding like the teenaged boy he was. My plate was still on the table, covered in plastic wrap. I picked up a fork and my own electronic tablet and carried them, my cell, and my plate to the stairs, far enough away to not be bothered by the sound track of Lucy roping Ethel into some kind of mischief, but close enough to keep tabs on my extended family.

I shoved in a mouthful of cold steak, chewing while I opened a file and typed in the pertinent info on the case, which I listed as KATIE'S GIRLS. When it was all in and documented, I located Reach's name under contacts on my cell. I hadn't called the intelligence specialist in months, not since we got back from Natchez. The reprieve had been good for my pocketbook, and with the Younger brothers as my new partners, I wouldn't be needing his services nearly so often. But somewhere inside, I had missed Reach's snark. I pressed the SEND button.

"Speak to me, oh Mistress of the Dark," he answered.

I let my mouth curl into a smile. "Mistress of the Dark? You used to call me Money Honey."

"You went for a much *Younger* man."

I chuckled at the play on words because it was expected, not because it was funny.

"Alex isn't as good as me, but he isn't bad," Reach said.

"Well, the Younger man is tied up in a search. Are my rates still current?"

"Vamp search rates?"

"No. Two missing twentysomethings, working girls who didn't come home from a party that was most likely a totally human sex party, but could have been a sex-and-blood party hosted by vamps. I have no data on that yet."

"Your rates on nonvamp stuff is good. Give it to me."

"First girl is a witch in hiding, Ailis Rogan, aged twenty-four, looks fourteen, street name is Bliss, Caucasian with black hair and blue eyes. Sending her DOB and numbers via e-mail." I double-checked the data from Troll's piece of paper and my tablet as we talked. "Next girl is Rachael Kilduff. Twenty-two. A new tattoo and multiple ear piercings. I'm expecting pics of both girls shortly. I'll forward them when I get them. The party was at Guilbeau's." I spelled it for him. "They called for their driver at exactly two twenty-two this morning. When their driver arrived four minutes later, there was no sign of them."

"Yeah? Nice place. Five stars and just as many dollar signs. Your party host had money, lots of money if it was a large party."

"Good to know. I'll check out the place tonight. Gotta go." I tapped the END icon and closed the cover. It was one of the newer models, part cell, part tablet, part movie theater, part reader, with more computing power than I would ever need, and with a built-in armored shell, designed by a tech company owned by Leo. The cell was designed for the military, but it came in handy for other violent lifestyles too—like vamp hunting.

I scooted over as Big Evan carried his two children upstairs to their room. Over his shoulder he said, "You can come up for story time." It was a grudging offer, but it was better than anything else I had from him lately. I sent the e-mail file to Reach and scraped the last of my cold supper off the plate and into my mouth.

"Yeah. Thanks," I said, satisfied that he didn't sound more irritated or tell me to choke myself, and followed him up the stairs. Whether he liked it or not, he needed my help, but that didn't make Evan Trueblood like me much. I settled onto the foot of Angie's bed, shoving the guns I still wore back and out of the way, and waited while the children said their simple nighttime prayers. After the "Amens," Evan pulled a padded wingback chair between the beds and sat, opening a thin copy of *Little Red Riding Hood*. The book looked ancient, the corners bent and worn, and the cover real leather, embossed and stained and dyed decades ago. And the author's name on the cover was Eldreth Everhart. Dang. An Everhart had translated Grimm's *Little Red Riding Hood*. How cool was that?

"Once upon a time," he read, "a little girl lived in a pretty village near Derbyshire, close by the forest, on the edge of a flowing stream. Her name was Philomena Everhart, but because she wore a red riding cloak, everyone in the villages nearby called her Little Red Riding Hood. One morning, while the dew was still on the roses, both red roses and white roses, Little Red Riding Hood asked her mother if

she could visit her granmama Theodosia Everhart, because
Theodosia had been visiting the queen for a long while, and
Philomena had missed her granmama."

"Daddy's a wolf-ees!" Little Evan shouted and giggled.

Wolf? Beast asked. *Hate pack hunters. Thieves of meat.*

This wasn't the first time the toddler had called his daddy
a wolf today. Just to be on the safe side, I took an explor-
atory sniff. No. Big Evan hadn't been bitten by a werewolf.
He smelled witchy. I curled up around Angie Baby's feet as
Big Evan continued to read.

"'That is a splendid idea,'" he read, in a high-pitched
voice, "her mother said. Philomena's mother packed a nice
lunch basket for Little Red Riding Hood to take to visit her
granmama."

The children giggled, and I laid my head on my arm, listening. No one had read me stories as a child, so this was ...
amazing. Really amazing. Big Evan reached the line about
Granmama. "The wolf crept up to the door, lifted the small
latch, and raced inside. Poor Granmama screamed, but the
wolf gobbled her up!"

"Our gramma woulda put a spell on him!" Little Evan
said.

"She would turn him into a frog!" Angie Baby said.

"A spider!"

"A ant!"

"Shhhh," Big Evan said, sounding stern, but with poi-
gnant laughter twinkling in his eyes. I knew without asking
that the poignancy was because Molly was missing.

Both children giggled and some foreign, incomprehensi-
ble emotion bubbled up from deep inside. I batted tears
from my eyes. When had I become so freaking weepy?

"The wolf burped, a full and satisfied burp, and patted
his tummy where Granmama poked and pushed and kicked
in his hairy belly," Evan said.

"He burped!" Angie said. Little Evan made a fake burp-
ing sound, long and gross-sounding. And I laughed through
my tears, caught in the good humor of my favorite people
in the entire world. And knowing it was up to me to find
their mother.

"But the wolf was wily, and he knew that Little Red Riding Hood would never come inside if she saw a wolf. So he
looked through Granmama's chifforobe to find a nightgown

and bed jacket that he liked. He added a lace sleeping cap to hide most of his ears and, to hide his wolfish scent, dabbed Granmama's lavender perfume behind his pointy ears and under his paws."

"'Cause wolf-ees stinks!" Little Evan shouted.

"Yes, they do," his father said. "Wolves smell stinky like wet dogs and rotten meat." Which wasn't far wrong for the smell of werewolves.

Big Evan went on reading and reached the last line. "Little Red Riding Hood and her granmama opened the basket packed by Philomena's mother, and shared a lovely lunch with the huntsman. And then they had a long chat."

Little Evan looked at me said, "He vomicketed her up. Buuurrrpurp."

"Yes, he did," I agreed. "Gross, huh?"

"Gross. Night, Aunt Jane."

"Night, Little Evan."

"Mommy and Daddy call me EJ."

"Short for Evan Junior," his father explained.

"I like EJ," I said. "It's a big boy's name."

EJ rolled into the curve of his arm and mumbled what sounded like "I'm a big bo." And closed his eyes. He was asleep. That fast.

I uncurled and kissed Angie Baby's cheek and left the room to their father. Standing just out of sight, I watched as Evan pulled out his flute and played a soft melody; he was setting wards on his children for protection and health, a form of prayer and power for an air witch. The notes were plaintive and melancholic and held all the need and loss he was feeling for his wife, the mother of the children he loved to distraction. When he was done, he stood for a moment, before leaving the room. In the doorway, he blew a last note, a minor key of longing. And stepped into the hallway.

He turned and saw me, standing there, watching. And stopped as if frozen. Before he could react, could tell me to get lost, could fuss at me for being some kind of desperate, childless Peeping Tom, I stepped into him and laid my head against his chest. My body rested against his huge torso, his heartbeat hard and steady on my ear, his breath arrested in surprise. My head was tilted down. It was a pose of submission, the nape of my neck exposed. I held my position until he exhaled, his breath warm on my neck. And his arm lifted to wrap around me. It was like being hugged by a heated brick wall.

After a long moment he said, his voice a rumble through his chest, "You *are* going to find her. Right?"

I nodded, his shirt rough on my cheek

"The wards are set to keep them safe and to augment their immune responses. If Angie wants to sleep with you . . . she can. I'll know when she gets up and where she goes, but I left the ward on the room open."

I sobbed once. Totally unexpected. And wrapped my arms around Evan. "I missed you too."

He laughed, the sound like logs tumbling over one another. "Yeah. Well . . . Oh. Once I go to bed, if you want to open the doors, come get me first."

"You'll set a big honking alarm?"

"Like the Fourth of July and the Blitz all at once."

There wasn't a human-built security system made anywhere by anyone that equaled one of the Truebloods'. They had started out as works of art, and then gotten better with time.

CHAPTER 3

She Calls You Sugar Lips?

It wasn't quite nine p.m. when I tapped on Eli's door and heard my partner laugh, his voice a soft caress. "Come," he said louder.

I opened the door and stuck my head in. His room was spotless, so well organized I wouldn't know anyone lived there if not for the slender, muscle-bound man stretched out on the bed and the e-reader on the bedside table next to the nine-millimeter. I looked at the gun and at him and he shrugged. "I know. We have babies in the house. It's locked up when it isn't on me."

I wanted to fuss but decided not to comment. I said, "We have a paying job—missing persons. I need to check out a restaurant. You wanna come along?"

"Gotta go, Syl. I love you. Yeah, tomorrow." He laughed, his face changing, going all soft and romantic. You could have knocked me over with a feather. I had never seen Eli laugh, not like that. And *I love you*? When did they go from *I'll show you my gun if you'll show me yours* to *I love you*?

Eli shut off the cell and grinned at my dropped jaw. "What? Never seen a man fall head over heels before?" I blinked as he holstered his weapon, strapped a small .32 above his boot, strapped a short-bladed knife to his inner arm, and grabbed a jacket. "We looking for vamps?" he asked.

I clicked my jaw shut. "No and no. Rachael and Bliss went missing this morning just after two. Looks like they were at a party, working without Katie's approval."

"Let's go. You can fill me in on the way."

We informed the other two adults where we were going, with orders to call us the moment any news about Molly came through, and went out the duct-taped front door. "The replacement windows and door glass will be here tomorrow," Eli said. "And I've been thinking about ordering some of the vamp shutters. What do you think?"

"Estimates would be nice," I grumbled as I strapped in and Eli started the motor. "But don't forget we'll have to go through the Vieux Carré Commission. And I promise, it'll be a pain." Dealing with bureaucrats always was, and every upgrade we made to our base of operations was a permanent loss, unless covered by Leo or Katie. We didn't own the building and I was iffy on tax law about real estate upgrades. And I hated that I had to even think about such things. *Business.* When did I become a *businesswoman*? *Eww.*

The SUV was nondescript and slightly battered, its internal lights worked only when you flipped a switch, the engine was powerful enough to drag several hundred horses behind us, and the back was modified to hold an abundance of weapons under lock and key. The blades and firepower were intended to kill rogue-vamps, Naturaleza vamps, and vamps who didn't abide by the restrictions set up in the Vampira Carta—the legal code that the Mithrans had lived by for centuries. Tonight, the SUV was carrying only us and the weapons we wore, nothing special. Well, that I knew of.

Guilbeau's, pronounced G'bo's, was in the French Quarter, a new restaurant in an old three-story brick building, replacing a business that hadn't survived the dearth of tourists after Hurricane Katrina. There was valet parking, and a red-vested boy who looked as if he were twelve years old raced out into the damp night and took the keys, driving away as we pushed through the revolving door. The restaurant had a venerable air, as if it had existed since Jean Lafitte's time, with deep burgundy carpeting and a roped-off area for patrons awaiting a table. The place smelled heavenly, if God were a carnivore and liked his meat seared and bloody. I had just finished my supper and my mouth was already watering.

Piano music played in the background; just ahead I could see a black baby grand and the black pianist, also wearing black, his fingers running lightly across the keys. Another man, wearing a tux, stood behind a little desk, like a pulpit poised at the wider entrance to the restaurant proper. I started for the guy, but Eli held me back, a hand on my upper arm. "Let me," he murmured.

I shot him a glare, but waited. Eli approached the guy, who I guessed was the maître d', and moved his jacket back as if to display something. They murmured for a bit, the words obscured by the music, something classical and springy that made me think of bunnies hopping through tall grass, before Beast swiped them with her claws and chomped them with her killing-teeth. Eli stepped back and whispered into my ear, "The general manager has been notified that we're here, and would like to see last night's and this morning's security footage. He's remarkably agreeable."

"Uh-huh. You wearing a fake badge?" I asked.

"You want to see the footage or not?" There was laughter in his breathy comeback and I shook my head, smothering my retort. I mean, yeah. I wanted to see the footage, but not by impersonating a cop, which was illegal. A lot of cops in this town didn't like me much. Go figure.

I pasted a smile on my face that attempted to look trustworthy and surely didn't succeed, but the manager, a small, lithe man wearing black, natch, and an ear wire, walked through the restaurant and, without introducing himself, motioned us to the side and up a narrow stairway. He must have wanted to get the big, bad, dangerous-looking people out of his lobby, pronto.

The stairs were not standard height—not even matching, nonstandard heights, each an inch or two off from the ones above and below, and I stumbled twice as we switch-backed up constricted landings to the second floor. The manager's office was small but tidy, with an old PC and flat-screen, some closed, leather-bound books, a small adding machine, pencils and pens in a green glass cup, a sturdy, scuffed-up desk that looked as if it had been there since World War Two, and had probably been put in place then, by a crane, through the window, since the stairs were so narrow. For sure they'd never move it any other way.

He sat in the desk chair and motioned us to the guest chairs, all three with low arms and narrow seats that made my knees stick up in the air. The chairs had been made for short, thin people, not tall, long-legged people. "I'm Scott Scaggins, general manager of Guilbeau's, and I had no idea anyone had gone missing. Give me the times you're interested in, and about ten minutes, and I can have the digital footage up, copied for you, and a list of employees who were on last night." He pulled a pair of spectacles out of his breast pocket, perched them on his nose, and punched keys on the keyboard. "We're in. Time?"

"We appreciate your assistance in this, uh, delicate matter. We'd like to see from two twenty through two thirty a.m.," Eli said, leaning back in his chair as if he owned the joint. "We've been told it was a private party. We only need to talk to employees who served for the party."

Scott didn't look from his fingers as he typed. "Which party?"

Which left me stymied, but Eli didn't even hesitate. "The governor's daughter and her friend didn't say, but from her recent interest in vampires, we'd assume the one hosted by the local vamps."

The manager snorted, again without looking up, which was a good thing because my eyes were bugging out of my head. *The governor's daughter? Did he just imply that we are looking for the governor's daughter?* I looked at Eli, thinking, *Are you insane?* He just smiled, if you can call that little twitch of lips a smile.

"I would hate to be raising a girl in this vampire climate," Scott said. "Everyone thinks the vamps are all sparkly and pretty, and forget that they drink blood. *Human* blood. The vamps throw a party and every teenager within miles is all over the place. We have to hire security to keep them out."

"Who did you hire last night?" I asked.

"Lewis Aycock's company. He's a Vietnam War vet. The owner likes to give vets jobs anytime he can. A boost back up, you know, and all Lewis' personnel are vets." He looked up under his eyebrows and back to his screen. "The client knew of him and was agreeable."

I didn't know him, and so let it pass. "And the client?" I asked.

"Not saying that without a court order," Scott said. "Bring me a piece of paper signed by a judge and I'll tell you everything—names, dates, alcohol consumed, hors d' oeuvres served, numbers of guests, cost totals, tips, and credit cards used. Not until then. And the waiters don't know who the host was, so don't bother asking."

"The governor prefers to keep this under wraps for now," Eli lied smoothly. "If it becomes a criminal matter, you'll get a warrant." I just shook my head.

"And it's up," Scott said. He flipped the flat-screen around and we watched for ten minutes as humans, blood-servants, and vamps left the restaurant, getting into cabs and limos, and a few walking. No one entered the restaurant during the ten minutes, not after two in the morning.

I leaned in when a pale-skinned, black-haired female appeared on the screen, showing only the top of her head and her hands holding the wrap she wore. *Bliss.* The woman beside her had scarlet hair and was wearing rings on every finger. She tilted her head and I recognized Rachael by the shape of her nose and the multiple rings through her ear-lobes. And the tattoo on her left wrist. It was a dragon, the body and tail wrapped around the wrist, the fire-breathing head on the top of her hand. It was new, and I'd seen it only a week past, when she complained about the pain and itching. Once upon a time, Katie had not allowed her working girls to get tattoos, but now things were different. Katie was different. She didn't seem to care about body adornment or other things that she used to. She was, on the other hand, way more territorial than she used to be. With them was a man who stood to one side, only the top of his head and shoulders visible in the camera—slender and muscular with spiked hair and dark clothes.

"That's them," I said.

Eli covered for me. "And the people with *her*?" he asked.

I hesitated only a moment, feeling my way, before saying, "The boss will be ticked off about the whole thing."

"So we shouldn't tell the governor everything. In fact, we shouldn't tell him anything," Eli suggested.

"And we've agreed to differ," I said, as if we had a long-standing argument about how to protect the interests of our employer—who was the freaking governor. Eli was insane.

On the screen, the man, possibly a waiter, handed the girls into a black cab limo and it drove off as he stepped back again.

Some humans left, one female wearing a hat and trailing

a long scarf. The arm of a man was around her as if to support her, her gait that of someone ill or unsteady after too much liquor, their faces never in view. Three other men left just behind them, the small group moving like vamps, breaking up at the door. One wore a tuxedo and seemed to move off fast, maybe in pursuit of the woman with the scarf and the other man, though all we could see from the angle of his head was dark hair and jacket and a satin stripe on the outside of his pants leg as he strode off. The other two, both in dark slacks and suit coats, stood for a moment, body movements suggestive of discussion, and then they too left, heading in different directions.

A scant two minutes later, a similar black car pulled up and waited, the driver a fuzzy form making a cell call. It was Troll. He waited. And waited. He made three more cell calls before eventually giving the valet the keys and entering the restaurant. And leaving moments later, tension showing in the set of his shoulders. He was on the cell, talking as he drove away.

To Scott, Eli said, "That's all we need, those twenty minutes of footage. And you have the governor's thanks."

"Yeah, well, tell him he has my sympathy. He has his hands full if his daughter's fallen in with that redheaded chick. She works for a vamp who runs a whorehouse. Seriously, he needs to consider chaining her up in the attic or something. If I'd known she was underage, I'd never have let her in, but everyone had an invitation." He opened a desk drawer and handed Eli a heavy, engraved invitation, the kind old vamps used, the paper made of mostly cloth, the words printed in gilt.

Eli handed the invite to me and I nodded my thanks, studying the card. The message was innocuous and uninformative. "The pleasure of your presence is requested at ten o'clock tonight at Guilbeau's for a coming-out soiree. Black tie." The party started late, like any vamp party. No names, and no RSVP. Not much help here.

The manager hit a button and his PC whirred. Behind him, a printer chattered. He handed Eli the printed paper first and again Eli passed it to me. It was a list of the waitstaff. Six names, with addresses and phone numbers. While I was studying it, he handed Eli a CD and stood, offering his hand.

"Thank you for your time," Eli said, standing and taking the proffered hand. I followed a moment later, out of sync with the bonhomie of the good old boys.

"I thank *you* for keeping the restaurant's name out of the press. Letting the governor's underage daughter into a vampire party would not be good for our reputation or good standing," Scott said.

I just shook my head and headed down the stairs. Back outside, the wet night had become a downpour, which totally matched my mood. The valet brought our SUV around and we drove away. I lasted a whole block before I busted out with "The *governor's daughter*? Are you *nuts*?"

Eli gave that twitchy smile and said, "We got what we needed, didn't we?"

"Yes, we did. And if he takes it any further, *our* faces are on the security footage now. You are insane. Totally insane."

"We just have to make sure we don't do anything that makes him take it any further."

I gusted a breath and looked out into the night. The windshield wipers squeaked slightly as they swept the rain away. I shook my head. "Okay."

"Just okay? No atta boy? No 'Heeey, duuude, that took balls'?"

I laughed softly and shook my head again. Eli Younger was entirely too pleased with himself. But he did do good. We had footage and names, neither of which we would have been given had we gone in with an honest request. But still. "I think you were *thinking* with your little brains, *dude*."

When we reached home, my first action—after getting Evan to remove the security spell from the house for a while—was asking for news of Molly, to which the Kid said, "No. Nothing. Nada. Not yet. The cops are searching the mountain roads for any car that might have driven off the road. She isn't in any hospital and I've checked them all. She hasn't used her cards or an ATM. I'll tell you if I get anything. Don't ask me again. Gimme the CD." All the words ran together, accompanied by a jittery hand-waving motion for me to hurry up and give him the data from Guilbeau's. He sounded grumpy, but I sorta understood that. His work space had been invaded by Big Evan, who had been pacing while we were gone. Pacing a lot. Passing by Alex's work space every few minutes and asking the same questions I was asking. It had to be nerve-racking.

I speed-dialed Troll from the living room, while watching the CD with Eli and Alex. He answered on the third ring. Instead of replying to his "Janie girl," I said, "What, exactly, did the girls say to you when you dropped them off, and what, exactly, did they say when they called you for a pickup last night? This morning. Whatever."

"Deon drove them out, and according to him, they were whispering and not sharing, which he considered way more than rude, and he sulked for hours. But when they called for a ride home, Rachael said, 'Hey, Sugar Lips. Can you pick us up at Guilbeau's?' I said yes. When I got there, they weren't out front, so I went inside. They weren't there either. I called Rachael's cell and was sent to voice mail. I asked to see the security footage and was told to get lost. End of story."

"She calls you Sugar Lips?" I tried to put the vision of Troll with the endearment of Sugar Lips and couldn't make my brain fit around the two concepts.

"Yeah, when she's feeling *friendly*. Whaddaya got?"

"We got the security footage from the restaurant."

"What'd you do, pretend to be cops?"

"No comment," I grumbled. "It shows several people, including the girls, leaving Guilbeau's, and I'd like you to take a look. Can you come over?"

"Yeah, but unlike you, I don't fly over brick walls, so I'll be walking around. Tell your shooter I'm on the way."

I closed the cell. Eli said, "Sugar Lips?"

"Yeah. Ick."

The Kid said, "Before he gets here, two things. One, Reach sent me his search on Rachael and Bliss. There have been no financial transactions or cell phone usage since they disappeared. He's set up an automatic ding if they use their credit cards, ATM, cells, anything, everything, anywhere, and will notify us if they pop up used. I can take over on the other parts of the search from here. Okay?" I nodded. "Two, I found security footage of Molly turning in her car in Knoxville. Evan and I already studied it and got nothing. You wanna see?"

Eli and I all but scampered over, to see footage of Molly entering a rental car cubicle. "McGhee Tyson Airport. High volume. High security, even on the rental agencies," the Kid said. Molly was clear on the camera, not hidden by a glamour or some kind of spell that would mess with the digital stuff, which could mean that she expected us to find this footage. She was wearing a coat, brownish, and sturdy shoes; she handed a woman behind the counter something—keys, most likely—and turned and walked away. The screen flickered to another angle and we saw her walking down the concourse, no luggage, no bag. Which meant she had other transportation already secured.

"That's it for the car rental security cameras," Alex said. "I can't get into the airport security footage without incurring the wrath of my parole board and my brother."

"I told him to stop. We'll find Molly another way," Evan said from the kitchen, sounding gruff. "Meanwhile, you have footage of the missing hookers."

"Call girls," the Kid said. "Very expensive, high-class call girls who my brother threatened with bodily harm if they gave me a freebie. Totally unfair, dude."

"When you're twenty-one," Eli said, sounding as if he'd said it a thousand times already, "and you're off parole, and your record has been wiped clean, you can break any law you want and buy any hooker you want and get any disease they have, and go to jail for your good time. Till then, I'll break your legs if you try."

"Not fair, bro. Anyway, here's the footage you got from the restaurant," he said. "I'll try to sharpen it, but digital can only go so far. That stuff on movies and TV, where they telescope in and make out writing on people's shirts and focus on tattoos and see eye color, is totally fiction. We won't get much better than the fuzzy stuff you already saw."

We were still watching the footage, the Kid trying to sharpen the digital images, and taking off still shots, when the knock came. I walked through the house, opened the front door, and said, "Come on in, Sugar Lips."

Troll grunted and moved past me, his bald head catching the foyer lights, his eyes taking in the repairs. "Whatever it is, Katie ain't paying for it."

"I know. My nickel." I closed the door and he followed me into the living room. I introduced Big Evan and Troll, and the two huge men sized each other up. I just hoped the floor joists held.

"Molly's husband?" Troll asked.

"The same," Evan said.

"You're the one who made the spell for Rick—my nephew a couple generations back. I owe you one."

"Nothing owed. Blood-servant for Katie?"

"Primo." The guys bumped fists and Troll pointed to the back windows, now covered with plywood. "Your work?"

"I thought my wife had left me and come here."

"Jane don't swing that way."

"That's not— Never mind. Jane is helping me find my wife."

"Good. I like Molly. Met her when she was visiting. She didn't look down her nose at my girls. I like that. High-class lady, your wife. If I hear anything about her, I'll let you know."

They bumped fists again and I made a little roll-'em motion at the Kid. The footage started. "We want to know the names of the vamps and humans leaving the restaurant, and the name of the driver of the car they got into." I handed him a spare spiral pad and a pen.

Troll started taking notes as human-shaped forms left the restaurant. Twice he asked to see a section again, and several times he pointed to heads and said, "Don't know 'em." But his list of names was twelve long by the time we reached the section of the girls leaving the restaurant and getting into a black cab limo. He watched that part four times before he finally said, "I don't recognize the driver, which I should if he drives for a vamp. And that isn't a regular licensed driver either. The car is personally owned." He pointed to something attached to the dash and said, "Radar detector. They're legal in the state, but no company allows them in their cars, and if a driver had one he plugged in, why have it in the city? Makes no sense. More importantly, these are heads." He tapped the screen and I studied what I had thought were shadows. They were sitting in the seat facing back, and while they were indistinct, we could see Rachael and Bliss clearly. Bliss' eyes were wide and her mouth was in a little O of surprise and delight. Rachael was laughing. "There were people already in the car. People they recognized and felt safe with." He sounded long-suffering.

His girls had gone off the reservation, to use a U.S. government line about my people. I let one side of my mouth rise with relief. "They weren't taken against their will," I said. "Good. We'll keep looking, but I'm guessing they got an offer they couldn't refuse."

"Yeah." He breathed out the word. "Someone at the party offered them something they wanted. It didn't have to be money either. Bliss and Rachael have been making noise about signing on for full-time service." At my blank look, Troll said, "Becoming full-time blood-servants to one master rather than working for Katie. They got money. Katie makes sure they have excellent financial portfolios. So whatever they were offered, it had to be worth stiffing Katie. She'll be"—he looked around the room to make sure there were no children present—"pissed. Sorry, Janie, but she will be."

I shrugged. Living with the Younger brothers was making me inured to mild profanities and minor vulgarities. "We'll keep looking, but it goes to the back burner unless we learn something else."

"Yeah." Troll stood and looked around, as if thinking. "One other thing. Probably not related. Two of the humans in the footage are blood-slaves looking for a permanent master. "They're both sick today, along with four others in the city."

"Sick?" I asked. Blood-slaves, like blood-servants, didn't get sick. Vamp blood kept them healthy, though it also kept them blood-drunk and passed around to be dinner and sex toys among vamps. "Sick how?"

"Fever. Malaise. Leo sent them to his vamps for healing. But . . ."

"But it's weird," I said.

"Yeah. Weird." Before I could ask, he added, "I'll find out if they all went to the party." Troll lumbered to the front door. "Later, y'all. And get this fixed." He pointed to the covered window. "You already put Katie on the bad side of the New Orleans Vieux Carré Commission with your last construction and repairs." He let himself out.

I looked at Eli and explained, "Historical commission. I fixed the door last time and it didn't match up perfectly and eventually Katie had to pay a fine, even though we matched the door to the oldest photos of the house."

"Last time?" he asked.

"Long story." I studied the list of names on the spiral paper Troll had stuffed into my hand. "He recognized four vamps and eight humans. We'll talk to them if the girls don't turn up soon. Any news on Molly?"

"Just one thing," the Kid said. "The mileage on Molly's rental car. According to an online mileage calculator site, the distance from Asheville to Knoxville is eighty-two miles. She paid mileage on one hundred forty miles. Molly took a side trip before she turned in her car and disappeared."

"My wife doesn't want to be found," Evan said, sounding surprised and deeply injured.

"Maybe the other things Molly mentioned in her note to you, the ones that needed putting to rights, are part of the extra mileage on the rental?"

"She took care of something nearby, close to home," Evan said. "Then she disappeared."

"Mileage," Alex said. "Lemme work on that."

The Kid spent an hour trying to figure out where Molly might have driven to account for the extra miles, but it wasn't happening. There were too many possibilities. Big Evan had stopped pacing and spent the time sitting on the couch, studying his hands. I didn't know him as well as I knew Molly, but I knew he was thinking about how Molly had deceived him. I needed to keep him feeling positive, so I said, "I need to know everything about Molly. What she's been doing, how she's been feeling, who she's been seeing, what spells she's been working—"

Big Evan's head whipped to me. "I told you her magic's been off. Plants dying around the house, her not being able to heal them. Her magic's the biggest part of the problem," he growled. "She hasn't been working any spells. None. Not since Evangelina died."

CHAPTER 4

A Touch of Tasteless Snark

The couple had been having problems, something Evan had confessed to us after an hour of silent hand-staring. He didn't know what had been going on with Molly.

"She stopped talking to me," he said, after lots of prodding. "She stopped sleeping with me. She stopped working in the garden. She stopped baking. She stopped . . . singing." He looked at me, his face stricken. "That was the worst part. Molly always sang. Always. I never remember a time when she didn't sing. Old songs from movies, or Broadway, or church. Children's songs. Always singing. The house was silent for months.

"The last time I saw her, she kissed me and said goodbye, just like always. There was nothing different that day, except for this look in her eyes. This . . ." His hands flapped as he searched for a phrase. "This determined happiness. I thought it meant she had worked through whatever was wrong. I had no idea she was leaving." He broke down then, and turned his face away so we couldn't see his misery.

I had patted his broad back, as if that might help. It hadn't. And I had no idea what to say to make it all better.

Now, lying in the dark of my room, I had a feeling that there was a lot of stuff going on with Molly we didn't know, and the secret stuff was the important stuff. Where had Molly gone on her fifty- to sixty-mile excursion? What had she needed to make right? Why had she said she was coming to see me and then not shown up? And most important, why had she stopped doing magic?

Magic to witches was as natural as rain was to clouds, as natural as the cycle of the moon, as the motion of the tides, the flowing of rivers, the eruption of lava, the growth of plants, the movement of tidal winds. It was nature in all its glory and all its power, and once a witch began using her gift, denying it was said to be impossible, which meant that either Molly was practicing in private or something had happened to her magic. Something bad, or she would have told her husband. Beast padded to the front of my mind and lay down, staring into the dark. Her tail tip, thick and rounded, was twitching just a bit, showing her inner agitation at all the humans and witches in her house. But she had been mostly silent about it all day.

I rolled over and stared out the window. The night and a cloak of fog had closed in the house, making it feel small, isolated, cocooned, and too full. I lay in the dark, wearing a long-sleeved tee and flannel pants for the snuggle effect, hearing people move through the house, little groans of floorboards, small squeaks of stairs, voices murmuring, the sound of breathing. Too many people. It reminded me of the children's home where I was raised, and none of those memories were particularly wonderful. Unlike at the children's home, these people were friends and family, but . . . I just wasn't used to having them all here, all the beds full, the house busting at the seams.

Like pack, Beast murmured deep inside. She wasn't happy for reasons I didn't fully understand. And if I would admit it, *I* wasn't happy. I flopped back over, my hands behind my head, the covers up to my neck, and stared at the ceiling, the fan above me hidden in the shadows. But if I was honest, I was unhappy for reasons other than the people in my house. I was unhappy because of Molly.

My best friend in the entire world was in trouble. She had told her husband she was coming to see me, though she had refused to see me or speak to me in months. *Why?* Why would she not just pick up the phone? Why lie? Why all the deception?

Unless . . . Maybe Molly left that note, because she knew if she told Evan that she was coming to see me, he would follow . . . and she wanted him here? Why? My stomach muscles clenched as things started coalescing in the back of my brain, straining to take a form that I couldn't yet make out. I slowly sat up in bed.

Either she was throwing him off the trail or she really was coming to New Orleans. Yet she had disappeared. And that side trip? All of Molly's friends and sisters lived in or around Asheville, North Carolina. Where had Molly gone for fifty or sixty miles? Why had she then turned in her car and disappeared? And how was she living without money? *That* was the real question. Sooo . . . Molly had a plan. And I needed to find out what it was. And where she was getting her money. And if she ever got to New Orleans. Or if something had changed her plans against her will.

Taking the cell off my bedside table, I texted the Kid: *Find where Molly's mother lives. Name something like Bedelia Everhart. Check mileage. Start file.* Whatever had happened afterward to change her plans, Molly's original scheme had included me. That could be the only reason for using my name. So where was she?

I struggled awake in the night, feeling/hearing/knowing my door was opening. A faint *scritch* of wood on wood. The air moved differently over my face. The sound of the central heater was less muted, with a more hollow hum. And I smelled Angie Baby. "Aunt Jane? I'm scared."

"Come on in," I whispered, lifting the covers.

She slid into the bed, whispering, "Scootch over," and she spooned into my tummy, pulling my arm across her. The smell of strawberry shampoo and witch child filled my nostrils. The bed, which had felt just fine only moments ago, felt wonderful now.

Kit, Beast thought, purring happily.

I was glad it was dark because I knew there was a silly, goofy grin on my face. "What about Little Evan? Don't you think he's scared?"

Angie Baby sighed and settled deeper against me. "EJ's brave. G' night."

"Good night, Angie."

Moments later, I heard small feet pattering down the stairs, and EJ raced into the room through the open door, saying, "Me too! Me too!"

The silly smile still on my face, I reached over and lifted

him onto the bed. He crawled across me, pushed me off my own pillow, and flopped into the warm spot. I pulled the other pillow over and fluffed it until it fit my neck and face, EJ's cold back nestled into the small of mine. I pulled Angie close and closed my eyes, more than satisfied. And Beast was still purring. Finally she was content.

Beast kicked out, swiping my mind awake. Instantly my hands found the children, safe and asleep against me. *What—?* My cell vibrated on the bedside table. By Beast's alert interest, I knew it was Leo. I took the cell into my hand, holding it as I pushed Beast away from control of my mind. She wanted Leo, always had, and the binding only made it worse. I needed to make sure that Leo never learned about the other soul that lived inside me, nor the fact that she was bound to him.

I eased out of the warm bed and padded into the living room, sitting on the couch and pulling the coverlet over me. I checked the time before I answered. Three eleven a.m. Like the middle of the day to a vamp. "Yellowrock."

"My Enforcer." The words were a soft rumble of sound, a possessive vibration that pulsed on the binding and made Beast ready to roll over and offer him her belly. Leo was using that come-hither tone the really old ones use when they are seducing for dinner and sex, and Beast liked it. My usual defense to all that was a touch of tasteless snark.

"Mornin', Leo. 'Sup?"

His hesitation was slight, but noticeable, and I grinned in the dark until he said, "You will attend me before dawn. We have much to discuss."

It wasn't a request, and because the MOC paid my quite hefty retainer, I had to obey. But I didn't have to kowtow to him about it. "Okeydokey, Your Royal Fanghead. You want I should bring my shooter? My tech guy? Or just me?"

He didn't answer for a moment and I could almost see him trying to find a response to my smack. "You alone will be sufficient," he said at last. "Shall we say half an hour?"

"Sure." I thumbed the cell off without waiting for his permission, which was totally satisfying. It wasn't much rebellion by anyone's standards, but it was all I could manage, and until I could find a way to break my binding, I wasn't going anywhere, so I might as well get paid for it. Moving silently in the dark, I dressed in jeans, boots, a fleece tee, and a leather jacket against the wind chill. I tucked the covers around Angie, picked up EJ, and made my way up the stairs to Evan's room, to tap on the door. When he opened it, he was wearing a robe, for which I was grateful, as I had once seen Big Evan in his version of sleepwear—boxers and not much else—and once was enough. He took in my clothes, seemed to reach a conclusion, and tilted his head in question.

"His High and Mighty requested my presence before dawn. Will you let the wards down and put them back up?"

Evan whistled a soft single note, and I felt an indistinct prickle of magics against my skin as the wards fell. "Kids were both in your bed?" he rumbled in his version of a whisper.

"Yeah. They might be confused when they wake up." I handed Evan his son, and watched with something like longing as he nestled the boy's head on one shoulder and the sleep-limp body across his barrel chest. EJ's arm came up and he hugged his father in his sleep, his lips making several smacking sounds as he adjusted his position. "I'll bring up Angie. When you hear Bitsa start up in the street, you can reset the wards."

"What's up?" Eli asked. I hadn't heard his door open and his voice came from the shadows. "Going somewhere?"

"Yes," I said shortly. Once upon a time and not so long ago, I could come and go with no problems. Now it was like a theater production. I half expected someone to shout, "Lights, positions, aaaaaaand *action*." But then I realized my tone might have been rude, and added, "Leo called. It's okay. Go back to bed."

I made my way back down the stairs, brought up Angie, and returned to the ground floor, where I opened the safe room door, hidden behind a bookshelf that moved on rolling hinges. The safe room was once used by Leo and his heir as a secret lair for their daytime trysts. Back then it had only one opening, through the floor from underneath the house, and was furnished with a bed and expensive sheets. The bed was still there, though now it was covered with sharp, shiny things and things that go bang and shoot, to kill big bad uglies. I chose a nine-millimeter semiautomatic handgun and two blades, strapped them on, and closed the door on its silent hinges.

Not speaking to anyone else, I took the side door, zipping my jacket as I walked. I helmeted up and pushed Bitsa down the narrow drive, unlocked the tall wrought-iron gate with the fleur-de-lis at the top, and relocked it behind me. I kick-started my bike and headed off to vamp HQ, face shield up, out of the way, so I could take in the morning scents. I could have walked, but arriving on foot was not nearly as impressive as the growl of a Harley, and with vamps and their minions, style is everything.

The gate opened as I tooled down the street, which was against protocol, but then I saw Wrassler in the shadows, heavily armed and ready for action, with low-light goggles in place. The security guy, muscle-bound and tough as nails, could surely see my face, and I lifted a finger to acknowledge him. He raised the goggles, lifted a finger in return, and closed the gates after me. I left the helmet on Bitsa and took the stairs to the front door of the white stucco-and-stone-faced building, my hip-length braid bouncing against my backside.

The door opened before I had to announce myself on the intercom and I strolled through the outer doors and into the bulletproof glass breezeway. Two black-suited unfamiliar blood-servants nodded greetings to me, standing at the tables in the breezeway, and I placed my weapons in the black resin trays on top. It was Security 101, protocols I had instituted, and I studied the newbies and their demeanor as I complied with my own rules. They could have been twins, perfect as bookends, Caucasian, nondescript, brown hair cut short. Both moved like former military, in top physical and mental shape, each about five foot ten, buff and somehow fast-looking, and they clearly had both been through the meet-and-greet lecture I had helped to prepare. They looked tough, yet managed to smile and come across as happy to see me.

Without being asked, I assumed the position and let one of the guys pat me down. The procedures didn't take long. I had brought only enough weapons to fight off and incapacitate or kill two vamps if they decided to attack me in the streets. I have enemies with long memories. Of course, if enough vamps decided to attack me at once, I'd be brought down by sheer numbers. Idly, I wondered how many blood-sucking enemies I had in the Crescent City. I ran out of fingers in my halfhearted count. I waited as my weapons were taken inside and locked away in the weapons safe I'd had installed in the nook near the front door.

"This way, Miss Yellowrock." My frisker opened the inner doors into the marble-floored foyer. The smell of mixed vamp, blood-servants, and human blood hit me like a landslide. It was the stench of a funeral home: herbal and floral scents—dry and desiccated—all the mixed blood, some old and some brand-new. Beast's ear tabs twitched, and I opened my mouth so she could taste/smell it all. She chuffed with reaction, whether liking the scent blend or not, I couldn't tell. But I could feel her desire for Leo as she automatically parsed his scent signature out from among the others and breathed it deep. The binding on her pulled hard at me as she pushed me to go find her master and crawl into bed with him. *Not gonna happen,* I thought at her.

She spat in reply and hissed, showing her teeth, but backed away, into the deeps of my mind.

"I can find my way," I said to the guard, testing.

"No, ma'am. It's our pleasure to provide you escort."

"Nice. Names?"

"Steven, with a *V*, Locke, with an *E*, and Stephen, with a *PH*, Hope."

"Mmmm." I stuck my hands in my pockets and followed Steven-with-a-*V* down the hallway and up the stairs. "Steven," I said, "not to quibble, but if I had a weapon still on me, say a garrote, I could bring you down fast and get your weapon. Suggestions?"

Steven-with-a-*V* stopped and gestured me forward, to walk beside him, amusement evident on his face at the thought of a lean, leggy female taking him down. "Yeah, that works. Unless there are more than one visitor. Then maybe two escorts?" Steven nodded and I said, "I'll adjust the protocols. Thanks." I knew all that stuff, and had already formed my own opinions, but working with the guys meant including them in the routine changes. Now, when I changed the paperwork, Steven-with-a-*V* would be able to say something like "Yeah. We discussed it. I suggested the change. Yellowrock's not bad for a chick. Even if she did imply she could take me with a garrote." Cue manly laughter at the little woman.

He knocked on a door and opened it, showing me

through before closing the door behind me. The papery, peppery scent of Leo flooded my nostrils and reached deep inside me, wrapping the silvered chain of the binding in an iron fist. Warmth flooded me. Beast sat up and looked out through my eyes, taking a breath and analyzing the scents. Leo's was heated with the smell of anise, old paper, and ink made of leaves and berries. *Good vampire smell*, she thought at me. I wanted to sigh, but kept it in, and shoved down on her to show her that I was alpha, not her. There would be no mating with Leo.

I walked down the short wide foyer into the room beyond. The office of the Master of the City had been rebuilt in the last few months, and once again looked just as it had the first time I was here. It was a windowless inner room: the walls were hung with tapestries and heavy drapery; Oriental rugs in every shade were scattered over the floors. Not that long ago, one rug had been heavy with werecat blood. That one was gone, probably with the cops and later stolen away by the vamps. Cops had a hard time hanging on to evidence when vampires were involved.

The room was chilly, even with the hickory wood fire, something the old ones all seemed to like, probably for the ambience of their own time as humans. The bookshelves around the fireplace were new, filled with antique books, and hiding two no-longer-secret escape passageways. I'd been hard on Leo's secret-keeping.

The furniture was wood, some hand-carved, some burled, others with gilt that glinted in the firelight and lamplight. Wingback chairs were around a small table, and the desk was so old it might have been hand-carved for a Spanish royal in colonial times. A thin laptop was open on it, in front of a modern ergonomic desk chair, the armoires locked behind it. They did double duty as file cabinets.

There was a chaise longue in the back of the office, a fancy one with tufted gold velvet upholstery and a velvet throw. Once before, I had been here and a naked girl had been sleeping on it. Tonight it was empty. Thank goodness. Though Beast disagreed and showed me an image of Leo and me on the couch having a grand old time.

I strolled in and plopped down into a wingback chair, uninvited. Put my boots up on a table and made myself look comfy. Leo was sitting at his desk in the leather chair, pa-

pers on the table before him, a pen in his hand, its nub
scratching as he wrote. The master vampire was wearing an
old-fashioned shirt, creamy silk with full sleeves and a tie at
the neck, hanging loose. Not like a modern tie, bright silk
with a pattern, chosen from dozens hanging in a closet, but
slender white ties that were part of the shirt itself, part of
the rounded band of the collar. The upper part of his chest
was visible, collarbone catching the light in a pale-pale sheen,
along with a few black chest hairs. His legs were stretched
out under the desk, encased in black pants, some sort of
nubby fabric with a dull sheen, and on his feet were black
socks and plushy slippers. His black hair was pulled back
into a little queue with a black ribbon, a loose tendril brush-
ing his cheek. I knew how preternaturally soft his hair was.
How silken his skin. Beast stretched out, purring.

I curled my fingers under to keep from reaching for Leo,
feeling the pull of the binding, and wondering again why
Leo never seemed to. It had to be because the binding was
completed while I was dying and changing into Beast. It
was the only thing that made sense. He put the pen down,
laced his fingers together on the desktop, and raised his face
from the desk to me. His eyes were French black, his skin
pale olive. From the darkness of the blue vein running
across his forehead and down his temple, I could tell he
hadn't fed tonight. I breathed in, and he smelled hungry,
which was an uncomfortable thought. Leo's eyes held mine,
without a hint of compulsion, curiosity in his expression
rather than a predator's gaze, and I let myself relax, just a
hair. Just a bit. Waiting.

"Things have changed since you arrived in my domain,"
he said slowly. "You are not entirely at fault, but you are . . .
a catalyst, a goad to transformation." That was true, so I
didn't respond. "We needed this stimulus that you have
brought, but it has been painful to many of us." Leo had
fought a war since I first came to New Orleans, killing lots
of his enemies, losing lots of his friends, disbanding half of
the established clans, leaving four instead of the original
eight, and that was only the most obvious of the changes. So,
yeah, painful. He had a point.

But I wasn't going to let it stand as totally my doing,
because no way was that the truth. At the same time, I also
didn't want to provoke him unnecessarily. It was one thing

to annoy the alpha predator over the phone, and totally different to bait the vamp in his lair. I said, carefully, "You used me and my presence here to achieve some important goals."

He shrugged elegantly, his head, shoulders, and arms moving as if choreographed. "I am the creature that nature and the Mithran blood has made me. I make efforts to rule with fairness and compassion, but I am not afraid to use the skills and abilities and people at my disposal as I see fit to accomplish ends that will keep my people and my lands safe."

Behind him, the door opened. I smelled Bruiser's scent even before he appeared. He was wearing a new cologne, subtle and citrusy, applied with the light hand of someone who lived with predators who had an excellent sense of smell and an aversion to strong perfume.

He entered the office proper and stood in the opening, his hands behind his back, as if at parade rest, though as far as I knew, he had never been to war. He gave a smile, his lips pulling slowly as he took in my boots on the table, my slouch, and Leo's studied patience. "Leo. Jane," he said, acknowledging us both, in order of social and dominant importance.

Bruiser—George Dumas—was elegance itself, some of that refinement coming from the upper-class British upbringing, and some from his years acting as Leo's chief blood-servant, head of security, and Enforcer. Leo's real Enforcer, as opposed to my part-time job as imitation Enforcer. Tonight he was dressed in slacks and a starched shirt, the sleeves rolled up to show his arms, lean and muscled, and worn, brown loafers, no socks. Which made me smile for reasons I didn't bother to try to understand.

"Sit, my primo," Leo said. When Bruiser sat beside me, Leo went on. "We have several things to discuss. First is the illness of several blood-slaves. It is not the plague. More . . . much like the common cold that is apt to infect humans who do not drink regularly." To me he said, "George is attempting to discover if they share anything in common. Worse is the disappearance of a Mithran in what appears to be a hoax or perhaps a kidnapping. I speak of this only to keep you informed," he said to me. "I do not wish you to engage in the search or the investigation at this time. George will deal with this issue. I have other needs for you.

"Tonight at dusk, I will receive a communiqué from the European Council. There have been rumors of what the call might mean, but rumors are faithless things, promising much and delivering little." I almost smiled at that, but he went on. "There will be a meeting of the full New Orleans Mithran Council just after midnight to discuss this call." He looked at his primo as he spoke and Bruiser nodded, understanding some unspoken command. "At that time, I will schedule a *gather* to announce to the clans the European plans and rulings, as well as to present the new Mithrans who have risen this season."

To me he continued. "I wish you to oversee the security for this *gather*. In-house protocols, safety measures for parking, vetting the waitstaff, and overseeing the caterer's arrival and exit."

A *gather* was a meeting peculiar to vampires. A powerful vamp could announce a *gather* and command all the vamps who had sworn him allegiance to show up. Then it was like—and yet very unlike—a democratic meeting. They might party, drink a few humans, maybe have a little sex, because for vamps, dinner and sex went together, or they might get right to business and discuss. Said discussions were not always peaceful; some required persuasion and a battle of compulsive power. Then the gathered would come to some conclusion and act. At least that was what had happened at the *gathers* I'd seen. "Okay," I said. "Standard security?"

"More than that. Many things may change in the next months and announcements will not all be met with joy." His voice went steely. "There should be no repeat of the events of our last soiree."

My lips tightened involuntarily, and I knew Leo saw the small movement. I had screwed up at the first vamp shindig I worked. Werewolves had gotten in by leaping from roof to roof and busting in through the stained glass windows in the ballroom. I had since figured out how they had gotten in and placed more security cameras to cover the roof system and the walls outside the grounds, and while no one could fault me for not knowing that werewolves could leap forty feet, my security measures had still been insufficient. I nodded once, feeling a bit as I had as a kid being reprimanded by a very proper and intimidating principal.

"We have arranged for enough human warriors to keep my people peaceful and safe," Leo said. "Derek Lee has been informed that you will be contacting him, and will need his men. There is a meeting of the full security team tonight before dusk. At the meeting, Derek will place himself and his men under your command."

Leo always meant more than just what was said, and my eyes narrowed as I took all that in. Derek was placing himself and his men under *my* command? I'd gotten the impression that he'd rather eat dirt than take orders from me again. It would undoubtedly tick off the former Marine . . . which could be fun. I should bring popcorn. Wisely, I didn't say that.

Leo turned his Frenchy black eyes to me. I felt their weight and the leashed power in him as he added, "At the *gather*, you will be acting as my true Enforcer."

If I'd been in big-cat form, my pelt would have spiked up. Leo had tried to make me his true Enforcer once before. It hadn't been a pleasant experience. But he had said, *You will be* acting *as my true Enforcer.* Acting. Not actually being. I glanced at Bruiser, who had polite interest on his face. It wasn't the expression of a guy who had just been fired in favor of the new girl in town. But something felt wrong with all this—wrong in a "Jane is about to be hoodwinked" kinda way. And Beast didn't like it, which was odd, because she was bound to the MOC and should be happy about anything that brought her closer to him.

To make certain that Leo was saying what I thought he was saying, I said, "I won't permit you to force a feeding from me again." It came out half growl, and my upper lip curled to show my teeth as Beast leaned in hard, showing her displeasure at the memory of pure predatory dominance. "I will not be bound to you against my will." Bound *more*, but I wasn't saying that part, since Leo didn't know. "I'll stake you or die trying."

Leo looked away and back up quickly. In a human that might have been a tell, a physical tic that indicated stress or a lie or— "Primo. A moment of privacy, please." Bruiser glanced from me to his boss and stood, gave a formal-looking nod that could have been a modified bow, and silently left the room. When the door shut behind him, Leo said, "I wounded you. I am sorry."

I sat up in my chair and put my feet on the floor. "Say what?" I felt Beast pawpawpaw into the forefront of my mind, and I breathed in through my mouth, taking in the MOC's scent. He wasn't lying. There were no stress hormones on the air. If anything, I smelled something that might have been called meekness, if such emotions had a scent at all. Inside me, Beast chuffed with confusion and flicked her ear tabs.

"A master," he said, studying his hands on the desk, "does not force his will upon others to feed or to bind. A master does not use violence on those under his care without need. A master, by definition of the word, should never have to resort to such methods." His hands went flat to the table as if holding himself down, and his eyes went unfocused. As if memories carried him to places he'd rather not revisit.

"I was close to reentering devoveo when you saved me from the hands and fangs of my enemies. I had been *drained*, Jane. Tortured. And you freed me. To save me, my people fed me full, beyond volumes even Naturaleza might drink. They brought me both humans and Mithrans and I drank deeply, nearly draining the cattle, in order to keep me from the brink of true-death. But it was not enough. My body healed, but my mind was . . . fragile. My . . . instability . . . was not an excuse for what I did, as Americans say, but this does offer some explanation."

My mouth had gone dry during his halting words and I had to fight to breathe slowly, but calm was far from me. I knew Leo could hear my increased heartbeat, and smell the shocked pheromones seeping through my pores, because his pupils dilated. It was a vamp predator reaction.

His control held and he went on. "Perhaps if my heir had not been recently risen from being put to earth. Perhaps if my primo had not been recently risen as Onorio. Perhaps if my Mercy Blade had not been acting upon agendas of his own, and perhaps if the priestess had not kept information from me . . ." He shrugged again, and this one was far less graceful. "Perhaps many things. I was powerful, full of the blood of my people, but I was not in control when I forced you, when I drank from you against your will and attempted to bind you. I was not myself."

Leo raised his eyes from his hands and sat back, moving

slowly, the way one predator moves in the presence of another, to not startle or give cause for attack. "Your eyes glow golden," he said, his voice like a caress. "There is nothing in the few histories of skinwalkers that speak of such a bright glow. Yellow eyes, yes. But not this glow."

I struggled with my heart rate, trying to keep it steady as Leo said aloud something that been my secret, mine alone, and then mine and Molly's, for so very long. But my flesh went hot as I thought about what he might mean by the histories of skinwalkers and I had to wonder what he had discovered. What his priestess might have told him.

Leo went on. "You are different from others of your kind, I think."

Beast's hackles rose and I shoved down on her, feeling her slink away, her surprise as intense as my own that Leo would talk to me about all this, about any of this. But like any cat, she was also amused and delighted at the power play and at Leo's . . . tentativeness, was the only word I could find. She sat in the back of my mind and extruded her claws, pressing them into my mind. It hurt. She intended it to.

When I didn't respond, Leo lifted the fingers of one hand, as if throwing something to the side. "But that is of no matter. What is imperative is that I make this right. I forced a feeding. I hurt you."

I nodded, the movements jerky. My hands gripped the upholstered arms of the chair as if to keep me in place. "When I took your blood, against your will, when I attempted to bind you against your will, I broke . . . not law, but . . . custom, perhaps. That which is custom for masters. For the forced taking of your blood, I owe you a boon," he said, "at the very least. A great boon. You could have half of my kingdom." He smiled, but I just stared, not acknowledging his use of scripture in the analogy. "Until such a time as you claim it, you own part of me. I am yours to command."

"Ummm." *Yeah, that's telling him.* But really. What was I supposed to say? And *You own part of me? Say what?* I said instead, "But you gave blood to help Misha's daughter Charly stay alive."

"That was charity for one injured by Naturaleza."

"Okay. You owe me a big honking boon. Gotcha."

He didn't smile. "And"—he took a breath, deeper than

the ones that simply allowed him to talk; it was a human breath in its depth—"at some time in the future, when you are able"—he looked back at his hands and said in a perfectly human tone—"I would have your forgiveness."

If one of my vamp enemies had been in the room, he could have meandered over and drained me dry, before I could react, I was so stunned. "Uhhh."

"George and my servant whom you call Wrassler have additional information for you regarding the *gather*. You are dismissed."

Like usual. But this time I didn't even care. I stood, walked to the office door, and out into the hallway. Bruiser was waiting for me. Leo's primo looked me over, lifted a single elegant eyebrow, and closed his mouth on whatever he was going to say. Instead Bruiser said, "You look . . . peaked."

"Yeah." I blew out my breath and stuck my hands deep in my pockets, my shoulders up near my ears. "I think that means I look crappy."

Bruiser smiled, the motion slow as he took me in again, his eyes roaming almost possessively. He gestured along the hallway, indicating it was time for us to move. When we were some ten feet from Leo's door, he said, "You do not look crappy. You look lovely."

I shook my head but I couldn't help the grin his words brought to my lips. I wasn't a lovely woman by anyone's estimation. Interesting, maybe. When I was all doodied up maybe a bit better than interesting. But never lovely, which implied more natural grace than I'd ever had and bone structure that was less strong. But I wasn't good with compliments and so I just shrugged and followed him. Which was easy. Bruiser had, by far, the best butt I'd ever seen on anyone, and it flexed as he walked toward the front of the building.

"The boss said you have info for me?" I asked, changing the subject from me and taking my attention off his backside, to something I could converse about. Like business.

"Yes." Bruiser's lips pulled down into a scowl and he turned to me, tilting his head down so our eyes were on a level. "We have a Mithran missing, in a strange manner, and I have a bad feeling she is true-dead."

"True-dead how? When you behead a vamp you have a

lot of proof, most of it bloody and gory and hard to get out in the wash."

He slanted his eyes at me again, dark humor lurking around his mouth. "Strange. Like something out of TV or film. One of Leo's newly freed scions disappeared from her sleeping lair overnight. The only thing left was her jewelry, her clothes, and her personal items."

"No body. No head," I clarified.

"No. And nothing to wash out." He smiled.

"She maybe left with someone?"

"No. Her new blood-servants went to bed with her. When the boys woke, all that was left was a pile of dust. Ash and some kind of granules, actually."

My mouth opened and closed. I had nothing to say to that for way too many steps down the hallways. I figured the term *boys* meant her young blood-servants. Ewww. I managed "That is weird, even for fangheads. The boys hurt her? Burned her to ash?" Though I had no idea how that might be possible.

"No. Leo sent a master he trusts to drink from them. At dawn, they went to sleep in a pile like a bunch of puppies and when the boys woke, she was gone."

From a side corridor Wrassler emerged. "You tell her?"

"I did. She seems as bemused as we are."

Wrassler popped the knuckles of his left hand, and then the right, and what would have been snaps in an ordinary-sized human were more like *thunks* from his meaty hands. "I've been handling it." He looked at Bruiser and something passed between them that I couldn't decipher in the heartbeat of time it lasted. "I got a minor promotion to security chief."

I thought about that for a moment. The primo was security chief as part of his duties as primo, but he seemed almost indifferent at the change in the status quo. I wondered if the change was due to Bruiser's own change in status to Onorio and if he'd share later, or if I'd never be told what was up. Never was more likely. Even if Bruiser was some kinda superblood-servant, that didn't mean he would be free from loyalty to Leo. I did wonder if Superblood-Servant warranted his own comic book and I had to smother a laugh at the thought of him in a black bodysuit and bat wings. "Huh," I said, fighting the laughter. That's me. So good at soliloquies.

"Reach is researching any similar occurrences in the histories," Bruiser said. "It's nothing to worry yourself over just now, but be aware. Wwwrrassler"—he stumbled over the nickname and I let a smile form—"will send you reports if we hear anything useful."

I'd rather not spend my time bent over a bunch of electronic gear researching, so I wasn't going to ask for the gig unless it got more physical—boots-on-the-ground kinda stuff. I shook my head. "Yeah. Okay. What do you know about the *gather*?"

"Boss is nervous about it," Wrassler said. "Which is why he's got Bruiser overseeing the caterers personally, hand-picking the blood-meals, getting his pet designer to make sure everyone's clothes *coordinate*." He ran his hand over his scalp. "Leo hasn't been this worried about a meeting since the leopards came to visit."

"Who's the visitor?"

"Don't know. But scuttlebutt says the *gather* will be to discuss a future visit by the European Council."

I stopped dead at the top of the foyer steps, and so did the men. Wrassler wore worry on his big, flat-featured face. Bruiser was watching me work it through. "Leo said he'd be getting a *communiqué* from the EC," I said. "Not a phone call or a chat, but something that might be considered an order or a plan of action. The *vamps* from the council are coming? Sometime soon? Not their human lackeys?"

"That's what I hear," Wrassler said. "If the gossips are right, it'll be the first time the top European Mithrans left the continent since the eighteen hundreds, and the visit could be, maybe, in as little as six months."

Six months seemed like a long time away, but to a long-lived vamp that was an eyeblink of time. I guessed the vamps had a lot to plan. The European Council probably traveled with their entire households, steamer trunks full of clothes, dozens of servants, a lawyer or two, interpreters, cooks for the humans, maybe provisions of food that their blood-servants couldn't get here. . . traveling like visiting heads of state. If visiting vamps was the kind of rumors Leo had been talking about, then no wonder he was worried. I would have to readdress every bit of security, both physical and protocols, for that kind of gig, which was why Leo wanted me as acting Enforcer. I was more up-to-date on

current security hardware than Bruiser, his real Enforcer. I
started down the stairs again, Wrassler beside me, Bruiser
following. And this time I could feel his eyes on my backside and legs. Bruiser was a leg man. I felt warmth rise in
me, settling deep inside.

"In addition to the announcement," Bruiser said, "we'll
have visitors for the *gather*, and an introduction of the new
Mithrans."

Wrassler looked disgruntled at that and rubbed his scalp
again, a gesture that meant he was disturbed. "Yeah. I got
details." He pointed to the waiting room cum holding cell
just off the foyer. I went with him. Bruiser closed the door
after me, leaving himself on the outside without a word. I
figured he would catch up with me later. Wrassler opened
the small fridge and handed me a Coke. I popped the top
and took a swig.

"Two months ago, Leo sent Grégoire to Atlanta, to reor-
ganize De Allyon's clans, to bring to the light the Naturaleza who refused to accept Fame Vexatum."

I knew Grégoire, Leo's *secondo* heir, had been sent to
clean up the mess there, but I'd assumed he was back by
now. And "bring to the light" was formal vamp-speak for
killing a misbehaving vampire true-dead. Fame Vexatum
was the way vamps lived in the modern world. They pretty
much starved, but the starvation allowed them stronger
mental gifts of compulsion and more mental control than
other vamps, Naturaleza vamps, had.

"It's a real mess," he continued, opening a can of Red
Bull. "De Allyon had a human breeding and slave program
on a farm in the hills near Chattanooga." Whatever he saw
on my face made him chuckle dryly. "Yeah. Federal cops are
involved, and PsyLED, and because of all the hoopla, Leo
has instituted the hostage chapter of the Vampira Carta
with Lincoln Shaddock."

"*Hostage?*"

"Yeah. When Leo put Shaddock on notice for a decade
of reorganization before he could apply for Master of the
City status again, he set up an exchange provision."

I thought back to the night, months ago, of the *gather*,
the ceremony where the chief fanghead of Clan Shaddock
heard the result of his request for an upgrade in status. I
remembered something Leo had said during the ceremo-

nies. I quoted, as nearly as I was able, "For a certain amount of time there was to be the 'customary and agreed-upon exchange of blood-servants and scions.'"

He pointed a finger of approval at me. "That. A couple of our vamps and blood-servants are in Asheville, dealing with organizational stuff, so we get a new human and a vamp in exchange." Wrassler drank down his Red Bull in three swallows and crushed the can. He tossed it into the recycle bin, where it clanged around with the rest of the aluminum. "Quarters are tight here as it is, until Leo moves into his new clan home, and no one's happy about the new people. We had to clear out two bedrooms with four beds each already, four more for the *gather*, and the rest of us are bunking in together."

I sipped to hide my smile. "Sounds cozy."

"Not. Anyway, none of this household stuff is your job, since you already updated the hardware, but the *gather* will be."

"I'm supposed to be here before dusk to go over security for the ceremony."

"Come hungry. Stephen is making his signature chili, so hot it'll melt your eyeballs and fry your brain."

I finished my Coke and tossed the can. "Somehow that sounds more dangerous than delicious, but I'll be here."

"You only live once. Unless you're a vamp or a cat."

I chuckled at the joke, ignoring his speculative expression. *Yeah, I got killed, turned into a big-cat, and came back to life in the back of Leo's car. Not going there.* And didn't say it aloud. "See you tonight," I said, and made my exit from vamp central.

CHAPTER 5

Molly's Dead Body

The sun was rising over the French Quarter as I tootled home, trying not to think about all the things I had to do today. Trying to relax and enjoy the morning air swirling inside my helmet, warmer with the sunrise and the promise of springtime. Spring came early this far south, and flowers were already blooming, hints of the coming season in window boxes and narrow courtyards.

The Quarter smelled of water from swamp, bayou, and the Mississippi churning nearby, of petroleum products and emissions, whiffs of garbage that hadn't been picked up yet, and food. This early in the morning the air was redolent of strong coffee with chicory, bacon frying, eggs, grease, and cane syrup, the fresh smells overriding last night's older cooking smells: seafood and grease and hot spices.

My stomach rumbled, and rumbled again when I realized that some of the smells were coming from my house. As was the babble of morning cartoons, the ringing of cell phones, and the chatter of news programs, so loud I could hear them in the street when I turned off Bitsa and pushed her down the narrow, two-rut drive. My quiet sanctuary was quiet no more, and I decided that I really didn't care. Especially when the side door opened and Angie Baby and EJ hurtled through and right at me, screaming a chorus of "Aunt Jane, Aunt Jane, Aunt Jane!" I nearly dropped Bitsa catching them. *Yeah. This was why it was all okay.*

"Morning," I said, hugging them and then easing them to the ground. "Am I in time for breakfast?"

"Uncle Eli is putting it on the table right now," Angie said. "He's makin' us *French toast*," she said, saying it like it was an exotic, mysterious food. And then I heard the term. *Uncle Eli?*

"And syrup," EJ added. "Lossa syrup." He whirled and raced back through the open door and inside, his tiny blue sneakers pounding. Angie pulled me in after him, and I shut the door on the chilly air. I washed up and locked my weapons in the weapons safe in my closet, since I didn't want to open the safe room. No need to make the kids think they should explore.

I joined the others at the table. Evan and his kids sat with their backs to the windowed wall over the sink; my chair had the best vantage point since Eli was cooking, my back to the kitchen windows, but with both entrances in sight. Alex dragged to the table and slouched into his place, still wearing his flannel SpongeBob pj pants and holey T-shirt, eyes glued half-shut, and his body stinking of sweat. He might have steered himself down the stairs while asleep, but if so, he'd picked up his electronic tablets on the way. Or maybe he slept with them cradled to his chest. I grinned to myself, betting the latter.

Eli shoveled two pieces of French toast onto each child's plate; onto the adults' plates, he shoveled bacon and eggs, with sides of French toast. I say shoveled, because the flexible spatula looked big enough to garden with. He slid the syrup down the table into Big Evan's hand and Evan poured syrup onto the children's toast. "Thanks, Uncle Eli," I said, letting my lips curl up on one side.

He grunted, sat, and started to eat, but was interrupted by Angie, the bite halfway inside his mouth. "God is great, God is good."

EJ finished with "Let us thank him for our food."

"Amen, dig in," they both said. And did.

Eli finished the bite and chewed, his eyes looking over the people gathered at the table. When he reached me, I waggled my eyebrows, as if to say, *Fun, eh?* He wiggled his eyebrows back, a bored, minuscule brow-twitch while he swallowed, and took another bite. *Yeah. Like having a real family.*

The Kid stuffed in an entire piece of French toast and chewed, eyes still closed. He drank down a half mug of strong coffee after and made an exaggerated sighing sound of happiness. It looked as if he'd had a rough night.

When the children finished and had been dismissed to morning TV, Alex managed to get his eyes and vocal cords to function and said, "I found where and when Molly came to NOLA."

Once the anger—on Big Evan's part—and the delight—on my part—ended, he pushed his tablets across the table and said, "It wasn't easy. That side trip she took? It was most likely to her mother's house to pick up a credit card." He took a swig of coffee and poured another mug, looking at Big Evan under heavy lids. "She lied to you, man. Your mother-in-law, I mean, when she said she hadn't seen Molly. She not only saw her, but she rented a car for her in Knoxville, on her home PC. And she gave Molly a credit card. Molly used the same credit card for gas, food, hotels, everything. But for the last thirty-six hours or so, there've been no charges on it."

The Kid handed me a slip of paper, folded. Evan's eyes followed the motion and he frowned, but Alex quieted his worsening anger with the words "That's for that Leo stuff you asked for."

Liar, liar, pants on fire, I thought. But it was a good lie, as it kept Evan calmer. I glanced at the page and said, "Hope you didn't catch Big Brother's eye on this one."

"No chance of that. I'll have more intel later."

"Okay." I pushed back from the table. "When you find where Molly went, let us know. I have an errand to run for this." I tapped the paper and left the house, wondering why the Kid hadn't wanted Evan to know what was on the paper— the words *The Hilton on St. Charles Avenue. Checked in two days ago, under name Bedelia Everhart. Paid up front for seven days.* The room number was at the bottom. And then I realized. Evan would have insisted he go with me. And what if Molly was dead in the room?

The hairs lifted on the back of my neck. Molly had been in New Orleans for two days and hadn't called me. I crushed my fear and pain deep inside and helmeted up, letting the Harley roar for me as I pulled out and headed for St. Charles Avenue.

I valet-parked my bike, entered through the center of three huge arched openings, and headed for the elevator as if I had the right to be there. I rode up with a bellman and got off on the second floor, took the stairs up to the third floor, and made my way down the hallways to Molly's door, checking the security camera locations. Molly's room was in a little alcove at the end of the hall and out of the coverage area of the stationary camera, with a Do Not Disturb sign hanging on the knob.

I was sweating and my palms were damp. My breath came a little too fast. I was nervous. Terrified. And I was angry. Molly came to New Orleans and she didn't call me or warn me or tell her husband. She abandoned her children. Whatever had happened that forced her here, it could not be good. Some panicked part of the back of my mind was cursing and shouting and weeping. Beast was close under my skin, her pelt abrading my flesh, making me feel itchy and tight. A trickle of cold sweat slid along my spine.

No one was in the hall but me as I knocked on the door. When no one answered, I gripped the lever handle and drew on Beast's strength. Twisted the knob down and shoved. I heard the sharp snap of broken wood, the faint squeal of bending metal, and the door opened. I stepped inside and shut the door, leaning my back against it to survey the room.

Molly's scent filled my nostrils, warm as a hug and a mug of herbal tea. But Molly wasn't here. I knew that by the fragile, old feel of her scent. But there was no trace of blood. The fear that had been my constant companion on the way over eased slightly. No blood. No smell of her death.

I had more than halfway expected to find evidence of a fight, or the scent of Molly's blood—or even Molly's dead body—and the relief that rolled over me was as intense and pounding as an ocean storm. But it was arrested instantly. Molly wasn't here. I didn't have to deal with the horror of a murder scene, but I *did* have to deal with the stink of vamp and fear.

I closed my eyes to take in the scents, breathing in through my open mouth, letting Beast help with the identification. *Three vamps*, I thought. My skin crawled, as if small snakes crept up my limbs, at the smells—vamp scent. Dry and arid, a faint hint of old roses, blooms wilted and hanging on browned stems, and the underscent of turmeric, slightly spicy and almost medicinal. Not vamps I knew. Nothing in the signatures that identified a particular vamp. Not yet. I opened my eyes.

Three vamps against Molly. Not last night. The night before. Over thirty-six hours ago, just after Molly got here, three vamps had come to her room. The door hadn't been broken until I broke it, so that meant either she had left the door open and vamps had somehow found her and kidnapped her, or followed her in at vamp speed or . . . Molly had let them in.

The room was neat, the floral spreads on the double beds folded at the feet, one with an indentation on a blinding white pillow and rumpled white sheets, as if someone had lain down for a moment, but not spent the night. Or been tossed there and then pulled upright. The drapes were open, no luggage in sight from the doorway; the TV armoire in the corner was closed, hiding the TV, which was on, the sound muted, the picture flickering through the crack.

I moved silently through the room, touching nothing. Molly's suitcase was on a foldable stand to the side of the closet, the case open. A black cocktail dress and two pairs of dark slacks were hanging in the closet beside two jackets, one a knit sweater, but short-waisted—like a bolero, one a traditional business suit jacket that matched a pair of slacks. Two T-shirts and a pair of jeans. One pair of pumps and a pair of running shoes were on the floor of the closet. I had seen Molly pack for trips before. This was her standard weekend-off attire. Still in the suitcase were two nightgowns, Molly's underclothes, slippers, and a robe. On the counter beside the bed was a bouquet of very wilted daisies, in a clear glass vase.

In the bathroom, her toiletry bag was on the cabinet, zipped open, toothbrush and paste, comb, bar soap, and dried-out face cloth beside it. On the top I saw something strange—well, strange for Molly. With one finger I pushed the small bag open and discovered a long, thin plastic case. Knowing what I was seeing, but not believing it, I flipped the lid open. To see birth control pills.

Molly was on birth control.

I stared at the pack, stunned. Last I heard, Molly and Big Evan were trying for more kids. Lots more kids. Either something had changed or they were waiting or they were having marital problems and Molly was protecting herself or . . . Molly was having an affair and trying to keep from getting pregnant? Or I was out of the loop. Yeah. That. And none of my business, unless I discovered something about her disappearance that might be tied to the pills.

But Molly had been out of the room overnight. If Mol was on birth control pills and she was planning to be gone several days, she'd have taken them with her. So she planned on coming back when she went out. Or was carried out. Which meant that however she had left home, she was now gone unexpectedly. This was not good. I slid the pills back into place and closed the lid. I moved back into the room proper.

It looked as though Molly had arrived in New Orleans, taken a short rest, and started to unpack, which sorta eliminated the idea of vamps following her to her room and then using vamp speed to get in. But what say Molly had been going for ice or something and the vamps had followed her in? It was possible. So Molly had come to New Orleans and checked into a hotel. And then been abducted? I closed my eyes again and breathed through my open mouth, searching for even the slightest scent signature. The fear I had detected when I entered the room was still strong on the air. Panic pheromones. Though without any trace of blood. Nothing to suggest she had been injured. But she was gone and her things were still here, which was suggestive of her leaving under duress. Eyes still closed, I tried to envision Molly walking in to the hotel, her suitcase handle extended, the bag rolling on two wheels. Walking down the hall from the elevator, wearing a coat against the weather. The coat was brown, and looked good with Mol's reddish hair. In my imagination, her pocketbook was hung on one shoulder, a pocketbook that was as big as a shopping bag, to carry all her kids' stuff and her paperback novel and her phone and her electronic tablet. I opened my eyes, searching for the coat and bag.

Neither was in sight. I walked around the room, looking. Gone. Could Molly have grabbed up her coat and left willingly? Not been kidnapped? Not . . . Frustration zinged through me like a bell ringing, leaving my nerve endings tingling with worry. *No.* That wasn't right. There was noth-

ing willing about the smells here, but they were so old, and
buried under the air-conditioning and air fresheners and
carpet cleaners and detergent.

Human stinks, Beast murmured. I sucked air in through
my mouth, across the roof and tongue with a *scree* of sound.
Letting Beast smell. *Fear. Purpose. Anger. Annoyance. But
I/we do not smell panic,* she thought. *Smells on air say she
was afraid but not lose-bowels-in-death afraid.*

*She went with them willingly, but also against her will. As
if she stomped out, slinging her coat. But as if she had no
choice,* I thought back, understanding what Beast was trying to say.

Molly went with the vamps. That meant I needed to call
Leo. Either he knew what had happened here, or he sanc-
tioned what had happened, or he could find out about it.
Unless someone was in revolt against him. It had happened
before.

I left the room, and stood outside the door as I punched
in Leo's number, trying to decide what I wanted to say. The
call went to voice mail, and I spoke softly into the cell, my
words as formal as I knew how to make them. "Leo, Primo.
My friend Molly came to New Orleans. Three unknown Mithrans took her from her hotel room about thirty-six hours
ago. She went unwillingly. She hasn't been back. Please contact me and tell me what, if anything, you know about her
situation." I ended the call.

Feeling a chill that had nothing to do with the hotel's
air-conditioning system, I forced myself back to work and
studied the security cameras on the way out. There was one
stationary camera pointed at the elevators and fire stairs,
which I avoided by keeping my head down and walking
near the wall. Provided there were no problems with the
system, hotel security should have footage of the vamps
who came to take Molly, and the four of them as they left.

If I had known all this stuff when I went to see Leo earlier, I might have gotten some info from him. And certainly
more help. Now I'd be asking the Kid to commit another
crime by hacking into the security system. I was going to
hell. Yeah.

Standing in front of the hotel, I texted a note to the Kid.
Can u safely access hotel security cameras on 3 flr frm time

Molly checked in to 12 hrs after? I hit SEND and got a text back while I was waiting on the return of Bitsa.

Can do. Erase text.

"Yeah," I said softly to myself, following orders and erasing the texts. "So your brother doesn't flay me alive for leading you to the dark side and putting your parole in jeopardy. Which, to him, would be just as bad as blowing up the planet Alderaan with the Death Star. And I've been living with the Kid too long if I know that geeky bit of trivia."

"Sweet bike," the valet said, pushing Bitsa back to me. "One of a kind?" he asked, his smile wide in a dark-skinned face. Approachable. Nice. Helpful maybe.

I patted the leather seat affectionately and used his intro. "Yeah. You know bikes?"

"I ride with a group, all black guys and sometimes a couple a' chicks. We volunteer with the community and the local po-po. Dress up like Santas on wheels for Christmas, and take gifts to families in financial trouble. I ride a Hog, the 2013 Street Bob, but I always wanted an older model."

I nearly gulped. A Street Bob started at thirteen thousand bucks. Being a valet made more money than I would have thought. All those cash tips, maybe. But I didn't say any of that. "A Harley Zen master put Bitsa together from parts of two old bikes I found."

"You ever want to sell her, you let me know." He handed me a card, and I replaced it with a five.

"Not gonna happen," I said. "Bitsa's like family."

"I can see why."

"Hey," I said, figuring it was now or never, "were you on night before last when three vamps left with a redheaded human woman?"

Some of the light left his eyes, to be replaced with a cagey uncertainty. "Yeah, I was. I didn't have the keys, but I saw them leave."

I handed him another bill, this one a ten. "Was the human upright and acting normal?"

"Standing on her own two feet. Looked pissed. Said 'Thank you' when the fanghead opened the door for her, but it sounded like she coulda been saying for him to, uh"—his voice dropped—"get friendly with himself, if you know what I mean." He glanced to the side where a man in hotel livery stood, watching, listening to whatever he could hear over the distance. "She was sounding all like, you know, like she was lying and not really thanking him." He fingered the ten. "For another one of these, I could get the plate number for you."

"For the plate number," I said, "I'll give you *two* more."

"We keep a log. I'll be right back. And if my boss walks over, this is between us and off the record."

I stepped to the side so his body was between us, pulled riding gloves out of my pocket, and gave them to him. "I'll tell him I left the gloves on top of the saddlebags and you're looking for them."

He flashed me a smile, pocketed the gloves as if he did sleight of hand at kids' parties, and disappeared. I straddled Bitsa and unzipped my jacket, turning my face to the sky. The promised warm weather was arriving with piles of gray clouds and gusty, humid wind, and I was starting to sweat under all the leather. Beast wanted to find a hot rock and lie in the sun for hours, and I felt my face try to relax as she sent me a mental picture of her muscular body stretched out and snoozing. But underneath her lazy image I knew she was pacing, as worried as I was about Molly.

"Here, ma'am." The valet was holding out my gloves, a bit of white paper sticking out between them. I took them, handed him the promised bills, and got a brisk "Thank you, ma'am! You have a good day" in return. I texted the limo plate number to the Kid and kick-started my bike, making my way home, my heart feeling as if it weighed fifty pounds at the thought of telling Evan what I had found.

When I walked in the side door, Big Evan looked up and scowled. He must have been reading my body language because he puffed up and turned red and looked pretty much ticked off. I sighed and pointed to the kitchen table. Evan sent his kids to the TV room and I poured myself a cup of hot tea from a pot that someone had left on the electric tea warmer. Eli meandered in and hit START on the fancy-schmancy coffee and espresso maker I had paid for, brewing himself and Evan coffee, black and strong. Alex wandered in too, a tablet in each hand, his head bowed over them, eyes darting back and forth between them. Still silent, we all sat, which was all surreal, since no one had said anything.

Taking a fortifying gulp of slightly scorched bitter tea, I filled the small group in on Molly's actions and her unknown whereabouts. It didn't take long because there wasn't much, and I wasn't about to tell her husband how bad it might actually be.

Big Evan listened in silence and when I was done, he turned piercing eyes on me and said, "And do you want to tell me why I wasn't informed?"

"Because you'd have run off and gotten in the way and made a stink and caused trouble and scattered your scent all over the hotel room and brought in the cops, who have little to do with, and no control over, vamps. Molly went off with *vamps*, Evan. And I have contacts with vamps. The cops don't. You don't." I let that sink in for a while and said, "I have a question for you. If Molly told you she was coming to New Orleans to see me, and then didn't come see me, can you make a guess why?"

"She was kidnapped," he growled.

I didn't let myself react, because it seemed a likely possibility. Even if Molly had left the hotel under her own power, it hadn't been by free will, and it didn't mean that she had been making her own decisions, and didn't mean she was still missing by her own choice. With only a slight hesitation to mark my thoughts, I said, "Molly came here for a reason. She expected you to come to me, just like you did, so that, if she got in trouble, I could keep her family safe until I found her. She also wanted *you* here for whatever reason—and no, I don't know what it might be," I said as he started to interrupt. "Molly *had* to want my help, Evan. And she had to be in trouble or she would have told us all the truth and called me and told you and none of this would be happening."

And Molly hadn't trusted anyone with her reasons for coming to New Orleans. Not her husband. Not me. Molly was in deep trouble. I didn't say that aloud, but Evan must have realized it because he swore, "Son of a witch on a switch."

"Pretty much." With Molly gone from her hotel room, and not checking in with any of us, things had gone bad. Maybe real bad.

There was little for me to do on any of my cases, and so when our confab was over, I did what all good vamp hunters do when nothing is happening. I lay down. I didn't expect to sleep, but figured things might come to me if I put my feet up and closed my eyes and let my mind wander, let things percolate and steep and find unconscious connections. Fortunately, it was also nap time for the Trueblood children and I got in three long hours of uninterrupted, blissful rest, some of it probably snoring, despite my worry.

I woke when Angelina opened my door and stood there, one hand holding the knob, her body dangling from it, her feet pivoting as she swung back and forth and around. She had a doll under her other arm, and I recognized Ka Navista, the Cherokee Indian doll I had given her. Ka had black hair in a braid and yellow eyes like mine, and a wardrobe sewn for her of traditional Cherokee clothes. Ka originally had black eyes, but Molly admitted later that Angie had complained that the doll wasn't "right," so Molly had painted them to match mine. "Hey, Angie Baby," I said.

"Hey, Aunt Jane. Uncle Alex Kid says he has something for you and to wake you up, biscause it's important. *Be*cause it is important," she corrected herself. Angie was growing up and had been trying to break herself of baby talk the last time I had seen her; still was, it seemed.

"Okay." I rolled off the mattress and checked the time as I tucked my phone into my jeans pocket. It was two hours before dusk. Plenty of time. "Let's see what *Uncle Kid* has to say."

Angie lifted her arms to me and I picked her up, adjusting her on a hip so that Ka wasn't squished. I slid my feet into slippers, but the floor wasn't as chilled as it had been. The promised warm front was fully in, and rain pattered outside. I went to the kitchen, where I could smell tea steeping. I poured a mugful, getting a whiff of a spice-flavored tea left over from the holiday season. I added sugar and a dollop of Cool Whip and carried the mug to the living room. I set Angie on the couch and bent over Alex. "Got something?"

The Kid tapped a tablet, bringing up a still shot from the video feed of Bliss and Rachael getting into the black cab limo. He pointed to the driver. "His name is Alonzo Nubbins. He owns a car service that caters to vamps and their dinners. The night of the party, he was driving himself because a driver called in sick. He wasn't willing to give me any more info on the phone, so you might want to pay him a visit." He pointed to one of the unknowns in the car. "I'm pretty sure she's a chick and that she has long, straight red hair because it matches the shade of Rachael's hair in this light."

I leaned in. *Molly's a redhead. She might have straightened her hair.* And then I realized how stupid that was. Molly was not tied in to my case. The timeline was impossible. I was reaching for straws. I was starting to panic about my best friend.

The Kid said, "The other one looks like a dude, with a nose ring."

Once he pointed it out, I could make out the ring. It was an aggressive piece of jewelry.

"From what Alonzo *didn't* say, I'm guessing the chick's a vamp, and was turned when she was about fifteen. He implied that she was classy, like an old-world vamp, though the words he used were 'like she was a movie star, like from the 'forties. You dig? Like, a real classy chick.'" I managed a partial smile, but I didn't think it fooled Alex at his mimicry. "The other one he didn't say anything about, but I'm guessing it's the vamp's blood-servant or primo or something."

"How many redheaded vamps have lairs or homes in New Orleans?"

"A few. I pulled up six. If we could get a name—"

"Yeah." I stood. "Anything on Mo— On the family case?"

"Nothing new. I made it into the hotel security footage, but it's a lot of work to locate the right floor and right day without access to their dedicated system. I'll text you the minute I get anything. The plates from the limo that the 'family case' got into were hard to trace because your source didn't give you a state for the rental agency. The car was rented out of Galveston, Texas, seventy-two hours ago."

My forehead crinkled in surprise. *Texas?* Leo didn't rule Texas. I didn't know who did, but it was in a database somewhere. The Kid went on. "Within an hour, but not on the same credit card, two buses were rented, all vamp-specific, which could have nothing to do with the limo rental. Or it could be related." He shrugged. "I can't rule it out, so I included it in my report."

"Yeah. Good," I murmured, trying to figure out what Texas had to do with anything in New Orleans. "Find out which vamp rules Texas," I said. "I'll ask Bruiser to look into who came here and who is on Leo's territory. Vamps are real careful about traveling into another vamp's hunting grounds."

The Kid snorted at the term, but that was the way vamps thought of land—space filled with humans to hunt and drink.

"I'm supposed to be at vamp HQ before dusk for chili and a security meeting," I said. "I'll go alone. You and Eli keep working. And maybe send Eli to the black cab limo company to talk to Alonzo?"

Alex laughed softly and looked up at me under his shaggy, curly hair. "Yeah. Big brother could probably get all the info we need."

"Tell him no broken bones, no blood, no witnesses—real or electronic."

"Hmmph. Eli will charm the dude."

"Eli? Charm?" I thought about the way Eli acted around me—no charm at all if you didn't count innuendo and verbal sparring, most of which had dried up now that children were on the premises. And then I thought about the way he had handled himself at Guilbeau's, with Scott Scaggins. The former Ranger had skills that were vastly underused. "Okay. Yeah. Eli can charm Alonzo." I drank my tea and the spicy warmth eased some of my internal chill away.

Before I finished the mug, Big Evan came in, Eli behind him. Evan was grumpy, glowering at me, but at least he didn't jump me in my own living room. EJ, unimpressed by his father's size and attitude, raced to him, squealing. There was no way to be out-tuded by any guy, no matter how big and gruff, when a toddler (holding his sister's doll) was hanging on his pants demanding to be picked up. I managed to keep my grin off my face, but Evan clearly knew the picture he presented wasn't overly formidable; he heaved a breath at lost opportunity and lost machismo, and lifted his son to his shoulder. "You got anything?" he asked after EJ kissed him on both cheeks and tugged on his beard.

I pointed to the couch. "Angie, will you watch your brother for a minute?"

"Okay," she said, not looking up from the TV, which was

playing a Disney film, one with fish, the title escaping me.
Evan set his son down beside Angie while I got him a mug
of coffee and a package of cookies that he had brought in
the travel supplies. Old-fashioned Fig Newtons, which I
hadn't had since I was a kid. I bit into one as Evan lumbered
back to the kitchen and sat down. He slurped his coffee and
said, "You're about to piss me off, aren't you?"

"Maybe." I turned my mug in a circle on the tabletop. It
made little scuffing sounds on the old wood. "I left a message for Leo that Molly was in town and missing."

"And the fanghead said what?"

"Nothing so far. It's been three hours and no reply."

"I'll bust—"

"Nothing and no one," I interrupted without looking at
him. "I'm heading there shortly. I'll deal with it. And if you
can't sit things out, then I'll start telling you nothing. You'll
be out of the loop, and anything you do might endanger
Molly. She's in trouble. She'll need you whole and hardy and
full of power. So stay here. Protect your children."

I felt magic swirl into the room, dark and stormy. I didn't
look up. I didn't want to see what was in Evan's eyes. He
kicked back his chair and it hit the countertop before clattering to the floor. Eli stepped into the room.

"Dude. Chill," Eli said.

A moment later, the spiraling wind eased to nothing.
"You really got a pair of big ol' brass ones, don'tcha, Jane?"
Without another word, Evan left the room.

"I'll take that as a yes," I murmured to the tabletop.

CHAPTER 6

Well-Trained Junkyard Dogs

The rest of the day was busy but fruitless. Eli got nothing much from Alonzo. The driver of the black cab that had taken Bliss and Rachael from the party had taken the driving gig through his Internet Web page, and it had been paid for with PayPal. Which was just amazing. Vamps using PayPal. Who'da thunk it? The driver gave Eli the PayPal info and e-mail, which went nowhere when the Kid tracked it down, and the address where he took the girls when he picked them up from Guilbeau's. Which was another vamp party, at the Arceneau Clan Home.

There was nothing new on any case by the time I got dressed for vamp HQ, and I was feeling pretty itchy at the inactivity, and useless in my own house. I wasn't going to a party or a fight, so I didn't dress for either. I was in jeans, ancient black Lucchese boots, a T-shirt under a silk shirt I'd bought in a consignment shop, my gold nugget on its doubled gold chain, with the mountain lion tooth wired on. And I wore only a few weapons. By my usual weapons' standards I was nearly naked, but, because of the rain, I was being driven to my appointment, and self-protection was never a problem when Eli was around. I could see no weapons on him as he steered the French Quarter streets, wipers on low against the drizzle, but I was betting he was carrying three handguns and as many blades, with extra mags easy to hand, and that the back of the SUV was full of weapons, secured just under the floor.

The drive was silent beyond me saying, "Thanks for keeping Big Evan from trying to hit me. Or blow me away."

To which he answered, "Big dudes bleed, and it's a pain in the butt to get out of wood floors." I laughed and Eli gave a slight smile—tantamount to a belly laugh for him.

After that there was only the patter of rain, the swish of wipers, the splash of vehicles plowing through standing water, and the hum of motors. It was pleasant.

When we slowed in front of the steps leading up to HQ, Eli said, "You sure you don't want me to come with?"

"Nah. Help the Kid keep Evan occupied."

"Alex has him looking at surveillance footage from the hotel."

I thought about that for a moment and said, "Stuff Alex has already viewed, and found nothing, so that Evan doesn't see something first, and go off half-cocked?"

Eli let his lips stretch to something nearly like a smile. "My brother came up with that all on his own. Devious. I think we're rubbing off on him."

"I think he's growing up."

"Yeah." There was a note of confusion in his voice. "Call when you need a ride. Call if someone else brings you home. Keep me informed."

"Will do." I opened the SUV door and scampered up the stairs and into the air lock in the foyer. Eli's SUV motored away, the powerful engine thrumming steadily. I went through the meet-and-greet with the two newest twins. None of them were really related, but whoever put the teams together was going for a look-alike theme. This time the team was male and female, with long blond hair in ponytails, dark eyes, sculpted bodies, and similar heights, about five-ten or so, dressed in black. They looked polite and deadly, as if they'd smile convivially as they shot you dead.

I deposited my weapons and the leather file on the tables and the woman frisked me, still smiling. I needed to get up-to-date on the names of new security personnel, and make sure that only teams with the most experience got access to the doors. Good gatekeepers were a necessity and I hadn't taken that into consideration when I redid the security protocol handbook. That was change number two. I hated the paperwork that went into being Leo's part-time Enforcer. Old blood-servants weren't always the easiest to

retrain, and the ones in security needed to be flexible, hence
me in the position, helping out the hundred-plus-year-old
Bruiser, Leo's primo. My weapons were locked away as I
watched. "You are aware that in a security situation I'd get
to keep my toys."

"Yes, ma'am," they said together.

"Right this way, Ms. Yellowrock," the woman said.

We entered the foyer and I stopped, closing my eyes and
breathing in over my tongue. *Vamp, blood, sex, vampvamp-
vamp, food, blood, and vamp.* No hint of Molly. No hint of
magic on the air. And if the vamps Molly had left with were
here, I didn't know the scent sigs well enough to identify
them. Just the stink of vamp that made me want to sneeze.
I opened my eyes to see the security woman watching with
undisguised curiosity. I narrowed my eyes at her and she
took a step back fast. I flipped a hand, indicating I was
ready to continue, and it was a moment before she turned
on a heel and led me to the elevator in the back of the
building. We went up a floor and down a hallway, to a room
I hadn't been in recently—the blood-servant lounge. She
opened the door for me and the air that whiffed out smelled
heavenly, of beef and pork chili with beans, rice, and beer.
Yummy. I also smelled humans, human blood, human sweat,
and blood-servants, scents that were axiomatic anywhere
vamps laired.

I entered and stood to the side of the door, inside the
spacious room. Two blood-servants were arm-wrestling,
muscle-bound, bald, tattooed, and sweaty. On one large-
screen TV a game was playing. A cooking show was on the
other. The clack of pool balls breaking, an exhaust fan, and
lots of voices filled the space, as potent as the smells. Though
some of the occupants were in business black, most were
dressed casually in jeans and tees, boots, barefoot, some of
the guys in shorts and no shirt, one of the women in camo,
boots, flak jacket, weapons, the works. The eyes of the men
followed her around the room, which allowed me to watch
them, unobserved.

My eyes fell on one familiar face, one that shouldn't be
here, no way, no how. Blond, blue eyed, sassy, elegant, and
gorgeous, Adelaide Mooney hadn't told me she was coming,
even though I had seen her two weeks ago in Asheville.

I put two and two together with the info about Leo's

hostages from Lincoln Shaddock's city, and felt a grin try to split my face apart, but I held it in and sauntered across the room. I drew on Beast's stealth senses to help me move casually, smoothly, as if I belonged here. Which I did, sorta. I was nearly on her when Adelaide turned to me and lifted a delicate eyebrow. I so wished I could do that one-eyebrow thing, but it wasn't something one could learn—the ability to lift one brow was genetic.

It was odd to look directly into the eyes of a woman. At six feet, I overtopped most females, and while I was never vain, looking directly at Adelaide Mooney always made me feel inferior and plain. Adelaide was drop-dead gorgeous, and since she was a blood-servant, that was funny on all sorts of levels.

"My mother said hello, and to remind you that she owes you one," Del said, rather than a more conventional hello.

I blinked. I hadn't expected her to lead with that. I had been part of the team that saved Dacy Mooney's life, but the researcher who developed the vaccine cure for the vamp plague had really been the hero. All I'd done was help to get her treatment until the meds were ready, but somehow Dacy seemed to think it was all me and this wasn't the first time she had sent thanks. "Okay. Sure. Whatever." Man, was I charming and suave or what? "Ummm. You're welcome. Again."

That got me a smile and I rolled a shoulder in a shrug. "Buy you a beer?"

She laughed, that feminine tinkle-bell sound so many women could do, which I never had mastered. "Sure." She reached into a refrigerated ice-filled bucket, one with beer labels on the sides, and pulled out two cold German ones. She twisted off the tops and I accepted mine. We clinked bottles and sipped. The brew was rich and malty and bubbly and delicious. Dang. I was feeling all warm and fuzzy inside.

"So, you're a hostage?" I asked.

"In a manner of speaking, yes. Luther Astor and I. He's the Mithran donation, but it's all very proper and polite. I get my job description tonight."

"Who went to Asheville in your place?"

"Dominique and a human named Winston Beavers."

I paused with the beer halfway to my mouth. Dominique was Grégoire's heir, and with Grégoire in Atlanta, that left

a hole in vamp politics in general and a huge hole in Clan
Arceneau's leadership. If I wasn't mistaken, that meant that
one of my archenemies—which sounded so comic bookish
that I grinned—was in the leadership of one of the city's
most powerful clans. And the girls I was looking for had
been on the way to that clan home to party-hearty after
leaving Guilbeau's—in a car with a redhead. Said archen-
emy was redheaded. Of course, I hadn't actually talked to
anyone who had seen them at the clan home party. All I had
was indirect evidence and I knew better than to trust that.
Well. Wasn't that ducky? I wondered why I hadn't been informed about all the changes in Clan Arceneau. Oh. Right.
I wasn't hanging around vamp central much these days.

"Hmmph," I grunted, and sipped my beer. "You know
anything about vamps from Texas being in town?" I asked.

"No. I'm still being read in, though. I'm supposed to attend this meeting tonight," she said, "so I'm guessing I'll be
on security somehow."

I chuckled and Adelaide laughed with me. She was a
lawyer, not a shooter, and all I could think of was her stopping an intruder and making him sign a release form before
belting him. I drained my beer and dropped the bottle into
the empties bucket; it landed with a satisfying *clink-clank*.
"Just to cover my bases, my friend Molly is in town and she
went off with some vamps I didn't recognize by scent." And
that felt all kinds of wrong to say aloud. "She wasn't happy
about leaving with them, though I'm not ready to call it
kidnapping. Yet. Do you know anything about her?"

"No." Del looked worried, which warmed my heart. I
sucked at making and keeping friends, so it was nice to
know someone cared about the people I cared about.

"We'll get started when Derek—" The door opened, ad-
mitting Derek Lee and six of his men, all former active-duty
Marines, all African-American, and each and every one bad-
ass to the soul.

Derek sought me out from the doorway. "Injun Princess," he called out. It sounded like a barracks full of men
being called to attention.

"Legs!" his men chorused loudly as they filed in.

All eyes in the room turned to me, and everyone and
everything went mute, including the TVs. My palms started
to sweat. I hated to be in charge of meetings. Derek, as if

knowing what I was feeling, snorted in mildly malicious amusement. The seven were all dressed in night camo and looking so self-confident that the tattooed arm wrestlers puffed up like junkyard dogs.

"Sit," I said to the room at large, and chuckled when they all did. *Well-trained* junkyard dogs, chairs scraping, gear dropping, space provided and taken. Wrassler followed Derek's men in and took up a stance against the wall beside the door. I nodded to him and he nodded back, putting one hand behind him, probably to be near a spine-holstered gun. Quietly paranoid. I liked that in a man.

"I'll make it quick 'cause the chili smells good and I'm hungry." That got a laugh and I leaned my backside against a table, stretching out my legs, pointing my toes. "For those who don't know me, I'm Jane Yellowrock, currently the part-time Enforcer of New Orleans, and we have visitors coming in for a *gather*." That startled them, even Derek. Leo musta told them about the guests, but not about the formality of a *gather*. Interesting.

"I don't know who's coming in, and won't until the day of arrival, but you've already been making guest quarters clean and secure?"

"Six guest suites in all," Tattooed Dude One said, after a quick nod from Wrassler. He had a tattoo of a hawk on his bald dome. It was meant to be intimidating, but I thought it was cute. And knew better than to say so. I nicknamed him Hawk Head. "Two currently in use. Four more in prep. Hallway cameras are operational," he said. "Sprinkler system and exit alarms tested and are a go. Elevators are capable of lockdown. Exits are clear."

"Thanks." I didn't know him, and needed to. I made a note in my book to read the dossiers of all humans in vamp HQ. "Electronic security?"

Wrassler said, "All suites have been swept. All conference rooms have been swept. Ballroom and party suites have been swept. No surveillance detected." Which was not the same thing as there being no outside surveillance. Got it.

"I know you're already under tight quarters," I said, "and this makes it even tighter, adding guests and their security to the mix, but it won't last long. So be cool, and if they try to stir up something, bring it to Wrassler or Leo's primo."

They nodded, including Adelaide, who was sitting at a table, beer in front of her, taking notes in a dark purple notebook. The notebook matched her tees, her boots, and the necklace she wore—a massive purple stone wrapped in copper wire. Huh. Color-coordinated all the way.

"Two changes to the protocol," I said. "I want three people at both entries at all times when we have guests or when we have a social event. Two will stay put if one guest needs escorting. The one guard escorting will walk side by side with said guest, not in front to prevent attack from the rear. When two or more guests need escorting, one guard will lead, and the other will follow. The remaining guard will call backup to the front, maintaining a two-man team at the entrances at all times. I want that fourth guard in place before the others clear the foyer.

"Back gates are to be treated like embassy security or prison security. Anyone here familiar with that protocol?"

A hand went up and it was Tattoo Dude's. "I worked San Quentin for ten years. Know all about the entrance protocols. If you got mirrors and other equipment, I can set it up."

"Get with Wrassler," I said. "Make it happen."

When Tattoo Dude looked confused, Wrassler lifted a hand. "Me. If Janie likes or hates you, she'll rename you."

"And if she doesn't?" Derek asked.

"I'm guessing she's withholding final decision."

Derek stared at me. That wasn't quite right. I didn't know Hawk Head or Tattoo Dude, but they got names. That said, Derek and I had issues—like, even though he worked for the fangheads and for me, he didn't like nonhumans. I shrugged at him and went back to my notes.

"Night of the *gather*, I want all hands present. All leaves are hereby canceled." Several people groaned, and I shook my head with a slight smile. "Next, I want everyone in teams. I'll be going over the list for security personnel, and will be putting everyone in place on the night of the soiree. Go over the protocols, especially the amended procedures, and watch your e-mail in-boxes." I made several more announcements, all of it boring stuff, and then said, "Derek, get with me early on the night of. Any questions?" No hands went up and I said, "Last thing. As of seventy-two hours ago, we have a new vamp in town. Rented a limo in Texas. Anyone know about it?" No hands went up, no one looked secretive. Wrassler looked baffled and troubled. Vamps did not enter another's territory without certain procedures being followed. To him, I said, "Take it up with Bruiser and Leo. See if they know anything. See if one of the visitors for the *gather* is coming from Texas."

Wrassler said, "No one is coming from Texas. No one."

That wasn't good. Vamps making trouble at a *gather* wasn't unknown. A new vamp in town just before a *gather* was worrisome. "Meeting's adjourned," I said. "Let's eat."

Moments later, Adelaide brought me a bowl of chili with beans, over rice, and a loaf of bread on a wood paddle, with a serrated bread knife. We sat with Wrassler and caught up on Asheville, and the new personnel in HQ, and shared info and files on our electronic tablets, including the dossiers on the new people. It was homey. Chatty. Fun.

Until Beast sank her claws deeply into my brain.

I saw movement. A smear of red and blue. A glint of metal—a blade, moving fast. I whirled to my left, lifting that hand in an instinctive block. Caught the descending arm on the meaty part of my lower arm. My right hand went for the bread knife on the table as I moved. Right foot shoved my weight, left ball of foot pivoting. Twisted my left arm around the attacker's right, securing it. Knocked away the attacker's knife with a right fist to his wrist. Heard the bone break.

Rising but still ducked, I blocked his other arm. Twisted my body under the attacker's arm. Slammed my shoulder into his stomach. Brought the knife in hard. Felt it penetrate clothes and slide off of leather, like a belt. Felt it press against flesh. Stopped at the first faint smell of human.

I chuffed in disgust and continued my pivot, torquing more power into the shoulder, drawing on Beast's strength. Tossed my blunt table knife into the corner. Lifted my attacker off his feet, his weight change part of the move. Whirled and dropped him.

He landed flat. The sound was like a dozen sandbags hitting, and an "Oomph" of lost breath. I fell across him, one hand under his chin, clawing at his throat, the other clawing into his abs.

"You're dead," he managed. It was a promise.

Hunter attacked in safe place, Beast thought at me. *Pack hunters!*

I blinked away Beast before she/I ripped into his soft

belly. In the same instant, I hit him in the side of the neck with my fist, with enough force to knock him out. His eyes rolled in his head. I leaped to my feet and put my back to the wall. No one else was attacking. I risked a glance down. *Dang*. Hawk Head was out cold.

I growled low, the vibration filling the room. *Fun!* Beast chuffed at me. *More!*

Everyone stared. No one else had moved. I was pretty sure no one was even breathing. Wrassler stood slowly and walked to my side of the table. He nudged Hawk Head with a pointed toe. "Derek, secure the prisoner," he said.

"Not just yet," I whispered. I swallowed, forcing Beast back down. I managed a breath that hurt all the way to my toes. Chuffed it out.

"Why not?" Wrassler asked.

"Whose clan is he?" I asked.

"Clan Arceneau," Wrassler said. His face fell as he put it together. Grégoire and his heir were both gone, leaving the clan home in the hands of Grégoire's secondo heir—who was well known to be my enemy, Adrianna.

The memory came back in an instant, rushing through me like a steaming deluge.

I had been at a vamp party. I had slid open the pocket door to the darkened powder room, seeing myself in a slanted mirror, haloed in shadows. Stepping in, I flicked on the light.

A blur swept toward me from the left, crossing the mirror. Time dilated and slowed. Beast screamed deep inside, shoving her strength and reflexes into my veins with a rush of power and heat. Vamp fangs and claws flashed in the mirrors, falling toward me.

The weight of two vamps crushed down immobilizing me. Fangs biting. The next few moments were desperate as I tried to fight my way free. But I was losing. Above me, another vamp watched, icy power flowing from her. Red hair, curly and wild, fanned out, a gold torque etched with Celtic symbols hung around her neck, a gold cuff shaped like a snake climbed one arm. I staked her just as Leo appeared. *"Adrianna,"* he had said, the word so full of power, it had made my skin ache.

Yeah. That had been a bad one. Me bleeding in a building full of vamps. It was amazing that I had survived. And later, of course, I'd staked her properly. But for reasons of his own, Leo had brought her back to her undead life, and kept her somewhere until she recovered from her own double death and the mind-breaking separation of anamchara with one of the Damours—black-magic-practicing witchvamps I had killed. Yeah. We had a history. None of it important, but all of it bad.

And now, with Grégoire and Dominique out of town, Adrianna was in control of Arceneau, one of the most powerful clans in the U.S. Adrianna, who had flaming red hair, like the person in the car with Katie's missing girls. And the girls had gone to Adrianna's territory and then disappeared. *Crap!* No way was this gonna end well.

I breathed in slowly and let the tension ease away from me. To force my body to calm, I walked across the room to the blade Hawk Head had dropped and studied it. It was a short blade, about four inches long, better suited to cutting than to stabbing, having a wide, curving edge and spine and a rounded point. I swiped a paper napkin from a table, wrapped it gently around the butt, and lifted the knife with two fingers. I carried it to the table where I had eaten and opened out several more paper napkins, placing the blade in the fold. I sniffed along the edge for anything odd. Because why would he try to hurt me with such a puny knife? It was hard to parse the scents with my human nose, especially with the pheromones and spice scents in the room, but . . . there was something there, something herbal and chemical both.

Like poison.

"Secure all personnel from Clan Arceneau," I said. "I want them in separate rooms. No food, no drinks, no TV, and no personal items." When no one moved, I snarled, "Now!" And they *moved*. Bliss and Rachael had been planning to leave the vamp party at Guilbeau's and go to another party at the Arceneau Clan Home. Something was really hinky.

CHAPTER 7

Sold Me to Leo

"So Leo's *not in*," I quoted.

A look of discomfort flashed across Adelaide's face for a beat, before she squared her shoulders minimally and lied to me. "No."

I pursed my lips. I didn't often tell people that I could smell the stress when they lied, and I wasn't about to tell Adelaide, but I wanted her to know I didn't believe her. "Leo's new clan home won't be ready to move into for another month. What'd he do, go *dancing*?"

"Really, Jane. Dancing?"

A tight smile set itself free on my face. "Leo can dance. Get him to take you for a spin on the dance floor. The fanghead is sex on a stick."

Adelaide's face turned faintly pink, and I realized she was blushing. "Perhaps another time," she said, and I wondered at the blush. Before I could ask, she went on carefully. "Even if he was in tonight, he will not be dealing with this issue."

Oh. I looked down at the names of the sequestered members of Clan Arceneau. All of them had been here for weeks, plenty of time to have been dinner for Leo—which meant something important. It meant that whatever was going on, Leo had to know something about it. *Got it.* "He wants me to deal with it so his hands are clean."

She shrugged, a delicate move of shoulder blade and collarbone that a ballerina might have envied. The light caught the purple fabric of her silk shirt, creating shadows and hollows and warming her skin.

"It wasn't a test?" I asked. "A way for Clan Arceneau security to see if the new part-time Enforcer was able to handle herself in a dicey situation?"

"No. Not without Leo's approval."

"Which he didn't give," I said, just to make sure.

"He did not."

I dropped the page of Clan Arceneau names and paced the length of the small room, feeling caged by the lack of windows, the narrow walkway, the oppressive stench of nervous vamp in the lounge off the foyer. I had sent the knife to Jodi Richoux, the cop in charge of the paranormal unit at New Orleans Police Department. She was testing it for toxins and fingerprints and anything else that might be weird on it, all as a favor to the MOC of her city. She was also frothing at the mouth to get inside vamp central and deal with the issue of assault and attempted murder in human legal ways. Leo had sent word that Jodi's services would not be needed. Which I'm sure ticked her off royally. Yeah. He was leaving this to me.

There were twelve Clan Arceneau blood-servants in vamp HQ today, six on security, six in services—meaning the kitchen, paperwork, yard work, and housekeeping. To keep the council chambers and headquarters up and running, the clans rotated in servants, sorta like a feudal system where the peasants and knights were sent in to serve the king as part of their liege lord's taxes or whatever. But in this case, the humans got to provide more than the usual services—they got to feed the chief fanghead his blood meals. And through that blood-taking, Leo could learn most anything they knew, and most anything he wanted. So . . . whether Adelaide knew it or not, Leo knew I would be attacked.

"Son of a gun. He did it to me again," I murmured. A slow heat burned its way through me. I was tired of vampire games. "Get me my weapons," I growled to the security twin at the door. "Now!" I added sharply when she didn't move quickly enough.

Moments later they were in my hands. I checked the mag and load, and strapped the nine-mil on beneath my left shoulder, adjusted the draw until I was satisfied. Stuck the throwing knives into my belt, into special tiny sheaths there. I was good with the knives, though not perfect yet. Beast liked them. She called them flying claws.

I strapped the vamp-killer on my right thigh and twisted my braid up into a knot on the top of my head, securing it with the ash wood stake. My hands high and twisted into my hair, I said, "Get me a vamp. One of Leo's *master* vamps. One who can read his dinner's minds. A hungry one."

Adelaide's eyes went wide as she understood what I was asking. Not all vamps could read the minds of their dinners. Some could only bedazzle and charm and allure. But some master vamps could take it a step further. They could read the minds of their prey. I know. It had been done to me. Del picked up a phone and stopped, staring at the receiver. It was part of the in-house security system, an old part, installed before my time, but I had seen no reason to tear it out of the walls. It worked as backup in case of system failure of my own hardware. The receiver was attached to the wall via a long tangled cord and Adelaide watched it swing, thinking. After too long, she punched in a single number. "The Enforcer shall be interrogating Clan Arceneau's blood-servants. She requests a hungry Mithran master. One capable of a forced reading of those from whom he feeds. I am not familiar with the Mithrans here yet— Yes. Of course." She put the receiver down, slowly, the thick plastic clacking quietly. She didn't meet my eyes and I felt compelled to explain.

"I have few options here, Del. I can ask questions and they will answer unless they were told or compelled not to. Then I can walk away or I could use harsher methods to make them talk. I could try waterboarding. Or bamboo shoots under their fingernails. Or drilling out their teeth. Or I can question them, and when they lie, get a vamp to drink it out of them. Which is the kindest method?" She didn't reply, her eyes on the far wall, and a thin line drew between her perfect arched eyebrows—the lawyer thinking.

"Leo drinks from every servant who comes here, Del, and every one of them on this list has been here long enough to be tasted. Leo knew they were going to attack me. And he didn't tell me. And he didn't stop it." Adelaide turned to me, the movement jerky, her blue eyes clearing, focusing in on me. "So clearly he wants me to find out something *else* too, something he only caught a part of, or a peek at."

"And since he can't look weak or uninformed, he's going to let you do his dirty work."

"Yeah. Kinda."

Adelaide crossed her arms over her chest. "Can you torture people this way?" When I looked away, trying to decide how much to tell her, Del said, "A forced feeding is painful. No human who is working against Leo will willingly allow a feeding. And it . . . *hurts*, Jane. It's a violation of body and soul."

My face softened. She had given me an opening and I decided to take it. "Yeah. Been there, done that." Her eyes, already wide, dilated farther. "Leo tried to force a binding on me. He attacked me and drank. And yeah. It was awful."

She breathed, the purple shirt moving with the motion, the only sign of her agitation.

My voice a burr of sound, I said, "He *apologized* to me for it." I heard the wounds in my own voice, the words hoarse with remembered pain. I forced down a breath past the tightness in my throat. "And he says he owes me a boon. A big one."

She shook her head as if amazed or disbelieving. "And you stayed with him? Even after that?" Her face changed again as she added two and two and came up with a total. "Oh no. The binding. He forced you to become his Enforcer. And now you *can't* leave."

"Not in the way you mean. He tried to bind me. It didn't work like it was supposed to."

"Because you're a skinwalker?" she hazarded, still adding things up in her lawyerly brain. When I didn't reply, her tone changed into legal-cool, and she asked, "If you aren't bound, why did you stay? Revenge?"

I sighed, realizing that Del was asking the kind of questions a vamp's lawyer might make, which told me where she stood on the matter—like Bruiser, she belonged to the vamps, no matter how much she might like me personally. Once, she had said she wanted to be my friend. I had a feeling that was going to be a lot harder than either of us thought.

"I'm sorry," she said. "That . . . sounded wrong. Unkind. You aren't the revenge type." I snorted in disagreement and Adelaide chuckled sourly. "Okay. Let me rephrase. Why did you stay all this time when you could have left?"

I stared down, focusing on nothing. Beast was bound. Couldn't say that. I settled on "Lots of reasons. I'd been killing vamps for years, and never thought of them as anything but monsters who deserved to die. I was acting on my own instincts. Me. Alone. When I got to New Orleans, I discovered that there was something more to it all. Something other than see-vamp-kill-vamp. Some vamps may have just needed more time to cure." I rolled a shoulder forward in a shrug. "But I killed them before they could finish the change that might have let them be something more. That said, according to vamp law, they deserve to die if they kill a human, no matter if they are technically insane when they kill. Once a human is turned, everything gets all mixed up. So yeah. It sounds stupid, but that's part of it."

Adelaide nodded in agreement with my legal judgment and said, as if clarifying, "But Leo hurt you. And you're staying anyway."

I nodded.

Softer, she said, "He *hurt you*, and you would do that to someone else?"

My old pal guilt squirmed under my skin. Knowing I was slipping down some slippery slope, ever farther away from any kind of high ground, I said, "Every blood-servant here has been drunk from. Every one of them signed away their rights to personal freedom. Being here, being dinner, isn't against their will. No one's going to refuse being sipped on except the ones holding out on me. I won't force them, but they will be turned over to Leo for judgment."

"And you think them signing a piece of paper is an excuse to let a Mithran hurt them?" This time her tone was curious, as if she were peeling back layers of me to see what rotted underneath, at the heart of me.

"They signed a contract. You're a lawyer; you know what that means. I could ignore it, but that person might have other orders, like, to kill Leo in his sleep, or set off bombs during the *gather*. Orders that will kill people, Del. Humans. Vamps. People I like. People I don't like but have sworn to protect. So yes. I'll hurt the guilty."

"And how will you know they're guilty?"

I smiled grimly. "I'll know."

"Skinwalker knowledge?"

I jerked my head down in an unwilling *Yes*.

A delicate tapping sounded on the door, and I squared my shoulders and pushed away my angst. I didn't have time for soul-searching or self-pity. "Come in." When the door opened, my jaw tried to drop. I kept it in place, but not by much. Edmund Hartley, former blood-master of Clan Laurent, stood there, looking meek and mild, which was odd enough, but my surprise came because he had lost in a Blood Challenge to Bettina, Laurent clan's new blood-master. "Aren't you supposed to be dead?" I asked.

He gave me a fangless smile. "I lost my title and clan in blood challenge, but Bettina is never wasteful. She accepted my clan and sold me to Leo."

"Sold—"

"Bondage," Adelaide said quickly. "He'll work for Leo for twenty years, at which time he may choose to remain in Clan Pellissier or move to another clan, where he stands a better chance of regaining a clan of his own. It's covered in a codicil to the Vampira Carta."

Twenty years wasn't a long time for a fanghead. I shook my head. *"Vamps."* It was nearly a curse, but not quite, and I said, "Ed, can you follow my lead and look threatening and spooky?"

Edmund smiled slightly and, with a dry tone, said, "I believe I can manage."

I nodded and stepped into the hallway. Edmund was an old vamp, and I could feel his power as he pulled it up and around him, icy prickles, like spikes of frozen air. He stood about five-seven or -eight, slight of body, with hazel eyes that seemed to give off a pleasant vibe, like that of a history professor. Nonthreatening. But if his power signature was anything to go by, his body was no indication of his ability. I wondered how he had lost to Bettina, who was powerful, but not nearly as old as I felt Edmund might be. I looked back at him and wondered. Would a vamp deliberately lose a blood-challenge? Questions for later, which I was sure he wouldn't answer. I checked my papers.

"I'm ready to talk to the prisoners," I said to Wrassler. Silent, he led the way.

The first blood-servant was listed as Imogene, who worked as a housekeeper, and had been placed in a comfortable room, like a sitting room, with a sofa and chairs and a small table. When we entered the room, she backed against the wall, her pulse beating hard in her throat, the whites of her eyes showing in terror. She stank of fear sweat. And I felt like an ass.

I blew out a breath of revulsion. My reasons for terrifying people were all valid. And all wrong. Still sighing, I plopped into a chair and gestured to the security twin to close the door. "Sit down, Ed, Del." While they were trying to figure out if I was being serious or giving them a hidden command to do something else, I asked, "Imogene, do you know who I am?"

She nodded once. "The vampire killer."

"Yeah. Among other things. One of Clan Arceneau's people attacked me tonight." Her fear stink spiked. "Did you know I was going to be attacked?"

"Nonononono." Her head shook back and forth as fast as her denials.

"Did you know anyone was going to be attacked?"

"Nonononono." Imogene put her hands behind her body. As if hiding them. Or as if proving that her hands were not involved in any plot.

Prey, Beast thought at me.

"Hmmm." I thought of how to phrase my questions to allow no opportunity for lying by omission or phrasing. "Were you made aware of any plans to attack anyone, anywhere?"

"Nonononono."

"Have you had any contact with Adrianna since you came to the HQ?"

"No. It's not permitted."

I sat up straight and gave her a little "tell me more" gesture.

"We're here as part of security measures, part of proving loyalty to our master's master. We don't call home. We don't talk with anyone during our stay and service here."

I turned that over in my mind and checked to see how long the Arceneau servants had been in the council home. It was two weeks. So if an order or a hidden compulsion had gone out to kill me, it was a long-standing order, one put in place weeks ago. The timelines were not quite right. Compulsions didn't usually last weeks without reinforcing.

I asked Imogene, "Did you have any sense or hint of anything wrong, or of anyone doing something against the Master of the City or his sworn servants?"

Her mouth turned down. "You mean like ESP or mind reading? Or body language or something? Or like they had been given a compulsion to kill you or something?"

"Yes. Anything."

"No. But . . . Louise said she had a bad feeling about the new security guys."

I looked at my list. Louise was two rooms down. And the two new security guys had to be the tattooed duo. I clicked on their personnel files. Hawk Head and Tattoo Dude had joined Clan Arceneau only two months ago, and according to their dossiers, they both had previous prison records, with assault, assault with a deadly weapon, assault with intent to kill, B&E, home invasion, and attempted murder between them. So the one who said he had prison security experience had meant from the inside, a totally different interpretation from what I had wanted. The lie by itself wasn't definite indication of current evil deeds, but it wasn't a rousing endorsement of high-minded actions either. And not the type of blood-servants vamps usually wanted. Trained mercenaries, yeah. Street thugs, no.

"Okay. Imogene, I'll have a meal sent in. I want you to relax. Thank you for sharing your worries with me." Her mouth formed a small O of surprise as I stood and left the room, my muscle behind me. In the hallway, Edmund and Del both stared at me in surprise. "What? You thought I was going to hurt her?" I shook my head and led the way to Louise's room, where I knocked and entered.

That went pretty much like the last interview, except when I asked the question "Louise, did you have any sense or hint of anything wrong, or of anyone doing something against the Master of the City or his sworn servants?"

Her head shook no, and then bobbed yes. "The new men had weapons."

"They brought weapons into this building that they didn't register?"

She nodded uncertainly. "I found them in the dirty laundry. I didn't tell anyone." Her voice dropped to a bare whisper. "I should have told someone?"

"Yes. You should have. Will you show us where the weapons are now?"

She nodded and stood, and her sweat smelled of fear and chili spices, heavy on the garlic. She led the way out of the room where she had been held and up the stairs with a fast-tapping toe rhythm, and down a short hallway. She let us into a room with a passkey. The small room had six bunks in a place that usually held two and it was a disaster: clothes everywhere, boots, candy wrappers, drink cans, fast-food packages littering the table and scattered on the floor, chairs overturned, wet towels dropped everywhere, the bunks piled with clothes and electronics and porn magazines. "I cleaned it this morning," Louise whispered.

"Yeah. I believe you." And I did. The Arceneau security roommates were apes. They'd done everything but throw feces at the walls. Not Grégoire's type at all. I had a feeling that all of them had been contracted since he left for Atlanta, and were sworn to Adrianna.

Louise went to the bathroom and scooted the laundry basket into the short entrance with her feet. She pulled back the few dirty clothes the guys had not tossed to the floor, to reveal three silvered blades and two small handguns—.22 semiautomatics. I knelt and tossed the dirty clothes out of the basket, sniffed the weapons. The blades were all coated with the same faint stench. I took the basket and handed it to Adelaide. "This hardware needs testing. Overnight it to Leo's private lab in Houston. I want independent confirmation if something is on the blades. And check the rounds. See if something is on them too. Just in case."

She nodded and took the basket, and I said, "Let's go visit the bad guys. Ed, here's where you get to be scary."

"With pleasure," he said, and his fangs slowly, so slowly, snicked down. They were a little over two inches long and bone white. His eyes bled scarlet and his pupils widened until they were black discs in bloody orbs. His mouth and jaw seemed to unhinge, growing longer and wider. Only the really old ones could show such control while vamping out.

Louise backed slowly away, her fear almost palpable in the room. Ed turned to her and hissed. I thought she would pass out, and Wrassler took her shoulder in his meaty hand. "It's okay," he said. But his voice didn't sound quite as confident about that as I might have wished.

"Yeah. That outta do it," I said to Ed.

Del handed off the basket of weapons to Wrassler. "See that these get to my desk, and relock my office door," she said. "And take Louise back to Imogene's interrogation room and lock them in for their own safety. Get them some food and drinks."

"I'll see it gets done, ma'am," he said, which I thought was awfully subservient of the big guy. And awfully polite. Del did cast an "I'm in charge. Don't mess with me" vibe, and she did it without weapons and without looking threatening.

A moment later we stood in front of Tattooed Dude's room. The two most likely suspects had been placed in real interrogation rooms—minimal uncomfortable furniture, no way to turn off the lights. I opened the door slowly and stepped silently into the room. With the grace of a hunting predator, Ed moved in as well, staying to my left. I drew my vamp-killer and let Beast shine into my eyes.

Tattooed Dude was standing with his back against the far wall, his arms crossed over his chest, and a great poker face in place. Or maybe with him it was a Russian roulette face. He had arranged the two chairs to either side and the heavy metal and wood table at a slight angle, perfect for bringing into a fight or using as defensive props. Without a single suggestion on my part, Edmund raced in front of me and tossed the furniture behind us. He moved so fast the three pieces landed with a single crash. Tattooed Dude flinched, dropping his arms to his sides and fisting his hands. And I grinned, showing blunt human teeth, feeling Beast in the front of my mind.

With this guy, I didn't waste words, just pulled a throwing knife and let the overhead lights glint off it. When I spoke it came out in a lower-register Beast-growl. "Who ordered you and your pal to attack me?"

Tattooed Dude snarled at me. I flicked the knife. I'd been aiming at TD's hand, but caught him higher up, the blade entering between the two bones of his lower arm and sticking into the wall at his back. He squealed like a stuck pig and Edmund was on him.

The squeal stopped, choked off. Edmund plucked the knife away and rode TD to the floor, perching atop the big guy's chest like a small raptor on the chest of a larger, fallen prey. Edmund drank once long and deeply, from the cut arm, his hand making a rotating "get on with it" motion to me.

"Who ordered you and your pal to attack?"

Edmund gave me the sign again, which I figured meant

he had the answer. *Dang*, the guy was fast. Below him, Tattooed Dude relaxed as he gave in to the feeding and the compulsion of a master vamp. Edmund might no longer be a clan master, but he'd lost none of his skills.

"Were you supposed to kill or just injure?" At the hand signal again, I sped up my questions. "What was on the blade? Poison? What herbs? Where did the concoction come from? Was a witch involved? Did Grégoire know about the attack?" Ed shot me a glance of ire but didn't break contact with the prisoner. "Did Dominique know? Did Adrianna know? Did anyone in Clan Arceneau know about the attack? Did anyone at *this* compound know? Are there any more attacks planned against the Master of the City? Are there other attacks planned against me or those I claim as mine?"

Edmund's eyes shot to me and he withdrew his fangs. He lifted the hand still holding the knife and checked his watch. "Get to your home, Enforcer. They are there now."

I said something crude, grabbed the knife that was covered with my attacker's blood, and raced out the door. Wrassler, back from running errands for Del, was on my heels, and for a big guy, he managed to nearly keep up with me, talking through his headset mic as we ran. "Secure the premises," he said into the mic. "Lock down!" But when I reached the front door I slammed the bloody knife tip into the table that held the trays for weapons and cursed again. "I don't have a car or my bike."

"I'll drive," Wrassler said, pushing ahead of me and out the door. We dove into an armored SUV, the powerful engine turning over. The roadway in front of HQ was wreathed in mist, the fog rising from the Mississippi and enfolding the entire French Quarter. Streetlights were halos of yellow, the mist capturing the light and keeping it close. Spell or natural, it made no difference. It would make fighting harder.

Wrassler drove like a maniac and we were at my place before my heart rate could settle. He braked about a hundred feet out. The street was silent, no radios played, no music or TV came through windows, no people wandered the pavement, drunk or homeless or bored. "This don't look right," he said.

The street in front and the houses to either side of my freebie house were free of fog, as a cold wind shunted through, dropping down from above, swirling around, and blasting away. With Beast-sight, I could see sparks of green in the wind; I heard distant flute music and a slow tapping, like a drum. It was Big Evan, warding the house with air magic.

Kits attacked in den, Beast hissed at me. *Kits not safe!*

I pulled my cell and called Eli. "Jane," he answered.

"We're out front. What have they done and how many are there?"

"They firebombed the house. Evan put it out, but it was risky. Wind tried to fan the flames at first. Four targets that I can see with low light. Two vamps, two humans."

Firebomb? Again? I needed to get a magical something put over the siding so it wouldn't burn. Low light meant he was using his toys to see in the dark. "Witches working with them?"

"Not so I could tell." A moment later, he said, "Evan says he can't sense anyone. The fog seems natural, coming off the Mississippi."

"Kids?"

"Asleep in the safe room. Front door is my twelve. Tangos are four, total. Human encoms are two: at two o'clock, on the side of the neighbor's house, and at six o'clock, outside the fence. Evan says that the human in back is coming over the wall. Vamp encoms are two: standing on the wall at our six, and standing hidden in the edge of the fog, in the street at twelve. I say again, four tangos." Tango was Eli's shorthand for unknown human or supernat targets. Encom was Eli's shorthand for enemy combatants, which meant they were armed.

"Okay. I'll take the front." I pulled my vamp-killer and palmed the blade that had cut Tattooed Dude. And smiled. "Tell Evan to let the fog closer at the street. I'm out." I closed the phone.

"Human at the side of the house next door, there." I pointed for Wrassler. "The space between houses is something like six feet, so it's close quarters. I'm going after a vamp in front of the door, hidden in the fog."

"I'll take the human." Wrassler turned off the engine, leaving the vehicle parked in the middle of the street. Reached up and disabled the interior lights, drawing a long-barreled semiautomatic with the other hand. "Go."

I went, sliding out of the SUV, leaving the door open. Beast rammed her power and vision into my bloodstream, adrenaline like a drug, speeding my heartbeat. Her night vision sharpened my own, the night glowing silver and green with tints of blue. The vamp standing in the fog was a warmer shade of pale melon, his body heat, slightly warmer than the fog, making him nearly glow. This was something I hadn't ever seen before, and I realized that Evan's spell must have now included a *search out vamp* component. *Nice*. Moving on little cat feet—which made me want to laugh—I circled around the vamp so I was downwind. He smelled of gasoline and the sharp stink of struck matches. If I'd been in Beast-form, my ruff would have stood on end.

I tossed the bloody knife through the fog, to land at his feet with a *clank*.

Distraction of blood scent and noise.

CHAPTER 8

B-b-b-b-bad to the Bone

The clatter and the smell of blood shocked the vamp, and he crouched. I was already launching myself through the air, right at him, intending to knock him to his back and place the blade at his throat. Beast took over the leap. The vamp and I collided, almost gently, my open left hand catching his right shoulder, gripping hard, my right hand moving across his body with a fast swipe, like claws. *No!* I thought at her. *Alive!* But I couldn't wrench control away.

The blade caught his throat just below his larynx. My momentum and mass-in-motion carried the sharp edge through his tissue with only the slightest resistance, to jar into his spine.

We hit the ground and I tucked, rolling across him, letting go the vamp-killer handle to keep from damaging him any more. Bending my arms to take the fall, cradling my head down, curling my spine into the somersault and instantly up to my feet. I was splattered with vamp blood, cool and sticky on my skin. He hadn't fed recently, which ruled out Naturaleza vamp.

I smelled the silver that finished the job of killing him true-dead. No one to question. I snarled at Beast, *I needed to question him.*

She growled back, *Hunter of kits. Must die.*

Furious, I pulled my blade free of his flesh, wiped both it and the throwing knife on his clothes, free of blood, and left him lying in the street. With Beast's vision and Evan's spell,

I could see two forms wrapped together in the lee of the house at two o'clock, both a vibrant orange, both human. Wrassler had the human in a sleeper hold, and eased him to the ground as I raced up. "It's me," I whispered. "Stay here. I'm checking the back." I sprinted around the brick fencing, pulling Beast's speed through me. I leaped high, grabbing the fence with one hand and swinging myself over, the brick grinding into my human-soft palms.

Stupid Jane. Needs paws.

Yeah. And living attackers.

Beast didn't reply.

I landed inside the fence, silently, in a crouch. From the second story at the back of the house, I heard a single shot. Rifle fire. An *oof* of pain and expelled breath was followed by the sound of a body hitting the ground. I found the human, the bright orange of her body warmth half hidden by the pile of mostly crushed boulders in the garden. I crawled to her on all fours, keeping the stones between me and the last vamp. The human didn't smell of blood, and when I touched her, my fingers found a vest beneath her clothes. It had to be one of the new combat vests just released on the market—Kevlar, silver mesh, and fibers spelled against magic. The woman was alive and unharmed, except for, maybe, a broken rib or two. Which was nothing short of a miracle, considering the range. But the breath had been knocked out of her.

To my side, I saw a pale amber form moving away in the dark. Vamp fast, she vaulted the fence and disappeared. I knew her. I'd been right. *Adrianna.* "When the cat's away, the mice will play," I muttered.

Beast snorted softly. Knowing that Eli would have me in his sights, I sheathed my blades and gave the "all clear" signal by tapping my head. I opened my cell and dialed Wrassler. "I got a human. Alive, but having trouble breathing."

"I got one taking a nap."

"Bring yours inside. Front door. Ring the bell. And just so you know, Adrianna got away."

The woman at my knees sucked in a breath that sounded pained—her first since she was shot. "Bet that hurts," I said softly. I confiscated a fully automatic weapon with a full thirty-round mag. There were other magazines on her person, enough rounds to chew through the back of the house and anyone inside. I lifted her up and tossed her over my shoulder, glad that my secret was out and I didn't have to hide what I was anymore. Her newly found breath *oof*ed out once again, along with her scent. She stank of Adrianna and something else, something vaguely familiar, but the blood and Adrianna's reek overpowered it and I couldn't isolate the scent marker.

I carried the human along the side porch and in the side door. And dumped her to the floor at Big Evan's feet. Without looking at them, I handed the weapons to Eli and he chuckled nastily as he looked the midsized subgun over. I yanked three zip strips out of his utility belt and secured the woman's hands. It only took about seventy-five pounds of force to break a regular-sized zip strip. Let's see her break three of the bigger ones at once.

"Let Wrassler in the front door, please," I said to Eli as the bell rang. "He has another prisoner." Eli headed to the door, his footsteps silent.

"You remember me telling you about the Damours?" I asked his retreating back. He made a waffling motion with one hand. "Adrianna was part of the Damours' blood family, and was a mind-locked anamchara to one of the top people in the family. When I killed the Damours vamps, Adrianna was there. Leo saved her when I killed her lover, for reasons I'll never know." I glanced at Big Evan. He knew all about the history of the Damours. The witch-vamps had been trying to sacrifice his children when I killed the fangheads true-dead. Though memory was a dicey thing—especially when one was technically insane— Adrianna had to know that I was the one who killed her anamchara. Vamps liked vengeance, so she thought she would kill me and mine. I got that. But it wasn't enough to make it all sit easily with me. There was still too much that didn't fit. Unless . . .

I looked at it another way. Unless there was more than one thing going on. Maybe some of the weirdness had something to do with the European Council coming to visit. I put that possibility on the back burner of my brain.

I dialed the council house and asked to be put through to Edmund Hartley. "We're safe," I said. "Thanks to you. Talk to me. I need to know everything pertinent that you drank out of Tattoo Dude."

"It was my pleasure," Ed said. And the way he said it meant way more than a simple "You're welcome." But he went on, his words succinct. "In order of your earlier queries, the man I questioned was under heavy compulsion. The two were supposed to alert Adrianna when you would be within their influence, and kill you while Adrianna attacked your home to steal something of value. They don't know what it was.

"Adrianna gave the men the weapons. They knew the blades were poisoned, but not what the poison was or if a witch was involved in making it. Neither Grégoire nor Dominique knew about the attack—a suggestion that was insulting but necessary," he added. "No one else at Clan Arceneau knew about the attack so far as he knew. No one else here at the council house knew of it. He did not know if there were more attacks planned. He was compelled, and quite well."

The men had been at HQ for weeks. So that put the planning of the attacks on me and my home back much earlier than that. It took time to set up a compulsion, even longer to get the men so deeply under that they would attack me in front of witnesses, though a violent compulsion might work faster in a violent human, last longer without reinforcing. I didn't know.

If Adrianna wanted vengeance for the death of her lover, then attacking my house and my friends and my person . . .Yeah. Adrianna had been busy. Vamps strategized with the long view and might wait decades—centuries even—to carry out a plan. Yet Adrianna had seemed too unstable to make any of this work. So, either I had read her wrong or her kind of crazy was the kind that got things done. Or I was missing something.

I needed to talk to Adrianna. And by talk I meant communication of a kind that made my blood run cold just thinking of it. But no one around me was safe as long as Adrianna ran around free. I wondered if Leo would give me leave to go after her. I need to talk to the MOC. I needed to decide how far I'd go to keep my people safe. I said, "Thanks, Ed. We'll talk later."

I closed the phone in its bulletproof case as Wrassler entered, his treads heavy on the wood floors. The door closed behind him and he dropped his burden on the floor beside the woman. The man made a satisfying *whomp* when he hit. Evan whistled a note and I knew the wards were back up. The big man stood in the foyer, watching us across the rooms; I figured he was trying to control his temper and not accidentally zap the prisoners. "Evan, you got any magical truth-serum-spell-whammies up your sleeve? 'Cause we need some answers from these two, and now." I rolled the human woman over, faceup. She was muscular, a bodybuilder who also worked on endurance training. Her arms were buff, and her thigh and calf muscles beneath the black skintight running suit were long and lean. She wore her hair short and slicked back with gel, and her eyes were darkly lined in black. She stared up at me with disdain.

Evan stepped closer and looked the woman over as I frisked her again, finding a knife I'd missed before, a thin, narrow-bladed weapon sheathed in a thigh pocket. "Cute," I said. "I guess it would be corny to say"—I pulled my vamp-killer with its fourteen-inch blade—"this is a knife." She narrowed her eyes and didn't laugh. Some people have no sense of humor.

"I got whammies," Evan said, "but they won't work on these two." When I looked my question at him, he bent down and yanked a metal charm off the woman's neck. The chain broke with a snap and she grunted again. Fear spread over her face, and she looked around, as if startled. Evan said, "Somebody's been mixing vamp compulsion with magic on them."

As soon as the chain broke, the smell of old blood hit me, and I realized that the compulsion charm had been activated with blood. I backed away, wrinkling my nose.

"Where am I?" the woman demanded, struggling to rise, her bound hands pushing at the floor. Her body took on the scent of confusion and, beneath it, the smell of fear.

Prey, Beast whispered to me.

"You don't remember coming to my house with a submachine gun and enough ammo to finish a small war?" I asked.

Her eyes went wide. "Are you nuts?"

"You came to my house! My *home*!" I shouted. I wanted to hit her with my fist, or with my claws, slashing open her face. But I controlled myself, gulped a breath, and shoved down on my fury, because the woman on the floor in front of me was truly, completely confused. Adrianna had been part of the Damours' black magic rituals. Seemed she had learned something from them. Maybe picked up a few magical things, like amulets that made humans willing conspirators in crimes. And I didn't beat someone to a pulp for being brainwashed by magic, no matter how satisfying it might feel while I did it.

I said, "Wrassler, would you be kind enough to drive these two to vamp HQ and see if Edmund Hartley will drink them and their memories. I need proof who ordered this." Because I was going to hurt that person. Badly. Yeah. And every dime I had said it was Adrianna.

"You do know that among Mithrans, such acts are said to be close to Naturaleza methods?" Wrassler asked, his voice neutral and without inflection.

I thought about Edmund's tone when he said it was his pleasure, and the spike in the center of my soul grew colder. "Noted," I said shortly.

Wrassler looked into my face and shrugged. "Sure. I'll ask." He held out a hand to Eli for more strips, and the two men zip-stripped the humans to within an inch of not breathing before carrying them to the SUV still parked in the middle of the street. I stood at the door and watched as they also loaded the dead vamp. If Leo's usual rates for killing vamps who acted out and put humans at risk applied to this guy, I'd just made a few thousand bucks. Somehow that fact, and the fact that I had just told a vamp it was okay to abuse a human, didn't make me very happy. Anger roiled under my skin, building up like steam with no place to go. I wasn't liking myself much. Not at all. But I also didn't know what to do different. I didn't know how to protect the ones I cared about without crossing lines. Lines I might not be able to cross back.

Once Wrassler was gone, Evan leaned against the doorway, one arm up to support and balance him, his head resting back against his palm as he stared up. Almost as if speaking to the painted wood, he said, "You asked if witches were working with the vamps. When we broke the chain on her charm, I heard a voice, whispering, like a spell being worked long-distance."

"Well, that's just ducky," I said.

The big guy nodded as if he agreed with my sarcasm,

dropped his arms, squared his shoulders, and walked to the safe room. He opened it with a touch of his hand, and the bookcase swung open to reveal the room beneath the stairs, narrow and tight, the stone-lined walls and wood shelves hung with weapons of all kinds, a bed and emergency supplies along one wall, and a trapdoor in the floor for escape.

He brought his children out of the safe room, the Kid following along. I expected Alex to look upset at having been placed with the children, and then he raised a long-barreled weapon from beside his leg and handed it to his brother. "You need to teach me how to use it," Alex said simply, his face tight with responsibility and the dawning reality of the world as a dangerous place, a place he wasn't prepared to survive on the training he had so far. "Something more than 'Point and shoot.'"

"Noted," Eli said.

The smaller children were sleeping deeply, a spelled sleep that had kept them silent, out of harm's way, and safe from playing with the weapons in the room. Evan carried them both up the stairs while Eli and I took care of securing the house, which meant putting weapons and noisemaker alarms at the windows and doors. You don't always need a fancy electronic security system. Fog can make some systems useless, and if witches are involved, they might have ways to eliminate or decrease even a magical system's effectiveness. I'd seen it happen—once—to an Everhart-Trueblood ward, a hole blown into it, leaving the edges tangled and frayed.

A pyramid of empty cans was a nifty, low-tech way to be alerted to a B&E.

When Evan came back down, I picked the conversation back up. "You can hear long-distance spells?"

"Sometimes. If the spell is directed at me, if the speaker isn't in a vault with no outside air flow, and if the working isn't warded against it, which most practitioners don't bother to do." He went to the kitchen and brought back three cans of Coke. We each popped a top and took a swig. "Warding against long-distance listening requires more energy, and not many witches have the ability. Since I'm not officially registered with PsyLED—yet—not everyone knows I'm an air witch." The weariness in his tone pulled at me. His wife was missing. His children were in danger. Because they were my friends and my extended family, they were my responsibility. And I hadn't helped much so far.

I looked down at my drink can for a moment. It was my fault that Big Evan was out of the closet in any way. Maybe my fault that Molly was in New Orleans, and therefore her family in harm's way. Again. "I'm sorry," I said again, feeling the weight of guilt. I stared at my hand and clenched my fist, remembering the feel of hot blood spurting over my hand as I killed the violently psychotic witch Evangelina, Molly's sister, the demon-caller. Remembering. Knowing I had no choice. Yet knowing that I'd hurt Molly beyond imagining.

"No help for it," Evan said, reading my body language. "Once Evie brought her power play public, in front of cameras, it was only a matter of time before someone looked closer at the Everharts and, by extension, me."

But I knew he was thinking about the children upstairs. The witch gene was X-linked, meaning it passed through the X chromosome. Molly was a witch, Big Evan was a witch. There was a one hundred percent chance that all their daughters would have the X-linked gene and be witches. There was a fifty percent chance that any son, like EJ, would be a witch, making him predisposed to the childhood cancers suffered by almost all witches, cancers that killed almost all males. And there was also a fifty percent chance that any girl child would have the witch gene on both X chromosomes, making her a weapon, dangerous, something to be feared or desired. The Trueblood children had already been in danger, as Everhart children, the descendants of a known witch, a danger made far worse by me when I let others in on Big Evan's secret. I had done it to save Rick LaFleur, my ex. I had done it with all good intentions. And like most of the things I do when flying by the seat of my pants, my action had unintended consequences.

My anger, my protective instincts, which had seemed to be cooling, flared hot again. "I have to go back to vamp HQ," I said, "and see what Edmund found out from the humans Wrassler took back. I'll be home after dawn."

Eli tossed me a set of keys, which I caught single-handed. "Take the SUV. Weapon up. And don't surrender them at the door. Be careful."

"Thanks, *Dad*," I said. But I did as he said, and weaponed up fully, holstering four semiautomatic handguns, my

Benelli M4 shotgun loaded for vamp with silver shot—
rounds made with sterling fléchettes—two vamp-killers,
and twelve stakes in my bun before I left—the new stakes
with small buttonlike ends to make them easier to shove
through flesh. As I departed the house, I heard Evan singing
softly, "B-b-b-b-bad. B-b-b-b-bad to the bone," George
Thorogood's version, his singer's voice low and rough and
not hiding the anger and fear inside him.

As Evan sang, Eli chuckled, his eyes telling me that I
looked good, real good, and that if other people hadn't been
present he would have been ragging me about being a totally kick-ass, hot chick. I just shook my head and closed the
door on the lyrics. The sad part? I probably was bad to the
bone. As if listening in to my darker thoughts, Beast whispered softly inside my skull, *Jane is killer only,* a litany she
had begun not that long ago, and which, for reasons I didn't
understand, made me feel really awful.

Vamp HQ was lit up like a ballpark, lights in every
bulletproof-glass window, humans and vamps patrolling the
grounds. I pulled to the security gate and let my window
slide down. "Jane Yellowrock to finish business and see
Leo." The words sounded harsh, half growl, and I felt Beast
pad to the front of my brain, shoulders rolling with each
step, sleek and predatory, and I wondered what the person
on the far side of the security camera saw in my eyes.

Without an acknowledgment, the gate rolled open. I
parked out front and strode up the steps two at a time, adjusting my bun stakes after the ride in the SUV. I pushed
through the air lock doors and stared at the triplets standing there, waiting to take my weapons. They musta seen
something because they looked at one another before
speaking to me. I beat them to the punch and gave them a
grin that couldn't have been pretty. I said, "You can try. I'll
leave you all three bleeding on the nice slick marble."

The three backed away, one of them speaking sotto voce
into his mic. "Jane Yellowrock is on the premises. She is
armed and dangerous."

"Good call," I said to them as I stalked through the
building, heading for the prisoners. Wrassler was standing in
the hallway when I got there, at parade rest, if parade rest
meant looking relaxed, feet spread on the carpet, with two

handguns drawn, held down beside his legs. "Did Edmund question the others from the security meeting?" I asked.

He nodded. "All but the one who actually attacked you. He saved that one for you."

"What did you learn?"

"No one liked the two tattooed security men, especially the women."

I narrowed my eyes, knowing what that likely meant. "Has Hawk Head given you any trouble?"

"Not a peep. We let the uninvolved ones go after Edmund fed on them, and vetted them. Edmund is looking pink and a little too happy, by the way."

"Which warms my heart," I snarked. But not hearing a peep from the prisoner was strange. Disquiet pattered down my back on sticky, padded feet, and I drummed my fingertips on my thighs before saying, "Okay. Open it."

The smell of blood hit first, and I shoved Wrassler aside, stepping into the room. At some point in the last instant, I'd drawn my weapons, a nine-mil in one hand, a vamp-killer in the other. But I wouldn't need them.

Hawk Head was dead. The hawk and scalp were on one side of the room, attached to his skull, which was sitting on the back of a chair like a stage prop. The rest of the body was on the other side of the room, on the floor, spread-eagle. Or spread-hawk. The body was posed like the raptor on the scalp. He'd been beheaded, like a vamp.

The room reeked with the stench of death. He'd lost control of bladder and bowels. Blood had sprayed over the ceiling and walls. *Prey,* Beast thought at me. *Meat.* I opened my mouth and sucked in the air over tongue and roof of mouth, through nose, in little spurts of breath. The blood smell was so strong I couldn't get a taste of the killer.

Wrassler was behind me, on his mic. The hallway was filling up with people. Filling up with smells. Filling up with voices. I growled and the place went silent. I studied the blood spray on the wall in front of me. "The killer was between five-seven and five-ten." Without turning around, I said, "Wrassler. Get on the cameras. I want to see every person who came and went down this hallway. And make a copy of the footage." The cops would want to see it too. Dead humans meant human cops on the premises. "And call Jodi. Give her a heads-up before you call nine-one-one."

I heard Wrassler move away and knew that Derek had taken his place. Didn't smell him or hear him. Just knew it. Beast was high in my brain, studying with me, taking over, evaluating death the way only a true predator can. *Closer,* she demanded.

I wiped my shoes on the carpet just inside the door, wiping them hard, to remove any trace evidence. It wasn't good enough. I should have on booties, but I/we *needed* to see/ scent/taste-this-on-the-air. I stepped around the blood spatter and squatted over the body to look at the neck. The cut was higher on one side than the other, clean, a single cut, like the kind a sword makes in the hands of someone who knows how to use it. And the killer's scent, buried beneath the stink of blood and bowel, was both unknown and familiar, hauntingly so. I swallowed hard, trying to figure out how everything that had happened fit together. And it didn't, especially the part about someone trying to kill me in the middle of vamp HQ. I could almost put the other stuff together, but that part fit nowhere. I had random puzzle pieces with no matching edges.

"Derek. Record." I heard a soft click and knew he had activated a recording device. "Killer was likely male, killed left-handed, but he knows how to use a blade, how to fight, so he might be right-handed and using his left to throw us off. I'm pretty sure this was done with a single stroke, with a sword. Blade got trapped in the spine and he tore the head off to free it, so he was covered in blood when he finished here. He's strong. Strong like a vamp."

"You think a Mithran did this?" a female voice asked behind me. It was the kind of question a lawyer asked, confirmatory and just a bit disbelieving. It was Adelaide.

I swallowed before I replied, pushing down on Beast, holding her beneath me. *I am alpha,* I thought at her. She hissed and twitched her tail at me as she padded away. I got a breath without thinking *prey.* And *meat.* "Few vamps would have wasted the blood," I said, hearing the harsh tone in the harsh words. "But maybe this time, a vamp did. Punishment, maybe?" For a job well bungled?

I holstered my weapons and backed out of the room, stepping in the same places I'd used before. In the doorway, I pulled off my boots and handed them to Adelaide. "The cops will be ticked that I entered the room. They'll need my boots for trace evidence. I know exactly where I stepped, so when they get into a pissing contest about it, let me know.

"I need to see the other guy. His partner."

In the room two doors down, I found Tattooed Dude, lying on the floor under a table. I thought he was asleep when I walked in. Then I thought he was dead. And then I realized that he was breathing, his head was still in place, and he was staring at the ceiling. I bent over him and sniffed, seeing the marks on his neck. Someone had been drinking from him. Recently. And they hadn't been gentle about it. But the scary thing was that there was no scent signature on the wounds or in the room. I didn't know how that was possible unless someone was carrying a don't-smell-me charm. Was there even such a thing? Had to be.

"Get Edmund in here," I said to the small group of people following me. "I want to know everything this guy knows. I'm going to security."

I pushed through the gaggle of blood-servants and out the doorway. Walking in my sock feet, I took the elevator down to the large security/electronic monitoring/conference area. The room was nearly empty. The bronze light fixture and track lights were dim, shadowing the corners of the room. The oval table was nearly bare, and the air smelled of coffee and Krispy Kreme donuts, the sweet scent from a box open on the table. The huge ceiling monitor was lit, showing twenty-seven camera angles from my newest upgrade, but as I watched, one view expanded to fill half of the screen.

"Footage isolated," a voice said. To the side, at the control monitors of the security system, Wrassler was standing behind a man wearing fatigues. Angel Tit looked up as I entered and gave me a faint nod, watching to see my reaction at finding him here.

"I brought him so none of ours had control of the system," Wrassler said, which was good thinking. Angel was one of Derek's men, and he'd been caught with his hand in the cookie jar once. He'd been working to rehabilitate himself, and while he wasn't worried at seeing me, and didn't stink of guilt, he was concerned. Being in charge of the electronics while in the middle of a crisis was a huge step forward to acceptance for him. I inclined my head to show I acknowledged all that; his expression of concern melted away.

Angel pointed to the monitor. "This one shows the hallway outside the interrogation room holding Jimmy Joe James. The guard looked down the hallway, as if called, and someone moving with vamp-speed appears for a moment, enters the room, and closes the door." The footage showed real-time speed as the guard walked away for a moment, still visible in the camera, but with his back turned. I caught a flash of darkness, a brighter light, and then the guard walked back, up and down the hallway, keeping watch. Moments later, when the guard was facing away, the vamp raced from the room. He'd been only a blur entering, then leaving.

"Can you show it in slow-mo?"

"Yeah. But it doesn't help. The guy was wearing a hoodie with the hood up, and jeans and sneakers."

Angel tapped some keys and I saw the same segment slowed down, the digital feed jerky. The guard walked away, the man in dark clothes raced in. Later he raced out. Something looked wrong. "Play the first and the last part again, the killer arriving and leaving."

The segment started in the dead time, when the guard pivoted and walked down the hallway. The interrogation room door opened. The shadowy figure showed, entering the room. Yeah. He was wearing a hoodie, and it was pulled low over this face, his only distinguishing features his broad shoulders and narrow waist. Angel clacked some keys and the same figure appeared leaving the room. I said, "One more time, this time cut out all the empty time. When the guard walks, I want to see the coming and going of our killer, as slow as you can make it."

I watched the footage. "Again," I said. "Freeze it with him on-screen, entering the room." The footage backed up and rolled forward to the correct digital frames, and froze. There were two frames, both blurred, but one showed what I wanted. "Print me out a still." I pointed. "Of that one."

A heartbeat later I heard a printer buzzing. "Okay, now the killer exiting." The digital shot appeared on-screen, and just as I'd thought, something was wrong and different.

When he left, the guy was wearing different shoes. I took both stills and studied the blurred photos. I pointed. "Entering, he's wearing brown lace-up shoes and carrying a bundle under his left arm. This shadow here might be a sword strapped to his waist. Exiting, he's wearing white running shoes. Maybe different clothes. And the sword is in a different position."

"Okay," Angel Tit said, but his tone added a "so what?" to the agreement.

"He changed shoes. Probably changed clothes too. Standing in the only blood-free place he could have."

"In the doorway," Wrassler said, "where you stood and wiped your boots."

I huffed out a breath. "Yeah. I'm an idiot."

CHAPTER 9

"Not Human," I Said. "Deal with It."

My idiocy summed up Jodi Richoux's thoughts nicely when she learned what I'd done. We were alone in the interrogation room where Imogene had been kept. "You contaminated my crime scene. You willfully walked into a blood-splattered crime scene to inspect a body. Not to check to see if he was still alive, which I could have understood and accepted. But you went in to look over a *dead body*." The last two words were nearly shouted. Jodi was not happy.

She stood in front of me, petite, blond hair bobbed at her jaw, fists on her hips, pushing back the dark gold business jacket that made her look stylish and tough. Tonight she wore her badge on her belt, and her gun in sight, clipped to a simple holster at her waist. "Talk to me, Jane. I need to know what happened."

I opened my mouth and closed it with a click of teeth. How could I admit to her that Beast had wanted a good look/smell/taste of air? I sat back in the chair, thinking about what I was about to do, and could see no other way out. However, there was no reason I couldn't establish some control of the info. "Off the record," I said. "Take it or leave it."

Jodi considered my requirement. "Unless it impacts a crime, I'm okay with that."

It was better than I expected. I nodded. "I'm not human."

"Tell me something I don't know."

"I'm a Cherokee skinwalker."

"What the hell is a skinwalker?" she snarled, in a fair imitation of a predator herself.

I gave her the short form. "I can take the shape and form of animals of my general size, provided I have enough genetic material to take a reading of it and copy it."

"So?"

"So my sense of smell is good. Way better than human."

"Keep going."

"I should have been able to tell in the hallway that a dead body was on the other side of the door. Just by the smell. I should have been able to smell the blood. I should have been able to smell the perpetrator coming and going. I couldn't. So I went inside. Stood over the body and smelled."

Jodi sat in the chair beside me and said, "Go on."

"I got a hint, but it wasn't much. You know how, if you glimpse something in the next room, out of the corner of your eye, your brain instantly starts to make a picture out of it? Because our brains are pattern oriented?" She nodded. "Well, I do that with my sense of smell. And I got a hint of a vamp I'd smelled before." I held her eyes with mine. "But I can't place it. It's been muffled, like with magic. And no, I didn't know scent could be tampered with, but it can."

"I'm listening." Which was cop-speak for keep talking.

"Adrianna, one of Leo's scions, and the secondo heir to Grégoire, attacked my house tonight, while I was at HQ. She was trying to kill my friends. They're okay, but it was close. Anyway, one of the humans involved in the attack said that Adrianna wanted something in my possession."

I blinked as a puzzle piece resolved itself. It should have been clear sooner, but I'd had too much unrelated stuff on my brain lately and it had hidden in the depths of my mind until I had time for it to push to the forefront. I couldn't guess what Adrianna had been after—besides death and destruction. It was *possible*, however unlikely, that she wanted the blood diamond and thought I had it. Which I did. Sorta. I asked, "Do you remember the Damours' lair?"

"Oh yeah. The crazy hideout full of long-chained scions and blood and death, which I got to see after a thousand paramilitary trampled all over." Her voice, which had softened, barked again.

I hadn't shown Jodi the Damours' lair. After my raid and

the silent alarm went off, a neighbor called the cops, after seeing vehicles take off with speed, and a motorcycle ridden off by a woman. The uniforms first on the scene had called the NOPD cops in charge of the paranormal cases, meaning my former boyfriend Rick LaFleur and Jodi. Rick had been okay with it all, but it had taken Jodi a while to get past the fact that she hadn't been part of the team entering the lair.

The Damours blood family had fallen into disgrace. They'd been stealing witch children and killing them in black magic ceremonies. Blood magic. Which Jodi knew, as she had been cop-on-scene when I killed the Damours. "Leo had to have known something was up with them, but he hadn't gone in and cleaned house. Until I showed up. And I don't know why they got a free ride, not yet." I was giving all my secrets away tonight, it seemed. I sighed and laced my fingers together, trying to look nonthreatening, which was hard with all the weapons I was carrying. Weapons Jodi had let me keep, which was a huge sign of trust in a cop.

Carefully, I said, "Our killer vamp? Has to be tied in with Adrianna. And that could mean tied in with the Damours. But I can't smell him—the killer vamp. Actually, I don't get a real sense of gender, which is odd. The only thing I can tell you with any degree of certainty is it wasn't Adrianna herself. And I can't tell Leo, because he let the Damours' work unrestrained in his city."

"Keeping secrets from the MOC in his own council house," Jodi said, her tone wry and unamused. "Better you than me."

I staggered out of the vamp council's HQ just before dawn, still in my sock feet. I hadn't seen Leo. I hadn't discovered what the humans might know, the ones who had attacked my house. I didn't even know where they were being held. Once Jodi showed up, I had been denied all access. It was her case and she was making sure I knew it. And to cap off my wonderful—not—night, all the way home I kept feeling as if someone was watching me, though I took three unexpected turns and never saw anyone. I was exhausted and worn and growing paranoid and wanted only to sleep.

But that wasn't to be. The Kid had found something and was sitting at the kitchen table when I entered, the smell of espresso and strong, hot black tea rich on the air. I didn't even ask. I just poured a megamug, added three spoonfuls of sugar, and topped it off with most of a container of Cool Whip. I sat at the table with a quiet groan and said, "Tell me."

"You do know that mug is for soup, right?" Alex asked.

"Yeah?" I looked at the mug and said, "Hughn." And drank. The black China tea hit my taste buds and my bloodstream at the same time. Caffeine and sugar are two drugs that have some effect on skinwalkers, and some days I crave the lift they give me just like a human does.

"And you do know you left your boots somewhere?"

"I noticed. I also noticed I ruined a perfectly good pair of socks." I lifted my foot and let him see the hole in the bottom. "I'm listening," I said, aware that they were the same words Jodi had said to me not long ago.

The Kid turned his screen to me. On it was typed *I drilled into a bank's security cameras. I got some shots of Bliss and Rachael.*

I knew instantly that we weren't speaking aloud because we had an air witch on the premises—and because hacking into a bank's system was illegal, and a surefire way for the Kid to break his parole. And if *Eli* was listening, we were so screwed. I sniffed, placing Eli by scent. He was upstairs. I nodded for the Kid to continue.

The screen disappeared. Behind it was a different screen, one with a fuzzy image on it. It was Bliss, her black hair and very fair skin in shocking contrast. Beside her sat a more fuzzy image of Rachael, her head tilted back, her eyes closed in what looked to be desire, but was more likely a bad case of blood-drunkenness. Over her, obscuring the lower part of Rachael's face and upper body, was another head. From its position I gathered that the vamp was drinking deeply from Rachael's jugular. The vamp had red hair, though not curly—just long and flowing. "Adrianna?" I murmured the question. But she still had curly hair when she attacked the house. So I was betting no. Some other redheaded vamp.

The Kid shook his head. He didn't know either.

"Any better shots?"

He gave me a waffling motion with his hand and punched a button. From another angle I could make out a portion of a face, but it was blurry. The nose was distinctive, maybe a bit too long, a tad too pointed for perfect beauty, which was odd for vamps. They usually only turned the physically perfect—no matter how mentally ill the human in question might be. I pointed to the nose and then drew my fingers along my own and pulled them together and out as if elongating my nose. The Kid shrugged and held up a finger to the side of his nostril, as if showing me that it could be something else and the poor quality of the shots might be involved in creating an effect that nature hadn't provided. So the photo was no help. Ducky.

The man beside her seemed delicate, his hair spiky, his face in shadow. Only the large nose ring and spiky hair set him apart.

Alex hit another button and a different car appeared on the screen. He typed out *This car was behind them. Following, as per three different traffic cameras and the bank camera.*

"Shadowing or tailing?" I whispered. There was a big difference. Shadowing might mean the lead car knew they were there and they were all working together. Tailing meant two forces in opposition.

Tailing, the Kid typed. "Way back. Can't tell that the lead car knew." He punched a button and a different shot of the second car came up. It showed a quarter shot of a man's head and part of his jaw—black hair, black beard, the kind that lines the edge of the jaw and usually moves up beside his mouth to form a goatee. His jaw was strong and sculpted, his chin might have been square, and something glinted gold on his neck. Dangling earring? If so it was a big one. Vamp? Not likely. Most male vamps didn't wear big honking hoops.

How many vamps have beards? I typed into his tablet. *How many blood-servants?* Thinking about the limo from out of state, I added at the bottom *How many Texans?*

Lots, he typed back. *Thirteen local fangheads scanned in already, no Texans. I'll try to do facial matching.* At my questioning look he said aloud, "Like facial recog programs, but this one matches parts of a photo with other known photos." He hit a key and a shot came up. It was from the other side of the street and it took me a moment to realign my brain with the car's spatial reality. I was looking at the tail car from the other side. Sitting at the passenger window in the backseat was a vamp. The one I'd killed earlier this evening. The now true-dead vamp who had attacked my freebie house had been tailing the vamp who drove off with Katie's missing girls, which made no sense at all. Another key punch brought up the driver of the second car. Below his face, the Kid typed *Macon Brown. Human. Blood-slave, not -servant, this info per your vamp census last year.*

I nodded. Blood-slaves were the hangers-on in a vamp's household, there for food and sex and odd jobs, and to be passed around to any visiting vamps. Or sold to another vamp to pay a debt. They were addicted to vamp blood and would do anything to get more. Literally anything with any-one. Blood-servants were much higher class. They were at-tached to a clan, had contracts that laid out their jobs, and were sworn to a blood-master. They were cared for, healed when injured or ill, and usually provided blood meals only to the one they were sworn to. I had started a file on them, keeping track of who was sworn to whom.

"So. We have a hired car in front, supposedly on the way to a party at Arceneau Clan Home, with one female vamp, an unknown man with a nose ring, and the girls, and a car in back with a former blood-slave, a now true-dead vamp who attacked our home with Adrianna, and an unknown bearded male, possibly a vamp, wearing an earring. Right?" I didn't expect an answer and I didn't get one.

The Kid shrugged, but added, "The girls never got to Arceneau Clan Home. They turned around partway and headed totally in the wrong direction. And the tail car must have lost them as they left the city. When the black cab went over the Mississippi heading west, the tail car was nowhere in sight."

"Huh. Keep me informed," I said. I punched in Wrassler's number and left him a message on voice mail. "The vamps who attacked my house were involved with the disappear-ance of two of Katie's girls, but may not have been working *with* the vamp who took them. They may have been tailing them, which makes the disappearance of Bliss and Rachael part of this." I hesitated. "Whatever this is." I hung up. Softly, I asked Alex, "Anything on Molly?"

The Kid shrugged, a typical teenaged gesture that was equal parts annoyance, frustration, and exhaustion. He didn't know and it was eating him up inside. "No," he mut-tered. "Nothing new except that I isolated a camera that views the valet parking. I'm trying to get the time and date differentiated."

I patted his shoulder, sighed, and rubbed the back of my neck, feeling the tension in the muscles. "On another subject, text Wrassler to call in someone with prison or government experience to go over the protocols in the back parking. The Tattooed Duo were handling that, and now we got nobody in-house, but I'm sure one of the clans has a specialist they can send over. Also, get him to go over all the security upgrades that were seen by the two." Which was sufficiently confusing, but I figured he could make sense of it all. I closed my door and fell across the mattress, rolling over to strip off my weapons and shove them under the bed. I was crashing. I desperately needed a nap.

I woke to the smell of coffee and bacon. Mostly the bacon. I had slept an hour, and felt worse for it. I rolled from the bed and again stowed my smaller weapons in the gun safe in my closet and the larger ones on the high closet shelf where the children wouldn't see them. I stripped out of my sweaty clothes, which still stank of blood and gore, and showered, the water almost scalding while I soaped and washed my hair, before I switched it to cold—or cold as New Orleans water ever got. I braided my wet hair and dressed—and because I lived with so many males, I started with a bra. Hated those things. Even a holster felt better most days. Over it went a T-shirt and thin cotton pants. It was March in New Orleans—cold one day, humid, wet, and warm the next. Already I could smell spring flowers over the stench of humans in the city. The house felt stuffy, and it wouldn't be long before we had to turn on the AC in the daytime. Back home in the Appalachians, we might still have snow on the ground. Deep inside, Beast rumbled something that sounded like *Home. Go home.*

Flip-flops and a nine-mil in a spine holster completed my ensemble.

I left my room and joined the breakfast mayhem in the kitchen, thumbing my cell open to check for voice mails. "Any messages or text from Wrassler?" I asked.

"Aunt Jane! Aunt Jane! Aunt Jane!" Two midsized projectiles launched through the air at me, in what was becoming a ritual, the strawberry blond one at midthigh and the redheaded one from much higher—directly off the tabletop where he had been standing. Beast shoved into me and I caught EJ in midair just as Angie Baby rammed against my legs. I staggered but caught my balance and hoisted EJ over a shoulder, juggled my cell, bent and picked up Angie, and deposited them in their seats. They were still squealing and the guys eating breakfast stared at me with open mouths.

Oh. Yeah. A normal woman would have dropped them or ended up in a pile on the floor. "Not human," I said. "Deal with it." Just saying the words was liberating. It was like shutting off a loud, out-of-balance motor, one that had caused an unstable vibration all through me, one I hadn't noticed until it was gone.

Pretending I didn't notice the sudden silence in the room, I picked a slice of bacon off the platter in the middle of the table and shoved it into my mouth. Chewing, I prepared myself a plate. It was scrambled egg day and I had regular eggs, Cajun eggs, and Western eggs. Cajun was cooked with red peppers and Western was cooked with onions and bell peppers and jalapeños. I served up most of what was left of each, scooped on a dozen strips of bacon, and sat, adding four pieces of toast to my plate. "Good," I mumbled as I ate. Around me the men started back eating.

"Glad you approve," Eli said dryly.

I said through a mouthful of eggs, "Report from Wrassler?"

"The humans who attacked the house have no memories of the attack," Eli said. "The last thing they remember is a party with some sailors at the Naval Air Station Joint Reserve Base out in Belle Chasse." When I looked up, chewing and lost, he added, "Belle Chasse is an unincorporated location in Plaquemines Parish."

I stopped chewing and swallowed the bite whole. Which hurt. When I got it down, I said, "Vamps and military guys?"

"Yeah," Eli said, concern lacing his tone. "NAS JRB is six nautical miles from downtown New Orleans. It's home to the 159th Fighter Wing, USCG Air Station New Orleans, a Marine Corps Reserve unit, navy and army units."

I felt as if I were being given a military readiness lecture. And maybe I was.

"Layman's terms: The base supports both the 159th FW's NORAD for air defense and Homeland Security, and the Coast Guard Air Station New Orleans search and rescue/

maritime law enforcement missions. It contains a military airport known as Alvin Callender Field. I've already notified your ex. Or your maybe sometime. Or your—"

"Rick will do," I said, sounding more prim than I intended.

"The info was confirmed by a vamp-feeding and Vulcan mind meld," the Kid added. "There were vamps at the military party. One had red hair. Wrassler said to call him after four p.m."

I snorted into my breakfast as I ate. Vulcan mind meld. It fit. "Hmmph," I said. "Now wayward vamps want a piece of Uncle Sam? Leo will be ticked. Cajun eggs are the best. More?"

"Good G—gravy, woman. You just ate a dozen eggs," Eli said. I shrugged. He got up and opened the fridge for more eggs and milk. I was nearly done when he flipped a pan of steaming eggs onto my plate and I dug in again. When I was satisfied, I pushed back the plate, swallowed the last bite down with a slurp of cold tea, and met Evan's eyes.

He was tired and fighting anger, tiny hot flames in his blue eyes. I said, "The Kid will update you on Molly, but we don't have a lot to go on. Yet. When is the last time you did a finding spell on her?"

"This morning," he said. "And I got nothing. But more like it's blocked, not like she's . . . gone." He meant *dead*. "Which is a relief of some sorts."

"Can you tell who's blocking her?" I asked. "Like, is she blocking all targeting and finding spells herself, or is someone else blocking her from others?"

The corners of Big Evan's eyes pulled down with his frown. I could tell he hadn't thought about her blocking him out. But now that I'd planted the worm in his skull, it was burrowing deep.

Go, me. With a little luck, I might make cruelest skinwalker of the year. "Can you tell if she's still nearby?"

"She's within fifty miles," he said.

"Mommy's okay," Angelina said. "But she's scared."

My mouth came open, but I stopped on whatever I was going to say, when Evan said, very gently, "You can tell she's okay?"

Angie nodded. "All the time. Can I have more syrup?"

"You've had enough sugar, sweetheart," Evan said, his eyes unfocused. "Can you tell where Mommy is?"

Angie scrunched up her face and thought, chewing her breakfast. "No. She's okay. But she's scared. You hafta find her soon. Can I please be excused? Me and EJ's gonna play in the backyard."

"Sure," Evan said. "Don't try to leave the yard."

"Biscause the alarms will go off," Angie said, nodding. "From your wards."

"Right." But it was obvious that he wasn't really hearing her. EJ crawled out of his high chair and he and Angie scampered out the side door, their footsteps hollow on the wood porch into the backyard. Evan looked down, fighting disappointment and fear and despondency so strong it crossed the table in dark waves.

My cell buzzed and I didn't recognize the number. "Yellowrock Securities," I said.

"Ms. Yellowrock, this is the concierge at the Hilton on St. Charles Avenue. Ms. Bedelia Everhart has trusted me with a missive for you. Would you prefer to have me mail it to you or would you like to pick it up?"

It took a moment to put the name with Molly, and when I did I stepped away so no one could read the expression on my face. "I can be there in a few minutes."

"It will be waiting for you at my desk, ma'am."

I clicked the cell shut. Eli and the Kid and I shared glances. As if covering for me, Eli said, "Windows for the back of the house come today. We'll have them installed by one."

"Well," I said with fake-sounding cheer, "I'll make a trip back to the hotel to see if anything new has happened, and then I'll be researching at NOPD." Mostly talking to Jodi at police department central. Asking if she knew anything about Molly or vamps out of Texas, or people in vamp society who wore gold earrings.

"Woo-woo room?" Eli asked.

"Yeah. No cell signal. If you need me, call Jodi."

"Will do."

I pulled on a pair of green Lucchese boots and left my house, hopped on the back of Bitsa, and took off to research—the tedious part of being in the security business.

When I got to Molly's hotel, I stopped at the concierge desk. "My name's Jane Yellowrock," I said to the slender, white-haired guy behind the desk. "I understand that Molly—Bedelia Everhart left me a message."

"Ms. Yellowrock, yes," he said, his smile professionally courteous. He extended a legal envelope. "She left it this morning."

My heart jumped into my throat. I smiled back, took the envelope, and found a seat in the lobby. Mostly because my knees were shaking.

I slid a nail under the flap and opened it, to see a piece of hotel paper and a room card key. The handwriting was Molly's. She had written two very short lines.

I'm safe.
Tell Evan I'll be in touch soon.

Mol

"Holy crap," I whispered. And then I closed my eyes. *Molly is safe.* Tears pooled under my lids and I squeezed them tight to keep the emotion and the waterworks under control. When I thought I could read without bursting into tears, I reread the letter.

And then I sniffed it. And I smelled blood. Molly's blood.

It was faint and fresh. And it made my heart stand still. Blood is composed of proteins, and as it ages it breaks down. Like with any other biological product, unless it's preserved, it starts to stink. Old blood has a sickly sweet smell. This was fresh blood. Maybe as little as four hours old. And mixed with the faint trace of blood were pheromones, the kind humans exude when they are blood-drunk, when they've been bitten and drained and the vamp was compelling them to become happy and docile and addicted.

I also smelled a vamp I almost recognized. I closed my eyes and sniffed. Slow and steady, then in little bursts of breath that I pulled over my tongue with a small *scree* of sound. Almost familiar. But not quite. As if maybe this vamp and some other vamp I'd been in contact with over the years had been kissing cousins. Or had been made by the same sire. Not enough to go on. The tears that had gathered when I first smelled Molly trickled down my cheeks. I slashed them away with the back of my hand, yanking brutally on my flesh. I would not cry. I had too much to do. I took three deep breaths and pulled out my fancy-schmancy cell phone.

I didn't want to call Big Evan. Not with this. But I had to. I dialed his number. "What?" he answered.

"Molly's alive," I said. "Or she was a few hours ago. Someone claiming to be her dropped off a letter at the hotel. If it really was her, then she's in the city." I steadied myself, a hand on the chair where I sat. "But you need to know that she's been fed on by a vamp. So nothing in the letter is necessarily real or true."

I read him the letter and listened to a prolonged silence as he digested the meager words.

"So where is she?" he asked. His voice sounded hoarse, as if he forced the words out through strangling emotion.

"Don't know yet."

"Who has her? What did she come here for?" he asked.

"Again, I don't know yet. I'll call back when I know more." Big Evan swore and ended the connection. I headed for the elevators, stuffing the letter back in its envelope.

On the way up, I pulled the envelope to sniff it again, confirming that she had been coerced to write the note. Molly had handled the paper. Her scent was fresh, though weak on the page. There were hints of fear on the note as well as . . . desire. And an undertang of vamp. I sniffed it again and remembered where I'd smelled it before. This vamp had been in her room the first time I went in. A vamp had Molly, was feeding on her. Anger was a low hum deep in my bones, but I breathed deeply, controlling it.

The card key worked and I stepped inside, noting on the way in that repairs had been made to the door. Inside, her scent was fresh. Molly had been back, and had left only a few hours ago. She was unharmed, if the scent signature was anything to go by. The underlying reek of blood was no more than would be left after a vamp-feeding. I detected only a faint trace of anguish, or fear, and far more blood-drunk pheromones. I stood in the entryway, breathing, scenting, studying the room with all my senses before I went farther, then quartering the room, starting with the bath. She had showered, and recently, if the damp, cream-colored towel and washcloth were indications. I sniffed the towel, and determined that she was okay. Healthy. Not stressed by a beating or some other horrible . . . indignity was the only word I could think of, and my mind sheared away from rape, settling on Molly not being freshly wounded. Her toiletries bag was missing. Her toiletries, including the birth control pills that I still hadn't mentioned to anyone.

Some of her clothes were missing from the closet, and her suitcase was gone. The covers were thrown as if her bed had been slept in at least once and she hadn't let house-keeping in to make up the sheets. There were indentations on one of the cream-colored pillows and the other was off to the side, and both pillowcases smelled strongly of Molly. The white sheets and coverlet were rumpled at the foot of the bed. Something in the room bothered me, but I couldn't figure out what. My nose said everything was . . . not fine, but not deadly horrible.

I remembered my thoughts when I had discovered the birth control pills. Was Molly having an affair? I went to the bed and bent over the sheets. No scent but Molly's. No humans, no witches, no vamps, no one but Molly had been in the bed. Beside the bed, the flowers that had been slightly wilted before were dry and crackling, brown as if they had dried in a desert. In the corner, two vamps had stood, wait-ing on Molly as she showered and gathered her things. A male and a female.

I closed my eyes, trying to find something, anything that would tell me who they were and where she was. There was nothing here. I had no leads. No ideas. Nothing except the stink of the vamps I'd scented the first time I came to the room. I stopped and sniffed again. No. Not Adrianna. Not one of the Arceneau Clan that she had been left in charge of. It had been stupid to think that in the first place. My cases were not interconnected.

I knew only this: Molly was in trouble. Someone didn't want her found. She was blood-drunk and didn't know she was in trouble. She had left me a note—or someone else had.

I had no conclusions other than to keep looking for Molly. Except that I'd used up all my own sources.

And that meant that I was going to have to ask Leo for help and soon. "Crap, crap, crap," I muttered. I hated to in-volve Molly with the MOC. Hated it. But unless I found something new in the woo-woo room, I might have no choice.

* * *

The woo-woo room was in the basement of NOPD Central. The first time I'd come here, it was dank and mostly unused. Then I'd discovered that witches had gone missing in New Orleans for decades, maybe centuries, and neither human nor vamp law had done a dang thing to stop it. The files of missing witch children had gone back for as long as the local cops still had records, all of them cold cases—unworked cold cases. Until Jodi's aunt—a witch-in-hiding and also a cop—came along and began to work the cases in her off time, human law enforcement hadn't cared that witches had vanished, in much the way that white cops had once ignored the violent deaths, lynching, and missing citizens of African lineage, perpetrated by the KKK.

I'd made a stink about it all. Things had started to change. Jodi got a promotion of sorts, which was really intended to be a career killer, by NOPD powers that be. She became the head of the woo-woo squad. Not the squad's real name, but one of the many names that I called them. Under her leadership, the woo-woo room had expanded into space for three offices and a conference room, carved out of the bowels of the cop dungeon. Unlike the upper reaches of the building, it was quiet and conducive to the kind of cold cases Jodi excelled in. Unfortunately it had no cell signal at all.

I skipped down the stairs, my visitor's badge bumping my collarbone, a box under my arm and a bag in the other hand, sloshing with my steps. I wandered the short hallway until I found Jodi, standing in the conference room, her jacket off, staring at a whiteboard. There were five whiteboards in the room, each and every one covered with photos of witch children. Some of the photos went back a long time, discolored with age, curling in, folded or creased. Knowing that there was nothing I could do for any of the victims, and feeling a sense of helplessness that curdled my stomach, I always tried to not look at the photos. Yeah. I was a coward.

The photo Jodi stared at, seeming mesmerized, was centered on the center board, with two other photos, file names, and numbers.

"Jane," she said, without turning her head to me. "Haven't seen you here in a while."

"Yeah. My bad." And here I was, not visiting, but bringing problems and asking for help. I needed to take this slow. "I brought peace offerings."

Jodi looked at me, her eyes tracking to the stuff I carried. A slow smile spread on her face. "Café DuMonde. You are evil. What if I'm on a diet?"

I didn't have the time, but I offered, "We can go for a run together this evening."

She huffed a breath. "I'm on a case. But thanks." Her eyes found mine. "Why do you have to be such a pain in the ass? Being friends with you is hard work."

"I know. So. Beignets and coffee? They're still sorta hot."

Jodi pushed papers aside from the long length of tables and I set the box and bag in the clear space. "Gimme," Jodi said of the coffee. I poured a cup from the travel box the café had put together and she took it, inhaling the aroma before she inhaled the coffee itself. "God, this is so much better than the swill we scorch here. I needed this." A moment later she took a beignet and bit in. Through the powdered sugar and fried pastry she said, "So. What do you want?"

I followed her lead, took a beignet, and bit in. The taste was incredible. Sweet, hot, and perfect. Through the pastry I said, "I need info. And I have something to trade." Jodi made a little "go ahead" gesture with her pastry and I said, "I need to know about any dark-haired male vamps or blood-servants who currently have short beards." I demonstrated with a finger to show her the shape. "And who may wear earrings. Hoops."

"Yeah?" Jodi watched me speculatively, and from the look in her eyes, she had something for me. "What do you have to trade?"

"Info on a vamp *gather*."

"Old or recent?"

I popped the last of my beignet into my mouth and pushed it in with one finger. Chewed. Swallowed. Grinned. Letting her wait. "Planned."

Jodi's eyes widened and her jaw dropped. "No shit? Uh, sorry. No kidding?"

"None at all. And if you help, I'll ask Leo if you can attend. He'll probably say no, but it's worth a shot."

"I'd give my ex-husband's left testicle to attend a *gather*. Actually, I'd give both. Wrapped up in a box with a bow."

I chuckled. I'd only recently discovered that Jodi had been married once. It hadn't lasted long and it had ended badly when the ex had tried to sleep with Jodi's cop partner. Who was male. And not gay. "Like I said. I can't promise anything. But I can tell you as much as Leo lets me about the *gather*, like date and time, info I'll get tonight. I do know that it'll be soon. Deal?"

"One of my sources spotted a new vamp in town. He goes by the name Jack Shoffru, and we have records on him back to the mid seventeen hundreds. Scuttlebutt from way back when, like ancient history gossip, says that he ran with Jean Lafitte."

"The pirate?" I asked, startled, talking around the pastry and thinking about the gold earring. I had been thinking gay vamp, but the earring could certainly have been piratical. I kept my smile in and swallowed my bite of beignet.

"Yeah. Him. Lafitte made Louisiana his stomping grounds, until he *disappeared* in 1823."

I stopped cold, another beignet halfway to my mouth. *Disappeared* was a vamp term, used when a vamp had lived too long unchanged and unaged in the human world. It also was a term they used when they were first turned and went into forced containment in their master's scion lair for the necessary ten years or so of curing, the time and the condition of insanity referred to as the devoveo. "Sooo, are you saying that Shoffru actually is Lafitte?"

"No. They hung together. A lot. Records suggest that he was a ship's captain in Lafitte's fleet and a partner in Lafitte's warehouse in the city in 1805. Anyway, Shoffru has been gone for nearly two centuries, and is now a big-time MOC in Mexico, which was also a stomping ground for Lafitte. Now he's back. I'll e-mail you his file as soon as I nail down some particulars."

"That would be great," I said. "A pirate on Leo's territory. Yeah. I need to talk to the MOC." I stopped. "When did he get here? To New Orleans? And . . . do vamps have passports? How did he get here from Mexico?"

"My sources are still tracking that down and trust me, it should *not* be taking so long. No one is saying, but I have a feeling that either he compelled humans to let him in without papers or he snuck in over the border."

I sat back on the tabletop, letting the formerly unmatched puzzle pieces find a few new empty slots. "So, does Galveston have a port where he could have come over?"

Jodi looked at me strangely. "Yeah. Why? What do you know?"

"Not a thing; just a wild guess. See if any record goes to Shoffru renting a limo in Galveston. If he did, then that would be the port he entered through, maybe, and the method he used to get here. And if my guess pans out, that would mean you would be willing to share all you have on him, right?"

"Deal. But right now I need info on the *gather*. Is security going to be a problem?" she asked, changing the subject.

"Shouldn't. Maybe traffic problems the night of. I'll keep you informed if we need traffic cops."

"And if you get me into the *gather* I'll be your biggest fan."

"I'll try to make it happen." I nodded at the photos on the whiteboards. "Anything new on the cold-case missing witches?"

"Not much." Her mouth turned down. Jodi's mother was a witch, as her aunt had been. For her, missing witch cold cases were a personal issue. "So many lost," she said. "So few bodies ever found. They have to be somewhere."

"Or turned and chained in a vamp's basement."

Jodi spun slowly on a heel and looked at me, her eyebrows forming a slight V. "Yeah. Maybe."

"My last bit of news is about witches," I said, taking a breath to start on the real reason I was here. "Molly Everhart Trueblood came to New Orleans a little over forty-eight hours ago. And went missing. A vamp took her."

I placed Molly's note on the table beside Jodi. She studied it and said softly, "Her note seems a little terse for a wife talking to her husband, but it also suggests she went of her own volition. Like a guest and blood donor. I doubt the FBI would be concerned enough to launch an investigation. I know NOPD wouldn't be." Jodi looked away from the dread in my eyes. "There's just not enough here, Jane." Her tone still gentle, she said, "It's not too early for a missing-person report to be filed, but you need to know that the switch in states makes it more difficult."

"You want me to go to Missing Persons?" I said, my tone incredulous. "Are you kidding me?"

"No." She lifted her eyes and met mine. "Her next of kin need to file it. And I'll keep an eye out for her or any news about her. But there hasn't been a crime committed. That's all I can do at this point, until there's more evidence."

I shook my head, disbelieving, and heard myself say, "So when I find her dead, drained body, then you'll take an interest?" Jodi pursed her lips as if to keep in words she couldn't say to me. On one level I understood. She had a job description and bosses she had to account to for the use of her time. But still. "This sucks," I said.

"Yes. It does. I'll help if I can," she said, soft and sympathetic.

Which was no help at all. Unwillingly, I said, "Her husband is in town helping me look for her. He'd be the one to file."

Jodi nodded slowly and went to a box on one of the long tables in the room. From it she pulled a loose bunch of cards and shuffled through them, handing me one from the middle. "Here. Lou Redkin is currently over Missing. Tell him I gave you his info. He'll help you work through the logistics. File the report as soon as you can. Meanwhile I'll keep a lookout. I promise. And if you get something more than a note, I'll push for an investigation."

"Yeah. Thanks. I guess." I felt blindsided by Jodi's lack of help. I kept telling myself that I understood it. But it hurt in ways I wasn't sure I comprehended yet. "Last thing," I said, and Jodi gave me a little smile. I interpreted it as being because I came to see her with a laundry list of problems. I gave a "so sue me" shrug. "Two of Katie's girls jumped ship after some vamp parties. It looks like they went of their own volition, but it's odd that they haven't contacted their friends, so I'm a little worried. I'll send you the particulars."

Jodi's expression changed subtly. "Let me guess. One of them was the witch, Alis Rogan."

Missing Persons would have no interest in missing working girls, especially a missing working girl who was also a witch. Which was why I'd brought it to her. "Yeah. The coincidence of Bliss and Molly missing at the same time isn't lost on me," I said. "Keep an eye out and call me if you hear anything?"

"Yeah. Ditto on Katie filing missing-persons reports, even though NOPD won't do much with them." I nodded. NOPD would bury everything I brought them.

"Before you go. The knives and bullets taken from the Council House?" she said, referring to vamp HQ by its proper name. She handed me a sheet of paper that looked like info copied from an Internet site.

I read aloud, "Datura: a native plant, common in flower gardens. It's also known as Jimsonweed. This deadly poison is related to nightshade and tomatoes. The toxins in Jimsonweed are tropane belladonna alkaloids, which possess strong"—I stumbled over the next word—"anticholinergic properties." I finished the article. "This is all about ingestion. Why put it on a blade?"

"Because it can affect people even through skin. Accidental poisoning by gardeners has been reported. And because it's easy to find and easy to use. Somebody was intending to send you on a psychedelic trip and/or kill you."

And had gone about it in a weird way, especially considering my skinwalker metabolism. I'd likely have . . . What? Would it have metabolized out fast? Or would it have interfered with my skinwalker shape-changing? Too many people knew about me and what I was. Maybe this was a test as much as a murder attempt? I didn't know how to feel about it. I folded the paper in half, over and over, until it was small enough to tuck into a pocket. I stood and gathered up the trash, tossing it into the nearby can, and putting the top on the coffee for later.

Jodi said, softer, "Jimsonweed is especially bad for witches. It makes them lose concentration, so they have trouble completing spells."

"So why would they use it on me?" I asked. I shook my head. "Unless they thought I was a witch. Not." I'd have to think about this awhile. "Beers when you're done with the case?" I asked.

Jodi studied me as if evaluating my nonreaction. "Beers and burgers," she amended.

I nodded and left the woo-woo room, making my way back up from the bowels of the building and back home in the SUV.

CHAPTER 10

Le Petit Chaton Avec Les Griffes

My orders came in the form of a call from Bruiser, which woke me from my nap. I flipped open my cell, shoved my hair back from my face, pulled it around, over my shoulder, and rolled into a sitting position on my bed. "Bruiser."

Instead of his usually flirty hello, or his pleasant British-style greeting, he simply said, "Bring your weapons tonight. The master wants to spar."

"Uhhh."

"Nine p.m."

"Spar?" I said, incredulous. But I was talking to the silent room. Bruiser had disconnected. I had never sparred with Leo before. Our only physical altercation was when Leo attacked me in the street one night when he was in the grieving process that vamps called the dolore. Basically, vamps just lived too long. Loss of a close loved one who had been with them for hundreds of years could make them lose it mentally, unless they had a Mercy Blade, the magical beings that helped vamps maintain mental and emotional control. At the time I killed his son, Leo didn't have one, and he had nearly killed me. I closed the cell. "I don't want to spar with Leo. Stake him, maybe. But not spar," I said to my room.

I remembered the last time Leo had put his hands on me, and I shivered. He had forced a feeding. It wasn't the only time I'd been attacked and fed upon by a vamp—most vamp-hunters have been bitten once or twice—I had even been healed from some bad vamp-fighting injuries by way of a vamp bite. But Leo's bite was the only time the feeding had been done to bind me to a master vamp's will. I thought about Leo's apology. And about fighting him. My lips parted slowly and I chuffed. Forgiveness might be a lot easier if I had the MOC under the heel of my boot.

I checked the cell and saw that I had hours before I would have to fight the Master of the City of New Orleans. Time for a long stretch, time to get dressed, and plenty of time to plan. I crawled from bed and started stretching, the smells of something rich, meaty, and spicy coming under my bedroom door.

After a meal of BBQ ribs and salad, I pulled up the dossier on Jack Shoffru that Jodi had sent me. The file was dense with material: pdfs of scanned, handwritten notes from decades in the past, more recent reports from Interpol and the FBI, and still more recent reports from the Drug Enforcement Agency. The info was well structured, however, evidence of Jodi's handwork and organizational skills. But the older, handwritten notes were the most interesting. It was historical documentation that Jack Shoffru had been contemporaries with Jean Lafitte, which meant he had been contemporaries with Leo. I sat slowly on my bed, making sure, cross-referencing dates, even downloading the file to my old laptop to see better on the bigger screen than the tablets.

I created a new file titled What-If, and typed in my notes, questions, and worries in bullet points. Mostly I had a lot of conjecture, and not a lot of facts. Okay—none. I had a lot of guesses. But they seemed to hint at a picture, or maybe several pictures, even if there was no mass to the smoke and mirrors at this point. I needed more facts.

Vamps' lives went on for so long that the past was knotted and woven into the present in layers, sometimes in layers of blood. Like the blood diamond and the vamps and witches who had used it over the centuries. My breath caught. What if Molly's kidnapper knew about the blood diamond? My what-ifs could be a lot of things and I shouldn't be getting paranoid.

Too late. I had thought about the diamond and now it had me in its claws.

I checked the time and patted myself down to remove weapons. Even though I was licensed to carry in most of the Southern states, it sometimes wasn't worth the hassle that could come from carrying them. Where I was going, weapons were a surefire way of getting attention from the po-po.

Weaponless, I grabbed my keys and left the house on Bitsa. There were eight or nine banks in the French Quarter/Central Business District area, and I'd picked the closest one for my banking needs and the safe-deposit boxes I rented. I didn't think about them much, but . . . I had a fair number of evil toys in my possession. Well, in the bank vault, but it was pretty much the same thing. I parked and walked into the bank just before closing.

Minutes later, I was standing in a private room, no security cameras, no bank attention, and three bank boxes sitting in front of me. It had been a little bit of a hassle getting them to let me open all three boxes, but when I told the teller that she'd have to open them back and forth so I could rearrange my valuables, she gave in.

I lined all the bank boxes in a row and opened the first one. It contained my personal stuff—passport, the paperwork that stood in lieu of a birth certificate, made out in the name of Jane Doe, the papers with my legal name change to Jane Yellowrock. My security business licenses and PI license. I closed that box and pulled the others to me.

In the one on the left I found two lead-lined acrylic boxes, called RadBoxes by the manufacturer, the kind used in hospitals for blood contaminated by radioactive meds. Inside was a clump of reddish iron about the size of the end of my thumb. The iron blob looked unchanged, and I closed the RadBox without touching it. In the other lead-lined box were pocket watches. Everything looked okay, but the black arts artifacts always made me feel slimy and the stink of old dead meat and spoiled blood clung to my fingers for hours after I touched them. This time, I didn't touch. Who says a cat can't learn new tricks? I closed up the box and pushed it to the side.

In the second safe-deposit box, there were two Rad-Boxes, but here things were a bit different. Resting on top of one yellow acrylic box top was the thing that should have been inside. It was a coyote earring, carved of bone, howling at the sky. It had come to me in a funky dream one night.

Like, literally it had come to me. As in appeared on the pillow by my head. And it moved around sometimes, like now, crawling out of its box. I tucked it back inside. "Stay there," I said to it, knowing it wouldn't listen. I opened the final RadBox, aware that I had been putting it off till last.

Inside, in a black velvet jewelry bag, was the blood diamond. I opened the drawstring, eased the gem to the lip of the bag, and trapped the blood diamond in the cloth with the tips of my fingers, careful not to let it touch my skin. It looked like a pink diamond or a washed-out, pale ruby, about the size of my thumb from the last knuckle to the thumb tip, and it was faceted all over in large chunky facets. It was on a heavy gold chain, a thick casing holding the gem, the casing shaped of horns and claws. The gem was sparkling and dancing with lights, internal lights, not just reflected lights. I had a feeling that it would glow with its own light in a dark room, though I'd never tested that theory. The gem was beautiful and ugly and quite possibly the most powerful thing I had ever seen in my life—and that counted all the witches I knew put together. The blood diamond had been fed the deaths of hundreds of witch children for centuries, in fatal blood-magic ceremonies that featured human sacrifice. The diamond was an artifact worth killing over. It had belonged to the Damours. Now I had it, hidden away. It was safe, for now, but it occurred to me, staring at the awful thing, that I needed a will. If I died, someone responsible needed to have charge of it.

Yeah. Happy thoughts inspired by the gem of death and destruction.

I closed up the bag, stuck it back in the RadBox, and called the teller to help me put everything away properly. Satisfied that the Icons of the Dark were safe, but not emotionally content with that fact, I rode back home, weaving through rush-hour traffic, which in New Orleans was a whole 'nother kinda awful.

I left the house again at seven forty, Eli driving. He had insisted on coming with me when I told my assembled pals and houseguests about my evening's plans. His exact words were "Leo'll bust your butt. This I hafta see. I'm driving." My roomies. So supportive.

In the SUV, I adjusted the stakes in my bun to keep from

stabbing my scalp when they hit the vehicle roof and didn't speak until HQ was in sight. "You did a good job on the door and windows."

"I did a little construction for Uncle Sam."

"Anything you can talk about?"

"Nope."

"You keep secrets like a madam," I said conversationally. "All tease and no share."

Eli made a sound like choking and I let myself smile, knowing he saw it when he glanced at me from the corner of his eye. He recovered quickly. "Holy sh—crap, woman. But you got that all wrong. I am never a bottom. Totally a dommes."

"Promises, promises," I said. He made the spluttering sound again, but I went on. "Okay. You know the vamps will try to take our weapons away when we get to the door. Yours especially," I added. "Security protocols that I put in place."

Eli grunted, lowered the SUV window at the gate to vamp HQ, and said to the little camera, "Eli Younger and Jane Yellowrock to see Leo Pellissier." The gate opened and the window rose. "Despite you not wearing a leather bikini, cuffs, and a dog collar, this is gonna be fun," Eli murmured.

I just grinned. "Someday I'll tell you about the mud wrestling." This time he swallowed down the choking sound.

We parked in the front of HQ, the only vehicle parked there tonight, and walked together up the stairs. Just as we reached the top, Eli asked, "So, what does sparring mean to a vamp?"

"No idea," I said sourly. "But I don't think I'll enjoy it."

Eli huffed a laugh as the air lock doors opened. "Sure you will. Just let your eyes do that weird gold glow. You fight better when that happens."

Deep inside, Beast chuffed and flicked her ears. *Fun*, she thought at me.

"Besides, I have an idea or two that might help."

"No backstabbing. And I mean literal backstabbing," I said. Eli just looked thoughtful.

Four security types met us inside the air lock, two pairs of twins, all male, all with military-length haircuts, and all dressed in black pants and white shirts. "Ms. Yellowrock, Mr. Younger," one said. "Your weapons, please."

"You can have the guns, but the stakes and knives stay

with us," I said. "I've been invited to spar with Leo and have
a feeling I'll need my claws. *Blades*," I corrected quickly.

"One moment," one said. He murmured into his mouthpiece, listened, and then looked at me. "Mr. Dumas says that
will be acceptable, but he insists that you each be accompanied by two security. You'll have to wait while backup ar-
rives."

"Fine by me," I said. Four security for two guests? Someone was taking my suggestions to extremes. However, Eli
and I together could probably take down an entire squad,
so maybe not. I unbuckled my holsters and started placing
my handguns in the black lacquered trays. Beside me, Eli
did the same, but with far greater reluctance. Eli liked his
weapons. "All of them, Eli," I said. "Next we get frisked."

Eli shook his head at that and said to the security, "Get
fresh and die."

The security guy who had been doing the talking said,
"Former SEAL here. I'll wipe the floor with you, army boy."

Eli grinned, showing his teeth. "You can try."

"Men," I muttered. And not in a nice way.

We were led through vamp headquarters until we reached
the elevator. I had never been entirely comfortable with the
elevator, knowing that it went to parts of the building that
were inaccessible by stairs. Which seemed unsafe in case of
fire, unless the vamps had escape tunnels. Which they did.
But I hadn't been shown where *they* all were either. I figured I'd have to become Leo's Enforcer for real for that to
happen, and I wasn't that interested. All six of us crowded
into the cramped area, the smell of blood and humans and
steroids filling the airless space as the doors swished closed.
Some humans were using gym candy. I wondered briefly
what effect anabolic steroids had on vamps who drank the
blood of servants who were using, then let the thought flutter away. I had more important things to worry about. The
leader twin swiped his card and the elevator moved.

We were let out on a floor I didn't recognize, though I
did recognize the same make and model of security cameras that Bruiser, Eli, and I had installed on all the other
floors. Too much to ask that I'd get paid for the design down
here too. Dang vamps.

The hallway was carpeted. We passed what looked like

storage rooms and locker rooms, one for men and one for women. We passed a lounge with couches and a small kitchen, smelling of old pizza and tacos.

The reek of vamp and blood and aggression swirled on the air currents, pushed by the ventilation system. Beast peered out through my eyes and purred, *Fun.* A small smile pulled on my lips, and her delight peered through my eyes. A sideways glance by one guard let me know that my eyes were glowing gold. Beast sent a shot of adrenaline through me. *Fun,* she thought again. *Like finding new territory filled with big prey.*

Down, girl, I thought at her.

The guard opened a door and the stink of sweat and blood and testosterone whiffed out at me. The room we entered was sized for a basketball court, one with various lines on it that allowed it to become tennis, multiple wrestling rings, and areas for martial arts mats to be placed. Tonight the martial arts pads were down. I had halfway been hoping Leo had something else in mind when he said spar, like verbal sparring, where my snark ability would come in handy. No such luck.

All along the white-painted concrete walls, there was also stadium seating, styled with padded benches with metal backs. They were full. On the center mat, two vamps were sparring, their movements so fast I could barely follow. Beast leaned into the forefront of my brain and studied the speed and flexibility of the two. It was like watching a dance, a dance with a loud drum solo sound track — *slapslapslap, oof, thudthudthud,* a rare sucking breath of pain, a rarer moment of stillness, and then more attacks, blocks, kicks, spins. I was so not gonna like this.

"We don't have a hot tub hidden away at the house somewhere, do we?" Eli murmured. I sighed, knowing the question was rhetorical. "I have a feeling you're gonna be one bruised babe tomorrow."

"Yeah." I mean really. What else could I say?

The match ended with a quick feint-punch-block move that sent one opponent flying off the mat and into the wall with a crack that I could feel through the floor and that left a bloody smear on the white-painted concrete blocks.

"That hadda hurt," Eli said. His tone was far too jovial and I slanted my eyes at him to see a huge happy grin in place. Before I could respond, a loud clap sounded and my attention was pulled to the center of the court.

Leo stood in the very middle of the padded center mat, dressed in loose black gi pants in a style I'd never seen before, with flaps that folded over the sides and ties that were stuck inside the waistband. His feet were bare, toes gripping the mat, his chest was bare, and his arms were out to the sides. He turned in a slow circle so the assembled could see him clearly. His skin was pale olive white after centuries out of the sun, his ribs standing out starkly. Scars showed evidence of piercings and slashes, and over his left ribs, beneath his arm, a huge scar traced the flesh like a spider's web, as if his ribs had been caved in by a massive mallet or a grenade or—

I felt Eli tense beside me. "That killed him," he murmured. His hand reached up as if to touch his collarbone and the scar there. He stopped and let his hand drop slowly. Leo had been a warrior for all of his life, fighting sorties, night battles, attacking out of the darkness, a demon from hell, a soldier's worst nightmare. And he had the scars to prove it. How bad did a wound have to be to leave a scar on a vamp?

Leo completed his circle. "Well done," he called out, his voice a sharp quick echo on the walls. "And now I call my Enforcer." I jerked, thinking he meant me, but he went on. "My Onorio, you may join me. We shall see what you are now." Which sounded like a threat in so many ways.

Bruiser stepped into the front, from where he had been standing behind a small group of people. He was wearing a gi, top and bottom, but he untied the black belt at his waist and dropped it, then shrugged out of his top as he stepped onto the mat. He topped Leo by several inches and maybe thirty pounds, all muscle, his skin darker than I remembered it, tanned. He was fit and brawny next to Leo's more slender body, but in a master, appearance is always misleading. I willed Bruiser to glance my way, but it would have been stupid to look away from an opponent, and Bruiser was never stupid.

Overhead, recorded music began, a violin playing something low and sweet, with a gypsy feel. The strings curling with emotion and defeat and love lost. Painful music. The two on the mat bowed to each other. And Leo attacked.

One heartbeat he was standing. When the heartbeat ended, Bruiser was on the mat, his face bleeding. "Get up," Leo said, bouncing on his toes.

Eli yanked me back, a hand on my upper arm. "No," he murmured, his lips at my ear. "I think this is for a purpose. A demonstration."

"He means to kill him."

"No. I don't think so. It isn't the way warriors think. A reprimand, maybe. Something. Not an excuse to kill. Not in front of witnesses."

Of course. That all made sense. I took a calming breath and stopped pulling away, but settled my hands onto my knife hilts. Feeling the rigidity of my delts, Eli kept his hand on me, holding me still.

Bruiser rolled to his feet. Before he was fully upright, Leo attacked again, spinning, pulling Bruiser's arm with him. I heard the shoulder come out of joint with a sliding pop.

Anger boiled up through me. Eli's fingers dug into the soft tissue of my arm, holding me in place.

Using the out-of-joint arm, Leo forced Bruiser to his knees. Bruiser went, with a grunt of pain. Leo let go the arm and kicked out, catching Bruiser with the ball of his instep, midabdomen, and spinning him. Up. Into the air. Leo's fist caught Bruiser's face as he whirled. Blood sprayed high. Splattered over Leo's chest. Bruiser fell and lay still on the mat. The room filled with the scent of blood, strange blood with a salty, sweet undertang. Bruiser's Onorio blood. I had smelled blood similar to it on the only two other Onorios I knew of—Grégoire's primos, both in Atlanta with their master.

"First blood," Leo said calmly. "Match to me." He looked around the room. "Someone take care of him."

Adelaide slipped from the small group of people Bruiser had been standing with and pointed at two others. Together, the three lifted Bruiser and carried him out a door in the rear. Eli's fingers held me still, but a low growl sounded in my throat.

Leo turned to us and looked us over, taking in the assortment of blades and stakes. A slow smile spread over his face, looking pleased and almost . . . *hungry*. My insides tightened and my lips parted, breath coming fast. I felt the

chilled damp of panic bud along my spine, the icy fear melding with the heat of anger in my blood. The door closed
behind Bruiser. My heart skipped a beat and then pounded
hard. I clenched my hands on the hilts of two vamp-killers.

"My other Enforcer," Leo nearly purred, "is here as part
of the entertainment tonight."

He held out a hand to me, almost as if he was asking me
to dance, his black eyes focusing on me intently. I wanted to
run. I wanted to scream and attack. I wanted to pull a gun
and fill him full of silver bullets—which was probably why
I'd been forced to leave them at the door.

Instead I dropped my hand and relaxed my palms,
walked toward him across the basketball floor, Eli at my
side. We stopped at the edge of the mat and I pointed down
at my feet.

"You may remove your boots," Leo said, managing to
sound very French, agreeable, and dictatorial all at once.
Around the mats the spectators started talking, low whis-
pers filling the space.

I started to toe the Luccheses off, but Eli was suddenly
kneeling at my feet, one hand on my ankle. I stopped mid-
move and Eli flashed that strange smile up at me. I realized
it was his battle smile. Eli *liked* combat. He'd missed fighting, missed pitting himself against an enemy, missed the
adrenaline rush. "One of those other things I mentioned? Is
this. Come on, Cinderella," he said, his voice dropping to a
register lower. "Off with the glass slippers so you can claw
the bastard."

I laughed. It was totally inappropriate, but I laughed. The
people in the stands stopped talking, all at once. I could tell
that they turned to us, as one, but I kept my gaze down, at
Eli.

The boots and the socks came off together, hooked in his
thumbs. From the boot sheaths, Eli removed the knives, one
at a time, holding them so the light glinted off the silver
plating and steel edges before setting them on the floor.
Silver was for one purpose only. To kill vamps. He was making sure the people watching knew who I was and what I
did. Pressure built in the room, hot and prickly as barbed
wire left in a desert sun. Eli spun on one knee and spoke to
Leo. "Weapons?" he demanded.

Leo studied us thoughtfully, me standing, Eli at my feet.

Leo's theatrical smile drifted away, leaving him looking curious and . . . *interested*. "Are you acting as Jane's second?"

"Does she need one?"

Second? Oh, crap. A second was what one had in a duel. A pal to make sure the rules were followed and to take the injured fighter home to die if necessary.

"Perhaps," Leo said. "Bare hands." Around us, the room went more silent, the final sounds of voices dying away, the small breaths and shuffles and cloth-on-flesh of movement ending.

"Rules?" Eli asked, his voice ringing in the silent room.

"No one dies . . . again." Polite laughter sounded from the stands, but hushed, as if they weren't quite certain why they laughed. I breathed deep, smelling vamp and human and fresh blood, my heartbeat speeding, but steady now. Deep inside, Beast prowled, back and forth, as if caged and waiting. Everyone knew that Leo intended to do to me what he'd done to Bruiser. This was a demonstration of power and control. And of who was in charge. He didn't want to kill me, but he did want to hurt me. I could turn and walk away. Or I could do what *I* wanted to.

From behind us, others entered the room and walked along the walls to the stands. As they moved, I reached down and unstrapped my thigh sheath. Handed the vamp-killer to Eli. He didn't draw the weapon, but he made sure everyone could see the length of the blade before he put it beside the others on the floor.

Eli extended his knee. It looked like an offering. Confused, I took in his face and he glanced to his knee, lifted his eyebrows. He looked urgent. Only a beat too late, I placed my right bare foot on his thigh and he rolled up my jeans leg, moving slowly, exposing my golden Cherokee skin. He unstrapped the sheath there.

Moving as if he did this every day, Eli rolled down my jeans and indicated my other foot with the barest of gestures. I placed my foot on the floor and lifted the other. Eli rolled up the left jeans leg, uncovering the weapon hidden there. Another knife. He unstrapped it as well and placed it beside the others.

"Wrists," Eli requested.

I held out my hands, palms up, and Eli rolled up my sleeves, removing the blade sheaths. These were small knives, throwing knives, well balanced. He pulled one, the silver plating only on the center of the flat blade, the steel edge so sharp it would draw blood before one could see it touch the skin. He leaned out and placed the knives to the side.

"Stakes," he requested, his hand extended. I lifted my arms and pulled the first two out of my hair. These were the new ones, custom-made of ash wood, fourteen inches long, wicked sharp on one end, rounded and buttonlike on the other, a shape that fit snugly into the palm of my hand. He took them and I lifted my arms again.

Overhead, I heard a faint click and the first strains of guitar music floated into the room. I hadn't noticed when the gypsy violin stopped. A moment later I identified the new music. Joe Bonamassa, playing "Living in a Dust Bowl," a live version, all hot electric guitar, blues, and sex. I drew up the last of my weapons, the sterling silver stakes with steel tips, holding them high for just a moment, letting them catch the light.

And I smiled. Beast padded closer, pawpawpaw.

Eli looked up from my feet and murmured, "Let it out. Let it go. Don't think, just move."

I laughed, the sound deep and cool and . . . ready. I lowered the stakes to him, and he took them with a soft click of metal on metal.

I felt the padded mat beneath my feet as I walked toward Leo. I matched my body to the beat, measured by the percussionist, famously shaking a plastic bottle partially filled with rocks. The music and the lyrics were primal and intense. And Leo watched me, standing with his shoulders rolled forward, his hands open and empty. Blood dried across his skin. Bruiser's blood. Dangerous, this being. Deadly.

Yet as Leo took a breath, the movement of his ribs looked oddly angelic—fallen angel–style. His hair was loose, curling around his face like strands of black silk. His sclera was white, centered with human-black but wide, dilated pupils. But he didn't exhale.

There would be no tells with this one. No hitches of breath for a being who didn't need to breathe. No change in tension for a being who didn't depend on a heartbeat to move.

From deep, deep inside, Beast padded. Settling into my

blood and flesh and bones. And I realized that she was tug-
ging with the silver leash that tied her to Leo. I *felt* him shift
his weight, only a hair, onto his back foot. Beast was sharing
her binding with *me*.

Letting *me* use *it*.

And Leo watched me move in sync with the slightly offbeat blues guitar. Again, I started laughing, a purr of delight. Bonamassa was singing the line "lifting me up." My
hips moved in a little figure eight. Enticing.

Leo struck, kicking vamp-fast.

But I wasn't there anymore. I was three feet to the side.
And Leo had a claw mark on his chest, centered over the
spiderweb of scars. Bright blood welled to the surface, long,
thin, deep gores. Beast claw streaks. I clenched my fist and
felt her claws press into my palms.

Crap. My hands had shifted.

"First blood," Leo said, "to my Enforcer."

I raised my left and made a tiny *come hither* gesture as
Joe sang the words "tearing me down." I didn't look at my
hand, but I saw the golden pelt that covered my arms halfway to my elbow, and the human-shaped hands with bigger
knuckles, longer fingers, and the extruded Beast claws.

My toes spread and gripped the padded mat, better foot-
ing than a human foot. But I didn't look down. I took a
short step to the right and flitted my fingers again. This time
it was a *come-and-get-it* gesture. And I grinned, showing my
blunt human teeth.

Leo took a breath. Time slowed, viscous as Bruiser's drying blood. The silver chain deep inside quivered in warning.
Leo's muscles rippled, his fists striking, feet shoving, body
twisting, torquing power into the move.

I didn't block. I shifted back a step, his fists passing so
close I felt the air cut my skin at the jaw and brush across
my chest. The music ground deep, the offbeat percussion
giving my hips a swivel as I stepped into Leo's move and let
his momentum carry him back across my leg, his balance
failing. I caught his arm and rolled him over my thigh,
swung him around, back to his feet. I danced to the side,
landing strikes as I moved, at kidney, spleen, and circling
around to his front, pounded the soft tissue between his
ribs, and lower down at the soft spot just slightly above the
navel. Kill targets had he been human, and had this duel

been with blades. The significance of the placement wasn't lost on Leo, who grunted with surprise, and what might have been delight.

Instead of dying, Leo laughed and his eyes bled scarlet. But his fangs stayed up, locked away. Vamps can't laugh and vamp out at the same time. It wasn't possible. But Leo . . . was doing it.

We danced around each other, feet out of sync with the music, but somehow in sync with each other, as I led him by the silver chain of the binding. "Come on, Leo," I murmured. "Dance with me."

"Dance of blood and death," he murmured back. And he kicked, so fast I didn't see him move. The blow landed, hard, knocking out my breath. I dropped and rolled and sucked in air that ached. As I was coming up, Leo kicked again. I ducked and bent my body inside the kick, against his thigh, shoulder to his groin. And I hit his knee with a well-placed elbow. It snapped. A crippling strike had he been human. He toppled. Over me. I rolled out, landing two more blows on his torso. Found my feet.

Leo was standing. And he was laughing. "Come, my Enforcer. Is that all *le petit chaton avec les griffes* has for me today?"

The next few seconds were fastfastfast. Slashing-punching-stabbing moves. Too close to kick, too fast to grapple. My heart beat hard, the air in my lungs like bellows beneath the music. I tasted blood and knew my lips were split. Saw the blood shoot from Leo's nose to splatter on the wall fifteen feet away, the blood spurting across my pelt as I backhanded him on the backstroke.

I heard a bone in his hand break as he misjudged and caught my shoulder instead of soft tissue. Distantly, I felt the punch that nearly dislocated my jaw and spun me away from him. With one hand, I worked my jaw, spitting the blood to the side. He was a vamp. He watched my blood fly. And I struck. The move was all Beast, torquing and lifting, kicking and hitting. The impacts lifted Leo off his feet. He landed off the mat. Flat. And lay there.

I walked over and looked down at him. Not close enough for him to grab an ankle, but close enough that I could see his purely human eyes and the pain in his face. My breath and the raw voice of Bonamassa were the only sounds in the room. I jutted my chin at his busted nose. "That's for Bruiser's beating. The rest of it was for my forced feeding, you bastard. Your apology be damned."

Overhead, Bonamassa sang, "living in a dust bowl," and the guitar wailed its plaintive notes. I walked away. A new Bonamassa started to play. It was "One of These Days," a slower-paced song, but grinding and hot. All I needed was to be wearing a red dress to make it all perfect. I laughed softly, the sound hidden beneath the guitar licks. Over my shoulder I said, "Meet you in your office, Leo. We need to chat."

CHAPTER 11

Decide. Now.

I walked out the door, into the hallway, Eli on my heels. The door shut behind us as Bonamassa sang the line "I'll be coming home." My second stayed silent until we reached the women's locker room. He pushed open the door and followed me inside. The room was long and narrow, with lockers down both walls and plain wood benches down the middle. Showers and toilets were on the far end. The music played here too, sultry and painful, but soft enough that we could talk. When the door shut I asked, "You think you should be in here?"

"I don't give a rat's aaa . . . ear for what the sign on the door says. Sit." He pointed. I sat. Eli laid out all my weapons on the bench beside me and checked out the room. I checked out my hands and feet. Human again. Mine. Satisfied with our privacy, Eli brought bath cloths and towels from a set of metal shelves in the back, one of which he wet in the sink and wrung out. "We're alone. Lemme see."

He pressed gently on my ribs, which hurt, but nothing was broken. He raised my arms, one by one, inspecting shoulders, elbows, wrists, hands. "Face," he said. I lifted my head. With the damp cloth, he wiped up the worst of the blood and tossed the cloth aside. He pressed a clean, dry one gently against my lips, blotting the blood on the outside and giving the still-flowing blood a place to clot. The pressure increased, and he placed a palm on the back of my head to give my neck a rest. I huffed out a breath and leaned into him, letting him hold my weight.

"Leo can heal this," he said. "I'll get him if you want."

"I'd rather die," I mumbled against the cloth. Eli chuckled, the sound sympathetic. The blood throbbed in my mouth. I was feeling that same throb of misery work through my whole body as the adrenaline stopped pumping and the fight-or-flight chemicals began to break down, making me nauseated. The door opened. I nearly fell as Eli moved. He was holding a weapon in each hand, both mine, grabbed up from the bench.

Edmund entered. He stood to the side of the door, his hands clasped before him as the door closed, his posture one of submission. "My master suggested that your wounds might need attention. I am to offer myself."

I caught the cloth as it fell away from my lips. "Tell me, Ed. Would you offer yourself if Leo hadn't sent you?"

The former blood-master smiled, the movement of his lips slow and measured. "Oh yes. As just reward for that." He cocked his head toward the sparring room. "It was a thing of beauty to behold."

"Especially the part where she beat the shit outta Leo?" Eli challenged.

"Especially that," Ed said, "though not quite so crudely phrased."

I laughed but stopped as the movement of my lips shocked me with pain. Fresh blood welled and fell down my chin. "Yeah. Okay. Thanks," I said.

Edmund sat beside me, one finger pressing one of Eli's naked blades away, and deliberately nicking his finger on the tip. Blood brimmed on the fingertip, and Ed touched it to my lips. The pain was instantly gone and I shivered with relief. He moved the finger across my lips, gently, rubbing slowly. Vamp blood merged with mine, and the healing moved lower down, warming me, making me want, as vamp blood always did. I opened my eyes and stared into Edmund's. He was watching me intently, his pupils wide, his own lips parted as his finger traced my lips. The vamp wasn't inhumanly beautiful. He had been an average-looking Joe in his human life, his best feature his hair, which he had worn pulled back in a tail the first time I saw him. Now it fell around his face and shoulders, an ash brown so fine it looked luminous.

Overhead the music changed to "Sloe Gin," the guitar

grinding sad, the kind of drunk-in-a-hotel-with-a-bottle-of-whisky-and-a-gun sad. Someone liked Bonamassa.

Edmund slid his hand up my arms to my cradle my face. He bit his lip and said, "I can heal the bruising. If you'll let me."

I knew he meant kiss me, mixing his blood deeper with mine, sharing breath. I hesitated, and Ed shook his head, amused. "I am under orders not to attempt to bind you or seduce you."

"Yeah, that'd be smart. Three's a crowd," Eli said, "and I got these. Two big silver ones."

If I hadn't been hurting, I'd have groaned at the double entendre. Instead I lifted my hand in acquiescence and Edmund bent his head, easing my face to the side and letting his chilly lips meet mine. Despite his promise, the heat of seduction was part of vampire blood sharing. His heat swirled into me, rushing from his cool mouth through my lips, down to my bruised hands and sore wrists, circling my ribs and tightening my breasts. Pooling in my middle. Moving down my body. Pain vanished where the heat reached. I sighed into his mouth and he took my life force into his lungs, our breath mixing, becoming one thing, one breath, one life—as much as undead can share life. When I breathed in, our commingled breath fed me. And suddenly the pain was gone. Just gone. And there was only the warmth of his lips, flesh to flesh. Nothing of passion or need. Just healing.

Edmund eased back. My lids lifted and I opened my eyes, as I whispered, "Thank you."

"No." His eyes, fully human, and a light, hickory-nut brown, held mine. "My thanks to you. I have never tasted blood such as yours."

The sound track had moved to "Black Night," the guitar licks complex and amazing. Edmund stood and stared down at me. "My master suggested you might enjoy a shower before joining him in his study. A maid will bring you a change of clothes and clean out a locker here for you, to use at any time you might wish."

"A shower might be smart," I said. "Walking around a vamp house smelling of blood and fighting sounds pretty stupid." I stood, feeling stronger, though I knew I'd be stiff in the morning. Even my skinwalker metabolism wasn't proof against a vamp beating.

"How's Bruiser?" I asked, and then clarified, "George Dumas."

"He is well. The priestess saw to his shoulder joint. His Onorio blood will do the rest." Edmund's mouth turned down and he looked grim. "Things are changing in New Orleans." With that bland, vague warning, Edmund Hartley left the locker room.

While Eli stood guard outside the door, I showered, using guest-sized samples of soap. Afterward, I slathered some lime-scented cream on my wet skin and dried off on the towels Eli had found. By the time I was done, the maid had delivered a change of clothes and taken my sweaty, bloody ones off to be laundered. I pulled on the undies, finding it mildly unnerving that Leo had my sizes on hand. It made sense, however. He paid for my formal wear, the fancy duds created by a wizened virago of a blood-servant who terrified me, but who made me look good in clothes that were made for soldiers—people who wear and carry weapons. So he might keep stuff here for nights like tonight. Or he might be having nefarious thoughts. I was betting on nefarious.

Beside the undies was a stack of black clothing—slim pants and a body-hugging, black silk, knit sweater. The sweater had a long turtleneck, which I didn't usually care for, but the neck on this one was wide and rolling and fell around my collarbones. The pants were just plain stupid. Who needed a zipper on the side? It was hard to get zipped and made me twist like a pretzel before I got the zipper up and the tiny inside buttons done. But when I looked in the mirror, I could see how long, lean, and dangerous the slacks made me look, and the turtleneck did things for my boobs that were surprising. Yeah. I was still going with nefarious.

The black socks and slippers were so comfortable I might never want to take them off, but they'd be impossible to fight in. Back in the center area of the locker room, I dried and rebraided my hair, twisted it up into a bun, and stuck my stakes in to hold it in place. I also strapped on my shin sheaths and wrist sheaths. The blade that went on my thigh looked good strapped a bit higher than I usually wore it. I checked myself again and wished for lipstick. I looked stark and pale in all the black. I pulled my gold nugget necklace to the front and nestled it, and the mountain lion tooth I'd wired to it, into the folds. The glint of gold added a hint of color and brought out the amber of my eyes.

Beast wasn't staring through my eyes now. No golden glow. She had hidden away since the fight. But she and I were gonna have a little talk later about how I was able to make use of Leo's binding on her. Something was hinky here.

I composed my face and pushed out into the hallway. Eli was no longer alone. Wrassler stood with him, face expressionless, leaning against the wall; both guys seeming relaxed. "Are you here to throw me out or take me to Leo?" I asked. "Because I need to chat with the chief fanghead."

"Yeah. He's all excited about that," Wrassler said, deadpan, pointing, indicating we should go to the elevator.

"Should I be worried?" I asked as we moved down the hallway.

Wrassler's forehead lifted up into little rolls. "About what? You just wiped the floor with the second or third best fighter the Mithrans in the Americas have."

"Who's better?" Eli asked.

"Grégoire for sure. Maybe a couple others could beat Leo in a purely physical fight. But not if he drew on the power of the clans. Then only Grégoire would win. Maybe."

I had felt Leo draw on the power of the clans before, the night Adrianna attacked me in the bathroom at a vamp party. It had been terrifying. Leo hadn't done that tonight, so yeah, I had beat him, but really, if he'd used all his metaphysical weapons or his weapons of war, like if he had challenged me to a duel with swords or flintlock pistols, I probably wouldn't have. Of course, if I'd brought my silver blades, and maybe a rocket launcher, Leo would have lost no matter what psycho mystical crap he might have pulled. It was all a matter of spin and possibilities and stuff that hadn't happened. But physically? Hand to hand? I'd beat the MOC to the ground. *Oh yeah.* Satisfaction flitted through me mixed with delight. I wondered if Leo had been surprised about ending up on the floor, and looked forward to finding out.

The elevator closed on us. "How's Bruiser?" I asked, wanting to confirm Edmund's information.

"Healing," Wrassler said shortly. His tone told me that he didn't want to talk about it, but from the stiffness of his shoulders, I knew he wasn't happy about something. "How often does Leo put on a show and beat up his people?" I asked.

Wrassler's mouth thinned. "I've been here for years. Never saw or heard of it till tonight."

"I see." But I didn't. Not really. Unless the show hadn't been intended for me. Unless it was for someone else. Not Bruiser. He could have beaten up Bruiser anytime. So . . . someone else. Someone in the stands. Watching. And since he hadn't drawn on the massed clan power, he had wanted that special someone to see his primo get beaten and then see him fight a skinwalker, win or lose. Even if he lost, it could work to his benefit. All without drawing on the power of the clans. He wanted someone to think he was a weaker master than he was. Maybe he also wanted that someone to think that Bruiser was out of favor. So he beat up his primo as part of some kind of vamp game? Interesting. Sick, but interesting.

Vamps had layers of plans piled up like sheets of snow and ice, some in the works for centuries. So maybe I was seeing one or two layers in the fight tonight. I just didn't know the context. Or why. Or who. Or what was to come next.

Eli and I entered Leo's office, walking through the wide entrance, Eli taking in everything. His shoulders tightened ever so slightly and I knew he wanted to look behind the tapestries on the walls, to make sure no one was hiding there. But even he seemed to know that might be kinda rude, because he forced his shoulders back down.

Looking awfully good for a guy who had just been beaten to a pulp, Leo was studying a printout while another page clattered in a printer in the open armoire. The rest of the armoire was filled with files, papers, and sheaves, and it smelled of parchment and ink, a lot like Leo himself. Inside me, Beast yawned and stretched, watching Leo through my eyes, like a well-fed and satisfied cat, lazy and taking no action. Moving slowly, Leo pulled the printed page, added it to the ones in his stack, and turned them facedown. He shut the armoire door and spun his modern chair to face us. "Sit, please," he said. We sat in two of the three chairs in front of the desk, and he said, "Report."

I gave him an update on the security status of vamp HQ,

in preparation of the *gather*, and finished with "We still have to go over the changes to parking area security, and we have two choices. We can let the limos drive to the front door and let off their passengers, then park on the street, or we can let them drive in back, park, and get out there and walk in. Parking on the street is safer for us and can be arranged with NOPD, but that means no privacy from the press and telescopic camera lenses. The second is way less formal and parking in the back means we could have a car bomb or other device in the backyard."

Still moving slowly, Leo put his elbows on the desk and steepled his fingers, tapping his lips with them as he thought. And I realized he was moving, not just slowly, but stiffly. I smiled, feeling my lips pull up in wicked glee. Leo was sore. *Go, me.*

"Can you get access to a bomb-sniffing dog?" Leo asked.

Still smiling, I narrowed my eyes and Leo inclined his head. I had suggested a bomb-sniffing dog once already and been denied. "I am sure one can be borrowed from the Federal Aviation Administration or NOPD or some other local law enforcement."

"Excellent. Then we will direct all vehicles to the back until the lot there is full. Any latecomers drive through, let off passengers, and then park elsewhere. Security from the other clans can patrol the outlying areas, freeing Derek and his crew and my own clan security crew to patrol inside the council house. There will be no need to involve NOPD."

Behind him and to the side, the door opened and Adelaide entered, carrying a tray with a teapot, a coffee carafe, and cups. Del, a lawyer, doing waitress service? And then I saw the marks on her neck, tiny, nearly hidden by the high collar of her shirt, but there. I took a slow breath, and over the vamp scent of Leo and the strong odors of the beverages, I smelled human blood. My hands clenched. Leo had fed from her and was now, likely, *breaking her in.*

I stood and took the tray from Del and set it down, and as I rose, I took her wrist, stopping her from pulling away. She stared at my hand on her arm for a long moment before meeting my gaze. "I'm fine," she said, no emotion in her voice.

"Reading my mind?"

"No. I know you. You're worried about me. You're wor-

ried about Leo using me." Her eyes were a cornflower blue
in the lamplight, matching the tiny flowers in her shirt. But
she didn't look worried or afraid or sad or abused. She
looked . . . shuttered. Closed. Detached. Determined. I
couldn't read anything more specific. "Leo and I have come
to an agreement," she said.

"What kind of agreement?"

She looked pointedly at my hand and I released her
wrist, sitting on the edge of my chair. "He has tasted me.
He knows I don't have an agenda regarding him. He
knows his home, his office, and his body are safe from me.
He is satisfied. And he will not demand a sexual relationship with me."

"What makes you so special?" I asked. Leo always demanded to sleep with his people. He considered it a vamp
perk.

"I threatened to sue," she said in the same emotionless
tone. She smoothed her skirt, giving me a chance to swallow
my shock and the bark of laughter, which would probably
have ticked Leo off. "After some discussion, he considered
it likely that I would win," Del went on, "and that such a
lawsuit would bring unwanted attention."

Leo raised a single imperious eyebrow at us, probably
for talking about him as if he were not in the room.

"Well, I'll be a monkey's uncle."

A slight smile, one that would have done Eli proud for
its minimalist style, found her lips. "We are now discussing
the end of his demands on his female servants and scions.
He was unaware that such practices are antiquated"—she
glanced at Leo and her smile widened—"and against the
law."

"Enough," Leo said. He pointed to the other chair. "Sit."

"Of course," Del said. And suddenly I got it. I beat Leo
on the workout floor, but it was really Adelaide Mooney
who was beating him senseless. Who'da thunk it? And *go,
Adelaide!*

"I now will accept questions," Leo said.

I blinked in surprise. *He would?* "Uhhh . . . ," I said.
Great rejoinder.

Eli said, "Why did you beat your primo to a pulp? Just
for starters."

Leo held the Ranger with his eyes. "My primo has been

acting contrary to my needs. He has placed another's needs before my own."

"And?" I asked, feeling that there had to be more to it.

"Onorios cannot be bound," Leo said simply.

It hit me hard and fast. Bruiser had told me he was free of Leo. Bruiser had told me a lot, but I hadn't put it all together. Onorios were rare, nearly impossible to make, and were considered free agents, as well as highly valued. They could stay with a master, but they couldn't be forced to do or be anything. And their master had a dickens of a time reading their minds. Which meant that Leo would be looking for a new primo *and* a new Enforcer. And I realized that Enforcer likely meant me. "No."

"I was not thinking of you, *mon petit chaton avec les griffes*, though I will have you assist in his training when he is chosen."

"Yeah." He'd called me that in the fight, and I had no idea what he was talking about, but I also wasn't going to ask. "Right. Okay. My turn. Adrianna attacked my house. What do you know about that?"

Leo's head went to the side. "Really?" He drew out the word into multiple syllables. He hadn't known, which gave me all sorts of relief. "The enemies of my Enforcer sew dissidence in my ranks. I will deal with this." He nodded at Adelaide. An electronic tablet appeared from a pocket as if she were some kind of prestidigitator, and she made notes.

"My friend Molly Everhart is in town and is missing," I said. "I left you a voice mail. You didn't answer. Do you know where she is?"

"The witch," Leo said, sounding bored.

"Molly was taken from her hotel room by three vamps I didn't recognize."

"You saw these Mithrans?" He looked interested.

"No," I said flatly. "I smelled them."

Leo nodded. "Scent is much more difficult to distort and hide. The witch is of no concern to me unless she encroaches upon what is mine. And no. I do not know where she is." Since Molly couldn't do anything to Leo, that seemed to eliminate her from the MOC's threat list, but I had hoped for a proactive approach. On to other topics while I had the MOC's attention. "Adrianna attacked my house. And two of Katie's girls are missing—Bliss and Rachael. They disappeared after a vamp party at Guilbeau's, on their way to a party at Arceneau Clan Home. Did you know all that?" Leo's head lifted, his eyes intent on me. I had a feeling I had surprised him again. "They left with two others, in a chartered black cab limo, and one was a redheaded female. Behind them, tailing them, was a personal limo, with a male in back. He had a narrow beard." I drew it again on my jaw. "And what might be a gold earring."

Leo's eyes went unfocused, but I had a feeling a lot was going on behind them. "Shoffru," he said.

"Could be, yeah. Jack Shoffru."

Suddenly I was in Leo's sights. It was a little like having a couple of blazing torches pointed at my eyeballs. Not comfy. "What do you know of Jack Shoffru?" he asked, his voice curious, silky with threat.

"Not much." I filled him in on the little I knew, and ended with "He knew Lafitte. And since he hung out in New Orleans in the seventeen and eighteen hundreds, you probably knew him."

Leo's face took on an expression of mild disdain. "We did not travel in the same social circles."

A pirate was beneath the Pellissiers. Got it. "So far as I know, his sire and original clan are unknown."

"Few mongrels know their sires."

I grinned, but before I could say anything snarky back, Leo said, "Research his ships. As I remember it, Shoffru and his partner captained two of Lafitte's fleet, the *Ring Leader* and the *Lady's Virtue*."

Oddly enough, something about the names of the ships were familiar, but I couldn't place them.

Leo nodded slowly, thinking, his face creased in concern, an expression he seldom showed to the world. "It is difficult to know how to treat with Adrianna. When I first knew her, she was a vivacious beauty."

"When *I* first knew her, she had been working black magic with the Damours," I said.

Leo didn't flinch, nothing so human, but something crossed his face. Maybe longing, maybe remorse. He said, "I was powerless to stop them, the Damours. My uncle had signed a . . . a treaty of sorts with them, to leave them alone as long as they left him and his alone. After he found true-death, I was still bound by that contract. Until you came and freed us of it."

I sat back. Thinking. Blinking in the light that suddenly felt too bright. "So you didn't go after the Damours because you couldn't—" I stopped. Leo had used me to break the treaty with the Damours and kill them for their crimes. I hadn't been his Enforcer back then, which had given me opportunity he hadn't had. "You sneaky bastard," I muttered.

Leo inclined his head, a small smile easing the pain on his face. He looked, in that moment, nearly human. "I have been called that. And worse. Though I assure you, I was legitimately conceived and born."

I waved away the comment. "Okay," I said, knowing I'd need time to digest all the knowledge he had just given me—freely—which meant there was a hidden cost somewhere, because vamps did nothing without a price tag attached. There was a lot of info I didn't have yet, but I decided to address this again later when I had my questions in line, and changed the subject from the past to the present. "And the girls missing? And Adrianna?"

Leo shook his head slowly, but I could tell he wasn't happy with the conclusions he was drawing. "Adrianna is declared outlaw. None may assist her, none may shelter her. Her blood-master has agreed that she is to stand trial when she is located, and will be given to the sun should she be found guilty."

I let that settle into me, not feeling anything. I probably should have felt something. Sorrow for her loss of undead life. Satisfaction that an enemy would be gone. *Something.* But I didn't feel anything, and that bothered me. I'd have to think about that later, along with all the other things I was stuffing into the dark inside me. I went back to the problem at hand. "So, if Jackie Boy's a Mexican MOC, why is he here, in your territory?"

Leo leaned back in his chair, his elbows on the padded leather arms, his fingers again steepled in front of his mouth. I could smell the leather as he moved, rich and earthy with tannins; I bet he paid a thousand bucks for the chair. "Shoffru is to be presented at the *gather.* Tomorrow night." I sat forward. It was nice to get some specifics. "Among others, he has applied for sanctuary in New Orleans. He claims that the drug cartels have placed his clans in danger and he wishes to relocate. What would you think if a Mithran requested such a thing?"

"I'd wonder if he was relocating here so he could have a base of operations to expand a drug cartel of his own," Eli said. "And maybe wanting access to a nearby U.S. military base. If he has delusions of grandeur."

Leo gave an approving flutter of his fingers. "That possibility has been under consideration. Upon the basis of that argument I have requested an investigation by the human authorities—undercover, of course—into his finances, plans, and his current situation in Mexico." Leo looked at me. "I believe that he intends to make my lands a *permanent* base of operations."

Oh, crap. "You think he might challenge you," I said.

"Of a certainty. Eventually. First, he will apply for sanctuary and offer me fealty. Should the Drug Enforcement Agency and the Federal Bureau of Investigation and other law enforcement agencies not discover reasons to the contrary, I will accept. Once he is ensconced here, he will apply for blood-master of the Shoffru clan. I can hold that off for a time, but eventually I must accept. At some point thereafter he will challenge me." Leo shrugged. "Or I can kill him now and avoid all the wretchedness."

"Ah," I said. I sat back too, keeping my frustration off my face by an act of will, but knowing Leo would smell it on my skin next time he took a breath.

Eli looked back and forth between us. "What?" he demanded.

Better to meet it head-on, rather than let Leo think I didn't know. "Shoffru," I said to Leo, "is the reason I got to beat the crap out of you tonight. Which, by the way, was immensely satisfying."

"As well as somewhat unexpected, *mon petit chaton.*"

I wanted to ask what the pet names meant, but that was a game I couldn't win. If I asked once, he might just talk French more often to get a rise out of me. I grunted instead. "Shoffru was in the audience, wasn't he?" I accused. Leo smiled, and I said, "I figured. You coulda beaten me to a bloody pulp if you'd drawn on all the clan members, but you didn't want him to see you doing that."

Adelaide nearly dropped her tablet, staring at Leo. And Leo looked totally nonplussed. "What? What'd I say?"

"You can draw on the clan members who swear to you?"

Adelaide asked. Leo looked away, thinking. "All of them?" she persisted.

"What?" I asked. "Can't all MOCs?"

"Some can draw on their own clan members," Del said. "Some can draw on the clan blood-masters sworn to them. Not too many can draw power from all the members of all the clans in a territory." Adelaide stared a hole through Leo. "Good Lord. That's why George became an Onorio instead of dying or turning—because he'd been sipping your blood for a century. No wonder the European Council is so interested in you. Is there a distance limit on how far you can draw? How many you can draw from at once?"

Leo pursed his lips and shot me a narrow-eyed glance. Obviously I'd spilled some beans, and he looked irritated. Flying by the seat of my pants had, just like always, put my feet into it when I landed. And this time it was vamp politics and Leo's secret that I didn't know was a secret. I remembered the night he'd drawn on all the gathered. Power had prickled in the air like lightning, harsh and painful, rippling across my flesh like sharp teeth. And he'd not drawn all he could. And maybe not everyone there had understood what was happening. Maybe Leo's power was—had been— partially unknown. "Oops?" I said, by way of apology. Eli breathed out hard, a huff that sounded amused, but said nothing. "So, that night you saved my life, and punished Adrianna for attacking me, you drew only what you needed to control them," I said. "You could have drained them into true-death."

The MOC held up his hand like a traffic cop, stopping me. To Adelaide he said, "Decide. Now."

"I accept."

I had no idea what had just happened, but Leo inclined his head and pressed a button on his desk. A tinny voice said over an intercom, "Yes, Mr. Pellissier?"

"Four glasses, and a bottle of the Chapoutier Cote Rotie La Mordoree 1990, please. And see that Quesnel allows it to breathe." From the way Adelaide's face went soft, I gathered it was an expensive wine, but I still didn't understand what was happening. Leo smiled at her expression. "Are you familiar with wines, my primo?"

I nearly choked. *Primo?*

Adelaide said, "The 1990 has a saturated dark ruby-purple color, an amazing nose with copious quantities of sweet black fruits, warm new oak, flowers, and smoky bacon fat. To the mouth it has a superb concentration of flavors, a sweet, expansive texture, like butter on the tongue, and a . . . mind-boggling"—she paused, and licked her lips as if tasting it already—"long"—she smiled, her lips lifting slowly—"finish. I tasted it when it was young. I am honored that you open a bottle now."

"What about Bruiser?" I asked, feeling the floor shift beneath me. I had known things were changing, but, this was . . . official. Too much, too soon.

"George is no longer suitable as the primo of the master of a city," Leo said languidly, watching Adelaide. "He has made other choices and, as Onorio, has other duties."

Adelaide was watching Leo back, her attention totally ensnared. And willing. And then I heard her description of the wine, as if it echoed from the tapestried walls. *Crap*. She was talking about a whole lot more than wine. So she would refuse his sexual attention while she was just sworn to him, one of the hoi polloi, but if she got the perks, she would add sex into the deal? Or maybe as long as it was her choice and not part of a contract, she was willing? Human women had always been confusing to me, even back in the children's home. Del just took that confusion to new heights.

"You have other questions, my Enforcer?" Leo asked, not looking at me.

"Yeah," I said, my voice too loud. "You knew about the witches disappearing in New Orleans, didn't you?" I had Leo's attention again and it wasn't the hot and sultry look Del had been receiving. For me, his eyes were bleeding black, and his sclera were taking on a faint tinge of pink. Not that I cared. Fury for Bruiser and anger at all the freaking vamp games burned hot through my veins. I stood and leaned in to his stare. "And I bet you knew about the witches in Natchez and the way the vamps were rising as revenants—a different kind of revenant."

I could see the truth on Leo's face. He had known everything. He had known it all. And he had never done a single blessed thing to stop it or warn me or fix it or . . . I stepped from my chair. "And instead of warning me, you let me go to Natchez, unprepared, to deal with it." A possible conclusion settled around my brain like a tourniquet. A headache started over my eyes and Beast hissed deep inside. Now I had the whole picture. "You were trying to find a way to keep from taking the problem to the European Council. You and your uncle before you were trying to keep the Council out of this situation and out of your territory for two hundred years. And to accomplish that, you signed and kept a contract with the Damours, let witches die by the dozens for centuries, and let Naturaleza in Atlanta and later in Natchez put witches into a circle and drain them slowly dry. You let them run a slave breeding ground in Chattanooga. You knew all about it. Everything.

"And"—I closed my eyes, letting the final picture come into focus—"you brought Adrianna back to life after I staked her because you thought she might know things you wanted to know. You kept her alive even though she was a ticking time bomb because she *did* know things." I opened my eyes and met Leo's. "And you let all that happen because you knew there were magical artifacts on these shores and you wanted them."

Leo sat back in his chair. His power rose in the room, a slow, coiling draft of energy, familiar and spicy, like black pepper on my tongue, this time mixed with blackberries and anise, a strange combination that signaled anger to the hind reaches of my brain. I backed two steps and my knees touched the chair, but I stayed standing.

"The witches are my affair. You are not my adviser, nor my priestess; you are my Enforcer. It is a position of power and honor, which *you* claimed, and which *I* allowed even though, like George, you are not one to be bound. Within the confines of that position, you will not work against my policies, my strategy, or my needs. And I will have respect from you, Jane."

I flinched and sank into the chair. He didn't know that Beast was bound. From Leo's viewpoint, everything I'd done, everything that had been done to me, had been a decision on my part or had led from a decision or choice I made. A court of vamp law might suggest that even the involuntary feeding and binding had resulted directly from the moment I had claimed to be Leo's Enforcer. By claiming the position, I had tacitly agreed to be fed upon and bound. The Mithran version of a forced Vulcan mind meld had been the result. It had been an intimate violation. *Not my fault. Not my fault*, some small logical part of me stated.

It wasn't my fault. It also wasn't right. It wasn't fair. It wasn't legal in a human court of law. But to a fanghead it was all that and more.

A memory flared through me, my body, flat on my back, held in place by the vampire priestess and Bruiser as Leo bowed over me, fangs extended. The pain as he ripped into me.

Not my fault. Not my fault. But that knowledge was not much help at the moment.

I had been such an idiot, and Leo had used my idiocy to his benefit. Though it might not be my fault, I hadn't looked before I jumped, flying by the seat of my pants.

Adelaide reached over and took my hand. The contact was a shock, my hands like ice. "She doesn't know, Leo. She doesn't understand about the council and the witches."

Which wasn't what I was reacting to, but I wasn't going to share my thoughts. Leo considered me, his eyes narrowed, his face still a thunderstorm. He took a breath he didn't need and blew it out hard. "That is not a topic to be discussed tonight," he said to Adelaide. "We have more immediate issues to resolve."

CHAPTER 12

Do We Call the Police?

Leo went on. "The *gather* tomorrow night will be for two purposes," he said, pulling my mind back to the present. "To welcome the applicants from Mexico, and to formally announce to my people the intent of the European Council to visit. The latter is known, of course, but the announcement must be accomplished pro forma. I have also been informed by Raymond Micheika that we are also to receive visitors arriving from Africa. They will be accorded the same respect as the last visitors."

Though I'd never met the man, I remembered the name. Micheika was a rare African werelion, and was the leader of the International Association of Weres, and the leader of the Party of African Weres—PAW. Surprised, I asked, "Is Kemnebi coming?"

"I was not informed of the identity of the arrivals," Leo said sourly, "only that three cats were to arrive, along with a grindylow and several servants."

"So you'll be housing Mexican vamps and African weres and parading your newest applicants for admission to the NOLA vamps all in one evening."

Eli chuckled. "That's a FUBAR waiting to happen."

"What is a fubar?" Leo asked.

Quesnel, the sommelier, entered through the door before I could reply and started pouring the wine. He held the bottle up high and let it gurgle into the glasses, which I thought was highly entertaining. As Quesnel passed the glasses around, Leo stood, the genial host. "A toast," he said, lifting a glass. "In honor of my new primo." He lifted his glass.

And the best part? The MOC was *still* moving stiffly. I had put a whammy on him. And that part of my night felt really, really good.

Eli, Wrassler, and I spent the rest of the night going over all the security protocols and implementing the changes to the parking area out back. The Kid called in the middle of the meeting and told us he had nothing new to share. It wasn't a necessary call from an informational standpoint, but it made me feel better to know that someone, somewhere, was still working on finding Molly, Bliss, and Rachael. We were going in circles trying to find them, and I was getting itchy under my skin just thinking about the passing time. The call kept me from screaming. Or lashing out and beating up someone. Neither would be productive.

We were nearly done when Wrassler got a text on his cell. He held up a hand to stop the discussion and dialed a number. "Tell me everything."

I didn't need my enhanced hearing to make out that the person on the other end was hysterical, crying, gasping for breath when she wasn't screaming. "Sonya's gone! She's gone! She went to her rooms to change and she never came back!"

I heard screaming in the background. Running feet. Eli looked at me and placed a hand on the blade at his side. I could almost read his thoughts as the other hand touched his chest. No flak jackets. No Kevlar. But all his toys were close at hand. He made a pointing gesture, I nodded, and he trotted off, to get our weapons and bring the vehicle around.

Over the phone, the woman was back, screaming, "We went to check on her. Her clothes are in a pile on the floor, like she just dropped them. Which she never would! She's so *picky* about her things. It's so anal it drives me— Never mind. That doesn't matter." I could almost see the girl waving the unimportant away with a frantic hand. "She's gone. Vanished."

"Jocelyn, take a deep breath," Wrassler said. He sounded calming and soothing. "That's right. Slow down. Take another breath. Good." I had no idea who Jocelyn or Sonya

was, but Wrassler knew, and from his expression he was
deeply concerned. "Now, tell me. Was there a pile of ash or
grit, like granules of sand, in or near her clothes?"

Jocelyn was shocked silent, and then we heard her take
a shaky breath. "How did you know that?"

Wrassler didn't answer her question. "Mr. Pellissier's Enforcer and I will be there in a few minutes. Touch nothing.
Do nothing. Understand?"

"Yes." She sobbed and gulped. "Like on those crime
shows. Evidence and all." Jocelyn sobbed again. "She's dead,
isn't she?"

"We don't know. But you are Sonya's primo." Which told
me who they were, and left me feeling gut-socked. I had
never heard of the two. As the Enforcer and head of security, I should know every vamp and primo in the city. And
clearly I didn't. "Take all the others," Wrassler said, "and
leave the suite. Go to the bar. We'll be there in five minutes." He closed the cell. "Come with me," he said, starting
back down the hallway, looking around.

"Eli's getting his gear," I said, mind-reading.

Wrassler pulled a mic out of his shirt collar and tapped
it active. "Bring my SUV around, one driver, one shooter."
He tapped the mic off and began removing the coms appa-
ratus as he led the way. Without me having to ask, he said,
"Sonya is a new scion, released into the world only two
weeks ago. If there's ash or grit, then that makes two killed
in just days."

"Any history on vamps turning to ash?" I asked, remembering that Reach was supposed to be researching that.

"Nothing that Reach has bothered to tell us," Wrassler
rumbled, anger in his tone. He pushed the way out of the
back of the building and rushed into the waiting car—a typical vamp-mobile, armored body, heavily tinted windows,
and armament in the side panels of the doors. The lead vehicle rumbled off as I hopped into Eli's SUV and belted in,
gearing up as best I could as he tore out the gates after
Wrassler.

In minutes, we pulled up in front of a narrow three-story
building just off Bourbon Street. There was no sign, no
neon, no nothing to identify the place, just three shuttered
windows, long and narrow, and a tall wood door bound with
rusted metal, a large ornate lock, and a door handle. On the

second story above was a wrought-iron balcony with columns shaped like leaves and flowers, and some kind of supporting iron filigree along the roof. Four long, narrow doors
and windows, closed and shuttered, lined up with the ones
on the ground floor. The third floor was similarly arranged,
but the windows and doors were out of sight from the angle
on the street as we pulled up, which I knew Eli didn't like.

"I'll scout around," he said, parking and taking off into
the shadows.

Much more slowly, Eli's extra go-bag slung over my
shoulder, I followed Wrassler and his shooter, a security guy
I knew served Clan Pellissier but couldn't name. For now he
was P. Shooter, which made me smile. P. Shooter wore jeans
and a sweater, and had enough guns on him to take out a
street gang. I tucked my braid into my T-shirts to dangle
down my back, out of the way. Unholstered a nine-mil and
readied it for firing.

Wrassler knocked and a tiny access panel in the door
opened and shut instantly. Stupid. They needed cameras. All
an invader would need to do was stick a gun in the panel
when it was opened and fire. The door opened and a well-
rounded, buxom woman fell into Wrassler's arms, breathing
as if she'd run a marathon. I could smell her fear-stink
sweat.

"Update, Jocelyn," Wrassler said, edging her inside.
P. Shooter and I followed and closed up behind us, looking
up the narrow, curving stairway to make sure no one stood
at the top. P. Shooter moved into the room, already quartering it.

"They're all in the bar," Jocelyn said, "and I had drinks
and food brought out." She shuddered a breath that shook
her to her toes—which were bare and painted and adorned
with rings and anklets. Pretty feet. Thick, beautiful arms,
skin the color of walnut, but soft and oiled to a sheen, large
breasts, and no bra. Long flowing clothes—a washed silk
salwar chemise in purples. "No one has been in or out of the
house—so far as I can tell—since we closed up for the
dawn. And I kept everyone out of Sonya's room."

I moved to the front windows and saw that they were
locked and secure. P. Shooter looked at me and gestured to
the back of the ground floor. I nodded and he left to check
it out. I paused and sniffed, smelling fear and alcohol and

blood and perfume. Humans and two, maybe three vamps. We moved into the main room, which was rectangular, the walls painted a pale mint color with darker green trim, the floor shrimp-toned tile, and the coffered ceilings twelve feet tall. Leather sofas were in one area with a merrily burning gas fire in the corner. The bar ran along the windowless right-side wall for twelve feet or so, and was stocked with enough liquor to satisfy a platoon of soldiers on leave for a month. Across from it was a library with books and shelves and an architectural-style desk. A long table with upholstered chairs marked the dining area. The back of the building smelled of cooking and a bathroom and old plumbing. P. Shooter disappeared into the rooms there.

Incense was burning, patchouli, I thought, in two burners, trying to mask the odor of marijuana. I didn't smile, but it was a close thing.

I counted the people sitting curled up together like puppies needing comfort on the sofas and chairs, coming up with eleven. Because of the incense, I couldn't tell by the smell, but two were vamp-pale. Vamps each needed a minimum of three humans to feed from, which totaled up at three humans apiece. The lair was running on a skeleton feeding crew. Which was funny. Sorta.

"Where . . ." *Are her ashes? Where did she die? No. Wrong.* "Ummm . . ." I floundered.

"All the bedrooms are upstairs," Jocelyn said, wiping her nose with a wrist. "Blood-servants are on the second floor. Sonya's, Liam's, and Vivien's are on the top floor." She sniffed. "Sonya's is the middle room."

Wrassler jerked his head to me, indicating I was to check out the upstairs. I nodded back and headed up the narrow, curving stairs by the front door. Pulling back the slide, I off-safetied, my trigger finger off the trigger, along the side of the weapon. I paused at the top of the stairs, feeling P. Shooter coming up behind me, and letting my eyes adjust, hearing my breathing, and Shooter's, slow and steady. Smelling everything. More blood and sex and humans and vamps and alcohol and more marijuana. Lots of marijuana, the smell overpowering all the others. In the fumes of dope, I could detect everything, but not parse the scents into the finer smells, like individuals and their previous locations. The kids had been partying.

"Downstairs?" I asked Shooter, sotto voce.

"Everything secure, all locked up for the day," he murmured. He gave me the hand signal for *I'll go right* and moved out. Using basic paramilitary procedures and hand signals, Shooter and I divided the place up, me taking the left half of the second floor. The rooms were tiny, like dorms that had been halved. They were cramped and messy, and the bathrooms were worse. There were only two baths on the second floor, one on the ground floor, for the nine messy humans. And no place for a killer to hide.

P. Shooter and I headed up the stairs to the top floor. Here there were three matching suites, each done up like a swanky hotel, lots of creamy Egyptian cotton, ebony king-sized four-poster beds, drapery that puddled on the black hardwood floors, the rare rug in large blocks of bright color, similar bright pillows everywhere. Squishy tan oversized armchairs and ottomans. The three baths were long and linear, done in white marble and black tile, everything sparse and very similar. Closets were free of hiding humans. Windows were actually doors, but all were locked and secured. Shooter and I met in the middle room.

In front of a long, beveled mirror on a stand was a heap of clothing. Tangled in the orange, pink, and shrimp floral dress were tiny gold sandals, two bracelets, a watch, a necklace, two earrings, and a heap of ash. It was brownish and white with granules of red. The brown for flesh, the white for bone, the red for blood, I guessed. I breathed in and out. Nothing had burned here. Nothing had bled here except for humans, and that some time ago. I smelled no magic, at least not over the mixed vamp/blood/weed/sex smells, already mixing with the patchouli rising from the bottom floor.

I knelt and sniffed again, short bursts of breath, my mouth open, the air scudding across my tongue and throat with a faint *scree* of sound. No. Nothing had burned. No smell of cremated human or roasted vamp. But the ash itself smelled like vamp—a thick and wiry smell that reminded me of cactus and hot sand. Something had turned a female vamp into an ash heap.

I pulled my cell and took pics of everything. When I was done, I pulled a wood stake and stirred the ashes. No bones. No fragments. *Weird*. I asked Shooter, "What's protocol on this? Do I call the cops?"

He frowned, and I realized that he was one of twins from the council HQ, blond and lean and sorta scary looking now that I saw him armed. I hadn't recognized him because his ponytail was tucked down inside the collar of his sweater, to keep an opponent from using it like a handle to control him, just as I had done with my own hair.

"The primo's call. Except the primo's new and won't know, will she?"

"Wrassler's call, then," I stated, and Shooter grinned. "What?"

"Maybe I'll have a nickname someday." He holstered his gun.

"P. Shooter. P for Pellissier."

"Yeah?" He nodded, thinking, securing all his weapons without looking at them, by muscle memory alone. "Can we drop the P? I haven't used a pea shooter since . . . ever. And it sounds kinda wimpy." He grinned again, displaying perfect white teeth, blue eyes bright and clear. He was pretty, buff, and deadly. My kinda man. If he hadn't also been a human-shaped bag of vamp food. Ick.

I grinned back at him. "Sure. Let's go talk to Wrassler."

Wrassler and Eli were in a corner of the main room, talking softly. Someone had turned on the fifty-inch TV to a home shopping network. The models were posing in tummy-shaping underclothing and long thigh-slimming leggings. Which looked really hot and uncomfortable. I joined the men while Shooter patrolled the ground floor again, his weapon back in his hands.

"Ash," I said softly.

Wrassler thumbed through his cell and held up a pic of some clothes and ashes with the odd brown, white, and red coloring. Same theory, different scene.

"Yeah. Like that," I said. "I see no way that the vamp—ire," I added, "was turned into ashes. No burn smell, no magic smell, no easy way in or out, no weapons found. Do we call the police?"

"No. Leo has people working on it. I'll collect the ashes. Thanks." He heaved a breath and ran his eyes over the people in the seating area. They had begun to stand, stretch, and move toward us. It was time for Wrassler to give them the bad news that their expressions suggested they were already expecting. And time for Eli and me to head home.

Or scurry away before the predictable emotional break-downs, take your pick.

We got home just after dawn and I fell into bed, exhausted, bleary-eyed, my head stuffed full of vamp business. It was only on the edge of sleep that I realized that Leo hadn't *really* talked to me about the witches or their disappearances or Molly or Bliss or Rachael or any of the things I had needed to discuss. He had given me a hint and changed the subject before I realized it. "Dang," I mumbled into my pillow. "He did it again." But he had given me one thing I hadn't had before—the names of Shoffru's ships, which offered me a line of research.

I rolled over at noon after too little sleep but with my brain whirling too fast to find dreams again. I rose, stretched, showered, and dressed in casual clothes and warm socks, braiding my hair into multiple braids and twisting them up into an intricate bun that made it look as if I had much thicker hair. Silver stakes kept it all in place. It felt weird to be able to do this on my own. Christie, one of Katie's girls, had taught me how to do the fancy bun. She had taught me how to put on makeup too, but I was always much more sparing than the dominatrix.

I laid my night's work clothes out on the bed, going for the side-zippered pants I had picked up at HQ the night before, with a slim, tailored white shirt, black vest, and black jacket. I needed to replace my black boots, and my dancing shoes were showing their age, but I ran a damp rag over my old black dancing shoes, the ones with the sturdy heel and the strap over the instep, and set them at the foot of the bed. There was nothing fancy about my ensemble, more useful and serviceable than swank, though the fabrics were top-of-the-line.

After doing some online banking, I traced the names of the ships Leo had given me, the *Ring Leader* and the *Lady's Virtue*. Shoffru and a cohort had captained both pirate vessels, and also had owned property on the island of Saint Domingue. I sat back, staring at the screen of my laptop, feeling a frisson of knowing, of being absolutely certain that I had found something important, but having no clue what it was. I cross-referenced notes from other cases, and when I found it, I was elated and horrified in equal measure.

The island had been home of the Damours, vamps I had killed during the black magic ceremony that had as the centerpiece the sacrificial deaths of witch children. The Damours who were part and parcel of Adrianna and why she wanted to kill me.

Bruiser had given me a history on the Damours' blood-family, which I had transcribed into truncated notes. I opened that file and read *Island of Saint Domingue: vamps' haven. Clans in strict social/political society based on race/wealth. White vamps on top, vampyres du couleur libre—free vampires of color (also landowners and slave owners)—in middle, slaves at bottom: workers, sex toys, blood meals. Slaves treated barbarously.*

The history lesson all came back. The slaves had wanted freedom. Duh. The vampyres du couleur clans had little political power because of their race, and they wanted equality with the white vampires. The whites wanted status quo. Some, both white and mixed race, had the witch gene and practiced blood magic, dark rites. Some with the witch gene never quite regained sanity, even after they passed the devoveo state and were unchained. I had read accounts of the atrocities the island's fangheads practiced. Their cruelty was legendary.

There had been a vamp of color, François-Dominique Toussaint Louverture. He had turned some of the discontented and helped plot one of the major uprisings. It had taken years, and it was brutal, on both sides. Three of the surviving vampire clans, including some who practiced blood magic, came to Louisiana in 1791, upsetting the local political scene.

They had traveled on Shoffru's boats, the *Ring Leader* and the *Lady's Virtue*. Had the Damours turned Jack? Was he a vamp when he worked with Lafitte? So what did an old vamp want with working girls? Was it possible that he had been friends with the Damours and wanted revenge for their deaths? If so, how had he figured out that I had helped kill them? Nothing made sense. Nothing connected. Nothing.

I checked my e-mail, and I saw notes from Eli and the Kid. Eli had talked to some of the waitstaff at Guilbeau's and discovered who had given the party, the one from which Bliss and Rachael had left and then vanished. The host's name was unknown, definitely not a local vamp, and not a familiar local blood-servant either. I set him and the Kid to working on IDing him. Or her. It was hard to know gender with a name like Bancym M'lareil, and there was nothing in a quick Internet search.

The Kid had info on the local vamps and humans that Troll had ID'd, on the security footage leaving the party. Troll had also sent the Kid a text that the other humans who had gotten sick had all attended the vamp party in Guilbeau's. Something had happened at the party that had made humans sick, but it wasn't like the vamp plague that had attacked both vamps and the humans they fed from. And I still didn't know how that related to the girls disappearing. Unless they were sick somewhere and not able to call for help? We had also discovered that the ashed-to-death vamps had attended the party. Something had happened at the party, and I needed to know what.

None of the people on the security footage had anything against Katie, Leo, or me, so far as Alex had been able to detect, so I created a note asking about info on the night in question—a formal one for the vamps and a much more casual note for the humans. But I signed both kinds of notes "The Enforcer, Jane Yellowrock." I cross-referenced my files for the vamps and humans who had e-mail addys and sent these notes out right away, then created printed notes for the Luddites and addressed them for snail mail. I really wanted to make an in-person visit while wearing enough weapons to start a small war, but there were too many names on the list to risk that. And even if I managed to find the right lair and locate the girls, a frontal assault would likely get them killed. When I left my room, I discovered a gift-wrapped box outside my door—gold foil paper with a bloodred ribbon. I picked it up and carried it to the front room, holding it up in question. Without looking up from his tablets, the Kid said, "Delivery. Special messenger. Card on the side."

And so there was—in a matching gold envelope. I pulled the card free and read the fancy old-fashioned script, *For my Enforcer. To replace that which you lost in my service. Leo.*

I thought about refusing—I always thought about refusing Leo's prezzies. But he considered it an obligation to replace things lost in his service, and who was I to keep him

from giving me what he thought was just compensation?
Besides, he always gave totally superlative top-of-the-line
gifts. I curled on the couch between the children—who
were watching a movie, natch—and unwrapped the box. On
the other side of the paper was a Lucchese boot box. From
the size and weight it was boots, not mules or ankle boots
or shoes. Delayed gratification was best, but I didn't have
the constitution for that crap.

I opened the box and peeled back the paper to reveal
boots. Black leather with green leaves and gold mountain
lions embossed on the shafts. These were hand-constructed,
hand-tooled, hand-stitched, hand-everything Lucchese
Classics, and they went for around three thousand bucks a
pair. Cooing like some kind of girly girl, I lifted them out,
the goat leather supple and softer than any piece of leather
had any right to be. I removed the stuffing paper from the
shafts and slid the boots on. "Holy Pan-hide, Batman," I
whispered. They fit perfectly. I was sure I'd never take them
off again.

Still wearing the boots, I curled on the couch, half dozing, Angie Baby on my lap, and EJ now on the floor making
"Bhupppp" noises with his lips as he pushed a toy truck
around the floor. The Disney movie was playing softly. The
Truebloods had a huge collection of kiddie movies.

I must have slept because when I nodded awake again,
the Kid was no longer alone working at his table in the
corner, running electronic searches. He now had a student.
I rubbed the sleep out of my eyes to make sure I was seeing
what my eyes said I was seeing. Tia was a working girl from
Katie's and she was currently bent over Alex's shoulder,
listening to him talk computer. She was also making the Kid
crazy, but that was another story.

Alex looked up and said, "Tia volunteered to babysit."

"For the honor of computer lessons," Tia finished, smiling coyly. Yeah, she knew what she was doing to the Kid.
But he was nineteen and able to send her away if he wanted
to. And they both knew his brother's rules. No visits with
any of Katie's Ladies until Alex was twenty-one.

"Big Evan is driving around the city, listening for Molly,"
the Kid said.

Weird things happened when I took naps, even unexpected naps.

The side door opened, rousing me, fully, and Big Evan came in. He looked worn and wan and dejected. Pretty much how I felt. "Anything?" I asked, realizing that I had been dozing with my mouth open. I checked my lips for drool and thankfully found none. I just hoped the Kid hadn't taken a photo.

"No. I drove all over the city, but I couldn't pick up anything. You?"

"Leo said a lot of nothing last night, but claims he doesn't know where Mol is. And I'm pretty sure he doesn't have her."

Evan shook his head and slumped up the stairs, even his footsteps sounding dejected.

Angie turned in my lap and craned her face up at me. "Daddy's worried about Mama."

My heart flipped over. How did I answer this? "I know, honey."

"Mama's coming back. Right?"

I forced the horror and fear and worry down deep inside. I had made promises to my godchild before and been able to keep them, but this time . . . This time felt different. "I'm—" I stopped, the words strangling. "I'm searching for her," I managed. "I'm trying to find her."

"Good." Angelina pulled Ka Navista from the crack in the couch and tucked the doll into the crook of her arm. The doll looked frazzled and tattered and much loved, the long black hair tangled. To the doll she said, "My aunt Jane can do anything." My heart turned over and went flat, as if the life had been sucked out of me. I looked away and batted my eyes to keep the tears away.

"I'll do my very, very, very best," I whispered.

Beast butted my soul with her head. *Will find Molly kit-mother. Will kill ones who took her.* She flexed her claws into me; the pain shocked the fear and worry away.

Okay. Yeah. We'll find Molly, I thought back, feeling inexplicably better.

"We're gonna have company." Angie crawled from my lap and sat in the corner of the couch, watching the doll with determined, hopeful eyes.

And then I heard the bike. It had the high-pitched whine of a Kawasaki. And it was heading our way. Despite my lingering worry and pain, heat bloomed from my middle, flamed up my torso, and folded itself over my shoulders while settling low in my abdomen. It was like being embraced by a big-cat, as Beast's interest fluctuated and changed.

The bike was familiar. It slowed in the street. And puttered close to the house.

Angie looked at the opening to the foyer, the front door, and the stairs, where her father had gone, and whispered, "I let the wards down."

"You let . . ." I stopped. Angie could manipulate her father's wards? Did he know? I had a feeling that he didn't.

The Kawasaki bike went silent. I stood and looked down at myself. Jeans. Navy T-shirt. Killer boots. I walked to the repaired door, hope joining the warmth that sat deep inside. A knock came. A familiar *tat-a-tat-tat*. I dropped my head against the jamb for a moment, fighting my smile, and when I was sure I had it under control, I opened the door.

CHAPTER 13

You Gonna Invite Me In?

He stood as tall as me in his black Frye boots. Black jeans, a short-sleeved black tee, his black leather riding jacket hanging on the Kow-bike. His hair was longer than I had ever seen it, finger-combed and looking even darker than its usual black, damp from the helmet. I could smell gun oil, spicy aftershave, cigar. And his cat.

"Let's go for a late lunch," Rick said, leaning in, supporting his weight on his arms, high, to either side of the door, stretching up to show his biceps and the damaged tattoos there. And pulling his T-shirt against pecs and abs. *Oh my* . . . "You can call Tom for an intro. Fair warning, though. He'll tell you I'm trouble."

My breath hitched to a stop. They were nearly the same words he'd used to ask me on our first date. "Yeah," I drawled, no longer holding in my reaction to him, leaning closer. "'Bout that. I *know* you're trouble, Ricky Bo."

His teeth flashed in a smile, his crooked bottom teeth pushing on his lip. "But I'm worth it, babe. Besides, even if I didn't make you crazy . . ." He leaned farther in, bringing his mouth near mine. "I have info you want."

I rested a hip against the door and considered, feeling my insides melt under his black-eyed gaze, his breath warm on my neck and jaw. "You let your hair grow," I said, wanting to touch it, to touch him.

Rick canted to the side, resting on the outside jamb, stretching even closer, so we were only a fraction of an inch apart. I could feel the warmth of his body, and his scent grew even stronger, jungle nights, heat, cat, and man. "My current job," he said, "doesn't have a dress code when I'm in the field."

"You on a job now?" I asked.

"Yeah. I got a party tonight at Leo's." His lips grew fractionally closer. "You gonna be there?"

I stood up and backed away. "Yeah. Lemme get this straight. You got an invite to vamp HQ for the *gather*?"

Rick laughed shortly. "He didn't tell you?"

"No, he didn't tell me."

Rick reached out a hand and pushed a stray wisp of hair behind my ear. His fingers were warm, werecat warm. I struggled not to lean in to his touch. "You gonna invite me in?" he murmured.

"Hey, Uncle Ricky Bo. You gonna kiss Aunt Jane?"

I tried not to laugh at the look on his face as he dropped his hand away from me. "Angelina?" he asked, his tone saying, *What are* you *doing here?*

"Uh-huh." Angie tugged on my jeans until I dropped my hand, which she took. "We staying with Aunt Jane while my daddy looks for my mama. You gonna kiss her? 'Cause I wanna watch. You never did kiss her last time I was here."

I snorted. Rick opened his mouth and closed it in a good imitation of a beached fish. "Uhhh."

"No, Angie Baby," I said. "Uncle Ricky Bo is taking me to lunch."

A terrible thunder of running feet sounded at the top of the stairs. "Jane!" Evan shouted. "The wards!" He went silent when he saw us standing at the front door. Out of breath, he leaned over the railing, staring. "Son of a witch on a switch," he whispered, the words explosive. "Angie?"

"Sure as heck wasn't me," I said. "I can't touch your wards."

"Me neither," Rick said. "Come on, gorgeous. Let's go eat."

"But I wanna see you kiss her," Angie said.

I picked up my sunglasses and keys where I'd dropped them on the way in this morning and closed the door on Angie's curiosity and her father's perplexity. Rick stopped me with an arm across my path, an arm that snaked around my neck and drew close. "I've missed you," he growled.

Trying to keep the goofy grin off my face, I pushed him away enough to drape an arm around his waist. He nuzzled my neck as I pulled him down the street. "Feed me or lose me."

As soon as we were out of sight of the house, Rick yanked me into an alcove, danced me back until my spine touched the wall of a house, and trapped me, one arm blocking the way out, the other around my neck holding me still. Lowering his face, he touched my lips with his, tentatively at first, as if giving me a chance to pull back. I didn't. I pulled him closer, feeling the gun at his side, the blade at his spine, and the welcome of his body that pressed against my belly.

I sighed into his mouth as he kissed me, deep and long. I might have made a little moan as his tongue touched mine and I arched my back to raise my body harder against his. Rick lifted me, the motion effortless as his were-strength kicked in. The smell of his cat intensified. His heart rate increased, and his pheromones shifted again, subtly, into adrenaline and something metallic and bitter. I realized he was in pain.

I shifted my head to the side, his lips trailing across my jaw and down to my neck. "Rick. Stop," I whispered.

His mouth opened. The scent of cat intensified. And his teeth clamped down on the muscle and tendon beside my jugular. A hold that a mating, male big-cat might use to grasp his mate. Heat spiraled through me. Beast purred, the sound coming from my mouth. *Mate*, she thought at me. *Mine*.

I shoved her down and gasped a breath. *If he broke the skin . . .* "Rick. Stop." He froze, his teeth clamped down, just to the point of pain. "Stop," I said softer. "Your cat is trying to come through. Your teeth? The were-taint?" His teeth-grip relaxed, but stayed in place, as if he was confused. As if his cat still held sway. I let a hint of amusement into my tone. "And I am *not* having sex in an alleyway."

Rick released my neck and swore under his breath, something crude about saints and testicles. I shuddered with laughter and easing heat. Beast padded away from me, chuffing in disgust. "This sucks," he whispered back, his voice a low growl. "But you have a point about alleys. I have a nice comfortable bed in a hotel. Room service, whirlpool tub."

"You are evil," I said, tempted, feeling my body respond to the images and memories of being with him.

"I could be," he said, nuzzling my neck again. He stopped, his breath hot on my skin, still damp and bruised from his bite. He sniffed, stiffened, and leaned his body back from me. "I . . . I bit you." He sounded surprised, and maybe horrified. He hadn't realized he had been biting me. Not good, but not totally unexpected. Rick had not been able to shift into his cat, held in human form by the magic woven into the tattoos on his shoulder, magic that might be attached to me somehow; the golden eyes, still visible among the scars, sometimes got hot when he was with me. Or maybe the magic had nothing to do with me. No one knew.

I touched his shoulder and felt the heat from the tats. Yeah. The magic—whatever it was—in them was activated. "Cat mating behavior," I said calmly, sliding my hand down his arm to his wrist. "You didn't break the skin."

"But I could have." He dropped his head to my shoulder, his mouth moving on my flesh as he added, "I'm sorry."

"No harm, no foul," I said, keeping my tone light. "But I was serious about feeding me. I'm starving."

I felt his lips move into a smile and he pressed them to my neck. Heat blossomed all over again, but sweeter and more tender. I batted tears away. I had missed this. "So am I," he whispered back, his meaning something totally different.

I chuckled and he eased back from me. "Fried everything?" I asked.

"And lots of it. But I'm warning you. Fried food is no substitute for sex in an alley."

"I don't wanna know how you know that," I said. "Ewww."

We ended up at ACME Oyster House on Bourbon Street, sitting at a table in back of the well-lit restaurant, surrounded by both locals and tourists, where Rick ordered and we ate servings of Boo-fries (which were covered with roast beef and gravy), char-grilled oysters, fried crawfish tails, and softshell crab po'boys. The entire meal was a heart attack on platters and so good I wanted to cry when I got too full to eat more. We finished off lunch with beer, which, considering our metabolisms, meant it was all for the taste and not for a buzz. And Rick paid with a "company" credit card.

"Sooo," I hedged. "Was this a date or business?"

"Yeah." And he gave me that smile. Oh, good merciful heaven. I remembered that smile, the one he used to give me when we woke up together. "Question," he said. "If I found that sex was safe—"

"In a heartbeat."

"Good to know." He smiled and licked a minuscule speck of hot sauce off his lips, which was what I wanted to do. Dang it. "There're differing opinions in the were community about sex and infection. Most say it isn't possible to transmit during sex, that the grindys don't kill for misbehavin'. The same people also say that it isn't worth taking a chance, so they mate only within the community."

Community. A were *community? Yeah. That.* A community that I wasn't part of. But I kept my reaction and the odd surge of disappointment to myself. Casually, I asked the question "Were community? In the U.S.?"

"No. The werewolves are too reclusive. The community is online, worldwide. I have contacts in Africa, which helps. Not Kemnebi," he said, before I asked about his onetime mentor and full-time enemy. "I've met this African werelion online, Asad. In human form he's this *huge* black guy, and some kind of war chief for his human tribe, the Fulani. He's been . . . He thinks he can find a way to help me."

Help him shift into his werecat, which would end the pain of his body always trying to free his cat. End the insanity-agony of the three days of the full moon when he was trapped on the verge of the shift, his mind held together only by a music spell woven by Big Evan. "That would be wonderful," I said. Deep inside Beast thought, *Could run with mate. Could hunt with mate.*

"So. What are you working on?" Rick asked.

"We're gonna talk about work?"

"That's something won't end with us in bed, you maybe infected, and us maybe killed by my own personal killing machine." He was talking about Pea, the neon green, kitten-sized grindylow that had been assigned to Rick to keep him from spreading the were-taint. "Spill it, babe."

"Not much." I filled him in on the missing girls, the tail car, and the presence of Jack Shoffru in town, and—mostly—on Molly going missing. Long before I was finished, Rick had his phone out and was pulling info on the names from a database I didn't recognize. It had a U.S. Government seal with vibrant black and gold lettering and graphics that I didn't have time to read before he clicked his password in. I figured it was a PsyLED thing and Rick would share if he got something good. Turned out I was right.

"We have nothing on Molly or Evan. Nothing new on witches missing—" He stopped and looked at me from the corner of one eye. "Other than cold cases, which you know all about. George told me about some blood-servants getting sick, and new fangheads going true-dead for no known reason. Said you'd update me."

Bruiser was talking to Rick? When did *that* start? "I'll e-mail over what I can," I said. "I don't have much yet."

Rick shrugged, indicating that would work for him. "Shoffru is a different matter entirely. He's a person of interest by law enforcement agencies all over. DEA for cocaine and brown tar heroin. DOJ, IASOC, and Interpol for human trafficking and racketeering. FBI just because they couldn't be left out. And you think he'll be at the meeting tonight?"

I twirled my empty beer bottle, taking in the hard planes and shadows of his face. I loved it when he talked cop. I just wish he had something to use to find Molly. "Yeah. He'll be there. Which is probably why Leo invited you and let me ask Jodi to attend. He wants ol' Jack to know he has cop friends locally and in high places."

"Huh. Dress code?"

"I'll be working. Guests are expected to wear black tie."

Rick gave me a slow smile, one with a twinkle in his black eyes, and said, "I look good in a tux. But I look better out of a tux."

"Yeah. I remember." I looked at the time on his phone and stood before I got myself into trouble I might not get out of. "I gotta change and get to HQ. Come on. Walk me out."

He slid an arm around my waist and half danced me back out into the warming, uncertain spring air.

"I'll take Bitsa," I said to Eli, my eyes on my cell, a thumb flipping through text messages, "and change closer to party time. You bring my clothes and the weapons and gear when you come, and get Derek and his guys set up in back. The New Orleans Police Department's gun- and explosive-sniffing dog and his handler will be at HQ at five p.m. I'll leave it up to you where you want to keep them, but I'm sure the dog will need water and a place to do his business. Ask the gardener. That's all I got." I looked up at Eli. "You got anything?"

"Just an undying happiness that I don't have to wear a tuxedo or get all dolled up like a girl. You polished your nails," he accused.

I curled my fingers under, admiring the bloodred color. "Tia did it for me. I'm just a working stiff like you, tonight."

Eli chortled, and before he could play on the word *stiff*, I said, "Yeah, yeah, yeah, I know. I'll never be stiff. I'll never have a stiffie. So don't go there." Angie walked down the stairs from where she had been napping, and I said, "Kids present," which put an end to any smart retorts by Eli.

"Aunt Jane? You going to a party?" Angelina asked, stopping at the bottom of the stairs. "Do I get to watch you become a princess?" Angie had watched my first-ever transformation into vamp security, and never forgotten it.

"Not tonight. Just lipstick and hair." I pointed at my head.

"Oh." She dangled by her arms from the banister. "You find my mommy soon, okay? And bring her home. I miss her." Her mouth pulled down and her eyes welled with tears.

I rushed to her. "I'll find her, Angie Baby," I said, cursing myself at the promise I might not be able to keep.

Angie threw her arms around my neck and hugged me. "I love you, Aunt Jane. But I miss my mommy." She smacked a wet kiss on my cheek and raced back up the stairs into her bedroom. She left me feeling all hollow inside, an emptiness that ached, and cooling tears on my cheek.

"Anything on Molly?" Eli asked softly.

"No," I said, heading out the door. "Big Evan is getting antsy."

"Tell me about it. I'm outta here."

I steeled myself against Leo's pull on Beast and walked into vamp HQ to see Wrassler and Jodi standing in the foyer.

She was dressed in her casual cop khakis and jacket, and nodded a greeting to me. "We're done for now. I'd like the crime scene to be left as is until forensics can take one last look."

Wrassler said, "Not a problem, ma'am. I'll attach a padlock right now."

"The body's gone, though, right?" I said, with a half smile.

Jodi ignored my question and asked one of her own. "You got any idea who killed him yet?"

"Not me," I said, "and if Leo knows he isn't saying."

Wrassler kept his face bland. Too bland. I had to wonder what Leo knew. And why he wasn't sharing.

"Oh. Forgot to tell you," Jodi said. "The guess about Galveston paid off. Shoffru came in at the port. We have records of passports. Vamps did it legally this time."

The news was helpful but not currently relevant.

"Okay. I'm for home and a shower," Jodi said. "Jane, what am I tonight, cop or guest? Because if I'm a guest I have no idea what to wear."

Wrassler said, "The house has a few cocktail dresses on hand for when the blood-servants have to do formal-wear duty. You look like about a size eight?" Jodi nodded uncertainly. He pulled out his cell and started keying in info. "I'll have something delivered. You want them sent to cop central or home?"

I wasn't sure whose mouth had dropped lower, Jodi's or mine, but Jodi managed a "Thank you," and gave him an address I knew wasn't hers. Smart woman. Sending a dress from a vamp to the NOPD was likely to get her a ribbing if not questions from the brass. Giving her home address gave the vamps too much knowledge. I wondered what friend would be getting a delivery. She left quickly thereafter and I watched Wrassler watch her go. Jodi made a trim figure, her stance capable and no-nonsense.

"She didn't give me her real address, did she?" he asked, his eyes tracking her out the front door.

"Nope."

"She's cautious. I like that in a woman." Wrassler was interested. As in *interested*.

I hid my smile, and while his upper brain was off duty, I said, "I'd like to talk to the humans who attacked my house."

CHAPTER 14

Fee-Fi-Fo-Fum. I Smell the Blood of a Witchy One

Wrassler's gaze jumped from Jodi to me and went from somewhat lustful to full-on intent. Blindsided. And he gave away something, though I wasn't sure what. I set a slightly interested expression on my face and said, "Now, if you please."

"Leo has read them. They're out."

"Out as in asleep? Blood-drunk? Anemic from blood loss? Or dead?"

"Blood-drunk." He sighed and rubbed his hand over his bald scalp. "Leo said not to take you to them, but I'm betting that won't work for you."

"Nope," I said again.

"So I made a video of them, with a time stamp." He thumbed through his phone and pulled up a video. "Here. They're breathing but asleep. Less than two hours ago. It'll be at least eight more hours before they wake enough to be coherent."

"And what did Leo find?" I asked sweetly.

"Nothing you didn't know. That Adrianna is in a lot of hot water. She got them blood-drunk, bound them, fed them the lie that Leo wanted you dead, and ordered the attack on you. She led it herself. Leo called her in, but she hasn't shown."

"Oh boy. Adrianna is rebelling against her sworn master

of the city, in the absence of her clan blood-master." This was like a soap opera, vamp-style. Not bothering to hide my delight, I said, "What does Grégoire think about all this?"

"Not funny. He's pissed that Leo hasn't found her. Scuttlebutt says he's leaving Atlanta and coming home to deal with her."

I chuckled. "Out-of-town guests, his heir missing employees, a missing witch in his town, and open rebellion in his ranks, the European Council on the warpath, and his second most powerful clan in the hands of Adrianna, a psycho Celt with fangs. Yeah. Leo's not happy."

"Keep that laughter to yourself," Wrassler advised. "Leo's sent his Mercy Blade to find Adrianna."

"Ah." And that said it all. My smiled faded. Vamp law in the United States was not yet the same as human law, with Leo having declared them to be independent, the way tribal Americans were independent. Sorta. So far, the political and justice systems seemed happy with that, because incorporating the superstrong, human-blood-drinking, daylight-sensitive vamps and the full-moon-shifting weres into the human legal system meant very expensive changes to police departments, jails, and prisons. For vamps, the Mercy Blades took the place of cops, acting under the direction of the vampire to whom they were sworn. Gee DiMercy had several duties, and one was to give the mercy stroke of death to vampires who were insane, but who were still part of a master's clan or house. The fact that Gee DiMercy had been sent after Adrianna meant that she had been given a death sentence by her master.

My job as a rogue-vamp hunter was a bit different. I usually tracked down the unaffiliated insane vamps and killed them. Or I had until I'd taken the job from Leo and gotten my Beast bound. Dumb move, that.

I let all the info shuffle through my mind. I didn't like Adrianna. She was totally psychotic. She had attacked my house when my godchildren were inside. She wanted me dead. I didn't necessarily want her dead, just . . . contained. Maybe in a silver cage. Not that I had any say in the matter.

I had a truly panic-worthy thought. Was Adrianna involved with Molly's disappearance? Terror rose in me, but I shoved it down, hard. Fear wouldn't help Mol. I needed to save the energy for when I found her, for the fight to get her free. I brought myself back to the concerns at hand.

Wrassler handed me his cell and I studied the video. The time stamp was just what he'd said—assuming no one had tampered with the electronics. The humans were asleep on twin beds, breathing smoothly. Both were fully clothed, if a little pale. One was drooling, the other was smiling. *Blood-drunk for real.* "Okay. Whatever. Let's go over the final security arrangements. Who's on electronic monitoring?"

"Angel Tit."

The rest was boring logistics.

Ninety minutes before the festivities, Eli arrived and sent my clothes to the ladies' locker room where I had showered before. He was already dressed in night camo, and together we did a final run-through of the house and the grounds. Everything was in place. Derek and his men had shown up at the same time as NOPD's bomb sniffer dog, and Eli and the former Marines had secured the premises. It wasn't exactly a lockdown, but it was close. Every car would pull through the gate out back, pause for the bomb-sniffing dog—who was a cute Jack Russell, black Lab mix—then motor up, beneath the little drive-through-roofed area that Wrassler called a *port kashar*, but spelled it *porte cochere* on my notes. French, probably. The passengers would get out and receive a good crotch-sniffing by the dog. Well, not really, but I could hope. The mental image of a two-hundred-year-old vamp with a dog nose in his crotch was giggle-worthy, but not something I could share under the circumstances.

And then the guests would be escorted to the elevator and the ballroom, where Wrassler and I would be. Not that planning and security measures would make the ballroom safe. The last big par-tay had ended in werewolves shape-changing and attacking through the stained glass windows. It had been a bloody mess. At least this time Leo hadn't invited the press to the event.

Before changing clothes, I checked the ballroom one last time. It was fancy, a sort of colonial Moorish mix, with pointed arches and domed ceilings, held up with fluted gilt-painted columns. There were stained glass insets in some domes, illuminated by artificial lights.

The floor was pink marble and the matching rugs were so rich my feet sank into them. Narrow, rectangular linen-draped tables were lined up in the middle of the room, and side chairs had been placed along the walls, all expensive museum-quality furniture. Also along the walls were curio cabinets filled with objets d'art, historical and archaeological items donated by vamps, and a bunch of macabre stuff. My favorites were the handmade items of tribal life from Africa, South America, and the U.S.: stone hammers, pottery that had been shaped without a potter's wheel and fired in open fires, spear points, and knapped weapons—not that I had time tonight to examine them.

Bouquets of aromatic flowers were everywhere, some standing tall in vases with water and some in little pots. The honey fragrance of sweet alyssum and the more intense scent of stock drifted in the air. The flower color scheme was a little of everything, pink, purple, white, and yellow, very springlike.

On the serving tables were gold-plated serving ware and utensils, nothing silver to harm the vamps. Platters for the humans were laden with cheeses, fish, meats, and a carved watermelon full of tropical fruit. A cute blood-servant bartender dressed in black tux pants and a black halter top was icing drinks at the alcohol bar and a blood-servant in similar garb, but far skimpier, stood guard in front of the blood bar, a small alcove off the main room. All the servers were loyal blood-servants, not hired, though Leo's usual catering service had provided and set up the food.

Satisfied, I went to the elevator and down to the locker room assigned for me to change clothes. My locker was on the end, in the corner, a tall, narrow one, from floor to ceiling, my name on the front, Jane Yellowrock, and beneath it, the word *Enforcer*. I opened the locker, to see shelves at the top, and hanging space in the middle with a shoe space at the bottom. But my slacks and shirt weren't there. Instead there was a designer dress on a padded satin hanger. I shoulda known. Leo had a thing about dressing me. He said it was part of my job description. I thought it was more that he liked being in control.

I didn't argue, and instead lifted out the dress and inspected it. It was made of a metallic-looking fabric that felt like silk, the bodice in an old-rose-gold color and the sleeves in a pewter-colored fabric. The flaring skirt was rose gold too, with bands of pewter sewn in at the waist, splaying

down the sides, and at the hem. The dress was so soft it
slithered through my fingers.

I wanted to find fault with the dress, but there were
openings at the sides where pewter fabric met gold, slits for
weapons, with holsters and sheaths built in for both my
guns and my blades. I thought the colors would make me
look washed out, but when I held the dress up to me and
inspected myself in the mirror, it brought out the golden
hues of my skin. It looked great, even without makeup.
Dang Leo. The only flaw was that the dress was one of those
stupid side-zippered things.

"Okay. I can do this." I stripped to my underwear and
slipped the dress over my head. It was tight, binding one
elbow to my side, then my chin to my chest. Maybe it was
part snake. I was struggling to get it on when the door
opened and Adelaide waltzed into the room. I say waltzed
because her dress moved as if she were dancing and she
looked like a million bucks. Dressed in a floor-length dress
of pale gold cloth, a shimmery color to match her hair, and
wearing jewels that looked like the real thing, she was elegant and perfect, and I was disheveled and off balance, one
arm in a sleeve, one arm and my head through the open
zipper, the dress off to the side.

"Do not laugh," I ordered.

But she did. It was a sympathetic laugh, I had to give her
that, even as she went to work on straightening the dress
and getting my arm in the proper hole and pulling the zipper tight, which made me catch my breath. The dress was
totally formfitting and I wasn't sure that breathing was part
of the form. "Shoes?" she asked, and I pointed to my new
boots and my dancing shoes. "Serviceable," she said, "but
not elegant. And even the new boots won't do for tonight
and with this outfit," she said with a cheeky grin.

"You like my boots?" I asked.

"Sugar, I picked those babies out, though I admit that
Leo had to make the final choice. I'll see about ordering you
a more dressy pair of dancing shoes. Perhaps several pairs
in different shades. Your gorget?"

"My who? Gor-jay?"

Del spelled it for me. "A gorget is a collar made of chain
mail. I believe that Leo had one made for you out of silver-
plated titanium."

I opened one of the few things that had made it from my house to the locker room—the black velvet box that held my throat protectors—and latched the titanium chain mail throat and chest armament over my neck. The undergorget was practical: the titanium would stop a knife, some clumsy sword strokes, and fangs. I latched the dressier gold link gorget over it, the one with the citrines and other gems. The set had been a present from Leo to replace the ugly but more functional one lost in his service. I had known from the beginning that it was too expensive for me to accept, but it was beautiful and I hadn't been able to say no to the shiny gifts, a reaction that was way too girly for me. The layering was perfect with the fabric. The set also fit perfectly into the low neckline of the dress.

"I see why the gown was made in this fabric—to match that stunning, layered gorget," Del said. "There is no reason why a woman's weapons should be ugly."

"Yeah," I said, feeling stupid that I liked the effect so much. I lifted a hand and touched the gold gems, one that was close to the color of Beast's eyes when they glowed through mine. "It's . . . sparkly."

Del kept her face bland, but I could smell her amusement. "Yes. So it is. *Sparkly.* All right, let me help you with your offensive weapons."

"None of my weapons are offensive. Most are kinda pretty."

Del chuckled dutifully and corrected, "So they are. Weapons for offense?"

"Yeah. I got 'em." I weaponed up through the little slits in the dress and strapped on the blades and the Walther .380 beneath the skirt. It wasn't as powerful as a nine-millimeter, but it was the best weapon when faced with potential collateral damage—humans in crowded situations. Last, I added the small box for com equipment beneath the back waistline, pulled the ear wire and mic up, and hooked them in place. There were two main channels on the system, one for blood-servant security and one for my guys. The third channel was a private one, directly from Angel Tit to me. I checked the channels, hearing chatter on two and hearing Angel talking to someone in the background on the third. Satisfied, I looked at myself in the mirror, expecting to be wowed, but I wasn't. I felt a bit like Cinderella in a before shot. Something was all wrong.

"Now, sit," Del said. "Your hair and your makeup need a bit of attention."

I sat and she went to work on me. When she was done, my braids had been rewrapped in the thick bun and the stakes had been stuck through it in a decorative fashion, not all out like a sunburst, but clustered, according to type. Wood stakes were placed with the rounded handle down, near my left shoulder; silver ones were handle-down near my right shoulder. It was an interesting way to wear them. I was wearing my trademark red lipstick, altered just a bit with a faint pink tint, some sort of smoky and gold eyeliner, a bronze blush, some shimmery, gold-flecked powder, and black mascara. I looked good, even if the neckline seemed way too low. In the three-inch heels, Del and I were of a height; standing side by side in the mirror, we looked great together, Adelaide like an angel, and me like an angel partially fallen.

"We'll do, I think. Let's get to work," Del said.

Fashionably late, the established vamp clans began arriving, in order of importance. Once upon a time and not so long ago, there had been eight vamp clans. Now there were four: Laurent, Bouvier, Arceneau, and Pellissier at the top.

At the bottom of the pecking order, Clan Laurent was first to arrive, the clan name called out over the speakers. Bettina, clan master, entered alone, the petite woman looking like a Greek or Latin model, full of curves. Once she had been so sensual that lust wafted off her like steam above a volcano. Now she was colder, reserved, but also looked more comfortable in her new clan blood-master status. Meeting her at the door and extending his arm was Edmund Hartley, the former clan master of Laurent. Bettina looked happy to see the man she had defeated to become clan blood-master, and they bent heads together. It had to be weird to attend society functions with the enemies you fought and subdued and drank from, but with vamps, everything was weird.

Her heir and two other vamps followed her, their blood-servants to either side and behind them. The reek of vamp swept in and was pushed through the room on the air currents, the usual dried herbs and fresh blood, but with the sweet, fresh, spring bouquets, the funeral stink wasn't as potent as usual.

Arceneau was announced next, and this one was the one I wanted to see, with neither Grégoire nor Dominique in town and Adrianna on the lam. The vamp was one I recognized but who was way down in the clan hierarchy, a fairly young vamp, indecisive and tentative, with preylike social skills, meaning that she was *way* down the hierarchy. She smelled faintly bitter with anxiety, like camphor and mint. I didn't remember her name, and the announcer hadn't bothered to share it.

Inside me, Beast was prowling, sensing the uncertainty the vamp brought into the room, the nervous tension. Her tail tip twitched slightly, side to side, as she paced. I breathed deeply and slowly to let her relax, but felt her staring through my eyes. From the looks I was getting from vamps and humans, they were glowing gold.

"Clan Bouvier," the announcer said. The clans comasters Innara and Jena entered together. They were tiny, one blond and one darker haired, five foot two in matching shoes, and their dresses were two shades of red, one ruby and one dark fuchsia. The girls were mind-joined anamchara; fully loyal to Leo, and though they looked cute, they were deadly. I'd seen them fight, and savage was a good descriptive term. Roland, their clan heir, stood behind them, dressed in a black tux, looking deadly and cold. Other clan members and their blood-servants moved out around them.

The stink of vamp was now so strong I wanted to sneeze, and pressed on my nose to stop it as I talked into my mic. "Everyone in, except Clan Pellissier, who are secluded with Leo upstairs. We have ten minutes before the guests start arriving."

In the ornate ballroom, all the humans went immediately for food and alcohol, some vamps slipping into the small alcove for a blood snack. Leo had approved the blood bar. I didn't like the practice, but I knew there were no weapons stashed in the curtained nooks, and really, what could I say anyway? The humans wanted the blood-servant relationship. I took the time to grab a bottle of water and walk the perimeter of the ballroom, hydrating.

The first guests to arrive were cops. "Special Agent Richard LaFleur of the Federal Psychometry Law Enforcement De-

partment and Detective Jodi Richoux, New Orleans Police
Department," the voice announced. Rick's tux fit him like
his own skin, or his own pelt, black and touchable. On his
arm walked Jodi, wearing a long dark chocolate brown
dress in some kind of gauzy material that flowed around
like veils. She looked good and she knew it. I was betting
the flowing skirts hid her service weapons and a backup. I
had left word that law enforcement was permitted to have
guns on premises.

The two had a good working relationship, from the time
Rick worked in NOPD, and, like good partners, they immediately split up and started working the room, meeting people and checking out my security measures.

Rick made it over to me faster than I thought possible,
considering his casual saunter. He didn't put an arm around
me, but he did ogle my cleavage, with an appreciative grin.
"Nice dress, babe. But I bet you look even better out of it."
I tried to force down an instant flush, but it rose anyway,
settling deep in my belly. Without waiting for a reply, he
chuckled and moved on past, to greet a vamp just walking
out of the blood bar.

"Dang," I mumbled under my breath.

Through the overhead speaker, stringed instruments
started playing. I listened to the com chatter, hearing that
the next guests had begun to arrive.

And then something changed. A voice on the full-
member-security channel stopped speaking midsentence,
and didn't start speaking again. I saw two of Derek's men in
the hallway adjust their headphones and look around, their
bodies suddenly hyperalert, so it wasn't my unit. I tapped
my mic. "Angel, security cameras. Do you see anything
odd? Someone not where they're supposed to be? Doing
something weird? Lying down like they just passed out?"

"Sound off," Angel commanded. The regular service
chatter was cut and a tense silence lay over the security
channel. One by one, Derek's people checked in, their
words preceded and followed by tiny clicks of the com system.

"T. Jolly Green Giant," the first said. "All is a go. Front
entrance is clear."

"T. Sweaty Bollock. All is a go."

"T. Antifreeze. I'm good. Back entrance is clear and shut

down." The *T* stood for Tequila. Derek named all his groups
of men after drinks.

"T. Sunset. Clear." "Trash Can, clear." "Red Dragon,
clear." "T. Acapulco, clear." "V. Martini, clear." "V. Lime
Rickey, I'm good." The *V* stood for Vodka. And no one else
spoke.

A long silence sounded before I heard, "V. Lee's Surrender, clear," Derek said. "We got one disappeared."

I tapped my mic. "Angel, who's missing? Cameras. Report."

I remembered to breathe, forced down my anxiety, and
drew my Walther, catching Jodi's eyes. Pointed to the guest
entrance. When she saw my gun, she nodded and drew her
service weapon, moving with it in both hands, pointed
down, trigger finger along the slide. She moved to stand
beside the entrance, but behind a column that gave her both
protection and a good angle of fire.

"Vodka Sunrise is down," Angel Tit said over the coms
unit, his voice calm. "I repeat. Vodka Sunrise is down. His
position is beside the elevator on the back entryway floor."

"Hold your positions," Derek said. "On my way."

My heart started racing. Something bad was happening,
and it had started at the elevator. Someone had gotten past
one of Derek's men.

Angel Tit said, "All I can see is his boots. Suggest you
take the nearest men with you. That would be Trash Can
and T. Sunset."

"Sunset, move midhallway and cover both ends," Derek
ordered. "I've taken the stairwell. I am in position. Trash
Can, approach the elevator."

"T. Sunset. I am in position."

"Trash Can. Entering elevator." I heard the soft *ding* of
closing doors over my com. Trash Can was in the most dangerous position. Whatever the cameras had missed could be
waiting for the doors to open. A second *ding* indicated that
the doors had opened. "Trash Can. Leaving elevator."

"Lee on bottom floor," Derek said softly. "I have V. Sunrise in sight. Repeat. Have a visual on Sunrise. He is on the
floor but he is moving. Repeat, man down, but he is mobile."

A string of curses came over the com, in the harsh,
slurred tones of Vodka Sunrise. "Somebody knocked out
my tooth." And then he started back cussing.

"Entering hallway from elevator," Trash Can said. "I have a visual of target. No encoms," he said. "Repeat, no encoms."

"Situation is secure," Derek said.

I gave Jodi a thumbs-ups and touched my mic. "High-alert status for entire team. Anyone, I repeat, *anyone*, who enters your area is to be stopped, ID-confirmed, and searched as you consider appropriate. Angel, go over security on the cameras in that area. I want to know what happened."

"Copy. On it, Legs."

Jodi reached me. "What?"

"Don't know. We had a man down. Something's wrong, but I don't know what."

"Vamp parties are so much fun." She moved away into the crowd, her gun once more hidden in the flowing folds of her skirt. I looked around. No one on the other communications channel seemed to have noticed anything odd. The blood-servant security types looked calm and efficient in whatever jobs they were doing.

"Legs," Angel Tit said into my earpiece.

"Go ahead," I replied.

"Something funny about the footage. It's all blurred. When it clears, Sunrise is on the floor, bleeding and not moving. Magic sometimes does this to digital footage."

"Magic," I said bitterly. "Copy it and send it to Alex."

"Copy."

A form appeared at my side, startling me. I had one hand on the blade at my thigh before I recognized Gee DiMercy. My breath went tight. The misericord was slim, slight, and deadly, dressed in black but not a tux. He was wearing an odd sort of outfit, tight but elastic, allowing him to move. He looked dark and deadly, like a modern-day ninja or hired assassin. Which he was, in a way. And worse, he was fully armed with knives strapped at both thighs; they had long blades for knives, more like short swords with carved ridges on the utilitarian grips. "We have a problem," he said, staring at the door the guests used from the porte cochere.

"Yeah, I — " And I realized he didn't have access to the communication channels. I followed his gaze, my right hand still holding the Walther .380 and my left on a knife hilt. A couple entered and my hands tightened on both. "Crap," I said. The place went slowly, uncomfortably, silent.

Much too late, the announcer said, "Ahhh. Jacques Shoffru, Master of the City of Veracruz and Cancún, Mexico, and all hunting territories between. And his companion, Adrianna, formerly of Clan St. Martin, currently of . . ." The speaker hesitated, not sure how to name a vamp who had been given a death sentence. He ended with the more polite "of Clan Arceneau."

Crap. Crapcrapcrap. Adrianna was working with Shoffru. Starting when? For how long? Did that mean Shoffru knew everything Adrianna did? Did she have anything to do with the attack on Sunrise? "How long has she been on the premises?" I demanded.

Gee tilted his head up and looked down his nose at me. "Only now. She has been in my sight all but about two seconds as she rounded from the elevator."

I tried to put that into the time that had gone by and the man down, as Derek took over the situation on the ground floor. I tapped my mic. "Derek. How many just came up?"

"Elevator full, two groups of fifteen. Coordinated movements. No one separated from the groups, no one unaccounted for." Meaning nothing looked hinky with them as it might relate to Sunrise hitting the floor and losing teeth. But if magic had been used, who knew what had really happened? I looked back at Adrianna. "How did Adrianna get past you? And is it okay for me to hurt her? Bad?"

Gee said, "We can discuss how she eluded me later. For now, she is on the arm of Jack Shoffru, and as his guest, she is in possession of an invitation, one that guarantees her access to the premises and personal safety while she is here."

I chuckled, the sound low but not amused. Along with every other eye in the room, I studied the pair. Adrianna had her scarlet hair up in a fancy do of braids and curls and pins and pearls. She was wearing a designer dress the same scarlet as her hair, the skirts flowing out around her, her shoulders and décolletage bare, the neckline covered with crystals and pearls and plunging nearly to her waist. Around her neck was a Celtic necklace, and a gold snake crawled up one upper arm, jewelry she had worn to a vamp function before—the night she tried to kill me. My heart rate sped at the memory.

"Got another smear on-screen," Angel said. "Sending men to intercept."

"Copy," I said.

Escorting her was the mystery man, Shoffru. He was swarthy-skinned for a vamp, his dark hair loose and shoulder length, curling toward his chin, like the finger of beard that defined his jaw. He was wearing a tuxedo, the suit, shirt, and cummerbund all midnight black, and his tie and shirt were both undone and hanging loose to reveal his chest and the thick black hair matted there. He was strong, athletic, and walked with a hip-rolling swagger that looked like trouble. He also looked as if he'd been drinking, and maybe he had been, vamp-style, on lots of blood. His dossier hadn't said anything about his lifestyle in the last hundred years, but he acted like a Naturaleza, well muscled and aggressive. And he was wearing gold earrings, thick, inch-diameter hoops that looked old and heavy, like booty he might have taken from a plundered ship. Last, and really weird, was the lizard on his shoulder. It was a bright green with darker green stripes down its sides, and its snout was up, tongue flicking as it took in the room. I had read about the lizard, named Longfellow, but hadn't expected to see it at a formal occasion.

Shoffru stopped in the entrance, taking in the room as if measuring it for carpet. Or as if imagining himself as owner. Proprietary. That was Jack. Oh yeah. Trouble in a Tux, with lizard. Should be a drink name.

Fanning out around the couple were vamps and humans. Lots of vamps and humans, including a woman who looked like a pirate herself, her face and ears studded and beringed, a sword hanging low on her hips. Why was she carrying a sword? No one but Pellissier security had been allowed weapons. But the thought evaporated. The woman was Jack's heir, I deduced, from her position beside him. I blinked and the vision of the woman drifted to the side. Something seemed important about her, but I couldn't figure what. She slid from my mind as insignificant, irrelevant. Shoffru had brought in maybe thirty of his people, all of them wearing black, encircling Adrianna like a rose delivered in a black velvet box.

I remembered the buses, chartered in Galveston, and had a mental image of pale faces peering out the windows at New Orleans, like fanghead tourists. The reek of unknown vamp filled the room, sharp and biting, and I bit my cheek to keep from sneezing at the commingled, acrid stench. When I could talk, I said, "So the invitation got them all through security, and the invite means we can't shoot or stake them here." Gee made a little "Mmmm" of agreement, and I tapped my mic, giving me a private line to Angel Tit. "You seeing this?"

"Yeah. You want it broadcast?"

"Yes." I tapped again and said, "Everyone check your cells. The woman with the pirate-looking dude is Adrianna, the vamp Leo is hunting. For now, she has what amounts to diplomatic immunity and is to be treated with absolute deference, unless she starts trouble." I thought for a moment, working it through. "With all the backup Shoffru brought, things could get dicey if she vamps out, especially with so many humans around, so everyone keep cool. In the event of trouble, hold fire, I repeat, hold fire, unless I give the word, and even then make sure you have only vamps in your sights.

"Wrassler, make sure Leo is informed of all this. Derek, send three more of your people into the hallway. Switch to infrared or low-light opticals as needed, should the lights go out," I said. The instructions on tactics were totally unnecessary—Derek's guys knew their business—but the human blood-servants who were working security might not be as well trained. Plus, I wanted it on tape, recorded, just in case the poop hit the prop. "Those with no low-light gear, hit the deck if the lights go out so the line of fire is free." That got me some insulted looks from the regular HQ security staff, but I ignored them.

"Copy," Wrassler said into my earpiece. "Copy," Derek echoed.

I tapped off my mic, not wanting what I had to say next to be heard. "Gee. Nothing says we can't follow them when they leave and take them then."

"True. If opportunity presents itself, I will follow them. They bear watching."

"I have a feeling they bear killing, but staking Shoffru isn't my call."

From across the room, Jodi strode toward me, her gait strong, her skirt trapped between her legs, the outfit not made for a determined stride. "Jane, why do I have a bad feeling about this?" Jodi asked, reaching my side.

"Because you're a cop and this has *problem* written all over it?" I asked.

She slid a hand into a slit in her skirt and I knew she was

readying her service weapon. "Yeah, well, when the dust settles, remind me that we need to chat. You can buy me that beer."

I nodded, and Gee said, "Our PsyLED guest may be less wise than you, Detective."

Rick was walking directly toward the couple who still stood framed in the decorative doorway, and moving with his cat's grace, he swept three champagne flutes off a waiter's tray. Jodi cursed. Without appearing to hurry, Rick quickly reached the arched opening and presented the couple with two of the glasses. They chatted, Rick's body language seeming jovial and introductory, and he lifted his glass, almost appearing to toast them. They responded in kind, all sipping, all smiles. And I had to wonder what game Ricky Bo was playing. But the tension the two newcomers were radiating did seem to decrease.

"Pellissier on the move," came through my ear wire. Leo was on his way down. Through Beast's binding, I felt the MOC's fury and his speed.

"Oh, crap," I said to Wrassler in the mic. He grunted. Beside me, Gee put his hand to his hip, and I realized he was holding the hilt of a long sword, one I hadn't noticed until now. I hated it when the people around me used magic to hide stuff. It seemed like cheating and the little girl in me wanted to shout, *No fair!* I evaluated the sword in an eyeblink. The blade was plain, a deep blued steel, but the quillon, *écusson*, and guard were etched sterling over steel in fleur-de-lis, leaves, and vines, and the pommel was a silver-gray stone that flashed blue with the light. The sword had a sheen of magic about it, as if it had special powers or something. A magical sword in the hands of a glamoured bird-creature. My life was so freaking weird.

As if they had heard that Leo was heading down—and maybe Shoffru's ears were that good, what did I know?— the pirate and Adrianna moved from the doorway into the ballroom, Rick keeping pace. My boyfriend-of-sorts glanced at me once and then back to Shoffru, his body moving like that of a cat intent on interesting prey.

Gee eased the fancy blade out partway and leaned in, sniffing as the vamp scent grew. Softly, for my ears only, he whispered, "Fee-fi-fo-fum. I smell the blood of a witchy one. Dark magics. Blood magics. Black arts all."

CHAPTER 15

Toss the Dress Away

He was right. Buried beneath the scent of vamp and human and blood-meals was the prickly odor of witch magic, indicative of a witch using magic or of a magical implement—a device charmed by a witch—being drawn upon. I thought about the blurring magic of a charm meant to elude a camera, and of V. Sunrise down, and I drew on Beast. She padded forward, peering through my eyes, lending me her vision. A bright mist seemed to cover the two vamps, a dark rose fog of a magical keep-away field. The energies didn't look or smell familiar to me, shaped by an unknown witch. But I did get a hint of cedar and sharp green, so maybe a vamp carried a charm made by an earth practitioner who had drawn on her own blood for a spell, and then added the blood of something else, maybe a small rabbit or large rodent. It felt vaguely like a keep-away spell, but with a dark, magical twist that made me feel itchy all over. There were hints of other magics in the room, other charms, but only the charms on these two seemed important.

To my left, Leo appeared in the house entrance with dual micropops in the air. Katie, his heir, stood behind him, her dark teal skirts billowing in the wind of their vamp-fast passage. Every person in the room turned to them, assessing the two in light of the many across the way. A tingle of Leo's power spread through the room, Leo's alone, not the power he could draw from the gathered, and Jack smiled, his lips closed, and slid his arm around Adrianna. The two looked cozy. If they were aligned, and especially if they were sharing blood and sleeping together, then Adrianna would have told him everything she knew about Leo, including Leo's ability to draw from the clans, making our little beat-the-crap-out-of-Leo scene an interesting but futile exhibition. And if she had switched alliances, then where did that leave Clan Arceneau? In the hands of the shaking panicked vamp standing in the corner, struggling to not vamp out, staring at her superior in stunned horror, surrounded by silent blood-servants. I saw someone I recognized, but couldn't place, move up beside the shaking fanghead and slide a solicitous arm around her. Brown hair. Familiar. Nothing dangerous about her. I looked back at the action.

The overhead speakers announced the arrival. "Leonard Eugène Zacharie Pellissier, blood-master of the southeastern United States, possessor of all territories and keeper of the hunting license of every Mithran below the Mason-Dixon Line, from the eastern border of Texas at the Sabine River, east to the Atlantic and south to the Gulf, with the exception of Florida. And on his arm, heir to Clan Pellissier, Katherine Louisa Dupre."

Leo's power rose higher, and I understood that by appearing as only two, Leo and Katie were giving a show of force of their own, all vamp power, and not just all vamp bodies, as Shoffru had done. The impression was that the two of them could take on the whole room, if they cared to do so. Leo's and Katie's blended scents seemed to whisper as they wove together and filled the space, and Shoffru's smile went stiff. Beast felt the pull on the binding, and my insides tightened.

Behind Leo, and late, stepped two humans—only two— Del and Troll, their primos. The humans looked cool, calm, and collected, though they must have dashed like mad to get here so fast.

Katie placed her fingertips on Leo's arm, and the Pellissier four moved across the room, so perfectly in sync it could have been choreographed. Through Beast's binding, I felt Leo directing his escort, and felt an urge to join them, to make my footsteps fall into rhythm with theirs.

As if in mirror image, Adrianna slid from ~~Jack's~~ Shoffru's embrace, placed her hand on his arm, and they started across the ballroom floor, their retainers circling behind them, leaving Rick standing in an empty patch of floor. His nose curled as if he scented changes in the air. I took a breath and smelled it too. Aggression. Dominance. Something was about to happen.

To the side, the woman with the sword put a hand to the hilt and looked around the room. I hadn't heard her speak, but she was communicating anxiety and anger with body language—all vampy-style, her head and spine twisting around in that inhuman way they have when they think no one is watching. For a moment I wanted, needed, to get her scent, but that desire faded as her gaze settled on me. Something seemed to tighten around me like a noose. Her eyes narrowed and I realized that she had been looking for me, for me personally. And then I *saw* the sword. I had seen it before and forgotten. Something was wrong with this. How had she gotten a sword in past security?

The sword-carrying vamp turned and watched Adrianna. As if feeling her eyes, Adrianna turned to the swordswoman. And she smiled. It was a purely sexual smile, full of longing and desire. And that thought too faded.

Beast slammed into me and I followed her instincts as I stepped toward the two groups, angling to meet them in the middle, rather than behind Leo. Jodi and Gee were at my sides and there was nothing I could do to keep them back and safe, short of shooting them myself. Beast was growling deep inside, but I didn't have time to deal with her, not now, and I shoved her down.

Leo's power rose, lifting and swirling Katie's skirts in a false breeze, and moving toward the guests. It raked across my skin like rose thorns, and met the witchy power of the keep-away spell in a small explosion of blue sparks. The skirt of Adrianna's gown lifted, and Shoffru hesitated, just slightly, midstride, as his spell-charm was countered by Leo's pure power. His mouth firmed and he seemed to push back. The sparks went green and scarlet, like Christmas lights. And Katie's skirts reversed course to swirl back as if in a strong wind.

Holy crap. It wasn't just a charm. Jack Shoffru was a witch-vamp, like the Damours. And he had Adrianna—who had allied with the blood magic family and who knew all their secrets—on his arm. No wonder there were magics all through the room. No wonder the woman had gotten a sword in through the humans. A master vamp with witch magics was crazy scary. Shoffru's power tightened, as if the air itself were growing thicker and harder to breathe. I searched out the swordswoman, but she was missing. Dang, where—there! At the entrance to the room. But even seeing her, I found it hard to remember why I cared she was there. Spelled, heavily spelled. Beast swatted at the spell from deep inside me, but nothing happened and she withdrew. And thoughts of the swordswoman slid away.

From the outside entrance spun a green . . . thing. Two of them. Grindylows. They raced past Rick, moving almost too fast for me to focus on them, but I knew what to look for, and this second shock made my breath hitch. The taller one came to my waist and had joints that bent the wrong way, limbs that were too slender and knobby for his body. His head was oddly shaped, his fangs were out, and when he ran, he was up on his toes, like a dog or cat, though he was generally bipedal, not a quadruped. His claws were out, looking like steel about three inches long. His pants and shirt were loose and baggy, hiding a body that I knew to be vaguely froglike, the skin hairless and green with darker green streaks, like dark serpentine stone. Darker and not as tall as the last adult one I'd seen, this grindy was golem-sized, about four feet high. And at his side was Pea, Rick's juvenile pet grindy. Neon green–furred and kitten-sized, she had her claws out and fangs showing.

They spun to a halt in the middle of the two parties and the taller grindy hissed, his shoulders raised high on his neck. Pea, standing on two back feet, claws swiping in threat, chittered. Shoffru stopped, his eyes on the creatures from myth and legend. His lizard had curled on his shoulder and darkened to a bronze brown. Clearly the pirate-witch-suckhead had never seen a grindylow, nor had the swordswoman, nor the lizard. It ducked back inside the pirate's shirt as the grindys herded Jack, his swordswoman, and Adrianna together. Derek and two of his men stood guard around them, weapons not exactly pointed at the pirate and his crew, but not pointed away either.

I said, "A *gather* is a place of peace, Shoffru. That means magical as well as physical. Back off or the guys carrying silver shot might mistake your actions as hostile and shoot you full of holes. And the grindylows might get ticked." And then I blinked. There were two grindys in one place. That meant that the African weres were here. And even as I had the thought, they walked into the entrance.

An African werelion in his human form stood there, his kinky coarse black hair streaked with lighter brown, his eyes lion-gold in a dark-skinned face. I had taken the time to study the names from the were-community that Rick had mentioned, especially the werelion who was mentoring him, and this was Asad. "Asad," the announcer said, "emissary of the Party of African Weres, and his wife, Nantale. With them is Paka."

Their scents filled the room, earthy, musky, the heated intensity of the sun on the African savannah. The two were-lions advanced, Asad wearing white robes in an Arabian style, Nantale looking like a Nubian goddess in cloth of gold, wearing beaten gold on her wrists, on her ankles, and around her neck. Behind her moved Paka. Her scent was different, but if possible, even more intense, and it was familiar. She smelled like Kemnebi, of the dark wet heat of the African Congo, of green jungle and rushing water and danger. She smelled of black wereleopard.

And she was, with no doubt, in heat.

I pivoted toward Rick, and pain flashed through me, as if I'd been socked in the gut. He was staring at the woman. The girl. I looked back at her. She couldn't be more than twenty-two. Her skin was dark, black as night, her hair lustrous and long, in a coil to the middle of her back. She wore a skirt in wildly patterned cloth, with a handkerchief hem, in reds and blues and purples. Her top was short sleeved, cropped to display her flat belly, the neckline round and gathered with a tie, which was open to reveal the curved tops of her breasts. The rounded mounds caught the lights, drawing the eye. Somehow I knew she was naked underneath the dress. That she would like nothing better than to toss the dress away and walk bare in the air currents and intense interest of the males.

The hot smell of her heat wrapped around me and tightened, and I was reminded of the snake thoughts from earlier. I couldn't breathe. She was beautiful. Full lips, black skin, wide dark eyes, cheeks like perfect fruit, skin glistening with youth and health. *I couldn't breathe.*

Rick stepped toward her. His face went slack and his eyes widened, like a sleepwalker or one who had been hypnotized. He took another step. Paka's eyes found him and she smiled, her lips parting in a look that was pure sex, to reveal perfect teeth. She moved toward him, stretching out a hand. Magics tingled on the air, hot and sultry and sexual. Werecat magics.

Beast slammed into me. *Mine! My mate!*

"Not anymore," I whispered back, feeling the shock of loss tingling through me.

Somewhere in the back of my mind I heard the words, spoken by Asad, "Paka. A rare unmated female discovered by the Party of African Weres. Paka agreed come to America, to provide succor to the only American black wereleopard, to assist the unmated male through the transition of his first change."

"The kindness is appreciated," Leo said. "Our leopard has experienced much pain since he was turned."

A roar started in my head, the roar of angry wind. Of stormy waves. *Our leopard?* Closer, a low growl sounded. At my side, fingers gripped my arm, and I realized I was being physically held back. And that the growl was mine. I wanted to slash and draw blood. I felt the tips of my fingers burn as Beast's claws once again forced through. My forearms ached as pelt broke the skin. I smelled my own blood as I clenched my clawed hands.

Mine. My mate.

Asad spoke again, and I heard his words through the roar. "The Party of African Weres believes that Paka's heat will offer the American a mystic path through the transition, from his human form in which he is trapped, to his animal form. She is here to assist. And"—I could almost feel his smile of pride—"to be a prospective mate."

I whirled and left the room.

Nearly half an hour later, I came to myself, my back to the house, my dancing shoes planted in the soil, in the middle of Leo's back garden. It smelled of fresh flowers: the stock and alyssum of the ballroom, and spring roses and early jasmine. Herbs. Fertilizers. And the reek of loss and grief.

I didn't smell blood except the stench of my own, so I hadn't killed anyone. I had just . . . lost it. Rick had a prospective mate, a black wereleopard, like him.

I made fists at the thought. My hands were human again, but my fingertips ached when I released the fists. I took a breath and blew it out. And I thought of a string of curse words I might use, but none of them were bad enough. And no dang way was I gonna cry.

It was as if the universe had it out for us. Or God. But no way was I gonna blame God, no matter how much I wanted to. This fell under the category of "life happens and it ain't always fair." Something a housemother at the children's home where I was raised might have said.

I huffed out another breath and forced my shoulders to relax. I had a job to do. A job that would let me use the pent-up energy, the anger that still crawled under my skin. A job that would let me focus on something other than my own unhappiness and the once-again-ex-boyfriend, be-charmed by a lovely catwoman who was sex on a stick. My ear wire was hanging on my neck, and I slipped it back around my ear, positioned the mouthpiece in place, and tapped it. I got Angel Tit.

"Sorry I went all girly on you, Angel. Update." And I was pleased that I sounded like myself and not as if I had been screaming at the moon.

His voice crisp, Angel said, "Leo and the werelions are chatting. Wrassler is still coordinating a room-by-room search for whatever knocked out our man. Shoffru and his nutso date are dancing. He has a lizard on his shoulder. A minute ago, the lizard reached up and bit his earlobe near the earring and held on, swaying like it was dancing with them. Tell me that isn't weird. The lady cop is dancing with a vamp, and keeping an eye on Shoffru. I think she likes lizards.

"The blood bar has a line and Gee DiMercy sent some more humans in to speed things up. And Leo sent word by Wrassler, and I quote, 'With the exception of the pirate, my petitioners will not swear to me tonight.' That mean anything to you, Legs?"

The name Legs came through like an endearment, and though I knew Angel meant nothing of the sort by it, it made me blink against tears. "Yeah. Got it. It means the young vamps won't swear to him tonight. The show is can-celed. More?" And by more I meant Rick, but I couldn't bring myself to say his name.

Angel didn't hesitate or sound pitying, and for that I was grateful. "The PsyLED cop and the leopard and the little green kitten left in a black cab, out the front door. Wrassler saw to it." Relief made my knees weak, but he wasn't done. "He also sent out word that you were checking a problem out back with the bomb-sniffing dog."

I felt my shoulders relax, steadied myself, and said, "Thank you." It might be stupid to care what anyone thought about my abrupt vanishing act, but I did.

"Copy, Legs," Angel Tit said gently. "You say. Copy."

"Copy. And thank you."

"Ooh-rah."

I went back through the porte cochère as if I owned the place, pulling on Beast to lend me her cat's grace and hunting calm. I had made a dramatic exit, I was certain, but if I entered seeming calm and centered, most of those who saw me leave would assume it was a security situation that called me away so fast, not a broken heart. It was stupid to appear weak in front of vamps. Weakness was a possibly deadly emotion, and I had a reputation to defend—the rep of a nonvamp who could beat Leo on the sparing room floor. Head up, I flowed down the hallway, looking neither right nor left, and stepped into the elevator. Appearing cool and collected would dispel or deflect many potential problems.

Just as the doors closed, a black form stepped in, the doors barely grazing him on either side. I caught his scent even as I drew a weapon and I looked up into warm brown eyes. I shoved the blade back into the special pocket sheath. The door sealed and the elevator moved. "Wondered where you were," I said. "New tux?"

Bruiser smoothed a hand down the satiny black of his lapel. "Yes. I think we should dance."

I don't know why that simple statement brought my pain to the surface again. I looked down at the small floor space, as much to keep him from seeing the fresh misery in my eyes as to inspect the floor. "Not much room. Besides, I'm working."

"So am I. And the location of our dance will be near the pirate and the traitor." When I didn't refuse or disagree, he went on. "When Shoffru goes to pledge to Leo, we will keep the defector company."

I thought about that while I spoke of more important things. "Was Adrianna around New Orleans when Shoffru ran with Lafitte?"

An approving glint lit Bruiser's eyes. "Oh yes. Adrianna ran with a fast crowd even then."

"The Damours."

"Yes."

"And Jackie Boy is a witch?"

"So it appears, though it isn't in his dossier, and Leo—who had to have met him at some point—didn't know."

I grunted at that. Hard thing to hide, but Shoffru had done so. Which made him smarter and more powerful than expected. He had to make really good charms to hide witch-scent from a vamp. "Are you still Leo's Enforcer tonight?"

"I am, though I am choosing my replacement. What do you think about Derek?"

I laughed shortly. Derek wasn't fond of vamps, not even Leo, and not even when Leo had healed some of his men from wounds suffered in his service. "Be sure to film it when you ask him. That should be interesting." The elevators opened and I took Bruiser's arm. The heat of his body was like a fever, and I felt it roar through my flesh like Beast hunting. Teeth showing, intent. Pushing its way through my grief.

We will scream out our pain to the moon at dawn, she thought at me. *Then we will kill our rival. And retake our foolish mate.*

"Sounds like a plan," I said to her and to Bruiser, letting Beast have her way for now. "We might have to revise the middle part a bit." I had no intention of killing anyone. "For now, let's go dance," I said. "Can you get some better music? I liked that track that was playing the night I beat the crap out of Leo."

"Which was a thing of beauty to behold."

I snorted. "His beating you was staged, wasn't it?"

"Not precisely." Bruiser tapped his mic, requesting a change in music. He didn't pause as we entered the ball-room to the opening strains of a Bonamassa instrumental I didn't recognize, clueing me in on who at vamp central liked the blues guitar player. Bruiser. He had set up the music for my fight with Leo. In advance. I put that realization away for later.

Bruiser led me forward into the middle of the dance

floor—the pirate and his scarlet-haired traitor to my left
and Bruiser's right—and into a slow, slow tango. Totally not
what I was expecting, totally not what my hidden heart
wanted, but I moved with him, my feet and body finding the
cadence of the steps in the odd rhythm of the song, one not
arranged for the Latin dance. I concentrated on his lead and
let the beat hold me to the floor, knowing that I might lose
myself in the music and dance through the pain if I forgot
that I was working.

Bruiser was a masterful dancer, my body moving like a
length of silk in his arms, bending and sliding and dipping,
my feet shifting perfectly, though my shoes were leaving
small bits of earth from the garden in our wake. There was
something mystical in the music and the soil dropping from
my feet, as if I had walked from a grave and into the dance.
My heart began to lighten as Bruiser bent me back over his
arm, his leg between both of mine, pressing into the center
of me. I wanted to pull away, but he held me there for a
moment, for several long beats, his eyes on mine. "They
have stopped dancing," he murmured beneath the music.
"Watching us."

I smiled, slow, so slow, and let my head drop back, exposing my neck to him. It was a position of submission to the
predators watching. A posture of a different kind of submission to Bruiser. His arm tightened across my back and I
arched deeper. Closer into him.

He rolled me up in his arms, trapping me, whispering in
my ear. "Some night soon," he said.

I let my smile slide away, promising nothing, but not denying him. Knowing I wasn't ready. Not right now. Especially not tonight. Maybe not ever. Yet he yanked my body
against his, a reminder of his intent. I slid away from him,
whirling, as I always had done before. And Bruiser laughed,
saying softly, "No, Jane. Not this time." And deftly, as if I
weighed a feather, he whirled me back to him.

The song ended with me at Bruiser's feet, one arm up,
resting at the top of his thigh, his Onorio heat blazing
though the cloth of his trousers. He leaned down and murmured, "Shoffru's heir, Cym, is no longer with us tonight.
We should wonder why that is so."

"Yeah. We should."

A different Bonamassa song started, even slower than

the first, and Leo stepped into the dance, replacing Bruiser as if they had planned it. And who knew? Maybe they had.

Leo pulled me to my feet and led me into his arms. His black eyes caught mine. And I felt Beast staring up and out at him through me. The silver chain that bound her to him tightened, vibrating, a slight tremor that reached into the deeps of me, through my grief, through my anger at him for the forced feeding.

My life was so messed up.

Leo held me for two beats, then stepped to the side, into a bolero. The dance steps were so slow and romantic, the pauses with our bodies at sharp angles to each other, our legs intertwined as the steps ground us together. His body was ice-cold, where Bruiser's had been inhumanly heated. Beast purred.

Inside, I wept.

CHAPTER 16

Ðead-Slab-of-Gravestone-Marble

The dance ended. Leo released my body and, following the pressure of his hand and arm, I moved out to his side, facing the partygoers. Our arms were out, clasped hands extended in the air between us. "My Enforcer," Leo said, releasing me. "Bring me the supplicant."

Shoffru's head lifted, his nostrils widening as he took a breath, hard and deep. But I had already pulled two blades, one a steel-bladed, silver-edged throwing knife, the other a twelve-inch-long vamp-killer. I drew on Beast-speed, racing to Shoffru's side and bursting through the witch magics, throwing green sparkles into the room, feeling them burn against my skin.

The keep-away spell was targeted, I thought, *but not against skinwalkers.* It's hard to spell against something you don't know exists or don't have a blood sample from. Shoffru had expected to be escorted up by vamps or humans, and planned a little witchy surprise for them. Leo had turned the tables. The fanghead was good at that.

I placed a blade at the pirate's throat.

His eyes widened and I grinned; it wasn't a sweet grin. He leaned in and sniffed me. And his fangs dropped down on the little hinged bones, a soft *snick* sounding in the suddenly silent room. The music had stopped, and the room's natural acoustics had taken over. "Hiya, Jackie," I said, the sound warm and bright and carrying everywhere in the quiet. "Welcome back to New Orleans. Things are gonna be a little different this time around."

Ignoring my comment, he asked, "What species of predator are you?"

"The kind who kills vamps for a living." I chuckled, letting Beast's power course through me and shine in my eyes. I could see the golden reflection in his pupils. The lizard poked his head up from the black shirt collar. It was sitting on Shoffru's collarbone, its long tail curled down his chest. It was watching me, as if unafraid, curious.

Shoffru's body was still, that vamp-style, dead-slab-of-gravestone-marble still. I could feel him trying to bring up the keep-away spell, but with me so close, it wasn't happening. I let my blade press against his neck, just enough to barely slice the skin. A line of red appeared. The scent of vamp blood flooded me, his caustic and sharp like cacti and desert nights. The lizard whipped his head to the cut. His skin turned a bright, interested green, a patch on his throat growing reddish and puffing out, as if he was excited.

Around us, Shoffru's vamps converged into a semicircle, starting to form a pincer movement, or a constriction like the mouth of bag drawn tight, to enclose us. Adrianna had vamped out, eyes wide black pupils in bloody red sclera. Her fingers were clawed with razor-sharp talons.

From the doorway, I heard booted feet, and the mixed scents of Derek's men blended into the room. Shoffru's people hesitated, and the pirate seemed to know his rebellion had been anticipated. "The world is always changing," Shoffru said. "Only the strong survive the evolution of life."

"Jackie's a philosopher as well as a pirate captain," I said. "Good. It'll help when Leo bares your throat and drinks." His pupils widened into black holes. He didn't vamp out. I gave him that. He stayed in control. "Tell your girl to sit this one out."

"Adrianna, my love," he said. "Please await me."

The nutso vamp hissed in displeasure, but she lowered her talons.

I said, "Let's go, Jackie. Move slow. It's like a dance, but *you* follow *my* lead without touching me or the blade slides home to nestle into your cervical spine. Got it?"

Shoffru didn't nod—not with my blade so close—but he did school his face in agreement.

I led Shoffru to the center of the dance floor, where Leo waited, Bruiser beside him. From the corner of my eye, I saw Wrassler standing behind Adrianna, and her facade was not the happy-camper face of a partygoer. It was the fang-down expression of a wanna-kill-something suckhead. I figured that Wrassler had a blade to her kidney. Good. And Derek had weapons leveled at Shoffru's peeps. Even better. Gee DiMercy stood to the side, watching the little game like an interested spectator.

We reached the center of the room, and when I felt Bruiser's body heat at my back, I stepped away, letting Shoffru go. Leo and Bruiser had him boxed in like a layer of vamp jelly between two slices of deadly bread. I walked to Wrassler, blades still out, and said into my mic, "Play us some music, something dangerous," knowing that Angel would hear. Just before I reached the traitor, the opening strains of "All I Wanted" by Temporary Empire began to play, soft and low. It wasn't what I had asked for, but the heartache in the song fit my own broken heart, pulling the anguish to the surface again. It played softly, at the edges of my hearing.

Grief and anger warred with a killing lust deep inside me as I reached Adrianna. "Hello, dead woman," I said. "I'll have your blood on my hands soon."

"Oh no, Enforcer," Gee DiMercy said by my ear. I hadn't felt him on my trail and I almost flinched, but I held it down, as if my other half had known of his presence. "That particular joy will be mine," he said.

I laughed, the sound only slightly louder than the near-silent music. "I'll fight you for it, Mercy Blade. But later." I whirled, my skirts spinning out around me, and I turned to the center of the room, giving Adrianna my back, in what any predator could only assume to be an insult, and I heard her hiss at the affront.

In the center of the room, Jack Shoffru stood before Leo. The MOC of New Orleans placed his hand on Jack's shoulder and pressed down. Jack's upper lip curled in resistance and his body locked upright. At the edge of my vision, the swordswoman snarled, her body poised to draw and fight, her expression suspicious and confused.

The announcer said softly, "Jacques Shoffru, turned by François-Dominique Toussaint Louverture, leader of the revolution in Saint Domingue. Survivor of the Purge of New Orleans, whereby two of the Domingue clans were slaughtered. Captain of the privateering vessels: the *Ring Leader* and the *Lady's Virtue*. Copartner with Jean Lafitte in the Whale's Tale Enterprises in New Orleans." Jack, locked beneath Leo's hand, looked as though he'd break a sweat if vamps did that kinda thing. Leo looked as if he were pushing down on a flower stalk, two fingers on Jack's shoulder. The overhead speakers went on. "Once, secondo heir in the now decimated Clan Rousseau. Currently, and for two centuries, Master of the City of Veracruz and Cancún, Mexico, and all hunting territories between. Seeking supplicant status from the Master of the City of New Orleans."

Shoffru's knees buckled. The vamp with all the interesting titles dropped to the floor at Leo's feet. Leo now had one hand on his enemy's shoulder; the other palm went to Shoffru's forehead, pushing the pirate's head back, elongating his throat. The posture was one of total submission, though it didn't really look as if Jackie was feeling very submissive. More as if he'd been forced that way, fighting it with everything he had. Leo, on the other hand, moved with effortless grace. And the MOC hadn't even pulled any power from the clans. *Go, Leo.* "Do you yield and surrender?" Leo asked softly.

Adrianna hissed again, but so did all the vamps that had come with the pirate, and it sounded like surprise. I looked around to verify that impression and saw that Leo's people were surprised too. So . . . yield and surrender meant . . . what, to a vamp?

Leo said, "My Enforcer, attend me."

All of a sudden, I didn't like this, not one bit. I still had my weapons out, however, and I stepped slowly to the center of the room, my dancing shoes making soft taps on the wood floor. I stopped three feet away and waited, but Leo didn't acknowledge me, so I said, "I'm here."

Leo didn't respond to me but repeated his question to Shoffru. "Do you yield and surrender?"

Shoffru ground out, "For now. Yes."

"For one decade," Leo said. "Or until we meet in formal Blood Challenge—which will be at a time of *my* choosing."

And then I got it. Somehow Leo had brought the wording of a Blood Challenge into the little tableau, and also somehow, that meant Jack was well and truly beaten, even though he was accepted by the MOC of New Orleans. The only leeway I thought might be in the wording was in the weapons used. Leo had claimed the time. Jack could choose the weapons.

"I yield," Jack said, "and surrender my titles and territories and cattle, for a time of ten years, or until I defeat you in formal Blood Challenge, at the time of your choosing."

Before Jack even finished speaking, Leo vamped out. He sank his fangs into Shoffru's throat. I turned away, making a point of watching Adrianna and Jack's peeps, not really wanting to watch Leo drink anyone down.

My throat tightened as my own memories surfaced again. Fangs at my throat. The priestess holding my head. Bruiser stretched out beside me, as much a prisoner as I had been. I shoved the memory away, deep down, into the recesses of the black cavern that was my soul. But I couldn't block out the sound of Leo drinking, flesh on flesh, soft sounds of swallowing. Before me, Adrianna was led off into the night by Wrassler and Gee.

I whispered, "Turn up the music, Angel."

Around me the raspy voice of Keeb, the lead singer from Temporary Empire, rose, the lyrics weeping into the air, ". . . . Everything is quiet, everything is calm. Everyone's a riot. Softer than a psalm." Behind me, I felt heat and warmth. And I knew Bruiser stood there, not touching, but there. Waiting. The band was a little-known one out of North Carolina. Only Bruiser would have thought to find it for me. Only Bruiser would have cared enough to find it. But Bruiser wasn't who I wanted.

I sucked down a breath and forced the tears away. *Damn you. Damn you, Rick LaFleur.* How had I let him do this to me again? I was an *idiot.* But I didn't have to stay one. It might take me several tries to learn a lesson, but it was well and truly learned this time. No matter how strong the mating magic and mating pheromones were, he could have resisted. He could have. I'd never trust Rick LaFleur again. Never let him into my life again. And the lyrics moaned, ". . . you're all I ever wanted in this world. You're all I ever needed . . ."

Never again.
Never.

The rest of the night went by in a blur. Shoffru accepting the
terms of his servitude. Leo and Jack toasting each other
with humans to sip from. Adrianna not reappearing. Vamps
dancing while drinking from their human partners. Humans
drinking hard, partying as if there would be no dawn.

Me, not crying. *Not* crying.

Not crying. Not where anyone could see.

It was nearly four a.m., and everyone was gone except the
humans too drunk to drive, and the vamps who were inebri-
ated from drinking from the drunk humans, and they were
all being offered rooms and bunks and lairs to sleep it off.

I went to see what the cameras had caught, watching the
night's anomalies over and over. I was certain it was more
than one. The first one was quick. Someone or some*thing*—
maybe more than one—had gotten inside HQ through my
great security plan. The blur was a prism of colors, like light
diffused. That one had injured Derek's man—had appeared
on three cameras, knocking out Vodka Sunrise's tooth, leaving him dazed on the floor, before heading up to the guest
quarters, and being turned around by Derek's armed men,
who admitted to seeing something but had no idea what it
was. Then the swirling bands of light had rushed out through
the front doors and into the parking area. A final camera
saw the blur jumping the gate. *Not human.* That one had
been something unknown.

Another one had moved through the hallways, jamming
the cameras, and out the front door as if chasing after it. The
security guys stationed there hadn't seen or noticed anything, though the doors opened and closed right beside
them. *Magic.* A don't-see-me spell. And then it reversed and
raced back through HQ, to the ballroom, where it disappeared.

And I still had no freaking idea what was going on in
New Orleans. Not a hint. Until I walked the hallways where
the blur had raced and the spell had taken place. And I
smelled magic and blood. The dry burned magic of a dark
practitioner. It smelled like Shoffru, except the pirate had
hadn't left my sight or Leo's sight all night. Someone was

with him every moment. So it couldn't be him. Could it have been the woman with the sword? Had that been how she got into HQ carrying a weapon? *Crap*. It wasn't just a don't-see-me; it was mixed with a forget-me spell. And it was a good one. Even now I had to struggle to remember her.

It all had to be connected somehow. How-freaking-how—I didn't have a clue. Except it was magic and vamps and a Damours witch I didn't know. My duties were done, except the security debriefing. To the assembled security personnel, I said, "You averted disaster. You did good. I'm putting in for bonuses for the injured." I looked at the guy who no longer had a full set of teeth. "And dental work. Gratis."

"Yeah? I want the best dentist in New Orleans. I used to be purdy."

Everyone laughed. I guess it was humor as a bonding experience.

When it was over, I found myself in Leo's office, alone, staring at the fireplace, smelling the warm scent of hickory smoke on the air and the stronger scent of cigar, something expensive left from some private discussion that had taken place during the night. Music played over the speakers, some blues singer I didn't recognize and lyrics I didn't want to hear.

Through the binding of my Beast, I felt Leo when he entered, and I was looking up when he stopped at the desk, our eyes meeting and holding. The silence was the silence of a graveyard when the mourners are gone, the leafless branches clattering softly together in the wind, sounding like desiccated bones clacking. The air smelling of dried tears and dying flowers, funeral scents, chilled with death.

I felt it when Leo took a breath, as the binding between us grew stronger, tighter. And I didn't know how to fight it anymore.

"You did well tonight, Jane Yellowrock," he said softly. I said nothing. There was nothing to say. It had been a play, a game, chess on a bloody board. He added, even more gently, "I did not know about Paka."

And my tears spilled over. My scream was half stifled, caught in my throat as if trapped beneath strangling hands. I caught myself, my hands across my chest, gripping my arms. And the tears fell, swamping me. My knees gave way. And I gave in to the grief. *No, no, no, no, no. I would not cry. Would not.*

Cool hands caught me, lifted me. Carried me to the velvet chaise. Lowered me to sit in his lap, his arms, stronger than any I had ever felt, wrapped tightly around me. Holding me. As I cried. I had promised myself. Never again. And here I was. Crying. *Stupid, stupid, stupid.*

"I am so sorry, my Jane. I did not know. I truly did not know. Even I would not have done such a thing to you."

He rocked me, slowly back and forth, cradling me as I cried. And cried. Knowing, even then, that I grieved for much more than simply the loss of Rick LaFleur.

The hour before dawn found me, still in his arms, us stretched out on the gold velvet chaise, side by side, my head on his shoulder, looking into his face. He was asleep. Leo Pellissier had fallen asleep, with me in his arms. Fully weaponed. Able to kill him easily for his abuse of me, had I still wished it. Did I still want him true-dead? Did I blame the predator for death, for blood taken? I wasn't sure anymore. When I was at my most fragile, he hadn't abused my weakness. He hadn't tried to drink or seduce. He had just held me while I grieved the loss of a love I never really had. I was so . . . confused. Torn. Ripped into shreds that lifted in any stray breeze. I hated him. But as a predator, I understood him. And I hated that about myself.

I studied this vampire, wondering how this creature of the night could hurt me, and then . . . try to make it right, somehow. I didn't understand fangheads—I never would—but especially I would never understand *this* vamp. His face was soft in sleep, human looking, though not breathing, and pale as death. His cummerbund, tie, and jacket were gone. His white shirt was open at the neck, the sleeves rolled up. His shoes were gone, his feet encased in thin black socks. Long black lashes lay against his cheeks. His black hair was loose from its queue. He looked so like Rick in coloring, but more slender. More powerful. And much more dead. His body was cold against mine, the temperature of the room.

I slipped from his arms and found my shoes. I didn't bother to put them on but picked them up and walked for the door. "Jane?"

I looked back at Leo. "What is the blood diamond?" he asked softly. I didn't blink, didn't react, didn't answer. He finally said, "Jack Shoffru came to retrieve it, believing it was here, in my possession or in the hands of Molly Everhart Trueblood. From sharing blood with Adrianna he then came to believe that you might have it. Tonight, he came to the determination that she was most likely correct. Do you have it?" I was caught in his eyes and knew that he was reading my faintest reactions. "He believes that the diamond is a terrible weapon when used against my kind." I didn't try to hide the truth in my eyes. "Ahhh," he breathed, sadness lacing the word like fine brandy. "Vengeance served cold. Do you still desire to take my head?"

Again I didn't answer. Leo's face didn't change, but I heard the distant threat when he said, "Will you use this weapon against me or mine?"

I thought how to phrase it in the words that an old, old, *old* vampire might understand. "No. I will not use the blood diamond against you or yours, so long as you and yours do no harm to me and to those I claim. I promise on . . . on the blood of my father. On the blood of the first man I ever killed."

Leo, the Master of the City of New Orleans, nodded once. "Jack Shoffru will not keep his word. He will be forsworn. He will attack me or those I claim, those I protect. Soon. You have my leave to defend." He closed his eyes again in sleep.

Well. Wasn't that just ducky?

I made my way down to the locker room, stripped, and changed into jeans and the new boots, pulling on a warm fleece shirt that was in my locker, but that I'd never seen before. In the mirror, my face was chapped and raw, my eyes red-rimmed, my nose red and swollen. My hair had come down, braids like long snakes around my shoulders, stakes hanging loose in the braids. I didn't care. I pulled the stakes and stuck them in a pocket. I strapped my weapons on and left the dress and throat protectors—the gorgets—on the bench in the middle of the locker room, along with the other clothes and shoes.

I had new information freely given to me by Leo. Jack Shoffru had an interest in the blood diamond. Which he knew about from his time with the Damours. I just didn't know how it all went together. I needed to think.

I walked out of the council headquarters into the dark gray of dawn. The world smelled fresh, of the flowers blooming in Leo's garden, of spring, of man and his modern-day foods—coffee, strong on the air from the kitchen at my back, a kitchen that had to feed all the blood-servants who fed the vamps.

I helmeted up and kicked on my bike, leaving vamp HQ, giving a two-fingered salute to the guards on the way out the gate. I wound slowly through the streets of the French Quarter, chill spring air on my skin. I lifted my head, my eyes half-closed, smelling water and petroleum products and fish and humans. Familiar now. Familiar as the mountains of home had been once upon a time, not so long ago. The last of the snow would be melting, filling creeks and streams, making them gurgle and chortle—

The weight slammed me to the ground. I hit, my knee, hip, shoulder taking the crunch. My shirt ripping. Legs tangled, boots and feet twisting. Wrenching. I bounced. Helmet banging into the curb. I saw white flickers on black. *Stars,* I thought. But only for a moment. They cleared for me to see the bike spin off and ram into an iron light pole, sparks flashing.

And the *thing* landed on me. Long and multicolored, like rainbows on white silk. No form, no shape. Just an impression of . . . something familiar. It wrapped around me and squeezed.

Anaconda, some reasoning part of me thought. Contracting, squeezing, to kill. *Snake!* my Beast shouted. *Anaconda!* Something I had been sensing but not understanding for two days.

Shift, Beast commanded. But I couldn't shift. I was trapped in the light. I—

A horn blew. Tires stuttered on the pavement as an antilock braking system took over. "Jane!" a voice shouted.

But I couldn't breathe. I couldn't move. I was suffocating.

And the change took me, carrying me into the gray place, into the calm of the shift and the painpainpain. But something was wrong. . . .

I/we were not alone in the gray place. *Other* was there as well. Gray-blue-green and sparking with energy like stars and moonlight. Smelling of lightning when it hit the earth

and burned through sand, making glass in its own image. I/
we swiped at the snake/energy of the *other*. Rainbow hues
and ice shot through the gray energy of me/us, seeing with
Jane-eyes and Beast-eyes together. Hot and frozen, sharp
and ripping, tearing through us in the place that was not a
real place, ripping, cutting, just as the pain of losing a mate
did to us in the vampire's den. Swiped back, using claws in
the gray place, using gray-energy-claws as weapons against
other. Felt/heard when *other* screamed with pain.

Other's teeth caught throat. Biting down. Coils of energy
took us and wrapped us and tightened.

Could die here.

Felt/smelled/*knew* . . . Bruiser stepped into the gray
storm that was us, here, in this place, his energies black and
silver and the red of the forge. He waded into battle. Steel
blade cut down into the storm of energies; sparks flew as
steel met electricity. Bruiser's blade exploded, metal shards
flying. Was injured. But *other* was injured more.

Beast clawed free from coils of energy. Through gray
place. Pulled self into world, pain like claws hooked deep
into flesh. Bleeding. Leaped out of Jane clothes, pushed out
of boots and leather and steel claws and guns. Pain. Deep in
bones. *Hurt. Jane was gone. Asleep in darkness.*

Turned fast, long thick tail whipping for balance. Knew
Bruiser was fighting *other*. He was pulled into gray place of
change. Was injured. Smelled his blood. Smelled steel and
lightning. Bruiser was screaming, like shout for war.

Raced in, claws out, swiping into gray place. Into wild
energy.

Pain like burning in fire! Leaped back. Away. Shaking
paw. *Burned!*

Jane? Jane! Screamed, big-cat scream. War scream.

Jane was still asleep in soul home. Did not wake. Could
not help. And Beast could not help Bruiser.

Backed slowly from gray place, from battle in here and
not here, pawpawpaw. Did not know what to do. Snarled in
anger and prey-fear. Saw Bruiser fall. Spun, paws on road.
Raced away. Into dawn. Smelling Bruiser. Smelling his
blood. Smelling a thing that was known but not known, a
thing made of light and dark and of energy like the gray
place of the *change*. A thing like Rick's Soul.

*   *   *

Noon. Sun high overhead, or as high as time of moons that Jane called *spring* allowed. Heat and warmth and sun held us still, lazing on branch over black water. Below, water swirled with good-to-eat fish. Or alligator, good to eat, not good to fight in water.

On bank of swamp, kill lay, buzzing with flies. Buzzards flapped in trees, smart birds to wait until Beast was finished with prey. Smell of pig blood and entrails was strong in nostrils. *Good smells. Good hunt. Good prey.*

Beast?

Jane.

I . . . What happened? Something landed on us. Jane stirred in remembrance. *Bruiser. Is he—*

Thing attacked us. We are safe. Bruiser is not safe. Rick is gone. Mate is gone.

Jane did not answer, silent like black water, slow and cold with winter rains. After long time, Jane thought, *Was that Rick's Soul that attacked us?*

No. Have thought like Jane thinks. Hard to do. Thing was same . . . species, Jane calls type of animal. But was not Soul.

Jane sighed in mind. *Soul. Not Rick's Soul.*

No. Rick is gone.

Yeah. He is.

Big-cats do not mate forever.

I know. I know. I'm done grieving. I have bigger problems than a cheating ex-boyfriend and a catwoman in heat.

Or we can find mate-Ricky-Bo and take him from lie-false-bad mate. Kill lie-false-bad mate.

No. Jane looked away, into the dark of me. *No. Tell me about Bruiser.*

I/we smelled his blood on streets when Beast became alpha.

Okay. I guess we don't have a phone.

Beast snorted. *Beast cannot carry phone. Beast cannot dial phone. Beast cannot talk on phone. And Jane cannot be alpha until sundown.*

Yeah. There is that pesky problem with shifting into you in daylight.

Beast twitched ears. *Am alpha. All day. We have prey to eat. Water to drink. Alligator to fight if Jane needs blood and battle.*

I'll pass, thanks, Jane thought.

We can go to Aggie One Feather's den. She is there now.

Yeah? You planning on eating her?

No. Snorted with amusement. *Old and stringy human.*

I promise to not tell her that.

Beast chuffed with laughter. *We are close. I will take us there and shift near stinky-smoke-fire-hot place.*

Thanks. The closer the better. I don't have any clothes, you know?

Jane should keep Beast pelt and claws instead of human skin.

I'll take it under advisement. And, Beast? Thank you.

I woke as the sun set, a hot red ball in the chill sky, tinting storm clouds vermilion, cerise, plum, and black-grape-purple. Tints that promised a long, wet, stormy night. I was on my side, lying in a painless location, on sand instead of pine needles, which was a kindness Beast seldom offered me. The sweathouse was just in front of me, smelling strongly of smoke from a long-burning fire. The scents of shrimp and hot peppers also hung on the air, coming from the small house nearby. Maybe étouffée and rice. Hot coffee.

I lay in the hard-packed sand, the night air wafting over me, currents cold and leisurely. I felt almost detached from my own inner pain. I was hungry. I was always hungry after a shift and I usually tried to stuff myself with grains and protein. Tonight, if I went into the sweathouse, there would be nothing to eat. Aggie One Feather liked me fasting when she took me through journeys into my own past, into memory dreams. Which had been both joyful and terrifying experiences.

In the last months, since I came to New Orleans, I had taken a lot of those journeys. Buried deep inside me, I had met the memory of my father and my grandmother. Had found what I was. Discovered the evil that I might become.

Since then, I had killed the only other skinwalker I had ever encountered. Had met potential mates. Had been bound to the Master of the City. Had found a family of sorts with the Younger brothers. And had lost Rick.

And maybe . . . maybe, had lost my God.

I lay on the cold sand, wondering if God heard me anymore. If he, the Elohim, the singular-plural God worshiped by the Christians and the Cherokee both, though by other names, even knew that I was alive. If he recognized what I was. Wondering if he had even created me, or if my kind had come into existence through some dark magic, as the legends had told. I shivered. "Do you hear me, God?" I asked into the night.

Instantly I remembered the resistance of steel slicing through flesh as I helped to kill my first man. God didn't answer. I wasn't sure he ever would.

Pulling my hands under me, I got up, my muscles aching, something I seldom felt after a shift. I went to the back of the sweathouse and turned on the spigot, holding on with one hand to the corroded metal as well water sluiced over me, cooling, raising pebbles of chill bumps on my skin. Physically, I didn't need a shower, but I wanted it. Wanted the drench of icy water over me, my hair loose and long and plastered to my body. I shivered hard, my stomach cramping, thigh muscles quivering with cold and the shock of the shift. When I felt cleaner, I shut off the water and shook out one of the simple, long, unbleached linen cloths hanging on the hooks. Long-legged jumping spiders fell, and scampered away. I shook it hard, to make sure they were all gone, before I tied the linen around me.

Barefoot, I went to the house, stepping gingerly across the shells in the drive. I climbed the stairs and knocked on the door. It opened almost instantly. I made out the features of Aggie One Feather in the dark. Smelled the étouffée, the shrimp and spices potent on the night air. Before she could speak, I said, "Help me. Please."

Aggie stared at me, taking in the long wet hair, the clothes that came from her sweathouse, the bare feet, and probably the desperation that sat on me like a bird of prey with its talons digging deep.

"Please," I whispered.

"Why should I help you, Jane Yellowrock, of the Tsalagi?"

I was too tired to even feel the shock of her question, the shock of her, maybe, not helping me, and I whispered into the night, "Because I'm lost without your help."

"You have not spoken truth to me. You have kept truth far from me. You have lied. Why should I help you, Jane Yellowrock, of the Tsalagi?"

I realized she was asking something ritualistic, something important. And if I answered wrong, I might never get her help again. I laughed, the sound broken and croaking, like a raven dying. What the hell? What the hell? *What the hell?*

"When I was five years old," I said, "I led my grandmother to two men, the two who killed my father and raped my mother. She took them. I don't remember how. She kept them in a cave." I laughed again, the sound now like the cawing of crows on a battlefield crowded with the dead. "I watched *Uni lisi*, the grandmother of many children—my own grandmother—kill the first man. When she hung the second man over a pit of stones, she gave me a knife. I helped her kill him."

Aggie drew in a long breath. It sounded like pity and pain, as if she suffered with me. But not for long. She wanted truth? Well, I was tired of hiding it, not saying it aloud to any who asked.

"I'm over a hundred and seventy years old, as close as I can guess. I walked the trail of tears with The People before my grandmother helped me to escape. I'm a skinwalker."

To give her credit, Aggie didn't go pale or back away as if she were facing a crazy woman. The silence between us stretched, like drops of sweat from a prisoner's back, long and thick and gelatinous. "You are not *u'tlun'ta*. You are not the creature called liver-eater. Spear Finger. You do not kill children and eat their livers or kill the sick and steal their hearts." She said, her tone growing vehement, "You do not!"

Hearing the certainty in her tone, seeing the belief on her face—belief in me—I closed my eyes. A sound, equal parts fear, pain, and relief, ripped from my throat before it closed up again. Tears tore out of me, the tissues of my throat rending and rough, tasting of my blood as I struggled to breathe past the obstruction blocking my airway. I couldn't name the emotion that raged through me. Too intense for peace. Too raw for acceptance. Maybe redemption of a different sort from what I'd experienced so far in my life.

I felt as if I'd been crying for days. I hated crying. Hated it. I'd been depressed not that long ago, and this felt a lot like that, a black cloud filling me. But this jag didn't last long. As quickly as it started, it ended, and I found myself leaning against Aggie's house, exhausted and empty. "Sorry 'bout that," I said, my voice a croak.

"Have you eaten?" she asked gently. I shook my head no. "Go to the sweathouse. I'll be there soon." I started to push away from the wall and Aggie said, "God does not condemn the children led into deeds by a War Woman. Such actions are not evil."

I stopped. "But does he condemn the adult who looks back and remembers? And is glad?"

"You were baptized, yes? Poured in the blood of the sacrifice? The redeemer does not condemn his own. He sees only his *own* blood when he sees you. Not the blood of those you have killed." She closed the door in my face. I blinked, hearing her words again. He sees only his own blood . . . Broken, as if I hadn't healed from a beating, I turned toward the sweathouse. And a vision of myself I didn't know if I could stand.

An instant later she opened the door again. "You need to tell someone you are alive?"

"Ummm." I wiped my eyes and they ached as if I'd been staring at the sun too long. "I'd love to borrow a phone."

Aggie opened the door wider. "Make it fast and go back out. Be quiet. Mama is watching *Wheel of Fortune* reruns."

Standing in the hallway, I dialed home and didn't bother to respond to the hello. "Have you heard from Bruiser or Rick?" I asked, Aggie's old-fashioned landline phone cradled between ear and shoulder as I braided my hip-length hair.

Eli said softly, "Good to know you're alive. George crashed on your couch about an hour ago. Evan is playing his flute, trying to heal him."

Bruiser is alive. My fingers twisted in my hair, pulling on my scalp as I breathed out in relief.

"Rick is a no-show here," he added. "Are you okay?"

"Ducky. Bruiser. Details."

"Bruised," he chuckled sourly at his own play on words. "Blood loss. Strange abrasions over his throat and back and one leg. Looks like he lost about twenty pounds. He keeps mumbling your name and stuff about snakes."

I closed my eyes in relief. And if a rather loud voice was shouting in the back of my head that I had left him to die and shouldn't be so worried now, I was able to shove it down along with all the other stuff I'd have to deal with someday.

"So tell me how your bike and your gear ended up scattered all over the street."

"Bruiser's snake. Or . . . I don't know what it was, but it kinda looked like a snake. My bike?"

"Busted. I don't know how bad. Jodi let me pick it and your gear up. You need to call her. But first, debrief me."

Bitsa! some small, bereaved part of me howled. I shoved it down inside too and, concisely, I filled Eli in on the fight and how I'd spent the day—which felt weirder than anything I had ever done before. I wasn't sure how to be honest about being in Beast form; saying the words made me feel as if I'd eaten something slimy. But Eli seemed to take it in stride, or maybe he was standing bug-eyed on the other end of the line and I just thought he was nonchalant. I ended the debrief with "I won't be home soon. Some stuff I need to take care of."

"Okay. Call Jodi. She has news she won't give me. Or maybe she wants to schedule mani-pedis and facials." He ended the call. I didn't call Jodi. I knew there wasn't time. And I didn't want her to have access to this number in relation to me. Her news or spa-day plans would have to wait.

CHAPTER 17

Killer Only, Killer Only, Killer

The sweathouse was still hot. Aggie had done an all-day ritual for someone, several someones by the sweat-stink on the air. I had to wonder how much she had left inside herself, drained of the toxins, yes, but also all the minerals that allowed a heart to beat and muscles to contract and expand.

Not choosing one of the log benches, I sat on the clay floor near the circle of stones that marked the fire pit. Heat radiated from the clay and the stones and the old coals. I shivered hard once more, and started to sweat as my body reacted to the change in temp.

From the metal bucket nearby, I took tinder—dry slivers of wood—and used them to brush away the coat of ash on the coals, dropping the curls of cedar into the red heat. The room brightened as the wood caught the flame, and I added more tinder, then larger pieces—stems and twigs. The flames seemed to dance with the shadows along the walls, a dance of day and night, of good and evil, like the dance of light energy and dark energy in physics, moving to an unheard beat. Sweat pearled and trickled down my spine in the heated room. I added a split log of hickory. The flames licked into the wood.

I was surprised that Aggie had let me use her phone. Usually the elder would tell me to put the things of the earth away, to concentrate on my breathing and the emptiness inside me. So I tried to do that now. I blew out my breath, trying to find a calm center in the darkness that swirled through me like a storm.

Aggie One Feather opened the door and slipped inside so fast that the heat didn't escape. She settled across from me and blew out a breath that sounded both tired and satisfied. "You came. You spoke truth. This is good."

I shrugged, my drying hair sticking to my sweat-damp skin. I leaned back, my body resting against the log bench.

Aggie swiveled to her side and hit a button, turning on the old boom box. The sound of a tribal flute skirled into the room. "Close your eyes. Breathe, as I have taught you. Slowly. In and out. In . . ." We both inhaled, slowly to a beat of three. ". . . and out." We exhaled together to a beat of three, syncing our breathing. "In . . . and out. In . . . and out."

We went through breathing exercises, which were a lot like yoga breathing, and I began to relax. The room darkened as the wood burned down. Outside, I heard a barred owl calling, hooting over the sound of the music. The track changed to drums, soft and slow, and I felt my heart rate slow to match.

My eyes were half-closed when Aggie dropped something on the fire. Bright flame burst out, devouring dried herbs. I breathed in the scents of rosemary and harsh sage and tasted something bitter in the back of my throat. Aggie poured liquid into a wood cup. I didn't ask what was in it. I drank it down, the bitter substance like gall.

And I remembered the first time I tasted gall. I was standing beside my father, his tall form blocking the sun. Before him were two trees, a length of rough board spanning them, the horizontal surface taller than my head.

"*A tsa di,*" he said, speaking the language of The People, which, in my memory, I understood as *fish*, "must be cut fresh, cleaned well, cooked and served quickly, or dried over a smoky fire for winter stew. In cleaning, the gall must be removed whole, not cut with the blade, or the bitter taste will pass through the entire fish and it will be no good to eat. Just as a bitter heart will poison an entire human, so the gall will poison the entire fish. Here. Taste." He squatted and pressed a yellowish white blob to my lips. The taste spread through my mouth and I spat. *Edoda,* my father, laughed, the sound filled with tenderness. "As with all things, *aquetsi ageyutsa,* my daughter, there is both good and bad in the *a tsa di.*"

"Is there both good and bad with the white man, *Edoda*?" I asked.

Edoda's face fell, the long lines pulling in more shadow.

He held up the steel knife, the blade kept sharp with the whetstone in the cabin. "*Yelasdi* made of white man's steel is good. *Yunega* himself is not good."

"Is his god good?"

There was a long silence after my question and *Edoda* stood to resume cleaning the fish. "His god is not bad. His god understands kindness, taking care of the old and the infirm. His god understands forgiveness. It is *Yunega* who does not follow the rules of living laid out by his god. Who does not forgive or offer respect to the land that his god said to place under the dominion and care of all people. *Yunega* thinks that he owns the land and can do what he pleases, when *dominion* means nothing of ownership."

"*Yunega* is stupid?"

Edoda looked over my shoulder and chuckled, a soft burr of his big-cat growling in his voice. "*Yunega* is very stupid," he said, but his attention was no longer on me.

I sucked a breath, started to turn to look over my shoulder, and was pulled out of the memory, back into the sweathouse, wondering what my father had seen behind me that made him laugh, made his face change with hardness, made his cat—his preferred animal—come close to the surface. Aggie asked no questions, she just handed me another cup of the vile liquid. And I drank. When the cup was empty, my hand went lax. The cup fell toward the warm clay ground. It fell slowly, as if gravity had forgotten how to pull things to the earth. When it hit, it made a hollow thump, like the sound of a bare heel hitting the ground in a dance.

Jane is killer only, a voice breathed. *Jane is killer only.*

The words echoed from stone walls, *killer only, killer only, killer.*

I was standing in a cavern, a familiar place, the place where I first shifted into *we sa*, my little cat, my bobcat form. But I was grown now, and wearing vamp-hunting leathers, making this a dream, and not memory. Light and warmth danced across the chilled wet stone walls from the fire at my booted feet. The rounded cavern over my head was lost in darkness. The smell of burning wood grew stronger, as did rosemary and the astringent sage. But nothing happened. I realized that my dream state had stalled. I asked, "What would you have me to do, *Egini*?" Aggie in the language of The People.

"Look around," her voice said to me. "What do you see?"

"Shadows and firelight."

"And the silver chain? What does the silver chain do?"

At my feet was a silver chain that hadn't been there only a moment before, appearing in the way of dreams. And as in the way of dreams, I was no longer in my human form. I was Beast, pelt, killing teeth, and huge paws on the stone floor. The silver chain was clipped around my foot above my paw with a silver clasp, leaves and cougar claws engraved on it. It gleamed in the light.

Tilting my head, I let my eyes follow the chain to the far wall, where shadows were darker still, piled up like cats in a den, against the winter temps. The chain entered the pile of shadows, its other end hidden. I padded across the shadowed floor, the silver chain dragging behind me, my paws silent. As I neared the pile, I made out Leo in the form of a cat, a black African lion, his mane full and commanding. His black eyes watched me as I neared, and he yawned, casually showing me his fangs. The chain went to him, and circled his neck with a loop. One paw was on the chain.

"This is your fear," Aggie said to me, her voice like the breath of the cave, slow and low. "Being chained. But you are skinwalker. You cannot *be* chained."

The cavern changed yet stayed the same. I was sitting now, on the cold floor in front of a different fire. My father's face loomed over me, half lit by flame, glowing with life and love; half shadowed, as black as death. *"Edoda,"* I whispered. His eyes were yellow, like mine. Not the black of The People, the *chelokay*, the *tsaligi*, but the yellow eyes of the skinwalker.

I struggled up from the cave. I knew this memory. I had lived it before in the sweathouse, and I didn't need it again. I needed something new. But it pulled me down, into the past.

Edoda smiled and I breathed in his pride with the herbed smoke—stern, yet full of laughter. *Uni lisi*, grandmother of many children, bent over me, her face crosshatched with life and age, her skin withered and drooping. Her eyes—yellow like mine and *Edoda's*—were lively and full of tenderness. *"A s di ga,"* she murmured. Baby . . .

The fire was harsh with the smoke of dried herbs. Drums were playing.

"We sa," my father whispered. Bobcat . . .

Time passed. *Edoda* sat close, his flesh hot in the chill air. *Uni lisi* sat near him, her fingers tapping on a skin-head drum. The echoes of her fingertips on the skin beat through me, vibrating deep. Touching sinew, bone, heart, and liver. Flowing through my blood. The beat reaching into my blood, my flesh, melding my heartbeat with it.

"A da nv do," she crooned. Great Spirit . . .

"Follow the drum," *Edoda* said.

I looked at the cave wall, at the shadows swaying with exhaustion. The beat of the drum filled me, slow and sonorous, echoing through my soul home.

Warmth settled onto me. Fur tickled me. On the wall of dancing shadows, I saw myself as the cat rested on me, a cured skin, with fur still on, ears pointed, tufts curling out. Pelt brushed my sides. My legs. *We sa* . . . bobcat. My face. The overlay of cat face, above my own.

Edoda settled a necklace of claws, bones, and fierce teeth over my head onto my shoulders. "Reach inside," *Edoda* murmured. "Breathe inside. Into *we sa*, into the snake within." The snake of the bobcat, the snake of my first shift, my first change. The snake of the double helix of DNA in the skin of the cat . . . Magic tingled along my sides, into my fingers as I slid down, inside the bobcat pelt. Dreaming. Floating in grayness.

For a moment, I remembered the gray place where Bruiser and the *thing* that was not Soul, but was like her, fought. I had seen her species playing in the black waters near Chauvin. I remembered the energies and the energy of the blade of steel, wielded by Bruiser. But before I could put it all together, I was pulled back into the memory.

Beneath the drumbeat, I saw the snake resting below the surface, encapsulated in every cell of the hunter cat, in its teeth and bones, in the dried bits of its hardened marrow. A snake, holding all that *we sa* was. The awareness of where the cat and I differed. Where we were the same. And how easy it would be to shift from my shape into the bobcat. So simple.

As simple as bringing steel with me into the place of the change, as Bruiser had done. This was important. I struggled to fight free of the ancient dream memory, but again it held me. Sucked me down into the past.

My first beast. My first shift. In the memory, I let go. I melted, taking the shape of bobcat. Pain, like spokes of the white man's wheels, radiated out, cutting me. The shadows on the stone walls merged and glittered, gray and dark and light. All color bled out of the night. The shadow was a young cat with a short stubby tail.

The past and the present merged too. And I understood. If I brought white man's steel into my cave home, I could cut the silver chain and free Beast from Leo. Freeing her, I could free *myself* from Leo.

I was back in the dream, the past and the old memories dissolved around me, falling like notes of the flute echoing in the distance through the cavern. In human form, I stood facing the pile of shadows. And I realized that Beast was there too. *Tlvdatsi*, but more than simply the form of mountain lion. This was the soul of Beast that I had pulled into my soul home when I was in *we sa* form, and stealing the kill of a bigger cat—when I had stolen both the living body of my attacker and her life-force to save my own life. This was darkest black magic among my people. But I could undo the evil I had done.

I could cut the silver chain. I could free myself from Leo. And I could free Beast. With the same steel blade, I could cut her out of me. Standing in my soul home, I could see how it would be done. Like cutting through the joints of prey, separating us, I could incise her from me, undoing the terrible sin that brought her soul inside with me. I could set her free forever. *Forever.*

I could be what nature intended—skinwalker. I could silence the second voice that clawed and tore at me, that demanded her way. I could cut her out.

In the dream Beast hissed and bared killing teeth. She said, *Jane and tlvdatsi are I/we. Jane and* Puma concolor *are Beast. Together Jane and Beast are more than Jane or Beast alone.*

I studied her, trying to read her body language, trying to understand what she was saying. Her eyes glowed yellow and fierce and her claws extruded, piercing the floor of the niche. Simultaneously, I felt them pierce my mind, painful and cutting, holding me in place like prey. *Don't you want to be free?* I asked her, flinching away, only to be caught by the claws and held down.

Freedom is death now, she said, her breath hot on my face. *Freedom was lost to me/us long ago. Long before last litter. Long before Jane became human again. Now I alone am no more. We have become we/us, I/we. Together.*

We've . . . merged, I thought. *Become one thing. And if I cut you free anyway?*

I will die. And Jane will be killer only. She blinked at me, her eyes closing and reopening slowly. *Beast . . . wants to live.*

Sucking a breath, I woke. Gasping. Shuddering. And I met Aggie One Feather's eyes across the dying embers of the fire. "Your eyes glow with pain and excitement," she said softly. "You have learned something."

"Yeah. I have." My eyes burned, as if I had forgotten to blink, and they had dried out. "Yeah," I said again, breathing as if I had run for miles. If I wanted, I could be a skin-walker only, a shape-changer with only one soul, and no Beast soul, no big-cat fighting to be in charge of my future and my life.

"Do you want to talk about this?" Aggie asked.

"I . . . I want to think about it." I had never told Aggie about Beast, about the unintentional evil that had bound Beast's soul with mine. It was the most foul black art, according to my memories of skinwalkers, according to the things I remember *Edoda* teaching me before he died.

I had been without Beast once before and it hadn't been fun. It had been difficult, a time when she was lost or hiding somewhere inside me, in the dark places of my soul. It had been troubling and lonely; I had hated the experience of not knowing where she was. Deep within me, Beast said, as if trying to convince me, *I/we are better and stronger and faster than Jane is alone. Better than* Puma concolor *is alone. Better than mountain lion. Better hunter.* Better. *I/we are more.* Beast *is more. Angel Hayyel made us even more than we together were before.*

Yeah, I thought back. *Yeah.* I looked at her, at her golden eyes, so like my own. Slowly, I reached out a hand and touched her face. The hair there was smooth and dense, softer underneath, near the skin, thicker and coarser near the surface. I scratched her face, up behind her jaw, and she leaned into me, rubbing her head into my palm. I scratched the base of her ears and stroked down her side, my hand closing on *her thick tail, and running its long length. The tail was warmer than I expected. Beast retracted her claws and the headache eased. She released me and I stood, looking into her eyes.*

"Water?" Aggie offered, holding out a glass to me. I pulled from the dream that wasn't a dream and looked at the glass. It looked like clear water, but with Aggie one never knew.

"More drugs?" I asked.

"No. You have sweated out the toxins of hate and troubles. You need liquid to be restored."

I took the water and drank it down. It tasted wonderful, like mountain spring water, or glacier melt. Fresh and perfect, and I could practically feel my body soaking it up. "More?" I asked, and Aggie refilled the glass from a pitcher. "Thank you, Aggie One Feather, *Egini Agayvlge i* in the speech of Tsalagi. Thank you for the sweat. For the cleansing. For the memories and the wisdom you share so freely."

"The memories are your own. Wisdom is there for any who seek."

"Seek and you shall find?" I paraphrased the Bible.

Aggie smiled slightly. "Yes. Knock and it shall be opened to you. The gift of wisdom can be found, if one wishes to search for it, and is willing to be altered by it. It is not a gift given without cost or transformation, nor one to be used lightly." Her eyes twinkled for a moment and when she spoke, her words sounded as though she was quoting, though I didn't recognize it. "Stand in the crossways and look, Jane Yellowrock. Search for the old and ancient pathways. These are the good ways. Walk in them, and find peace and wisdom. This is old philosophy. Ancient teaching." She shrugged slightly. "I changed them a little. You have done well, *Dalonige'i Digadoli*. But I sense you have questions."

"Yeah. One. Earlier, you—or maybe it was your mother—used the term War Woman. And once you called *me* War Woman. In the history of our people, what does War Woman mean?" At her puzzled look I said, "What were their—our—duties?"

"In *Tsalagi* society, before the white man changed who we were and are with their God and their ways, women were of great value in the tribe. We owned all property. We farmed and were in charge of all commerce. All arts and crafts. All children. Men were for use in hunting and battle and war and husbands when the winter was cold, and for as long as they amused or satisfied us. But War Women"—I could hear the capitalization of the words, the importance of them—"War Women were more. They were Beloved. Wise. Stern. Gentle. Demanding. They sat on the council of men as equals, voted in council, fought in wars with their husbands, took their husbands' place in battle if they fell. They were strong. Fierce."

I nodded, her eyes holding mine. And in her words I saw the promise. The memory. The equality of women in the tribe.

"In war," Aggie said, her voice going softer, "it was important that the losses in battle be compensated. If warriors of the tribe were killed, no matter if our people won a battle or lost, those warriors had value that had to be replaced in some way. After a battle, the *Tsalagi* would take the same number of prisoners, scalps, or lives that they lost."

Aggie paused, watching my face. Even more gently, she said, "Women led in the execution of prisoners. In the torture of prisoners. In the buying and selling of prisoners as slaves to recoup the financial cost of war. In the adoption of prisoners into the tribe. Such was the right and responsibility of women. As mothers. As widows. As warriors in their own right.

"There was no one more fierce than a woman avenging her husband or son."

I closed my eyes. Understanding. *Finally* understanding. I felt again the hilt of the knife as my grandmother put it into my hand, too large, hard to hold. I saw the blade, bright gray steel, the same blade *Edoda* had used on the fish when he gave me gall to taste. I saw my hand as I reached out and made the cut in the white man's flesh. Watched as he bucked. Heard the strangled sounds he made as my grandmother, a woman of another age, another culture, a War Woman in every way, started to train me for my life's work—to avenge the losses of the tribe. And then I remembered the feel of the hilt in my hand as I killed Evangelina, her blood a hot flood over me.

Evangelina, who had once been something like a friend, a woman I had always respected. And who had died because she . . . had killed the innocent. Was trying to kill oth-

ers. Who had broken all the laws of her own kind. No one
else could have killed her in time. Had I not acted, many
more might have died. I knew that. But my soul still held on
to the grief and guilt, because I wanted there to have been
something, anything, different that I could have done.

Hot tears coursed down my cheeks. Burning.

I hadn't forgiven myself for either death. Not yet.

Aggie went on. "Our women celebrated the capture of
prisoners. They sang and danced and joined in the torture
of their enemies at the stake." I nodded, closing my eyes,
understanding, remembering, and Aggie's voice softened
yet more. "Women had the right," she insisted, making certain that I heard and understood what my grandmother had
been doing when she led me to torture and kill, "and the
power to claim prisoners as slaves, or adopt them as family
and kin, or condemn them to death, 'with the wave of a
swan's wing,' as the old words go. The *right*." Her fist struck
the clay floor. "And the responsibility. Sometimes . . . oft-
times . . . it sat heavy upon them."

"Oh," I said. I opened my eyes and wiped my cheeks, to
see Aggie patient, drenched in sweat, her hair plastered and
salty. She needed nourishment and electrolytes and water.
And I knew that somehow, Aggie One Feather had come to
know what I was some time ago, without me saying anything. She had discovered that I was a killer, a rogue-vamp
hunter. And she had taken me in anyway, because the duties
of a War Woman, a woman of the Cherokee culture, were
not so dissimilar to my own. My eyes burned, but my tears
had stopped. I was too dry, too empty for crying.

"Ghigau," Aggie said, and repeated the word again, so I
could learn it, "Ghee ga hoo. She was wise and full of
knowledge, a person of great respect and value to a clan and
to a tribe. War Woman. Beloved. You are all of these things."

"Maybe not wise," I said, a hint of humor in the words.

"But learning. Growing. Such things are precursors to
wisdom." Aggie gestured to the door and I led the way, out
into the dawn. The air was nippy and the sky overcast with
rain clouds. I looked up and a splatter of rain spat over me,
icy and sharp, pelting. But the rain stopped, as if the micro-
shower was a promise of more, or maybe a warning. Or
maybe Mother Nature was bored and teasing.

Twenty-four hours ago, I had been attacked in the streets of the French Quarter, crashing my poor bike, and running away from a fight with an energy *thing*. Running away and leaving Bruiser there, wounded and hurt and bleeding, to fight alone. I had run away from people. I had spent the last day and night trying to find myself, and when I did, I was different from what I had always thought, always feared. Not necessarily better, but certainly stronger.

I thought about losing Rick to Paka, to the magic of black-wereleopard heat. To the bristly and powerful magic of the African continent, and the were-taint, and the mating needs that had claimed him. And I smiled, my teeth baring with Beast's fury.

My mate, Beast thought. *Mine!*

Oh yeah. Ours, I thought. *I could tell by the way he fought against Paka. Not.*

But before I could deal with Beast's claim and Ricky Bo, I needed to go discover what had happened to Bruiser, find Molly and the missing girls, Rachael and Bliss. And make sure that Beast understood that she and I were . . . the I/we of Beast.

Yeah. That.

Deep inside, Beast lifted her head and screamed, the shriek that planted terror in the hearts of the Tsalagi long before the white man came. *I/we are Beast,* she cried. *This is our place! Our hunting grounds! Our mate for as long as we choose him!*

I heard a soft sound and turned my head as Aggie stripped off the unbleached linen and balled it up in a plastic container that smelled of other people's sweat and a little of mold. Naked, she turned on the spigot and stood under it. I had figured out that, to Aggie, being naked in ceremony was not the same thing as being naked in public. *Tsalagi* had no shame of the human body in ritual.

I stripped and stood beneath the other spigot. And as the water rushed over me, I at last discarded the guilt and the grief. I was a lot easier than I had expected. More a thing of letting go, releasing it, rather than cutting something foul out of my soul. I would grieve no more for Evangelina. No more for the death of my first human. No more for the loss of Rick. I was *Tsalagi*. I was washed in the blood of a redeemer and in the blood of my enemies. And I no longer needed to take back what had been stolen. I dipped my head beneath the rush of water and felt it sluice me clean.

When we both were sweat free, Aggie handed me a towel and I dried off with it, then took another of the linen drapes and shook it out before wrapping it around me. This one was free of spiders, thank goodness.

Aggie looked at me, curiosity on her face. "Where are your clothes?"

"Last time I saw them, on Royal Street." I met her eyes. "I was attacked by something. It was a coil of energy, like a snake, pulsing with power. It landed on me from over-head, though if it came at me out of the sky or had been waiting on a rooftop, I don't know. It wrapped around me like a big snake, like an anaconda, and constricted around me. I've seen something like it before, but I still don't know what it is."

Aggie's eyebrows nearly met her hairline. "You didn't think it important to tell me this before I took you to sweat?"

"Do you recognize the thing I'm talking about?"

"Maybe. How did you get away?"

"I changed into my Beast, which should have saved me, but the snake followed me into the place of the change and kept squeezing. George Dumas was there, and he was pulled into the change. I ran away. Or rather my Beast ran away. I don't remember it."

Aggie blew out a breath, pursing her lips like a bird's short, thick beak, wrinkles around her mouth making her look older. "Jane Yellowrock went from telling me nothing to telling me more than I can understand." She tied the fresh linen around herself with a jerk on the ties, gathered up her clothes, and canted her head, again like a bird, but not the weird bird-neck-twisting thing vamps do. She said, "I can find out what the elders know of such a creature. But it sounds as if you left a battle. You should deal with that first, Jane Yellowrock."

I let a smile pull up my mouth and it felt weird, the way it did when I hadn't smiled in a while. "Thanks, Aggie. I will. Um. May I use your phone?"

Aggie chortled and jerked her head at the house. "I smell coffee and bacon. Mama's up and cooking. You come in. Call your people. Eat. By the time they get here, you will be full and ready to fight any battle you must. And *Lisi* might have a gift for you, something in that regard."

Lisi was her mother, and a shaman like Aggie, maybe more powerful and knowledgeable than Aggie herself. But—for reasons I had never been able to articulate—*Uni lisi* was much more scary. "Oh. Goodie," I said, meaning *Oh, crap*, but one did not refuse the gifts of an elder.

CHAPTER 18

We Never Found the Body

"What the—" I jumped back from the table, standing, knocking over my chair, sending it crashing to the floor, and nearly exposing myself to Aggie and her *uni lisi* in my haste. There were long bloody scores down my thigh, and something hanging from my linen drape. "What *is* that thing?"

Uni lisi said, "Oh, you don't be silly, lil' girl. That's just a tabby kitten." With a gnarled hand, she reached over and removed the kitten still dangling from my sweathouse dress and cuddled it with the other, much bigger cat in her lap. "You a good kitten, ain't you, KitKit? And you a good mama," she said to the larger cat in her lap.

To me she said, "KitKit is a adventurous li'l thing. Gonna be tiny, but smart. Good mouser. Already litter box trained. And goes outside most times."

I narrowed my eyes at her. I knew a pitch when I heard one. "No."

"Oh yes. I see in a vision. You gonna take KitKit. She gonna save your life, she is." *Lisi* tittered a laugh, happy as could be.

"No." I backed away from the table. "I leave home often, and she'd be alone. I don't have a car. I can't take her places, like the vet. And I don't have mice. I do not want a cat."

The old woman squinted her eyes and met mine full-on. She was determined in the way only the old ones can be, and it was like being pinned on an insect board, steel through my wings and legs. I felt my shoulders draw in in defense. "Hmmpf. You taking this KitKit. You don't fight it. She yours."

A knock came at the front door, and I raced away to answer it. Eli stood in dawn's dark, blinking against the porch light, and I jerked the bag from him, hoping it was my clothes. "Wait out here," I demanded, and slammed the door in his face. Buying time, I hoped. I was doing a lot of hopeful things, but I had a feeling things were not going my way.

I raced to the tiny powder room and slammed that door too. It wasn't the first time that Eli had come to my rescue with clothes and a ride, but it was the first time he'd been to the One Feathers', and I'd just as soon keep them all separate. But I could feel disaster lurking.

I shoved my legs into my panties and jeans and my old, worn black boots, not bothering with the socks in my haste. Yanked on bra and shirt and raced out. And was too freaking late. Eli was sitting at the kitchen table, the Kid to his left, chatting with the two women. And the dang kitten sat on Eli's lap.

"We do not have time in our lives for a pet," I said.

"He's cute," the Kid said.

"And one does not turn down the gift of an elder of the people," Eli said, obviously quoting information he had just been given, and not bothering to hide his evil twisted grin. He stood, cradling the kitten in his arm. "Thank you for the gift, Mizez One Feathers. We'll take good care of her."

I rolled my eyes; it was childish, but I couldn't help it. Yet I still remembered my manners, the ones pounded into me at the Christian children's home where I grew up. I forced out the proper words. "Thank you for the sweat and the dreams, *Egini Agayvlge i.* And thank you for the hospitality of your home and food, *Uni lisi.* You have been most gracious hostesses. And" — I plastered a smile onto my face and lied through my teeth — "thank you for the kitten." If it sounded as if I was cussing instead of offering thanks, who could blame me?

"You welcome," *Uni lisi* said, standing, patting my face. "You a good girl."

"You'll need to buy a litter box and cat food," I said as we crossed the Mississippi River on the way home. Rain splashed at the windshield, and Eli turned on the wipers and the heat. I slouched against the front passenger door and shoved the kitten off my thigh and into the backseat. "And don't look to me to feed it or clean the box. I'm not gonna."

"I'll take care of it," the Kid said. "And hey, call Jodi." He handed me my official cell, which seemed to have survived the accident. I checked my messages and saw that Jodi had called four times. I hit the button and the fancy cell dialed her private line at NOPD. I knew that Leo and any of his people would now know I was back in service, as he kept tabs on me through the electronics he paid for, but there was nothing I could do about that. Leo was like a big black spider spinning his web into everything, even my soul home.

"Detective Richoux."

"Yellowrock here."

"So you aren't dead." She didn't sound happy about me being alive.

"No. Sorry about the mess."

Jodi laughed roughly, and I could nearly see her rubbing her head as if she had a headache. "Yeah. Well. Your good-looking roommate cleaned most of it up. He taken?"

"Yes. By a cop in Natchez. But if they have a spat, I'll send him your way. He likes crappy coffee and guns."

"My kinda guy."

Eli slanted his eyes my way. "You pimping me out, Legs?"

You should be so lucky, I mouthed at him.

"I told you last night that I have info for you. I started a search on your missing working girls, something I could do because of Bliss' connection to witches," Jodi said.

"You found Bliss?"

"No. Just info. I discovered that she was adopted at the age of two, and when she reached puberty and her gifts started to express themselves, her parents kicked her out. I have an address for you if you want."

I shook my head, even though she couldn't see the gesture. "I'm not interested in talking to people who would kick out a kid for being who and what she is. Even if the kid is torturing cats, she needs help, not kicking out."

"Okay. So anyway, just today, when researching Bliss' connection to other witches, I found a link to somebody you might be interested in. Someone who relates to Molly. Shiloh Everhart Stone. Name ring a bell?"

I sat up slowly, fingers tightening on the cell. Shiloh was Evangelina Everhart Stone's missing daughter, a runaway who went missing, here in New Orleans ages ago, and who had been dead for years. She was also Molly's niece. *Shiloh?* Pieces started dropping like dominoes falling, but I couldn't quite see the picture they made. "Tell me," I breathed.

"We thought we had identified her body back last decade. We were wrong. The dentals didn't match and we didn't catch it. Change of investigators. It fell through the cracks." Her breath made a moaning sound over the line, an electronic, mournful noise. "We never found her body."

I hadn't known they had an ID. I hadn't known they were wrong. But it all fit the picture that I couldn't quite see. "Okay."

"She might be alive."

"We'll be right there," I said, closing the cell. To Eli I said, "NOPD. Yesterday."

The SUV pulled off the bridge and headed for the main police department building. As we drove, I texted Rick's Soul about the thing that had attacked me in the street. It was short and sweet. "Something like you attacked me in the street in NOLA. Call for details if interested." Duty done. Now I could stop thinking about it. Then I checked the e-mails from the vamps who had responded to my query about the party at Guilbeau's. And came to a stop on one.

According to a vamp from Clan Arceneau, Jack Shoffru had been there. At the party. So had Adrianne. And they had gotten together then. *Hooked up* was the phrase the vamp used, and while it felt all wrong for a vamp to use the modern phrase, it also felt all kinds of right. Jack and Adrianne had met at the party. And everything since then had gone wrong for the rest of us.

I was still putting things together when we reached the woo-woo room. "You look awful," Jodi said to me. "And is that cat hair on your clothes?"

I looked down. "Yeah. Sadly." I looked back at her. "Thanks. You look awful too."

She was still wearing the shoes she had worn to the vamp shindig, her body smelled of exhaustion and anger and sweat, mascara was smeared under her eyes, and if she had started out wearing other makeup, it had succumbed to the hours since, all of which led me to believe that Jodi hadn't been home yet to shower, change, or sleep. She looked at her watch, which was odd to see. So few people wore watches these days, using their cells to keep track of the time. Cells that didn't work down here. Right.

"Long day. Long two days," she amended. "I need sleep." She looked over my shoulder, which was difficult for a woman so much shorter than me. "You have no social skills, so I introduced myself to Eli and Alex this morning, after the party, when they came to pick up your busted bike, clothes, and other assorted crap strewn all over the streets. And let me tell you, that is not my job, keeping track of you. You made a huge mess, and tied up traffic in the Quarter for two hours. . . ."

Yada yada yada. I tuned her out, set a hip on the table edge, and let her rant for a while. Eli leaned against the wall and took in the woo-woo department's war room, the room with all the whiteboards and the pictures of missing witches. Alex sat in a chair, head bent over his electronic tablet in the typical geek way of avoiding contentious situations.

When Jodi ran down, I said, "Shiloh?"

"She was turned shortly after she disappeared," Jodi said. "She's still in the devoveo, in a lair somewhere. Probably."

Now, that I didn't see coming. A peculiar icy distance flowed through me, crackling with surprise, as I tried to fit that into the picture of vamp history and politics I had put together when I talked to Leo and Del and—

"Made by who? Leo?" Eli asked.

My head wrenched around so hard I feared my neck would twist right off. "*Leo?*" Something else I hadn't considered. Heat raced through me, furious, blazing anger. "That lying, evil bloodsucker," I growled. "I shoulda staked him after I wiped the floor with him."

"That sounds like something I would like to have seen," Jodi said wryly, "but no. Not Leo. A vampire named Renee Damours, formerly of the Damours blood-family and of Rousseau Clan, now presumed deceased."

The anger racing through me had no place to go, and I took a breath, trying to calm it, but deep inside, Beast was growling. Showing killing teeth. *Kitssss*, she hissed inside me.

My fists bunched and my fingertips burned with pain. I

had killed Renee, as Jodi well knew. She had been there the night when I killed several Damours at the same time and place where I had staked Adrianna. And taken the blood diamond. And if Adrianna hadn't been crazy as a loon ever since, Leo would have known I'd had the diamond because he'd brought Adrianna back from her second death. Which meant that Leo had done the Vulcan mind-meld thing with her to bring her back from whatever insane and broken place she had been in, but the shattered shards of Adrianna's brain had clearly not given him that info. However, maybe he had learned from her that that Shiloh was a fanghead, chained to a wall somewhere. But he hadn't told me.

And Adrianna had hooked up with Jack Shoffru. Which meant that what Leo knew about all that stuff, so did Shoffru. The vamp Leo had subjugated and drunk from. Full circle.

Leo knew about Shiloh. And he hadn't told me, even when he held me, comforted me. But then Leo was nothing more than a cruel, sick suckhead.

My head started throbbing as anger heated my blood and all the domino pieces began to form a pattern. I had been about to put it all together when the soul-thing hit me in the street. And I had forgotten. Memory loss? Maybe part of the head-banging I'd taken in the wreck?

If Adrianna knew about the chained vamp-scions and who they were, then that also meant that Jack Shoffru had learned it all at some point. Jack, who had possibly taken the Damours to Louisiana from their island hell, who might have known about the blood diamond from way back when. I'd bet every dime in the business account that he had been in New Orleans off and on long before he applied to Leo for a safe haven. Leo might not have known that before he drank down Jackie, but he surely knew it now. Which was why he gave me tacit permission to kill the pirate or his people if I thought it necessary.

"Alex?" I asked, my unfocused gaze on the ceiling tiles. "The party where Bliss and Rachael disappeared, trailed by Jack Shoffru. It was a coming-out party for vamps newly released from the devoveo. How many newly risen vamps were there?"

He started keying on his little tablet, his head bent so low I could only see his crown and his curly, lank hair. "Not sure how many actually showed," he said, "but it looks like twelve were invited," the Kid said, his tone telling me that he was putting it all together too. "No names on the info we have yet, but young vamps."

Like the ones turning to dust. The falling dominoes, which had been creating a pattern, stopped dropping. What if Jack Shoffru had been there? In the building. Not just tailing Bliss and Rachael. But in the building itself. And what if Shiloh had been there too? Without Leo's permission.

"The tail car with Jack Shoffru in it, following the car Bliss and Rachael were in. What if it didn't lose them? What if the car caught them and took them and then went over the bridge?"

"Checking," the Kid said.

"And I'm going for a cola," Jodi said, when she caught a glimpse of the screen on the Kid's tablet. "There are things I do *not* want to know."

I gave her a halfhearted wave as she left the room.

If Shiloh was at the party . . . what if Jack had taken her on the way home too? I took a slow breath, remembering the unknown vamp in the car. What if Shiloh had been the redheaded vamp? "Holy crap," I whispered. And who was the other vamp? The one with the nose ring?

And Molly? If she knew her niece was in the city and newly risen as a vamp, and if someone had told her Shiloh was in danger, would she have come here? *Yes*. And without telling Big Evan, in order to protect him. She would have come to New Orleans, and come to get me, just as her note to her husband said she intended. But Molly hadn't called me.

What if she thought I was mad at her for not calling before and thought the best way to get me over my hurt feelings was to show up on the doorstep? And what if someone was watching for her and took her as soon as she got to the city . . . ?

But why? Why take her? Why take the girls? But Molly had gone back to her hotel room. Slept there. Or . . . someone had switched the pillows. Left the damp towel. Taken her things. Left a note Molly had been forced to write.

"No . . ." The pillows on my first visit to the hotel had been blinding white. On the second visit they had been cream colored. The pillows had been full of Molly's scent, but I hadn't bothered to sniff the sheets. Someone had exchanged the pillowcases, and I had been so scent-involved I hadn't noticed it until now.

It all fit. And I was an idiot. I cursed under my breath.

I turned back to Eli and Jodi. "And Leo was planning a swearing-in ceremony at his soiree, to welcome in all the new scions, but Adrianna caused a scene and someone got in through security, so he called that part off. What if—" I stopped and waved that thought away before it was fully formed. I had been about to ask what if Leo was in on it, but that made no sense and Leo always made sense even if it was only vamp sense.

"What if Shiloh was one of the new scions?" I asked instead. "What if he didn't know she was an Everhart? Her last name was Stone." The pieces were there, but still suspended, hanging in space. Waiting for . . . something. But what? "Do you have a picture?" I asked Jodi. "A picture of Shiloh?"

Jodi walked to the center whiteboard and removed the center photograph, one of three she had been studying the last time I had come to see her. *Crap*. She had been researching Shiloh, probably ever since I mentioned her. The girl in the faded photo was about fifteen, with long straight red hair and dark eyes. And a pointy, not quite perfect nose. I handed it to Alex and the Kid twirled his tablet so I could see the photo taken as the girls rode away from the party. The red hair and the nose were a good match for Shiloh. I pulled my cell and started to dial Del, but remembered that there was no reception in the bowels of NOPD's woo-woo room. I didn't ask permission as I picked up a landline and dialed Adelaide's number.

"Adelaide Mooney," she answered.

Fury whipped through me; unexpectedly, I felt pelt abrading my skin. "Primo," I spat, trying to keep the threat out of my voice. "Tell me about Shiloh Everhart Stone."

Adelaide huffed a breath. "What are you? Psychic? I just put it together. We had her as Shiloh E. Stone. She wasn't one of Leo's scions, but just another rescued scion from a failed blood family."

All the domino/puzzle pieces shifted again and even before I asked, I saw the picture they all made, and I knew the answers. "It's all my fault," I said.

I settled slowly to the floor, cradling the landline receiver to my cheek. *Idiot, idiot, idiot.* I should have put it together the moment Leo said Shoffru had come for the diamond.

"The party at Guilbeau's was hosted by one Bancym M'lareil," Del said, "but we believe that being was an agent of, or an alias of, Jack Shoffru. We think he was after a lot of things, the Damours' estate and real properties, the Damours' scions, and when he tracked down the scions, that meant that he also had info on Shiloh. And who she was before she was turned.

"And he brought, to the party at Guilbeau's, Molly Everhart, as his guest. I just discovered that from one of the attendees."

My heart plummeted and thumped painfully before settling into a fast, irregular beat.

"I'm. . . I'm so sorry, Jane. I should have looked into it earlier."

It all made sense. I closed my eyes. And it *was* all about the Damours' estate—the most important and powerful part of the estate—the blood diamond. Except that Jack thought Molly had the black magic jewel because she had been there, on camera when Evangelina died. It never occurred to him that I had it until much later, after he had Molly, and had drunk from her often enough to learn most of her secrets. And because Jack hadn't come directly for me already, Molly had somehow kept that from him for a long while.

Earlier, I had considered the possibility that Shoffru had hired someone to search out something. There had been plenty of time for a good detective to put together the events the night the Damours died. A good investigator— maybe like Reach—would come up with my name in about two seconds of research. Was Reach working for someone else and giving them info on Molly? On me? I could end up hating Reach, if he was involved with this in any way.

I loathed that gem. It was cursed.

Almost as bad, there were other magical toys from the time of the Damours and the blood magic they practiced on

Saint Domingue, and later in Louisiana, like the charms used on the two humans who attacked my house. And maybe someone had even more of them and was using them, just as the vamps had used them in Natchez. Maybe they were using something that helped mask the killer inside vamp HQ when he killed Hawk Head.

It all made sense if Molly knew that Shiloh was alive—undead—when . . . What? Jack, maybe, called her in Asheville, and told her, and maybe told her he already had the girl, even though he didn't. Yeah. It all made sense if Molly had come to save her niece from him. And with Molly his captive, Jack had gotten Shiloh, taken her—after the party.

"Talk to me, Del," I said. "I think Shiloh and Molly and Bliss and Rachael may all be in Shoffru's hands."

Adelaide hesitated for a moment as if weighing the wisdom of giving me more info, and then she swore softly. "I got most of this secondhand. But after the Damours were brought to the sun," which was vamp for killed true-dead, and this by my hand, "Leo found the Damours' lairs and confiscated all their chained scions. The long-chained ones were taken care of by Gee DiMercy." Which meant the ones who had been insane for more than twenty years had been killed. I thrust out my jaw, trying to decide if the Mercy Blade was really merciful or just another killer like me.

"The others, well, when you finished with the problems and the hoopla in Asheville, Lincoln sent a first-generation Shaddock Mithran home with Leo. They've been using that Mithran's blood to bring some of the witches caught in the devoveo to health and sanity. Leo wanted to make sure it worked before he announced it, and then he wanted to make a big production of it as a way to impress the European Council," she said. "As a way to keep them from coming. But the timing didn't work."

"Holy crap," I breathed. "The night of the Guilbeau's party, Shoffru already had Molly under his control. He was tailing Molly's niece, the blood-child of the Damours, who, according to vamp law, was part of their estate, and who he probably knew was a witch, and who shouldn't be sane yet because of that. If he was in with, or at least talking to, the Damours before I killed them true-dead, he probably also knew her history and her full name. But either way, he knew who she was—he had to—and therefore who she was related to—Molly."

"And so, he wants Molly, why?" Del asked, sounding confused.

And there it was. I took a slow breath and said, "Leo drank it out of Shoffru. I guess he didn't tell you. I have a piece of the Damour estate. I have the blood diamond, a black magic artifact, powered for centuries by the souls of sacrificed witch children." I heard a hiss in the doorway and opened my eyes, looking up from the floor to see Jodi standing there, shock forming on her face.

"Is it in a safe location?" Del asked, her voice cutting, lawyer-sharp.

"Yeah. It's safe." I stared into Jodi's eyes, seeing the betrayal, the fury starting to form. Yet, inside me, the pieces continued falling into place, and I *almost* saw the picture they made . . . if . . . "Del? How many people knew about the young Damours vamps being brought out of the devoveo?"

"Everyone," she whispered. "Everyone."

I closed my eyes. The last of the uncertainty and anger filtered out of me, leaving an empty hole in the center of my gut. Everyone knew. Everyone but me. Because I had been out of the loop, hiding away from Leo because he had hurt me and I was bound to him. And now Molly and Shiloh were in danger because of it. And somehow, possibly, though I couldn't see how now, the vamps-into-dust problem could be—had to be?—related. Because Shoffru had been part of the Damour clan? Yeah. So he probably had some black magic mojo artifacts himself. Like something to make the magical blips on the security cameras in Leo's HQ during the party. I dropped my head and cussed again, softly, under my breath.

I heard shoes tapping quietly on the floor and Jodi appeared at my side, her dancing shoes in my field of vision. She reached down and put a hand on my shoulder, squeezing slightly. My face must have been a mess for her to do the whole pat-pat, there-there thing, especially after I kept info from her. Jodi didn't do girlie any better than I did most times. And it must really be bad for her to be kind when she was so angry.

"If people would just tell me things," I whispered. Louder, my voice sounding tired, I said, "I need any and all addresses for the Damours' estate property. Send them to my cell. And tell Leo that he was right. Shoffru is after the blood diamond and he now knows everything Leo knows about it. He lured Molly here to get it only to discover that she didn't have it. And he knew about Shiloh and he took her after the party at Guilbeau's. At some point, he and Adrianna got together and shared blood, and went to work together. By now Shoffru may know I have it. I'm surprised he hasn't contacted me to demand it in exchange for Molly and Shiloh."

Though I had to think that Leo had put all that together already and was using me to get rid of Shoffru for him. I shook that thought away and went on. "Shoffru is using the people closest to me to get the diamond." I closed my eyes. "Del? Wake Leo up. Tell him that I'll give Shoffru anything he wants to keep them safe. Understand?"

"Not really," Del said, sounding all prim, proper, and lawyerly again, "but I think from your tone that Leo will understand perfectly. I don't have the Damours' estate addresses at my fingertips. I'm still trying to get settled here and learn my way around. But I'll send you the addresses and coordinates of the lairs the moment I get them, along with the addresses of any locales where Jack Shoffru has been seen or might lair."

It could be too little too late, but it was a start to making sense of the vamp-into-dust problem, the missing Bliss and Rachael problem, and finding Molly. I forced a smile, my lips feeling stiff and thin as I focused on Jodi. "Thanks. I'll keep you informed."

"Yeah. You better," she said. "And if humans are in danger in my city, you let me in on the action. Understood?"

I nodded. I understood perfectly. And I had no intention of obeying her. I wouldn't be calling in any law enforcement until I had done what needed doing, but I wasn't going to tell her that. I was learning to control my big mouth.

I hung up the phone and looked at my pals. The Kid's head was still bowed over the tablet, a smear of black and gold visible on the screen, oddly familiar. I pushed myself to my feet and said to Jodi and Eli, "I need to talk to Bruiser

and Big Evan. And then we're going to find and rescue
Molly and Shiloh Everhart Stone, the newest vamp in New
Orleans. And probably Bliss and Rachael too."

I had finally understood what was going on. But more
important, I had finally understood what I was, who I was. I
was War Woman. And this was my fight.

CHAPTER 19

Beast's Angel Tolded Me So

My bike was on the back porch, bent, busted, and twisted. Paint was scored off to reveal asphalt-scraped metal beneath, like the worst case of road rash in Harley history. The front wheel was a goner. It looked as if I had hit the curb head-on. The body was bent, as if I'd wrapped it around a light pole. Oil and gas dripped with a silent splat, leaking out like blood, to pool on the cardboard someone had placed beneath, like a blood-soaked mattress on a death bed. My bike smelled like petroleum products and burned rubber and defeat.

The Kid patted my shoulder and went inside, leaving Eli behind with me, his thumbs in his jeans pockets. Silent.

I squatted and placed a hand on her gas tank. Her once-smooth skin felt rough under my fingertips, cold. The mountain lion claws painted on the gas tank were mangled. The bike was . . . broken. "Oh, Bitsa. I am so sorry," I whispered.

"We can ship her to North Carolina and get the original mechanic to work on her," Eli said softly behind me. "You told me he's a genius."

"He's like a Zen Harley master," I said, hearing the grief and acceptance in my voice. "Nobody works with bikes like him. Yeah, he can fix her. Eventually. If I get you his address, can you handle the shipping?"

"Yep."

I stood. "Okay." I looked from my broken bike to Eli and felt some of the heaviness lift off me. "You're awfully nice for a big bad fighting machine."

"Let's keep that between us, okay, Legs?" He gave the twitch of a smile that was his version of a belly laugh. "I got a rep to maintain with Uncle Sam's second finest."

I figured he meant Derek and his Marines cohorts. "Deal. Thanks."

"Your fancy new boots are already back at vamp HQ. Adelaide is returning them to the company for repair or replacement. Your ruined clothes are in your room. And it's no wonder you're single. No lace, no black silk. I gotta tell you. I was terribly disappointed."

"That breaks my heart. *Not*." I shrugged. "I'm kinda hard on clothes," I admitted.

"Yeah. I noticed. Go see George. He was in pretty bad shape too, maybe worse than your plain cotton undies, but I think *he'll* survive." Eli opened the door and held it for me, grinning enough to actually show some teeth. "For next Christmas, I'm buying you some decent underwear."

"You mean indecent underwear."

"You know me so well," Eli chuckled, the sound filling the yard with amusement. I left him on the porch and entered the house.

I stood, looking down at Bruiser, sleeping on my couch. He was scarred, pale, and looked like death warmed over, but he was alive, breathing evenly, his eyes moving in REM sleep, Angie Baby sitting next to him, holding his hand. "He's gonna be okay, Aunt Jane," she said, her face solemn and encouraging, nodding like an adult health-care worker, trying to assure a family that a loved one was healing. "He's hurt but he's gettin' better. Daddy played his flute for him, and I'm helpin' make him better too. Can you see?"

She took my hand and instantly I could. I could see healing energies moving like a stream reflecting back a starry black sky, from Angie's fingers into Bruiser. The stream was magic, Angelina's magic. Magic she shouldn't even have yet, let alone be able to use. "Angie," I asked, "does your daddy know you're healing Bruiser?"

"No, ma'am." She shook her head, red-blond curls swinging. "Don't tell him, okay? Him and Mommy's both scared of my magic."

Ohhh. This isn't good. I let myself slide to the floor beside Angie. "They're not scared of you, Angie. They're not scared of your magic. They just want you to grow up some before you use it, so you don't make mistakes and get hurt or hurt someone else."

"And so the special policemen don't come and take me away," she added solemnly. "I heard them talking a bunch a times. The policemen will take me away from them if they find out I got my magic before I'm all growed up. But Uncle Ricky Bo knows and he isn't taking me away."

"Oh . . . Angie." I took her free hand in mine and scooted closer on the floor. How was I going to fix this? "It's just not fair for you to have to deal with all this when you are so little. I'm so sorry."

"I'm not little anymore, Aunt Jane. I'm seven years old now. I had a birthday party and everything, but you didn't come to it. Why didn't you come to my birthday party?"

I laughed through my nose, silently, knowing I was wrapped around Angie Baby's finger and she was using that to her advantage. "Your mama was still mad at me. I bought you a present, though. I sent it to you."

"Ka Nvista's new dress." She nodded. "It was pretty. I left it at home. I forgot. I'm sorry."

"You don't have anything to be sorry about, Baby. Not a thing. But for now, I want you to stop trying to heal Bruiser, okay? And stop using your magic when you don't absolutely have to."

Angie tilted her in perplexity, her eyebrows drawing together. "But people need me, Aunt Jane. I'm supposed to help. It's why I'm here. Beast's angel tolded me so."

Beast's angel? Hayyel? That interaction between the angel and the people gathered in the room in Evangelina's house, not long before I killed the witch, had lasted all of five heartbeats. A single moment of bright light and darkest chaos, the sound of swords clashing, and the scream of darkest evil fighting a blinding, killing light. But in that single moment, the angel had done a lot of things, and I was nowhere near figuring out what all he had done or how to undo any of it.

I wanted to say, *Angie, do you know what the word* inscrutable *means? 'Cause God is inscrutable. He gave us life with no promises. And that life sometimes just slaps us silly for no reason, out of the blue, and leaves us to deal with the problems. Sink or swim.* But Angie wasn't ready to hear all that. And how did you tell a kid that the angel who talked to her might have his own agenda and that what the angel wanted might not be the best thing for the nonangelic?

I was getting in too deep with this. I was floundering. "Ummm, the angel didn't mean you had to do it all now," I said softly. Yeah. That sounded good. "Aaaaand . . . um . . . the angel wants you to grow up a lot more first."

Angie straightened her head and grinned at me. "You're funny, Aunt Jane." But she let go of Bruiser's hand and the black motes of dazzling magic vanished. Relief shuddered through me like a jackhammer. Angie went on. "Mommy's hurt. She was okay, but she's not okay now. You gotta go help her."

My heart crawled up my throat on pounding feet. "Can you tell me what's wrong with her?" I asked.

"She's got dead stuff all around her. And she's scared. She's talking to God and you gotta help her."

Molly was talking to God? Molly hadn't really believed in God for a long time. "Okay. I'm trying really hard." And then I grinned. "Your other birthday present? Is this." I reached over and picked up the kitten, depositing her in Angie's arms. "Her name is KitKit."

Angie's eyes went wide as saucers. "I been holding her! I love her!" She hugged the kitten close. "I always wanted a kitten for my own! Hi, KitKit! I love you already!" Angie Baby threw her arms around my neck, squishing KitKit between us. "Thank you, Aunt Jane! Thank you, thank you, thank you!"

I glanced up from the floor to the Kid, sitting at his table, working, and shamelessly listening in. He shook his head at me slowly, perplexed, baffled. Or maybe amazed. It *was* pretty brilliant of me.

I opened my cell and checked my e-mail to find one waiting from Del. In it were three addresses, all of them out of the city, west of the river. I dipped the cell at Alex, indicating I was sending him info. He nodded, and I hit SEND. "Directions, sat maps, anything you can get," I said to him. "We have a couple of hours before sundown and we need to be done before nightfall." Or Molly might not make it.

He nodded once and bent over his tablets. I caught another glimpse of black and gold graphics, dark and bold, which seemed familiar, but I couldn't place where I'd seen it before, and I shrugged, pushing my way off the floor. I lifted Angie up in my arms and headed up the stairs, the kitten hot on my feet, managing the steps with clumsy determination. "So. I'm guessing that you're supposed to be in your bed for a nap," I said to her, "and that EJ is in his bed asleep, and your daddy's exhausted from healing Bruiser and he's in his bed. Would I be right?"

"Yes, ma'am." She crooked a tiny hand around my ear and whispered, "Don't tell Daddy." I felt a tingle of magics from her words, a compulsion that she was not supposed to know how to use.

"Stop that," I whispered.

Angie jerked back, her eyes wide. She covered her mouth with the fingers of one hand. "You felted that?" she whispered.

"Yes," I whispered as I reached the second-floor landing. "I *felted* it. Don't do it again."

"Okay. I promise."

I squinted at her, seeing her magics recede into her fingers. "Hey, can you use that on your parents?" If Angie's eyes had gotten wider, her eyeballs would have popped out and rolled around on the floor. "If I ever see you using that on your parents, I'll turn you over my knee and spank the living daylights outta you."

Angie's mouth went as wide as her eyes. "You would hit me?"

I paused on the landing, my feet coming to a complete stop, considering my godchild and wondering just how mischievous—and how dangerous—she was and might become as she got older. In a normal voice I said, "If EJ was about to touch a hot stove, would your mama and daddy grab him and spank his bottom to keep him safe?"

"EJ wears trainer-diapers," she said, her face going mutinous. "He wouldn't feel it if they spanked him."

"Don't dodge the question, Angie."

Her bottom lip poked out and her eyes narrowed to slits. She huffed a breath, thinking. "Mommy and Daddy would spank him." She frowned hard. "And they would spank me for doing magics."

"And would you deserve it for sneaking around and doing things they told you not to? Things you knew they would disapprove of?"

Angie took her arms off my shoulders and crossed them, her curls bouncing, and I was reminded of an old black-and-white movie with a little girl actress. Shirley somebody. Mutinously, as if the words were dragged out by pincers, she said, "Yes. I would deserve it."

"I'm proud of you, Angie," I said, letting my face soften.

"Why?"

"For taking the high road. The hard road. For being honest and for having . . . honor. Not many people in this day and age have honor." The corners of her mouth pulled down farther, quarrelsome and confused. "And I have honor too," I said. "Which is why, because I'm your godmother, if I see you using magics without the knowledge and permission of your family, I'll spank you."

Angie huffed, watching me.

I smiled fully. "I'll spank you to keep you safe and alive, the same way I'd spank EJ to teach him about hot stoves. The way Beast would swat a kit to keep it from falling out of the den and to teach him to stay away from the mouth of the cave."

"Spanking babies is wrong," she stated. But she uncrossed her arms and waved them in the air in front of us. And I felt the magics that had crisscrossed in front of us and under my feet vanish. I hadn't even noticed them until she dispersed them. I heard Big Evan roll over in bed. Angie had been keeping him asleep while she healed Bruiser. *Good heavens.* What was this child gonna be like in ten years?

"Soon I'm gonna be smart and all growed up and using my magic," Angie said, anger darkening her face. "Damn it."

Without even thinking about it, I swatted her. It didn't hurt her, but it got her attention. I schooled my face to neutrality. When had my godchild started cussing? I had to talk to Molly about this. *But Molly isn't here.* "I won't beat you. Yes, beating kids is wrong. But now you'll have a time-out and no movies and no dessert after dinner. Because you knew what you were doing was wrong. And you know language like that is not accepted in my house."

Tears welled up in her gorgeous eyes, wavering and pooling. Horror and guilt welled up in me, but I swiped the kitten off the floor and into Angie's arms, gathered the little girl and her new pet close, and carried Angie to her bed, laying her on top of the covers. Emotion made me gruff. "One-hour time-out. No dolls, no TV, no nothing but the kitten." Tears rolled down her cheeks and I forced my voice to soften. "I love you, Angie Baby. I love you with all my heart."

"I hate you," she said to me, and rolled over, presenting me with her back.

"No, you don't. And if I die tonight, saving your mama, it'll be too late to say I love you." With that, I turned on a heel and left the room, going back down the stairs. Some life lessons are hard. They just are.

Big Evan followed me down the stairs, his face creased in sleep. Instantly I was reminded of the time I saw him sleeping and I shook my head, trying to make the picture memory go away. "What?" he asked. When I just shook my head again, he said, "I'm hungry. Who wants food?" and moved sleepily to the kitchen.

"Jane?" Alex called softly from the living room. "I found footage of Molly leaving the hotel."

Big Evan was instantly awake and standing behind the Kid. I didn't even see him move. Sometimes Evan was just plain scary.

On the Kid's largest tablet was a still shot of an empty hallway. "Put it up on the big screen," Eli whispered from the doorway. We were all talking quietly, to allow Bruiser to stay asleep.

The empty hallway appeared on the wide-screen TV, looking blurred and pixilated. "This is why it took so long to find in a search of security footage. Nothing really shows up when you're looking fast, with multiple screens running at once," Alex said. On the screen, a blur appeared, like four swishes of color caught on old-fashioned, regular-speed film when something fast happened. But it wasn't fast, it was just swishy. "That was them leaving."

"Magic," Evan said, frustration in his tone. "Someone hid them leaving."

"Yeah," the Kid said, something odd in his voice. He tapped his screen. "This is the vamps arriving."

Movement appeared on the screen again, moving in the opposite direction. Three forms, this time. Still all swishy.

Big Evan said, "That's active magic, not something canned. One of the vamps can use magic. One is a witch."

"Angel Tit sent you some footage captured during the *gather*," I said. "He said something was odd on the digital feed. Put it up."

"Yeah," the Kid said. "I haven't had a chance to look at it."

The security footage was just as blurred as the hotel footage. In fact, it looked so similar it had to be the same kind of spell, if not the same practitioner. "Okay. Run the hotel footage again." The blurred footage ran: three forms in and four forms out, looking much like the footage sent by Angel Tit.

"Huh," Alex said.

"Same magic worker?" I asked Evan.

"No way to tell," he said. "All low-level magic would look like that on a digital camera unless you had a really good camera."

"Oh."

The Kid looked at me. Eli and Evan looked at me. I breathed out in resignation that sounded suspiciously like a long-suffering sigh. I hadn't wanted to tell him this way, because the big guy had a temper to go with the red hair and the big magic, but I saw no option now. "Evan." I stopped, not sure how I wanted to say this. There wasn't an easy way that I could see. I heaved a breath and took the plunge. "I found out this morning that Shiloh is alive. Well, undead. She's been turned." At his blank look, I said, "Molly's missing niece. Shiloh Everhart Stone, the one presumed dead? She's a vamp. And I'm pretty sure Molly came here to rescue her."

I saw gears shifting in Big Evan's eyes and the silence stretched out. He propped his meaty fists on his hips, and his face darkened from red to slightly purple. I wasn't sure he was breathing, and his heart was suddenly pounding so hard that I was afraid it would explode—things I notice when my Beast is close to the front of my brain. He took a slow, whistling breath, and there was compressed magic in that minor key note.

Musingly, thoughtfully, Evan said, "I wonder what Leo looks like without his head." The words rattled around in my brain searching for meaning, but before I found it, he went on. "Because no way did that chief fanghead not know that Shiloh was alive and that Molly was with her. This is his city. Nothing happens here without the MOC knowing."

Oh, crap. This was gonna be trouble. I just knew it.

"Yes, about that," a scratchy voice said from the couch. Bruiser levered himself up on an arm, moving stiffly, his face twisted in pain. He coughed, the sound dry and harsh. "Since no one will allow an old man to get some sleep." He looked at Evan, his brown eyes exhausted but clear. "Leo's new primo called and spoke with me about your concerns and conclusions, and she suggested that you might believe Leo was involved. He had no idea," Bruiser said. "None."

Bruiser had gaunt cheeks and a yellowish pallor. He was shaking slightly, a fine tremor that spoke of dehydration and calorie loss.

"Wait," I told him. I went to the kitchen and found a sixty-four-ounce bottle of blue Gatorade in the pantry area. I thought about bringing a funnel to get it into him faster, but figured I might accidentally choke him to death. I settled on a wide-gauge rubber straw currently in a water bottle Eli used to hydrate while he worked out, grabbed some energy bars and a bag of dried dates, and returned to the living room to see Eli tucking a blanket around Bruiser. Big Evan looked as if he might explode if not given all the info soon, but I opened the Gatorade and tucked one end of the long straw into it, the other into Bruiser's mouth. "Drink." He did, draining half the blue liquid in about sixty seconds.

Bruiser pushed the straw away, but accepted a handful of dates and tossed them into his mouth. I didn't think he'd actually taken the time to chew them, and was sure he hadn't when he went back to the Gatorade and struggled to swallow at first. He finished off the bottle and placed a hand over his mouth in what might have been a polite British burp, but I heard nothing. "Excuse me," he said.

Impressed but not surprised, I went for another large bottle. By the time he'd taken in about a quart of the second gallon, he looked better and he had stopped shaking, but Bruiser's voice was still rough when he said, "Leo took Shiloh in last summer." My mouth dropped open, but Bruiser ignored it. "He didn't know who she was, beyond her given name and her witch status. No history, no information at all. He didn't know who any of the Damours' scions were. He should have allowed her to be given the mercy stroke, given that she is a witch, and showed no indication of ever return-

ing to sanity. But he asked Lincoln Shaddock to send Amy
Lynn Brown to feed her."

I dredged my memory and came up with the name of the
two-year wonder, a scion who was turned by Shaddock and
went through the entire curing process in two years, finding
sanity and reentering society in a brand-new record time.
She had been brown-haired, slender, unremarkable, but
with a good head on her shoulders, calm under fire, smart.
Aaaand yes. That was the familiar female vamp I'd seen at
vamp HQ, sliding an arm around the panicked fanghead
standing in for the leader of Clan Arceneau. "Okay."

"She brought Shiloh out of the devoveo in less than two
months, though your niece," he said to Evan, "had been in
thrall to the madness for years by that time." Bruiser
stopped and drank again. All I could think was that he'd
have to pee like a racehorse, which was totally inappropriate under any circumstances, and I'd never say it aloud. I
was, however, unable to keep a crooked grin off my mouth.
Bruiser, as if he knew what I was thinking, shrugged with
his eyebrows. He needed a shave, a shower, and new clothes,
but he looked . . . good, sitting on my couch. Long and lean
and dangerous.

Beast focused on him intently and started to purr. *Mine,*
she thought.

"Unrelated, but pertinent," he said, "Leo is having Amy's
blood tested to see if it's something genetic, a fluke, or some
reaction to Shaddock's blood, that she went through the
devoveo process so quickly and now is also able to help
others through it faster.

"Before Leo could learn the girl's history or true name,
Jack Shoffru entered New Orleans, far in advance of Leo's
approved timeline, and held a party at Guilbeau's. He took
Shiloh, which means he knew who she was. And no one
knew until you told Adelaide to look for her. And worse,
something went wrong at the party and two scions who attended died."

"Then Leo had his own shindig," I said, and something
went wrong. "Something got through security. Two some-
things."

"We think they tried to search Leo's rooms," Bruiser
said, sounding more and more like himself.

"The blurry things," I said, remembering the footage

from the night of the party, and remembering Vodka Sunrise's missing tooth.

Bruiser looked from Big Evan to me and back. "Leo fed from Jack and learned about the diamond. Quite honestly, we didn't know that they were searching, or what they were searching for, until then."

"All nice but I don't give a rat's ass about it," Evan said. "What I want to know is, why did Leo not inform her family the moment Shiloh's identity was known?"

Bruiser would have to be a block of stone to not hear the threat in Big Evan's voice. He bowed his head slightly, formally, to the larger man. Even with him sitting, in his unkempt state, the gesture looked formal, ceremonial. "It was a mistake, seen in hindsight. And when the young scions who had attended the party began to vanish, leaving behind only a pile of ash, and their blood-servants began to fall ill, Leo attempted to right the wrong and find the girl. It was too late. Shoffru had her. He failed."

"And what?" I demanded. "Leo figured it all out the night of the party and he still let me leave, knowing everything was coming down around his shoulders? Knowing my family was in danger?" I stopped as a flash of anger burst through me. I didn't look at Big Evan because I could feel his reaction on the air, sparking and sharp with barely controlled magic. I pushed down on my own reaction because I might set him off if I let it go. "You didn't think I should know this before I left vamp central?"

"Yes, I did. And when I insisted, Leo kicked me out."

"Kicked you out?" Evan said, his magic stuttering and going still.

"Permanently," Bruiser said. He looked lost for a moment, a scant instant of shocked surprise. Then he pasted a cocky grin on his face and said, "Which was timely considering that I followed Jane and assisted her in her difficulties."

"Which nearly got you killed," I said.

Bruiser shrugged. "Leo and I have had difficulties over the last few months, but this was"—his face drew down, frowning—"different. Much more acute. I believe the proper phrase is, I need a new crib."

"Dude," the Kid said, still sitting in the corner, watching us all. "I can bunk with the bro. You can have my room."

I sat up straight. *This can't be good.* But before I could say no, Bruiser said, "Thank you. I won't stay long. I promise."

Mine, Beast said. *Will take Bruiser.*

"Uhhh," I said, thinking, *Rick . . .*

Will take Rick back soon, she growled. *Will have Bruiser now.*

No, I insisted. *I will be alpha in this one thing.*

Bruiser turned his gaze to me. And held me in it, as if he cupped his hands around my face, as if I was precious and . . . special. As if he would never hurt me. Ever. Or something. And . . . Beast purred, which I swallowed down. Hard. *Oh, crap.*

Eli looked back and forth between Bruiser and me and his lips twitched.

"Shut up, I said to them both, and Eli chuckled softly, the sound pure suggestive wickedness. I said to Bruiser, "This place is already pretty crowded."

"Yeah. Whatever," Alex said, ducking his head. "I gave him my room. I took his stuff up there last night. So it's, like, a done deal."

"His stuff?" I asked, and my voice broke into a tiny yelp on the end.

"Yeah," the Kid said. "I'm sending you info on the Damours' potential lairs, to add to any Adelaide sends you. You shouldn't need to fight once you find them, but you never know. And it's less than two hours before sunset. You better get weaponed up."

Not knowing where else to go, but absolutely certain that I didn't want to stay in the room with all the guys, I went to my room, shut the door, and started changing clothes. As I left the room, I muttered just loud enough for them to hear, *"Men."* They laughed. Great. I was an amusing tension reliever for them.

Deep in my mind, Beast said, *Mine.*

And deeper still, I ached quietly for Rick. Which was just too incredibly stupid of me.

It didn't take long for me to gear up. But it was weird. We were taking orders from the Kid. When had that happened? He texted our cells with the addresses for the Damours' possible lairs and GPS coordinates and sat maps of the locations. Back in the foyer, we checked com gear and turned for the SUV parked out front.

Big Evan stepped in front of the door. "Shotgun," he said.

He wasn't asking for one. He was claiming the passenger seat, intending to ride along. I nixed the idea fast. "You are the only one who stands a snowball's chance in Hades of controlling your daughter," I said. "You can*not* leave her with the Kid or Tia without her making them think they need to follow us." At his confused expression, I muttered, "Trust me, big guy. Your daughter is doing magic, magic with raw power and no math or spells. And she's got scary good control. So move. *Now*. I'll find Molly and bring her home to you."

"And if you need magic to help?"

"Then we'll back off and call you. Deal?"

He heaved a breath that I felt across the foyer, and rubbed his face, sliding his hand down his beard. He smelled of sweat and fear, a slightly sour stench. His massive shoulders slumped. "Okay." He went back to the sofa and sat down beside Bruiser.

"What's wrong with this picture?" Eli asked.

"Too much to list," I muttered. "Let's go while we can."

CHAPTER 20

What Took You So Long?

The first place on the Kid's list was on Ulloa Street, near I-10, and out of the French Quarter, a world away from the lair of the three vamps, well, two, now that one was true-dead, a bag of ash. It was a narrow single-story building— empty of inhabitants but full of a mixed ethnic bag of carpenter types, a plumber, and maybe an electrician, standing around doing that guy thing that looks lazy but is actually part of working. Or so they say.

Eli stuck his head out the window and called out to the man closest, "Yo. How long this place been empty?"

"We been here, like, six weeks," the Latino guy nearest said. "It was a doctor's office till then, man."

"What are you turning it into?"

"Some rich dude's digs. Guy's got it all." He rubbed his fingers against his thumb to indicate money. And made another gesture that suggested the client was getting a lot of other kinds of action too. The men all laughed, Eli too. He gave a lethargic wave—another one of those manly gestures that suggested they all understood one another—and raised the window so the men wouldn't get a good look at me as he drove off.

I snorted. Eli just slid his eyes to me and headed for the bridge and the Mississippi. "No rich guy's gonna live here," I said. "They'll buy something in the Garden District or out at the lake."

"He was shooting a line," Eli agreed, with what might

have been a teasing note in his voice, "'cause he saw I was with a woman."

"Oh. Suave." I would never, *ever*, understand men.

We accelerated down the street and I felt a prickle on the back of my neck. I looked around but saw nothing, and the unease dissipated into exhaustion and lack of sleep. Behind the seat was a blue cooler I hadn't noticed before. I heaved it over the seat and into my lap.

Eli glanced at it and warned, "The Kid packed it for us. It's probably full of crappy food."

He meant it would contain sweets and carbs and he was both right and wrong. We had snack cakes stuffed with creamy centers and slathered in icing, energy bars, nuts, dried fruit, trail mix with Chex cereal in it, three kinds of meat jerky, two energy drinks, and cola. I downed a Coke nearly as fast as Bruiser had drunk the blue Gatorade and opened a pack of the snack cakes. "Caffeine and sugar," I explained to Eli, who hadn't asked. He shook his head but held out his hand. Without asking what he wanted, I popped the top of an energy drink before handing it to him. Then I opened a stick of jerky, which smelled like vinegar and preservatives. "Whatever floats your boat," I said.

Again, I felt that prickle of . . . something on the back of my neck. I pulled the visor down and studied the traffic behind us, but saw nothing odd.

"Only thing that's been sticking to us is that old red Ford van," Eli said, reading my worry. "We passed it ten minutes ago. It's got a yellow Baby on Board sticker on the back window and is driven by a woman in her fifties. Brown hair, wrinkles, about a hundred fifty pounds overweight."

"Not vamp food, then," I said. Vamps had a predilection for skinny, and their dinners tended to be fit, young, and pretty for a long time, one of the side effects of sipping on vamp blood in return for dinner and service and sometimes sex. Still, I kept an eye on the van until it turned off into a strip mall.

The second address on our list was on the west side of the river on Lake Cataouatche, in an area that was green with impenetrable foliage as far as the eye could see, houses popping up between swampy land, sitting on acreage too large to be called lots. The houses we passed all had canal access out back and thick, wild vegetation all around, the air already thick with mosquitoes this early in the season.

Eli made a left and slowly puttered down a recently graded dirt road, rocks and shells flipping onto the under-carriage. I checked my cell as the vehicle crawled. The house at the address fit the swank image of one of Leo's scions, with a three-car garage and a pool to go with the pricey palms, dense landscaping, and red tile that roofed a brick house of maybe five thousand square feet. From the dirt road, we could see a powerboat docked on the water beyond the house and a furnished, screened room in the backyard, bigger than the house on Ulloa Street in town. But the kids' toys in the yard were a clear contraindication to newly risen vamps. We didn't even speak as Eli made a three-point turn and headed back the way we had come. Waste of time.

We were almost back to the paved road when I spotted something. "Stop! Back up." I strained to see what had caught my eye. Whatever it was, it was across the narrow canal. Eli backed up and braked in an opening of the vege-tation, black water visible past the thick greenery.

On the other side of the canal was a barren lot with a house situated in the middle. The house was new, with green tile roofing, brick facade, paved drive, separate garage, and blackened earth instead of greenery in a wide arc around the house. Not plowed. More like burned. Debris floated on the faint breeze. It looked as if the landscaping company had scorched the earth prior to new plantings that were scheduled to arrive any minute. It looked dead. It smelled wrong. Even with the wind against me, I should have been able to detect the scent of burned plants and scorched earth through the open window. "What?" Eli asked.

"Is that place on our list?"

He checked his cell while I kept my nose in the open, taking in the few scents that came from that side of the ca-nal. "Not ours, but I just got a list from Adelaide. It's on that one."

Something about the barren home site pulled at me. "I want to see that place. Up close."

"Not a problem," he said, raising the window and easing on down the dirt road. "I'm pretty sure there's a bridge somewhere." He might have been being sarcastic. Getting from one side to the other in the bayou country often meant long detours. Too bad we didn't have a boat hitched up in back.

It was dusk when we pulled up in front of the house, the engine rumbling. I lowered my window to see better. A gray tree stood, leafless, the bare wood showing where the bark had peeled away and fallen to the ground. Littered around it were twigs and leaves, shriveled and dark. The shrubbery around the house was dead too, looking burned. Dead grass stood, spiky and broken, black earth in patches, showing beneath. Up close, it still looked burned, and the yard seemed to move as the night breeze lifted the debris. It was ash. *Ash.* Yet I didn't smell anything burned. The house showed no signs of being touched by flame.

The moon was rising over the black water, easily seen beyond the house. A low white mist was rising off the water, buffeted gently by slow-moving winds like huge hands were fluffing it.

Dead vamps and granules of ash, I thought. And then I remembered the bouquet in Molly's hotel room. Dying, the first day I went there, shriveled to ash on my next visit. Molly, not doing magic anymore, according to her husband. And then an older memory. Molly and her sisters fighting Evangelina. Molly, an earth witch, drawing the life force out of the garden, killing every plant, every garden snake, every mouse and squirrel, to save her younger sisters from the elder one.

"Oh. Holy crap on cheese crackers. I am an idiot." I should have known right then, the moment that Molly used her power for death instead of life, that there would be problems. "A total complete idiot."

Eli might have laughed through his nose at my swearword, but maybe I was too sensitive. He pulled past the drive and shut off the SUV just down from the house. "No car in the drive. No lights in the house," he said. He reached over the seat and pulled a low-light monocular forward. This was a new toy, which allowed him to see in the dark with one eye and keep his other eye safe should anyone turn on a light and blind him. "Looks empty. I'll take the right."

He slung a hunting rifle over his shoulder as he got out

and readied the weapon. "Cells off," he reminded me. We
had agreed to drive unweaponed. Even in Louisiana, citizens might report armed and dangerous-looking drivers. So
all the gear was stowed in the floorboards behind us.

Much slower, I turned off my cell and opened the door,
the lights off in the vehicle. The night smelled of plants in
the distance, water all around, some stagnant and some
moving. I smelled a skunk somewhere far off, and something dead closer, something that had been left in the sun to
rot. The dying smell of exhaust from the SUV.

The night breeze touched me with tenuous fingers. Hairs
that had worked their way from my braid brushed my face.
In the distance, a night bird called, but closer to us, nothing
moved. I sniffed, smelling old, faint magic. Nothing fresh.
No hint of Molly herself on the air.

The magic I smelled was different from anything I had
ever scented. It was metallic and brittle, like heated steel
and old bones. It smelled like a man's magic, though why I
thought that I had no idea. Evan's magic was sexless, no
more masculine or feminine than Molly's or her sisters'.

From the backseat, I pulled my M4 shotgun and checked
the load. Seven rounds ready to fire, six more in the ammo
holder clipped to the weapon. A nine-mil went in my spine
holster. I slid a fourteen-inch-bladed vamp-killer onto my
calf-strapped sheath.

Eli had moved to the garage and stood to the side, dipping his head back and forth fast, looking in the windows
with each forward move. He turned to me and held up one
finger. A car was in the garage. From there, my partner
crouched and moved right, into the shadows. I moved left
across the front of the house. I was exposed, should anyone
be looking out, say a vamp or two, with their near-perfect
night vision. But nothing moved.

I circled the house, meeting Eli in the back as we both
continued on our circuits. He pointed to the side door as
the entrance he would use. I nodded and pointed back to
the front of the house, miming ringing the bell. He flashed
white teeth at me and moved on. He thought I was an idiot
for announcing myself instead of busting in, but really . . .
We had parked within sight of the house. There were
alarm company stickers on the doors and windows. No
way would we be able to enter undetected. Why get ar-

rested for B&E when someone might just open the door and invite us in?

I climbed the short steps to the door, set the weapon on safety, and slung the M4 back around. I readied the nine-mil and held it in my left hand, down by my leg. I rang the bell. It chimed inside, three soft, soothing notes. I heard nothing else, but my Spidey senses went on alert. I took a slow breath and stepped back from the door just as it opened. The girl who stood there was willowy and pale, about five-seven, wearing khakis and a long-sleeved T-shirt. She smelled familiar. She was one of the vamps who had been in Molly's hotel room.

We stared at each other, the night bird starting to call again from far away.

The girl smelled of vamp—leaves and wilted flowers and, oddly, desert air. She had red hair, long and straight, but it was lank and dull, unlike the lustrous hair of most vamps. Her brown eyes were yellowed and sunken, her skin sallow. She looked far more mature than the sixteen she had been when she disappeared. She looked *old*. But she had Molly's mouth. Molly's nose. And a wreath of magic about her head and on her hands, held in place with fingers that worked and braided the magic as I watched. She was a witch, like her mother and her aunts, and her magic smelled of roses with long thorns and the heat of the sun on stone. "Shiloh," I said, the word a breath of sound. Shiloh took me in from the top of my head to my boots, lingering on the necklace at my throat before dropping to my hands. "Are you going to shoot me?" she asked, her voice a croak, her eyes on the gun at my side. "Because you might as well not bother. I'll be dead before dawn anyway."

"What? No. Not planning on it. You gonna try to drink me down?"

She ghosted a worn, wearied smile at me and stepped back from the door, saying, "Come in, Jane Yellowrock. What took you so long?"

I sat in the darkened living room, on a chair across from the cold fireplace, staring at a dead girl who was still dying. She was vastly different from the picture I had seen of her in her abandoned bedroom, in her mother's house outside Asheville, North Carolina, and in the NOPD's woo-woo room.

Older than the photos, indicating that she hadn't been turned immediately after they were taken. Skinnier, paler certainly. Probably a bit taller. Her hair was a browner shade of red than Molly's.

She didn't move with vamp grace, the way they do when they want to charm or disarm, but all lizard-y, bird-y, snake-y, the way they do when they're fearful or angry. Or sick. She was sitting on the sofa, her spindly legs drawn up onto the cushion, arms held up in the air, the skein of magic still working, providing the only light.

"Where's Molly?" Eli asked. He was standing in the corner, weapon at ready, ocular perched on top of his head like a science fiction cyborg.

"He took her today while I was sleeping, after Bliss got sick," Shiloh said, still staring at me. It wasn't the regard of a predator with prey in sight; more like being regarded as uninteresting, unnecessary, and I remembered her question at the door, "What took you so long?"

Beast padded slowly forward, into the front parts of my mind, studying her. *Witch-vampire. Dying,* Beast murmured.

"Your eyes are starting to glow, just like Aunt Molly-Lolly said they would," Shiloh said.

Molly-Lolly? I hadn't heard that name before. I took a breath and pulled myself together. Someone took Molly. I had work to do. "You look sick," I said. "Bliss is sick too?"

"Yes. Something's wrong with Aunt Molly-Lolly's magic. Jack is a witch like me. Or not like me, but he's a witch. He got Aunt Molly-Lolly blood-drunk, cast a spell, used his compulsion on her, and redirected her magic. With the death magics, he can make people sick and kill Mithrans. He's going to use it on Leo Pellissier, as soon as he gets him away from his power base." Shiloh smiled, the skin of her face pulling into wrinkles, as if she was badly dehydrated. She looked worse, if possible, than she had when she answered the door, but maybe it was the lack of light. She still hadn't turned any on.

"Death magic," I said.

"Yes." She took a breath and her fingers, still manipulating magic, trembled like dried sticks in a winter wind.

"That's why the grounds are dying. Because of Molly," I said.

"Yes. If it isn't used, it spills over. She's fighting him, but he's draining her, and when she fights him, other things die and people get sick. She can't last long." Shiloh chuckled, and there was nothing amusing in the laughter. It was raspy, dry, the laughter of the grave, full of despair. "She'll give up soon and let him use her. She'll have to. And then I'll be dead."

I pointed at the magic she was doing. "You're fighting the death spell." When she nodded I said, "If it can be fought, it can be defeated." I pulled my cell and dialed Big Evan.

"Stop," Shiloh said. "Don't. He'll know."

I looked at the cell and back to the girl. And it all made perfect sense. "Someone is telling him stuff about us. Stuff we say on our cell phones."

Shiloh nodded, her neck like a thin stem, overbalanced by her head.

"Did he use the name Reach, by any chance?"

"Yes," she whispered.

I wanted to scream, but I didn't have time just now for vengeance. I would take care of Reach later. Once I found him. I pulled a burner phone from my pocket and dialed Evan. When he answered, I said, "Jane here. Don't talk. Just listen. Jack Shoffru has Molly, but I have Shiloh. Molly's magic went bad and turned into death magic."

"Magic doesn't go bad. It takes—"

"I said shut up." He did, but I didn't have time to enjoy it. "Shoffru is directing Molly's magic against her will, killing vamps and making humans sick. Shiloh is fighting it, but she's losing. I need you to play something disruptive. And *now*." It took a few seconds, but over the cell connection I heard the first strains of flute music. It was a melody similar to the one he had devised for Rick LaFleur, and tears prickled under my lids. But I didn't have time for grief either, not for Rick, and not even for Molly. I held the cell to Shiloh, forcing all emotion down inside, where it raged and shrieked and slashed at the cave walls where I confined it.

Shiloh's eyes shot to the cell vamp-fast, and her fangs snapped down on the tiny hinges in the roof of her mouth— the thin needles of the young, newly risen vamp. The magic in her hands swept to the cell and enveloped it in sparkles of green and white and pale blue, colors of light that I could see in Beast's vision. The cell in my hand began to heat and the screen flickered for a moment. The battery wouldn't last long at this rate. Neither would the electronic guts of the machine.

Strength returned to Shiloh, and her head moved upright, her fingers grew steady. But Shiloh's eyes began to vamp out, and I knew she needed blood. Eli must have known as well. He said, "Bliss is sick. How about Rachael?" I closed my eyes and slumped in my chair, breathing deeply, scenting, trusting Eli to keep me safe while I was busy. Beneath the smell of vamp and the sting of magic, there was a scent on the air, like sweat on sickbed sheets. The girls had been here. They still were here. "Bliss? Rachael?" I called. "Come in, please."

The door to the kitchen opened, revealing the two girls standing in the dark. "Hey, Jane," Bliss said as she and Rachael walked into the living room. They looked horrible, as if they'd had the flu for days, but Bliss went straight to Shiloh and held out her wrist.

"You don't have to," Shiloh said, sounding stronger, but staring at the proffered flesh.

"Drink. You have magic help now, so I don't think you'll lose control," the little witch said.

My brow crinkled with confusion as Shiloh bit down and sucked, greedily and hard, ravenous. Bliss flinched at the pain before the pleasure in the vamp saliva made it bearable. Shiloh still had stuff to learn about being a vamp and making her dinners happy. But the witch part, she was getting pretty well. In front of her body, her fingers kept working, braiding her own magic with Evan's that sounded from the cell.

"Someone want to tell me what's going on?" I asked.

Rachael said, "We were stupid. We went to a party at Guilbeau's, looking for a little fun on the side. And we saw Molly standing with this guy. He looked like our type—rich and vampy. She looked drunk."

"We went over to say hi," Bliss said. "You know, because Molly was nice to us when she stayed with you and high-class ladies don't usually treat people like us as"—her hand made a waffling motion—"people. Anyway, we don't know what happened." She cupped Shiloh's head with her free hand, a grimace of pain on her face, and her voice showed strain. "Everything seemed great. The guy seemed hot, like

Mr. Wonderful, great in bed and with wads of money. And he introduced us to Shiloh."

"And next thing we knew, we woke up here," Rachael said. "Chained to the beds upstairs and a newly risen fang-head loose in the house."

"Hungry," Bliss added. "Which kinda sucked, pun intended. Okay now," she said to Shiloh. "*Greenwitch*. That's enough. Remember what we said. *Greenwitch*. It's time to stop." Shiloh's fangs slid from Bliss' wrist and she licked the wound to close it. Or to get the last drop. Or both. To me, Bliss said, "*Greenwitch* is our safe word. So far it's keeping her need in check."

Shiloh looked less ill, as if there was more flesh cushioning between bone and skin, and she looked more in control. She clicked her fangs back into her mouth. "Aunt Molly-Lolly said I probably need more blood than the average Mithran. I had been talking to two blood-slaves, Devin and a guy named Ozzie, and two of their pals at the party. But then I saw Aunt Molly-Lolly and Bliss and Rachael. And then I don't remember anything else."

"Jack has a bottle of wine," Bliss said.

Rachael said, "Honey wine. And if you drink it, you get, well, let's say you get real suggestible, real fast."

"Molly said it was probably the bottle that was spelled, because he would pour wine into it, cheap stuff, and it would turn into honey wine. And the spell transferred to the wine and then to the drinker. And according to him, it works on every species."

"Enough," I said. "Let's get you three back to Katie's house."

"You're going to bring a hungry fanghead and the two"—Eli hesitated a bare second—"*ladies* back into the city?" he asked.

"Yeah." Into the cell, I said, "You hear that, Evan? Make sure things are safe at Katie's. Make sure she knows what happened so she doesn't kill her girls or Shiloh." The young vamp's eyes went wide at that, but really, what else could I say?

CHAPTER 21

Went to the Dark Side

The ride back to Katie's was anticlimactic. The blood had given Shiloh strength, and Evan's magic had given her something to use to keep the black magics at bay. And contrary to what I expected, when Katie saw her, the older vamp invited the younger into Katie's Ladies instantly. Katie was changing, and so far, the changes seemed positive—barring that possessive streak and the quick temper.

Eli and I filed in after her, and I was doubly surprised to see Amy Lynn Brown sitting on the couch in Katie's office, next to Big Evan. The young vamp and devoveo prodigy didn't even stand, she just lifted her wrist. Shiloh fell at her feet and drank. When the young vamp had taken all she safely could, Katie offered the girl her own wrist.

I had never seen Katie do that for anyone. Katie's blood was special, composed as it was now of the blood of eight clans, and I had to wonder why the old, cagey vamp would be so generous, until she turned her teal green eyes to me and asked, "Do you claim this one?"

I hesitated, knowing that either way I answered, I wouldn't like the result. I nodded and Katie smiled, showing her fangs. I almost backed up a step at her expression but stopped myself in time. Katie said, "My master insisted that I offer apologies to you for the blood I forced."

Instantly I was on the cold floor in the warehouse, Katie's fangs buried in my flesh, pain like lightning shooting through me, hearing Big Evan's niece slurping my landlady's cold blood. I lifted my chin, waiting, knowing that she could hear my heartbeat suddenly racing.

"My blood is valuable," she said, "far more than yours. We are now as blood equals, owing each other nothing."

I thought about that, about agreeing with her, wondering if that meant I, and the people who looked to me for protection, would still be safe from her. I said, "I agree to . . . not kill or injure you or yours? And you agree to not kill or injure me or mine? And I get to keep the house."

Katie narrowed her eyes before it hit me what I had just asked. I had meant that I would get to keep my rent-free status on the house, but it came out different. And it suggested that my blood was worth as much as her own. Maybe even more. Very carefully, I didn't move as Katie's eyes slowly bled to black. With her fangs down, she was fully vamped-out. However, when she spoke, her voice was even and without inflection. "Agreed. I will have the papers sent over to you via messenger. Taxes and insurance are due. Pay them."

I gave a minuscule nod. I had just accidentally outbargained a powerful vamp for a house. And won. *Go, me.* But maybe it was smart to not acknowledge that win for fear it would sound gloating. Carefully I said, "We are even."

As I spoke, Shiloh slid to the floor in a boneless glide that ended with a muted thump of her head on the thick rug. She was grinning and rosy-cheeked, a tiny drop of cherry red blood on her lips. Drunkenly, she licked it away. "I will keep the girl alive," Katie said, "for three days. On the third day, if you have not ended the death spell that is draining her, she will die. I will also care for and respect the blood-servant tie between the Mithran you claim and her new blood-servants." She looked at Bliss and Rachael. "I will not treat with them as traitors to my household but as former employees who have found a new master. You are released from my service."

It was a better bargain than I expected, and it gave a place of safety and service to Bliss and Rachael. It also made me wonder about the value of my skinwalker blood, but I knew better than to ask. "Done. Eli, Evan, we need to go now."

And then the doors blew off the house.

I leaped for the front entry. The windows smashed in,

glass shattering everywhere. My ears popped as the pressure changed, midleap. Wind blew through, whirling and smashing things to the floor. Batting me out of the air like a fist to the gut as my leap took me clear across the entry to protect the humans and the vamps.

Magic ripped across me, scoring like knives, stinking of burned sage and scorched human hair. The lights went out. It was as dark as it had been in Shiloh's lair, and as I watched through the open door, lights all down the street popped and went out. I knew, somehow, that Jack Shoffru's magic interfered with electricity, which was how he cast such great don't-see-me spells and charms while in Leo's headquarters. A weird silence settled over the French Quarter as the lights continued to go dark. I stepped for the open door, the M4 in one hand, the stock between my elbow and my body, held close, a vamp-killer in the other hand.

Talons and fangs out, Katie raced past and I caught her with the shotgun, swinging her by the waist back toward the office. "Stay put," I whispered. "Keep them safe."

Wind ripped through the house without warning, battering me back into the office, as if the air itself knew where its prey was. I shouted over the roar as I rolled the sofa over the humans and bent my own body back to a crouch.

The wind stilled to nothing again. In the distance, I heard sirens. I drew on Beast's night vision. The house looked silver, black, and gray, with hints of green. I didn't see Molly's niece anywhere. I smelled blood—human and vamp. And my own. Flying glass had ripped into me, right arm and thigh. Probably face. Worries for later. I said, "Eli?"

"At your two," he said softly. I oriented him at my right to the side of the front door. "Company," he said softly. "I count three. Two vamps, one human." To know that, he was using his low-light monocular. Vamps moved faster than humans, often with a herky-jerky rhythm when they thought they were unseen, and it was easier than they thought to pick them out with modern technology.

I heard them, moving fast, knowing that it was one of my enemies. "Eenie, meenie, miney, mo," I muttered, readjusting my grip on the vamp-killer.

On the wind, I smelled Molly's magic, cued by fear and by addiction. My body tightened. "Evan. Play that disruptive melody. Now!"

A blast hit the house again. It wasn't the magic of an air witch. It was something else, something darker and blood-ier, icy air and heated magic, smelling of sage and burned hair. Candles in the office lit, brightening the room. So did the gas logs in the parlor, a whoosh before everything went dark again. Eli cursed and I knew he had lost his low-light vision in the burst of light. The air went still. Evan began to play.

I heard the sound of footsteps. They were inside. This was not good.

I said, as conversationally as I could manage, "The En-forcer of New Orleans is on the premises." Which was so not scary. "Withdraw. Or suffer the consequences," I added. Could I do a hot C-grade movie line or what?

In the office the melody became discordant, a flute played by an air witch with a gift for undoing spells.

The next seconds were overlaid, like images seen be-neath fireworks, broken and disjointed. From the doorway, a burst of magic hit, lighting everything—smelling of burned hair. Out of the bright, a form leaped at me through the doorway, vamp-fast, a flash of bright scarlet red. Diving at my throat. I fired a single round. Silver shot. Caught her midbelly. A split instant later, to keep from shooting off my own hand, I lifted the vamp-killer. Brought the weapon in hard. Dark fell again, taking my vision with it.

I was body-slammed. I smelled Adrianna as she rode me down. I kicked out and up, catching her abdomen, my foot sinking into the shotgun wound there, flipping her over me. She held on, knocking us into a back somersault. Momen-tum pulled at me. I flipped her over me into the wall. Rolled to my knees. Not fast enough. She tackled me, knocking me to the floor. I tried to roll up, but she crawled up my body, vamp-fast. I smelled burning vamp flesh and boiling vamp blood from the silver shot as fangs tore into my right shoul-der, going for maximum damage, tearing. I lost the M4, heard it clatter to the floor, my arm instantly numb. No pain yet, just hot blood. With my left arm, I stabbed up. Feeling the rubbery resistance of flesh. She screamed, the ululating wail of vamps dying, heard even over the deafness from the shotgun blast. I dug up with the blade, buried to the hilt. Cold blood flooded over my hand, across my body. Mixing with my own.

A burst of the light-magic lit the room, the burned hair smell gagging. Adrianna yanked her fangs out of my shoulder. Her eyes were vamped-out, lips snarling back from extended fangs.

Adrianna was supposed to be in custody with Gee Di-Mercy.

My blade was buried in her gut, and I angled it higher, aiming for the heart. Her blood was slippery, almost oily, and the hilt slid in my grasp.

"Stop or he is dead."

The lamps came back on, bright after the black-night fighting. I blinked against the glare. Jack Shoffru stood in the opening to Katie's Ladies, Eli against his chest. Blood was everywhere, cascading over my partner. Not arterial. But too much. Shoffru's fingers were around Eli's neck, the talons buried in the flesh. Eli was human. He would die. And there would be no bringing him back. Images flashed through me of Eli dead, flesh pasty white. Of Eli in a coffin.

I released the hilt of the blade buried in Adrianna.

She hissed, bloody mouth open like a cat. Lifted herself off me and stumbled into the corner, against the wall. Away from the office and the sofa that hid Bliss and Rachael. I was happy to see my blade still buried in her, the hilt in her right side, where her liver had been when she was human. The point tented her clothes on her left side, poking through between her ribs, under her arm. I had missed her heart, the thrust too low, but I smelled scorching blood, the silver on the blade burning her. Poisoning her. Though not fast enough. I remembered my words to her at the *gather. "Hello, dead woman. I'll have your blood on my hands soon."* I'd been right.

I reached across my body and lifted my own hand. Pulled my damaged arm to me, feeling/hearing broken bones grate against each other. My breath was fast and shallow, my heart sprinting. But no blood spurted. It just ran down my arm and off my fingertips. The pain was already starting, a throbbing, distant gong echoing through me, like a great bell of pain, gathering and building, but still distant. I set my face in emotionless lines as I tucked the numb hand into my waistband. It was cold and bloody. I needed to shift. *Beast?* I asked. She didn't answer, but I felt the skin beneath my fingers ripple and bristle. Pelt was forming on my numb hand. Intense pain flashed through my arm, lightning hot. My eyesight tunneled down, black at the edges. I was close to passing out.

It's never smart to show weakness to a vamp, and fainting from blood loss probably fell into the category. I huffed a laugh at the thought. With a foot, I flipped up a stool that had found its way into the foyer from elsewhere. I sat a hip on it. My eyesight widened. I managed a single deep breath and my field of view widened again.

At his side, Eli's hand was pointing. In his other hand, hidden in the shadows, he held a fragmentation grenade. I clamped my teeth against a pained breath and huffed a laugh. "Yeah, that'd do it, but it's sorta overkill, dontcha think?"

Shoffru looked confused and then dismissed my comments. "Give me the blood diamond."

"Let him go, heal him, and we'll chat." Eli, trusting me to get him out of this, tucked the grenade back in a pocket.

"You have nothing with which to bargain," Shoffu said.

"He dies, and neither do you," I said.

Evan stepped up to me, his music playing. In Beast's vision, I could see Evan's magic pushing back on the directed death-magic. Molly's magic. And I knew the moment he realized that the magic was familiar. Was his wife's. His music nearly died as he breathed it in, but he played on, with only that single hitch in the melody. His scent changed, though, and I smelled the panic flooding through his body. Fight or flight. And with Big Evan that always meant fight.

"I have your friend."

"Not with you, you don't. See, I'm not human, and while I smell her magic, I don't smell Molly. You have her somewhere safe. But not here." My words were spoken to Shoffru, but were meant for Evan, to keep him from doing anything stupid.

To my side, Adrianna slid to the floor, leaving a long smear of blood on the wall. Sitting, she gripped the blade and pulled. It dragged from her body with an awful sound. She moaned softly, like a child in pain, holding the knife out. Her blood poured from both sides, bubbling and dark as the silver poisoned her. She had started the night dressed in white. Now she looked like death served cold. Her arm slowly dropped, until the blade touched the floor. Her fingers went limp and released the hilt. She took a breath, released it, and went still. She wasn't exactly true-dead. She could be brought back if a master vamp was in the mood to save her. Or she could rise as a revenant if no one took her head. But for now, she was no danger to anyone. At most she was a bargaining chip, though I had little reason to suspect that Shoffru cared for her.

Through the busted windows I heard more sirens far off, growing closer. Someone had figured out where the problems were. Big Evan played on. He knew we were in trouble, big trouble, and he wanted me to know he wasn't going to fly off the handle, that he understood that Molly wasn't here. Wasn't just outside, in need of his help. I turned my attention back to Shoffru. Eli was pale and sweaty in his grip. His black camo was wet and even blacker, drenched with blood. "I'll let you take Adrianna. In return, you let Eli go."

"I bargain for only one thing. The blood diamond."

Eli's eyes rolled back in his head. He wasn't breathing. His knees turned to water as he went limp. I wasn't sure Shoffru even noted the extra weight as the Ranger passed out. Panic shocked through me and I saw Shoffru sniff as my fear pheromones charged the air. I had to keep Shoffru from killing him. I had to keep the people in the house safe. I had to find Molly and save her. The goals could not be merged. "It's not like I carry it around with me," I snarled as Eli's dark skin went ashy gray.

"Pity," the pirate said. "It seems our rapiers are locked."

I made sense of that metaphor. He was talking about dueling with swords. "Yeah, life sucks that way sometimes." I jutted my chin to the nearly dead vamp on the floor to my side. Using the gesture to hide my other action, I palmed a throwing knife. "So what about your girlfriend?"

He tilted his head to the side, one of those weird moves that looks like a bird cocking its head. Not human at all. "I do not require the female." He lifted his head and sniffed. The lizard poked its head out of Jack's collar and raced around the vamp's shoulder to the back.

Behind me the notes of the flute changed, rising an octave, now sounding like a challenge and not pure defense. At the same moment, the stench of Molly's death magic stopped cold. Either she was dead or she was temporarily free of

Shoffru's control. "Your pet sorcerer is a nuisance. If you want the soldier back alive, bring the blood diamond to me."

Left-handed, I threw the knife. It shot through the air and buried itself in Shoffru's chest. Inches from his heart. The pirate didn't react. He tossed Eli up into the air. My partner landed on Shoffru's shoulder like a rag doll, his blood spraying across the room and onto the wall, spattering like a swan's wing. With a loud pop of air, Shoffru—and Eli—was gone. Silence settled on the house, expectant and full of despair. The sofa rolled over, thudding on its feet. Rachael rose from a crouch, holding a wicked-sharp kitchen knife, a boning knife, maybe. She had a hand on Bliss, holding the little witch behind her. "Shiloh?" she called. When nothing happened, she called louder, "Shiloh!"

The redheaded girl leaned in through the broken back window. Somehow she had ended up outside, and she was crying. Thin bloody streaks marked her cheeks. Rachael rushed to the window and pulled Shiloh through into the room. "I'm sorry," Shiloh whispered. "I'm sorry."

"You panicked," Rachael soothed. "It happens. It's okay."

"But I left you to die," she wailed. "I'm a horrible mistress. I suck at being a vampire."

I couldn't help it. I laughed. Rachael and Bliss both shot me evil looks. Shiloh looked nonplussed for a moment and then she laughed with me. Beside her, Katie laughed too, her fangs *snicking* back into the roof of her mouth.

Still laughing, maybe sounding a bit hysterical, if I listened closely, I slid off the stool to the floor, landing in an ungainly pile of legs, a half scream of pain as my arm jostled horribly, and my body landing sent out a puff of air. The stool rocked up, twirled on one leg, and clattered over beside me. The gust from my fall reached Shiloh, and her nostrils widened as she sniffed. Instantly she vamped out. Tiny needle fangs snapped down on the hinges in the roof of her mouth as her eyes bled black and wide in the bloody red sclera. Not very stable, was our little, youngest fanghead. And me bleeding all over the floor.

"Shiloh?" Evan's voice came from the side, and Shiloh whipped her head to him, sniffing. And licked her lips. Her uncle was a body full of blood that an emotional vamp might need, badly.

Without looking, Evan reached out a hand and touched Bliss' shoulder. "Help me here," he said to her. He lifted a flute and blew a soft, breathy note. It was a note full of compulsion, and I let myself fall into the ease and peace it offered. Magics danced across the room, to spark on Shiloh's skin. Even Katie looked content, almost serene, and I had never seen her look that way. Never.

Shiloh's fangs hinged slowly back into her mouth. Her pupils contracted, the sclera paling out to streaks of red and then to white. She blinked, humanity and understanding flooding into her expression. "Ohhhh," she breathed.

And with that, I slid down, falling face-first into a dark pit that was free of pain.

When I woke, it was to the sound of flute music. There was no particular melody, just low notes, each seeming a hint off, followed by chirps of bird calls, piping and bright, all merging into a pleasant, easy sound, like egrets murmuring to one another as they settled into nests for the night. I was lying on something soft that smelled of female bodies and vamp and blood and arousal. I was in a vamp's lair, in her bed. I thought about that. About moving. About how I happened to end up here. In a rush I remembered most of it. I decided that as long as they weren't feeding off me or inviting me to join in a group . . . whatever . . . I was good with that.

"She's awake," Shiloh said. "Her heart rate changed."

I grunted, but I didn't want to move. I wasn't hurting bad, and that almost-pain-free feeling wouldn't last if I moved. But the music stopped and heated hands gripped my good shoulder to pull me upright. I met Evan's eyes and managed a smile, or I intended it to be a smile, but from his reaction, I must have failed. *Yeah. So much for the pain-free moments.*

"How many times can you be injured that badly and survive?" he asked, almost gently.

I just grunted again, pulled the neck of my shirt down, and looked at my shoulder. The muscles beneath the thin pink, scarred skin were mangled still, but I was no longer bleeding. As I watched, one of the muscles making up the rotator cuff twisted, moved to the back about a quarter inch, and relaxed. Vamp healing mixed with Big Evan's witch healing. Pretty good. Not as good as shifting to Beast and back, but pretty good. There wasn't much left of my shirt, my bra was torn and bloody, and I stank of old blood and fear and sweat. "Eli?"

"The *fanghead*," Rachael said, drolly, "took him."

"The Kid is working to find him," Evan said. "What can you tell me about Molly?" He looked at his niece and added ominously, "The girls won't tell me."

I looked at my injured hand. No pelt. Good. I tried to make a fist, and pain spiraled through me. Not good. Still some healing to do and no time to shift. "Yeah. About Mol," I said. "I think her magic went to the dark side, during the fight against Evangelina in the yard. The fight when Evie nearly killed all her sisters," I said.

"Shoffru thought Molly had the diamond and threatened her niece to make Molly bring the diamond to him. Molly knew I had it, so she came to New Orleans to get my help with getting Shiloh free. And then he took her and the girls Shiloh was partying with. He realized she was a powerful death-witch and a brand-new weapon in his hands, so he got Mol blood-drunk and started using her magic. That's the timeline I've figured out so far and maybe it's right. I don't know for sure yet.

"But I think Molly killed off every live thing around the house where she was being kept hostage, and when her magic couldn't be controlled any longer, and started draining *them*"—I nodded to the three females—"she rebelled."

I also thought Shoffru was keeping her blood-drunk, which spelled addiction for her, but I didn't say that. "And I think Reach is working for Shoffru and called him when we got near the house. He took Molly and left." I shrugged and the shoulder moved with less pain from the ongoing healing that Evan had started and that one of the vamps cozied up next to me had improved on. Lovely, wonderful feeling. I sighed and stretched very, very slowly. The shoulder was weak but better. Much better. Not as good as if I shifted to heal, but better, and I didn't have time to shift and still find Molly.

I looked around Katie's love nest, seeing pretty teal, aqua, blue, and green fabrics, with prints of violets and orchids on the walls. The ashes of a dead plant stood in a purple bowl. *Molly*. My best friend had sent a death spell against Katie's. I had the feeling that we were alive only because her husband knew her magic so well that he could combat it with his eyes closed. Molly was blood-drunk, living on the dark side, working with a witch who wanted a black magic artifact. Wasn't that just ducky?

"Okay. Enough of this." I tossed my official cell to Evan. "Call Reach. *Now*. You tell him what happened here. Tell him I have the blood diamond and I want to talk to Molly. Remind him I'm a dangerous enemy to have. And then hang up. Don't let him talk. He can make it happen. I know he can." I pointed at Evan. "When Molly calls, *you* keep silent. If she wants to talk to you, she will." I reached for my burner cell phone, turned it on, and dialed the Kid.

"Speak," he said.

"Track your brother's cell. A fanghead took him."

Alex cursed like the brother of an army Ranger, low and fierce, but he didn't waste time. I heard tinny clicking sounds in the background. "His cell's off," the Kid said.

"Oops. That was your brother's idea."

"Sometimes my big bro is an idiot," he spat. "How bad off was he? What are the chances he'll turn on the cell?"

"Uhhh." How did I tell Alex that his brother was bleeding like a stuck pig and tossed over a vamp's shoulder like a sack of feed, the last time I saw him? "I don't—"

"Got him!" Alex said. Relief fluttered through me and I closed my eyes. If the cell was back on, then Eli was alive and functioning. The Kid went on. "Got Eli's and two more cells in what looks like one location, moving together." More tapping, more silence followed. "Yeah. They just passed a tower. One cell in use, three active. Starting searches on each one now. Old suckheads got no idea how easy it is to track them if they have a cell and the tracker has access to certain governmental Web sites."

I didn't ask what governmental Web sites. Alex might get arrested for using them. Eli might die if he didn't. No contest.

"Hang on," he said. "Merging with the other cells in close proximity."

Katie looked at me and leaned over to push a button. We were in her bedroom. And I was in her bed, squished in with vamps and blood-servants like a pile of puppies. Ewww. Not something I wanted to think about just now.

Katie said, "I've waked my computer system. It's top-of-the-line, and I've compiled a databank of all properties ever owned by any Mithran in this state for over three hundred years. Your Kid has my permission to merge our systems. The screens in the office are newer. Come."

My eyes didn't bug out, but it was a near thing. We all gathered in the office. Troll, who had been out picking up a girl from a "date," went to work covering the windows with plywood that he had already scavenged from my house. My house. How weird was that? Maybe now I'd put up vamp shutters and do some more improvements, like install a hot tub for soaking. *I have a house.*

Time passed. Everyone got itchy, twitchy with unused energy. Waiting was never easy. My pain waxed and waned, my shoulder muscles and tendons healing, aching, moving under the skin as they rearranged and regrew. And it freaking hurt. Over the cell at my ear, I heard static and Shoffru say, "—will try to keep him alive until we get the diamond." I jerked toward the sound, but it cut off. Eli? Was Eli the one he wanted to keep alive?

"Come on," the Kid said, cajoling. "Come on, come on, come on."

And I realized that Alex had lost the cell connections. I put the cell on speaker and set it in my lap as the reason for the loss occurred to me. "Alex, were you using your regular cell or a burner?" The Kid cursed and cut the connection. With my free hand, I rubbed my shoulder. It throbbed deep down inside, but as I rubbed, something else popped and the pain eased further.

Bliss brought me a tall glass of water and a wet purple washcloth. I drank the water down all in one gulp. Magic heals, but like any magic, it requires energy, and healing my shoulder had taken a lot out of me. When the glass was empty, I handed it back to her and scrubbed the dried blood off me. It stained the washcloth, but I figured that Deon knew all kinds of secrets for getting blood out of cloth. He had to, living here and taking care of the girls.

When I was cleaner, Bliss handed me a purple T-shirt and I spread it out on the bed. It was fuzzy, long-sleeved, with a dragon on it. Not a pretty dragon, but one of the eats-virgins types of dragons, with a body striped like a coral snake, its wings spread wide, covered with striped red skin and feathers. Weird. And so ugly the dragon was beautiful. Through my fingertips, I felt magics tingle over my hand.

I raised my eyebrows at Bliss, and she shrugged. "I figured it was time to see what my magics did. Turns out I have"—she shrugged again as if searching for the words—"some ability with healing. The shirt has a healing spell woven in it. Molly taught me how. I brought it from the lair where we were kept."

"Yeah? Cool," I said, trying for nonchalant. Bliss had denied her power and heritage for a long time, running away from it for myriad reasons. That she was embracing it was, well, yeah, amazing. Despite my worry over Molly and Eli, I nodded approval at her. She ghosted a smile at me.

I pulled off my tattered shirt. Big Evan turned away, closing his eyes, which made Rachael grin evilly, her silver earrings catching the light. Poor Evan. The former call girl would never take pity on him now. He was in for a difficult time if he hung around Katie's for long. When I eased the shirt over my shoulder, I sighed with relief. "Nice," I said to Bliss. My cell rang and I picked it up again.

"I'm back. Okay," the Kid said into my ear, frustration lacing his voice. "I got an address for the cell billing, but it won't do us any good. It's in Galveston, Texas." Where the limo had come from. All the pieces were coming together but were leading us nowhere. Unless we had an address for Eli and Molly, we were lost.

"Do you have a broad location?" Katie asked.

"I lost them near Belle Chasse, heading east."

"Hmmm. . . . I'm sending you my databank file," Katie said casually, keys tapping, as if she used and talked about computers all the time. "According to my records, a house, the kind I believe you call a McMansion, in Lakewood Golf Club is a rental, owned currently by the Damours' estate while the property is in probate." More keys clacked, both in the office and over the cell. "Of course, there are other properties, but I assume Jacques would prefer a large, ornamental house for his temporary clan home."

"Got you, you bastard," Alex muttered. I smiled. He could cuss and swear all he wanted right now. I just needed him to find Eli. "Yeah. Yeah, yeah, yeah. The car with the cells is heading in the general direction of the golf course. Yeah. Sending a map and a sat view to your cell."

"We'll head that way." I closed my cell and looked at Evan. "Well?"

"I told him. He cut me off without a word."

I closed my eyes. If Reach was working against us, we were really in trouble. I'd never find Molly or Eli. I pointed to the front of the house and asked Big Evan, "Are the keys still in Eli's SUV?" He nodded. To Rachael, I said, "You know how to use a gun? A knife?"

She grinned wickedly. "How about a whip? A gorgeous calf-skin cat-o'-nine-tails with tiny sterling-over-steel blades in the ends. Christie taught me how."

"I spelled them for her," Bliss said. She shrugged when I looked at her curious. "One part of healing is to decrease the ability of blood to clot, for people having heart attacks or clot-made strokes. There's a spell for that; Molly showed me how." She looked down and then back up, holding me with her eyes. "If I push the spell a little, and put it on the metal barbs, then whatever it cuts won't clot over. Instead it will relax and expand the vessels it cuts, making the person bleed out faster. Vamps would bleed out really fast unless I reversed the spell, or they had help from a master vamp."

"How fast can you reverse it if needed? Like an instantaneous reversal?"

She nodded, knowing I was going to ask her to use her magic against another sentient being. But to have created the spell in the first place, she had already planned that. So I wasn't leading a witch into dark magic, I lied to myself.

I pulled a throwing knife. "Can you do that with this too?" She nodded again, reaching out a finger to touch the blade. I felt the hilt go cold. The blade seemed to frost over, a spiderweb of power that vanished as quickly as it appeared. The hilt warmed again, as if it had never been cold. "Nifty." I grinned at her. "I promise to use it only for good, and to the benefit of mankind."

Bliss dropped her head, her black hair sliding forward, hiding her face, but I had the feeling that she was pleased with my promise, no matter how silly I had phrased it. "I have a passel of knives that need the spell. And when we get where we're going, can you keep an eye out for anyone who isn't trying to kill us as we rescue Eli, and reverse the spell if they get cut by accident?" She nodded again. "Good.

And just in case," I added, holding out a silver stake, "can you make this one already reversed, so I have it as needed?"

Bliss' forehead crinkled, as she tried to figure out how to reverse a spell that wasn't there yet. Then she just touched it twice. The first time, the sterling stake iced over and went cold; with the second touch, it heated, fast.

"I can shoot," Shiloh said. "I used to hunt with my dad." Her face closed off for an instant as she thought of her dad, who had been killed by her mother. That had to be a tough thing for a kid to remember, even a blood-sucking kid vamp. "Rifle," she went on, "shotgun. But a rifle is better. I don't like a shotgun's kick."

"Good. There's probably a hunting rifle with a scope in the SUV. Let's roll."

"One little problem," Shiloh said. "What do we do with the dead Mithran in Katie's living room? We can't decapitate her. It wouldn't be right."

Why not? But I didn't say it. Shiloh was still human enough to have morals, not a trait common to most vamps, and a quality I wouldn't harm.

I looked at Katie, who said, "Such is not my responsibility. It belongs to the Mercy Blade."

I flipped open my burner cell again and dialed Leo's new primo. When Adelaide answered I gave her an update and said, "Adrianna is close to being true-dead, but still has her head. Would you be so kind as to send the Mercy Blade to Katie's to, uh, pick her up? You can have the Council accountant deposit my fee electronically." I could almost feel Del's single elegant eyebrow rise. "Just tell Gee DiMercy. He'll explain it all."

I closed the cell and looked over my small band of warriors, finding a smile somewhere inside and plastering it on my face. "Let's go." I grabbed up my weapons and headed for the car, not arguing when Big Evan shoved the driver's seat back as far as it would go and turned the key. Not arguing when Shiloh and her vamp blood-servants piled in back. Not arguing about anything, as Big Evan and my coterie of fighters drove out of the city.

We were still on the east side of the river when Shiloh's cell warbled a punk rock tune from the 'nineties. She looked at the screen, but rather than answer, she held out her phone to me. It was purple and studded with bling. A teenage vamp from the 'nineties. Go figure. I looked at the number on the screen. It was Reach's number. I didn't let my face change. I couldn't. If I did, Evan would rip the phone out of my hand and crash the SUV.

"Hello?"

"Jane?" *Molly*. The connection was awful, but her tone came through anyway, sounding disbelieving, as if she didn't really believe it was me. Sounding guarded as if she was expecting me to lash out at her. "How . . . ? Really you?"

"Yeah. It's me."

Molly laughed softly, sounding broken, even over the static. "Your voice is coming out of the intercom. I'm either crazy or . . . dreaming."

"Neither. I have a tech genius who made it work." I blinked back tears. "We don't have long, so just listen and let me recap. I have the diamond," I said. "Everyone wants it, including Jack Shoffru, who used to hang out with the diamond's owners, the Damours. He scammed you, thinking you had it, and got you here. Then, when you didn't come straight to me for help, he kidnapped you, found you didn't have it, so then he took Shiloh, one of the Damours' scions, thinking she could tell him where it was now that she was sane." Or maybe vice versa. Whatever.

Big Evan's face went tight as he realized I was talking to Molly. But he didn't backhand me or accidentally drive off the bridge into the Mississippi, so that was good. Molly said softly, "How could he know I was in town? I didn't call anyone. I thought I had time to put my head on a pillow for just a short rest before coming to you. And he was there before I even closed my eyes. I'm so stupid."

"No. Not stupid. Someone was tailing your cell's GPS, overriding it. And that same someone is letting you talk to me now." I went on, outlining Shoffru's actions. "Jack sent some of his people to look for the diamond at Leo's the night of the *gather.*"

"I don't know," Molly said. "I'm handcuffed in a room in a house with steel shutters on the walls. And he keeps me . . . he keeps me blood-drunk," she finished, and I understood. It felt good, so good, when a vamp drank, the lure of seduction, the chemicals in a vamp's blood making it seem right and good to give everything he wanted. I didn't know how far the seduction had gone, but I could hear the shame in her voice as she said, "Every time I try to get away, he comes in and he . . . he drinks from me."

Another burner cell rang and Bliss opened it. "We have an address," she said softly. "A house on that golf course. And according to Alex, the car with Shoffru is still en route."

"He isn't there now, Molly," I said. "He's in a car and he's close. Can you get away?"

"I can't." Suddenly she sobbed, speaking through the tears. "I can't break through the shackles without draining someone. I can't. I can't . . ." She stopped, her breath ragged. "I can't kill —" Her voice stopped and I knew she was about to finish with "anyone else." I figured it was the first time Molly had admitted to anyone, except Bliss, that her magic had gone bad, and she didn't want to be talking to me now. She was drunk and ashamed and wanted to hide away until things miraculously fixed themselves or she found a way out of her troubles. Bad thing about that was, troubles didn't just go away or get all better. They took work and effort and maybe some danger. And unfortunately she didn't have some sweet, kind, gentle person on the line. She had me. And I didn't have time to be figure out how to be nice.

I considered what I was about to do, and stared at Evan, telling him with my eyes to keep driving and stay back. "I know about the dead plants and the danger to your family," I said. She took a harsh breath over the connection. It was a sound one might make while peeling back a bandage to see the wound beneath. "I have a feeling that Jack Shoffru has convinced you that the blood magic contained in the diamond might be strong enough to help you control your own magic. Might keep you from killing your husband and your children."

I saw comprehension and horror settle into Evan's eyes. He hadn't known. Softer, I said, "Tell me, Mol. Are you aware that you killed two vamps true-dead this week with your death magic?"

Her only answer was a sob so heart-wrenching that tears filled my eyes, and I couldn't say anything for several heart-beats. I blinked away my misery, waiting for her to find some control. Molly exhaled, and it sounded as if she was being tortured. Evan took the exit off the bridge and onto the west side of the Mississippi. We didn't have long, but I needed Molly, if the stupid plan I had in the back of my idiotic brain had a snowball's chance in Hades of succeeding. I shoved down my nerves and fear and talked.

"You put a protection around your magic and around your niece and it probably protected her blood-servants through her blood," I said, "but your magic is too strong for it. I'm thinking that it leaked out and attached itself to other vamps in the city, the youngest and weakest vamps. Your magic likes vamps because it's death magic and they're undead. But it's spreading to humans too. Humans are getting sick."

That made no sense at first, but then I got it. Somewhere in his plan, Shoffru found Adrianna, and learned about me, but Adrianna already had plans in place to kill me. Plans she couldn't call off. It was the only reason that made sense for Hawk Head to attack me once Adrianna was with Shoffru. Molly's magic going wild and Adrianna joining up with Jack made everything that didn't match up, come together.

Molly was half sobbing, half choking. Her voice was muffled as if she had stuffed something against her mouth, but I heard "Yes. And I can't live with this."

"Shoffru's getting close to the house," Bliss whispered.

To Evan, I asked, "Can you break Molly's shackles? Over a cell phone?" And the connection from electronic hell.

As answer, Evan yanked the car off the road, braked to a hard stop, and pulled out his flute. And I realized he had tears running down his face. "Molly, love. Get out. Now!" He placed his lips to the flute and blew.

The note was high pitched. Piercing. My eardrums vibrated. A headache stabbed through me. The girls in back screamed. I dropped the cell. Fell out of the SUV, I unbuckled and opened the door so fast. Landed with a rolling thud on my bad shoulder. And lay there sobbing, cursing, covering my ears against the horrible spearing notes that sounded from the vehicle. Beast screamed and disappeared from my mind. When the notes ended, I heard muffled words, Evan's voice. And then the big guy had me in his arms, shoving me back into the SUV. He gunned the motor as I buckled in and wiped my face. "Well, that sucked," I managed.

Evan grinned at me, and I saw the face of some ancient Viking warrior, all teeth and fury. "She's free," he growled, me mostly lip-reading around his beard. "Heading out a window that appears to be on the side of the house. But she sees headlights in the front."

"Run, Molly," I shouted. And I thumbed off the cell. Molly was free. Not safe yet. But free. I closed my eyes, feeling the tears gather and forcing them back. *No time for girly crap,* I told myself. *Not now.*

"You're going to use her, aren't you?" Evan asked when I could hear again.

"Molly needs direction," I said. "She needs to accept that she killed someone. And she needs to use the gifts God and genetics and bad luck gave her to do some good, so she can get her self-worth back. She doesn't need to be coddled or pampered or indulged. She needs to get up off her ass and use what she is and fix this situation." And I knew, somehow, that without Molly I couldn't do what needed to be done. I massaged my injured shoulder through the healing purple tee. I felt blood, and now that I felt it, I could smell it. I'd broken the skin again when I landed on the ground. Gravel, I thought, but the kind Louisiana uses, mostly shells, brittle and sharp. Pretty sure that was what I landed on.

"And you know that how?" he growled.

Well. This was the last secret. Once I spoke in this car, it was out there for good. But maybe secrets are evil things. And maybe once the secrets were revealed, I'd be free of their weight and their remembered pain. Maybe. Still rubbing my shoulder, I said, "I know that because when I was five years old, my grandmother put a knife in my hand and made me help her kill a man."

Big Evan blinked. Bliss drew back into the shadows of the backseat. Rachael leaned forward with interest. Shiloh just stared, her eyes bleeding red. Or maybe she just smelled my blood. Whatever. I kept an eye on her as I continued and Evan drove.

"I've spent all the years since full of guilt and misery, even though I didn't remember it. I've let it run my thoughts, my plans, my whole life. But the experience doesn't own me. I own it. What I do with it is up to me, just like what Molly does with her death magic is up to her."

CHAPTER 22

The First Day I Woke Up Dead

Molly was nowhere in sight when we got to the address we thought Jack Shroffru was using as a lair, but I knew we had the right place as I walked around the house, looking it over from a distance. The foliage was dead and shriveled and wisping in the wind. There were no bird sounds, no stealthy motions of mice or rabbits or feral cats. There was no smell of anything live anywhere except the far-off stink of skunk.

As Beast and I reconnoitered, the Kid stole in to the security system and disabled the important parts—like the part that sounded an alarm. And the part that called the police. Everything still worked. Everything still showed little green lights on the monitoring system. It just wasn't going to do the occupants of the house any good for a while. Go, geek—electronic hero in SpongeBob SquarePants flannel pj's. I really was gonna buy him a cape and tights.

And the best part came in three pieces. First, Molly was no longer inside—her scent and footprints running off out of sight, downwind. Second, the place reeked of vamp and magic and lizard. And third, it was poorly defended. Shoffru believed the numbers of vamps he had brought with him kept him safe. He was about to learn a painful lesson.

The house was two stories of stucco and tile on a tiny lot that barely qualified for the designation. I could smell water from everywhere, pools, bayous, and the scent of rain on the air. Fertilizer stink came from the golf course, adding to the pong of vamps, human blood, and the prevalent skunk smell. I realized it was mating time for skunks and wondered if it was possible to lure skunks into a house. With their superduper noses, vamps would likely asphyxiate. Except for the fact that they didn't need to breathe. Yeah. That.

The house was equipped with electric vamp shutters that worked as well for hurricanes and security as they did for keeping the sunlight out of a lair while vamps slept. It also had a three-car, pull-through garage, pool, gated yard, and golf course access. I imagined a foursome of vamps in plaid knickers and those white shoes with frilly collars golfing at night by the light of a full moon. Tams on their heads. A mental picture that made me inappropriately giggly.

I smothered my reaction and went back to work. The first-floor shutters of Shoffru's rental house were closed, leaving the best access on the second floor, where the shutters were open and doors leading out onto the balcony were open as well. I didn't have a ladder, but I had Beast strength and I was betting on her lending me enough power to jump, grab the railing on the second floor, and pull myself up. Well, except for the shoulder. Which was nowhere near a hundred percent.

I had perched Rachael behind the house on the golf course side, in a short tree, within whip length of the back door. Bliss, terrified and uncertain, but determined to stay, was with her. I didn't want them so close to any potential action, but it was give them a real job or have them pick a job for themselves, probably one that included them going into the vamp lair. Rachael was strangely eager for that, and it would surely result in injury or death for them.

Big Evan was positioned on the golf course, upwind, so that when he played, even the air itself would assist his spell. Unfortunately the skunk smell was coming from that general direction, and I wondered how well he was dealing with the stink. And the amorous skunks for that matter.

With everyone in place, I headed back where Shiloh waited. It was across the road and down the block from Shoffru's house, about a hundred feet away, in a vacant house that was being remodeled from the first floor up, including the windows and doors. Shiloh was sitting at an open space where a door would eventually go, on the second-floor porch, Eli's gun on a tripod that she had assembled like a pro. Southern country girls are no pushovers even before they acquire fangs.

I chuckled under my breath and nodded at the rifle and scope in Shiloh's hands. "Keep an eye on the house. Once the action starts, any vamps who try to escape, you shoot. Humans you can let go." I paused. "You *can* tell the difference from this distance, can't you?"

Shiloh gave a ladylike snort of derision and repositioned her rifle. "I could do that the first day I woke up dead. Prey don't just smell different, they *look* different." I wanted to shudder at her casual use of the word *prey*, but she added, "They look beautiful and desirable and tasty." Her voice went dreamy and dropped into a lower register. "They look like something you want to protect and love and savor as you drink them down. It's just a matter of deciding how to blend all the desires into one, and then take control of that desire."

There didn't seem to be much left to say to that one. "Ick" seemed counterproductive to keeping her balanced and useful to the plan. I settled on "All righty, then." I didn't know her well yet, but already Molly's niece gave me the willies.

A human form was moving slowly down the road behind the house we had appropriated. At this hour, it was either a dog walker, a sleepwalker, or Molly. "Gotta go," I said. One-handed, I swung off the second-story porch and landed on the walkway below.

Pulling on Beast's speed, I skirted through backyards, swung over low fences, and up to Molly. She stood for a moment, staring at me, lit by a security light from a house nearby.

She had cut her hair, and wild red curls danced in the night breeze. Her skin was pale in the dim illumination of security lights. She had lost weight. A lot of weight. She was wearing skinny jeans and a dirty T-shirt with a way-too-big sweater. She looked afraid—shaking, her hands trembling, her heart rate too fast and uneven. Molly stood there, waiting. And I pulled on Beast's eyesight to see her magic. It was no longer vibrant and spangled with motes of power, like rainbows on steroids with diamonds. It was black and dense and pulled tightly to her, as if she wore a black cloud.

Flashes appeared within the cloud, like lightning, but clutched close and well contained. For now.

"Jane?"

"I'm here," I said.

She looked toward my voice and smiled, her face looking lined and more wrinkled than I remembered. "I'm glad I got to see you again."

What? I analyzed that short statement and came to a conclusion I didn't like. "Why!" I huffed out. "Because you intend to end things tonight?" I steeled myself against my next words. "As in jumping off a bridge or something? Because that's just selfish, Molly."

She turned her head to the aside, and I knew what she intended. *No!* Beast screamed, the fear echoing inside me.

Molly turned her head to me, wrapped her arms around her body as if from an inner chill. Quietly, she said, "If I . . . stay around." She chuckled as if that was funny somehow. "I'll keep killing people. And I will eventually kill my husband. My children. I have no choice, Jane. You know all about choices, about sacrifice. After all"—her voice went gruff and cold—"you sacrificed my sister. And my friendship when you killed her."

The wind changed directions and I smelled Molly strongly. And Jack Shoffru, his scent on her, mixed with hers. And I realized she was trying to make me mad, trying to make me go away and let her do herself harm. I didn't respond to her hurt, but to her intent. "Don't be an idiot," I spat. "Because I'm not dumb enough to get mad at you."

Molly dipped her head and looked at her arms wrapped around herself. The smell of shame filled the air, overriding the stink of vamp and blood.

"I also know about running away," I said, "when staying around is so much harder. And I know the happiness, the"—I searched for a word and had to settle on—"the joy when sticking around and fighting things means I get to keep the people I love near me."

Molly seemed to hear that, her head lifting a fraction. "I'll help you figure this out. We all will. But"—I took a deep breath that ached all over at what I was about to ask—"I need your magics, your death magics, now. I need you to drain most of the life out of a vampire for me. I need you to find a way to use the magic that you have right now.

I need you to accept it, control it, and use it. For good. For the light."

Molly made a choking sound. "No," she whispered, strangling. "You can't use death magics for the light. I have to end it tonight before I do something horrible."

Claws scored my gut and I grabbed myself, holding my middle as I broke out into a hot sweat. How was I going to fix this? How? And how did death magic react to the death of the magic user? Would it even let her die? Or would it take her over? Stop her? *Force* her to drain others to sustain itself? Did witch magics even work that way?

Deep inside, Beast growled and leaped to the forefront of my brain. Crouched. Padded forward. I could feel her, pawpawpaw. She stopped and extended her front claws, pressing them into the place where she and I joined. *Beast is not prey to Molly.*

My breath hitched as I tried to figure out what she meant. *You can protect us from death magic?*

The I/we of Beast can do many things. Cannot change her magic. Cannot bring back earth magic. But can keep Molly alive for kits. Can protect the I/we of Beast.

I wasn't exactly sure what Beast was talking about, but I had paused too long already. I'd have to fly by the seat of my pants. "Molly, Magic 101," I said, making my tone demanding even though I was breaking inside at the thought of her taking final steps to protect others. "If you don't use your magic, what happens to it?"

"It dies. It shrivels. It becomes inert," she whispered. "Or . . . or it goes off, feral magics everywhere around you."

"Like your magic is doing," I said, "like it started doing to the woods behind your house, to the flower in your hotel room." She snuffled agreement. "And it may not let you die," I said baldly.

Molly went still, considering my statement. "No. Oh. No . . ." She shuddered hard.

"You have to use it, Mol. You have to drain something or it will kill everything and everyone around you, even from a distance, like it did the two vamps, like it did the humans who got sick and had to be healed. You have a choice. You can practice on the vamp who stole you and hurt you. The witch vamp who wants to kill Leo and take over New Orleans. The witch who wants to use the blood diamond, which probably means he'll reinstitute blood sacrifice, probably of witch children," I said carefully, still piecing it all together. "You can take the steps you're talking about, and let Shoffru win. Or you can help stop him. Your choice. Run"—I meant die—"or play the hand you were dealt. Bring good out of the evil."

Molly took a breath that sounded painful. In the dark, I couldn't see her tear-streaked face, but I saw her hands fist in her dirty shirt. Deep inside me, Beast's claws eased out of my gut. I was able to rise straight. I caught my breath as Molly thought about what I was offering her.

"And if I kill him?" she asked. "If I turn him into a pile of ash like the plants in the hotel room? Like the plants I passed in the yard as I ran away tonight?" She gusted out a sob. "What if I lose control?"

I remembered the wash of blood on the wall, the splatter made as Shoffru lifted Eli and tossed him over his shoulder. It had been shaped like a swan's wing. And I remembered Aggie One Feather's words. Women had the right and the power to claim prisoners as slaves, or adopt them as family and kin, or condemn them to death, "with the wave of a swan's wing." Part of an ancient ritual. But Molly wasn't ready to hear that she was about to become a War Woman.

"If you start to do too much, I'll bonk you on the head and knock you out," I said softly.

Molly stuttered a laugh. She managed a breath that sounded like tires on wet earth, grinding. "Ah, hell." I blinked at the swearword. Molly never swore. Of course, she never killed two vamps either. "I've missed you, Jane. Okay. Okay. I'll do it."

I had a single heartbeat to worry. *Beast, you better be able to do what you said.*

Beast sniffed and looked away, bored.

Boots crunching on the ground, I walked toward Molly. "Don't get too close," she said, the fear making the lightning of her magic flicker around her, the shadows wavering and splintering on the ground.

"Nah. I'm not worried," I said. "We're gonna do a little experiment." I pointed to a container full of flowering plants. "Without killing anything but that, I want you to kill every plant in it."

"That's someone's property," she said instantly. I sighed,

pulled a twenty from my back pocket, and set it under the edge of the pot. "Kill it. Just that. Nothing else."

"I've never done this—"

"Do it!" I snarled.

Molly jumped, glared at the container, and her magic coiled. Like a spring-loaded, compound archery bow, it aimed, released, and exploded with power. Lightning flickered, hot and fast. Everything in the pot shriveled and died and turned to ash. It took maybe two seconds. Maybe one and a half. Molly let a breath out with a whoosh, as if she had been holding it for days. The lightning around her settled into a slow pulse, and I realized that her magic was synced to her heartbeat, her adrenaline, her very life force.

"Impressive," I said blandly. "How did it feel? To use your magic?"

Molly closed her eyes, her mouth pulling down in a frown. She turned away, crossed her arms again, and gripped them in her hands as if holding herself together. "You *know* how it felt."

"Yeah. I do," I said gently. "Say it. Accept it. Own it."

"I." Her voice shuddered. "Don't." Her grips tightened. "Want. To."

"Tough. It's yours. Deal with it."

Molly whirled on me. "What do you know about it? What do you know about *anything*?" The lightning flickered, gaining strength from her emotions.

I hooked my thumbs into my jeans waist, going for moxie and guts over kindness and compassion. This story was getting told a lot tonight. Soon I'd have no secrets left anymore. "My grandma gave me a knife when I was five years old," I drawled. "She took my hand, holding that knife, and helped me kill my first human." Molly stepped back once, her eyes going wide, her mouth in an O. "She was trying to make me into a War Woman. A woman who could kill when needed. Who could go to war with her husband or in his place if he fell in battle. Who could protect her children and her tribe. Who could use wisdom and violence as needed. She succeeded.

"Life is trying to remake you too. So. How did it *feel*, Molly, to use the magic that kills?"

"It felt good. You *know* it felt good. You could smell it on me."

"Yep. Now kill that." I pointed to a small tree. "I'll pay for it."

Molly bared her teeth at me, and Beast looked up, interested. Molly pointed at the sapling. Her magic coiled. The instant she released it, I stepped in front of the burst of death magic. And took it.

It was a gamble. A big one. And if part of the willingness to step in front of a burst of death magic was the knowledge that living without Molly in my life had sucked, and living with her permanently gone would be unbearable, well, I'd have to live with the knowledge that I offered my life to her on a silver platter. Or be dead, if Beast was wrong.

The death magic hit me in the solar plexus like a great big honking fist. I fell to my butt on the grass, rocking back, booted feet in the air. The darkness wrapped around me, burning and tightening, sucking the air out of my lungs.

"Jane!" Molly whispered, dread in her voice. Horror.

"Oops," I gasped. My heart stuttered. And stopped. Agony sat on my chest like a pink elephant. My vision started to go dark. *Maybe this wasn't so smart.*

Beast reached out a paw and swiped, claws bared, catching and hooking the death magic. With an underhanded toss, she pitched the magics away. They landed on the driveway, where they sizzled and burned the white concrete. Flame licked up. And then it was gone.

My heart beat. It was so painful I thought I'd rather go ahead and die anyway. Then it beat again. And I took a breath. And it hurt as if I really had died and come back, fatally wounded. "See?" I grunted, breathless, aching. "Not a problem." Inside I was thinking, *That officially sucked scummy pond water.* But I didn't say it.

Molly didn't approach me. Didn't kneel at my side. She just stared at the blackened place on the white concrete drive. I rolled to my side, and somehow to my knees. All without screaming, grunting—too much—or throwing up. That last one was a near thing.

When I reached my feet, moving like an arthritic eighty-year-old human, I looked at the blackened place. It was shaped like me. I didn't know if that was because it had already latched onto me and shaped itself to fit what and who I was before Beast ripped it off, or if the magics shaped themselves as they were thrown, before they even hit.

"Yeah. Like that," I said, as casually as I could manage between gasps, "except with more control, because I'd like him weakened but still undead."

"Are you insane?" she demanded, eyes wide.

"Probably," I groaned. "But now you know you can't kill me with your death magic." I managed a breath that almost didn't hurt. "And now you know you can control it. Instead of hiding from it."

"Insane. Totally insane."

"You aren't the first person to suggest that." I managed to stand upright.

Molly pivoted and studied another sapling. Pointed at the tree. Her magic was slower this time. More controlled. The tree wilted, leaves drooping, young branches sagging. But it stopped dying at the early-wilt stage. I figured that with enough care, the tree might survive.

"Oookaaay," I said.

"Evan?" she asked. She sounded uncertain, worried, and with the vamp stink on her, she probably had reasons to be worried, reasons I didn't really want to know about.

I shook my head. "He's in place already. You two lovebirds get to make up later." I described to her what I wanted her to do and when she agreed, I finished with "Let's go kick us some undead butt."

She nodded, but halted the action midnod. Her head whipped across the darkness. "He's here," she said. She licked her lips and I could almost feel the desire for blood kicking in. On top of dealing with death magics, Molly was addicted. *Just freaking great.*

"I knew, logically, that there wouldn't be time, but I had hoped to make a run at the house, disable all his vamps, and be in position before he got here. I guess we'll play the hand we're dealt. Come on." I gestured toward the house where Jack Shoffru was getting out of a car, a body over his shoulder.

Ideally, now would be the time to take Eli back, but before I could figure out how to attack five vamps and as many humans, they were inside, the door closed. "So. We'll do it the hard way."

Getting into a house, finding a hostage, rescuing him, and getting out again without casualties was usually a job for a big, well-trained force. We had me. And a few charms Big

Evan had put together for me. I had a look-away charm, a
feel-better charm, an obfuscation charm—the closest thing
to invisibility that witches could make—and a pain charm,
what witches called a curse, one that gave pain instead of
relieved it. I carried spelled and silver-plated knives, silver
shot in my weapons, flashbangs, and some old holy water.
Holy water had worked well one time against vamps, but it
seemed to have an undeclared expiration date. One day it
would work; the next it stopped, without warning. It wasn't
something I could depend on.

My biggest advantage was Eli himself. He wouldn't do
anything stupid to make my job harder. He would help if he
could. And I wasn't smelling his fresh blood on the night air.
That had to be good. It had to be.

Observing the house from the driveway next door, hidden behind a Hummer painted a horrid hue of warning yellow, I adjusted my coms unit on my head and ears. Tapped
the mic. "Kid? Can you hear me?"

"Copy, Jane. Bruiser is on the way over. He can hardly
stand, but he says he's coming for moral support. And before you ask, Tia and I are watching the babies."

"Yeah, okay. That means no rolls in the hay. Eyes and
attention on the job at hand."

The Kid laughed evilly, and I rolled my eyes. Teenagers
can make double entendres out of anything. "Rescuing your
brother," I enunciated.

"I know. I'm just yanking you. According to the house
specs, online with the builder, the ground floor is an open
plan, with the exception of a kitchen and a safe room in
back. The second floor has a game room at the top of the
stairs, four bedrooms, three full baths, including one Jack-
and-Jill-style. Master bedroom is up the stairs, to the right,
at the end of the wide hallway. There's a spiral staircase
from the master bedroom down to the safe room on the
first floor near the kitchen. The stairs can be wheeled away,
sealing the upstairs opening. The first-floor entrance to it is
from the laundry room, off the kitchen, and then out along
the shed in the backyard, through a narrow hallway along
the garage, where another safe room is set up. This one
leads into the garage where a vamp could get away in a
vamp-mobile, even in the daytime, as long as he had a
driver."

A car moved silently down the street and into a driveway, seven lots down. My gut did a little somersault as the MOC glided out of the car. Bruiser, who had been riding shotgun, also got out, moving like the walking wounded. The driver was Derek Lee, who was wearing black camo and who weaponed up fast as I watched. From the passenger side of the back, Gee DiMercy emerged and melted into the night. A sense of relief washed through me. I wouldn't be doing this alone.

"Surprise," the Kid said. "Backup. They all know what you know."

I chuckled softly. "Thanks."

"Yeah, yeah, yeah. Remember this at bonus time."

"Pony ride on your birthday?"

I heard Tia giggle in the background.

"Sorry," I said. I hadn't been aware that she could hear. I was pretty sure I'd embarrassed my partner. *Dang it. Social skills zero.* The Kid gave a long-suffering sigh.

The men slid through the dark like wraiths and up to me, and joy like the morning sun rose in me. We could save Eli. With this group, I could do anything. I smiled at them, and it must have been a brilliant, really good smile, because Bruiser and Leo both hesitated midstep.

Bruiser was dressed all in leather, bristling with weapons. Leo wore a long sword at his side and two short swords. And several knives strapped to his thighs. Derek looked the way he always did—one of Uncle Sam's finest—but I was still surprised to see him here.

I flipped a hand at him in question, and he said, "I always did wanna save a Ranger."

"Ah. So you could rub his nose in it."

"Forever. Ooh-rah."

"Just so long as your priorities are straight," I agreed, grinning. To the group, I said, "The downstairs shutters are closed. We have magical assistance in the tree out back and in the golf course. Don't shoot them. Molly"—I pointed at the house under renovation—"is trying to see if she can pinpoint Shoffru. She sent a search and locate spell inside a bit ago. Since it's dead magic, Shoffru might not notice that magic is being used against him. You know—undead flesh and all that. No offense," I said to Leo.

"None taken, *mon petit chaton avec les griffes.*"

I had learned what the phrase meant. "I'm not your kitten."

"Perhaps. But you hold my soul in your claws, *mon coeur*."

Which could *not* mean that he knew about the binding. No way. Could *not*. Oh, *crap*. Did he know? Something else to deal with later. Much later. "Yeah. Okay. Whatever." Gee DiMercy slid up to me in the dark. I said, "There's a back entrance. Make sure Shoffru doesn't make it to the garage. And maybe you could also puncture his tires?"

"I would be mortified to be assigned such mundane tasks," Gee said. "I will simply kill anyone who tries to escape. Except your human." He slid back into the darkness.

"Okeydokey." Working with supes was weird. "Leo, can you get Shoffru's attention and hold it for a while?"

"Of course. Contrary to his vow to me as his master, he attacked one of my people. I am within my rights to demand a Blood Challenge."

"We don't need to be getting into the middle of a sword fight until Eli is safe. I'd rather you trash-talk him for a while instead."

"You wish me to discuss the garbage industry with him?" Leo was confused and I wanted to chortle but had to settle on a mangled cough. I needed him too much to make fun of him. When I got myself back under control, I said, "Ummm . . ."

"I'll explain," Bruiser said, putting a hand on his master's arm. His former master. Weird. Weird-*er*. Maybe not weird-*est*.

"Bruiser," I said, "once you explain, can you hang with me?"
"Yes."

"Good. Hey, Marine," I said to Derek Lee, as Bruiser explained trash talk to a five-hundred-year-old fanghead. "I got a rocket launcher in the back of the SUV. It's been modified to toss flashbangs. You up to finding a weak spot in the downstairs windows or doors?"

"Hell yeah."

His delight at mayhem and destruction was a bit unsettling, but I nodded anyway. "Whatever. After I reach the second floor, count to ten, then fire. If you can find openings, start left to right. I'll enter the far right room. Oh. There's a headset in the SUV too."

"Copy. Hey, cute dragon, Puff." With an expression of wicked delight, Derek merged into the shadows toward Eli's SUV. Guys and stuff that goes bang I'd never understand, but the reason for that might be as much physiological as anything else. I was also gonna be stuck with a new name. Puff the Magic Dragon, courtesy of the T-shirt. Great. Just freaking great. But not my biggest problem.

As plans went, mine wasn't much of one. Mostly it was distract, make a lotta noise, some bright lights. Evan and Molly outside, one in front, one in back, with their magical woo-woo stuff. Bruiser and me inside, with Leo close behind.

And then I heard the muffled scream. I caught a whiff of something. I was smelling blood on the night wind. I opened my mouth and drew air in over tongue and the roof of my mouth. Eli's blood. I could hear his pained breath, and soft, female laughter. Eli was hurt. Eli was dying. Someone was torturing him. And that someone was enjoying the process.

CHAPTER 23

Hey, Bitch! You Want Some of This?

"Come on, Derek," I said, hearing Eli's ragged breath on the night air. Derek had used some of Eli's fancy equipment to tell me that the Ranger was in a second-floor room, with a human and a vamp. Even without electronics, I knew which window the sounds were coming through. I could smell the blood and hear the pained breath of my partner. I could tell he was gagged. I could smell his pain and fear. "Come on, damn it!" I snarled.

Over the headgear, which the Kid had routed into all of our cells, I heard the others checking in. Big Evan was ready. The girls in the tree were ready. Molly and her niece were ready. Only Derek was left.

"In position," Derek said over my earpiece. "But you'll have to open the shutters or doors. I've been all around the site and there is no, repeat, no, access on ground floor without use of explosive ordnance."

"No bombs. No explosives," I said.

"Copy. But you ain't no fun, Legs."

I knew he was trying to lighten the tension, maybe as part of some battlefield routine, and for the sake of my team, I forced a tight smile onto my face and countered his gibe. "Not the first time I've been told that."

"We can talk about your love life later. Focus, woman. We got a man to rescue."

I smiled for real then, stretching my arm. It was not a

hundred percent. But at least I still had an arm. There was that. "On ten, Evan. Count down."

Evan, his voice tight, started counting up from one. Irritating man.

Casually, Bruiser said, "I can toss you up."

I measured the distance from ground to second floor. I thought about having to use my strong arm to catch myself if I jumped, which would mean holding my weapons with my injured arm. "You think you can toss me up so I can just step onto the railing and drop to the porch floor?"

"Piece a cake, doll face." Which sounded like something out of the 'twenties or 'thirties. The *nineteen* twenties or thirties.

"Ten," Evan said.

"Gogogogogogo," I said.

Big Evan began to play a haunting melody, the flute notes low and sonorous. Air magic flowed toward the house from the golf course. Molly's dark magic began to flow through the air from the second floor's unfinished porch across the street from our objective. Leo, though he practically flew ahead of us, moved at a speed that humans—and witches with spells aimed against vamps—could follow. He stopped in the middle of the yard, his body going from a slow vamp-jog to a dead stop. He drew his long sword, propped it over his shoulder, and grinned at me. His fangs were down. Leo was having fun. The smell of blood and fear on the air was probably making him happy.

Our boots nearly silent on the fresh-cut grass, Bruiser raced in front of me. Dropped to one knee, his hands up high to grab mine. I raced up his body, my feet landing on knee, hip, and his shoulder, my body bent, taking his hands as he leaped to his feet. I leaped with him.

My body straightened, elongated, and I flew up and forward, drawing my weapons as I flew. Bent-kneed, I touched my right toes to the iron banister. With a shove I propelled myself in through the open door. Into the room where a fanghead had her fangs buried in Eli's neck. I landed on the carpet with a double thud.

The vamp-killer took her head almost as if it sliced through the air all by itself. My throwing knife buried itself in the man's throat. Silently, the bodies of both vamp and human went down. I caught the vamp's head in both hands, holding the fangs in place in Eli's throat. Blood, watery and pale, burbled out around the fangs still buried there. Bruiser landed beside me and raced to the doorway, securing the room. I eased the fangs loose and tossed the bloody head. Blood spiraled out from the stump of neck, creating weird patterns on the bedspread. I pulled the charmed stake from my thigh sheath and pressed it to Eli's neck. Instantly the blood clotted over around the stake, a gelatinous glob of blood that spread until it clotted over the entire wound. I raced to a bureau, opened it, and pulled out a handful of folded clothes. T-shirts, maybe. I removed the stake, tucking it into a pocket, and pressed the clothes to Eli's throat. I cradled his head in my palm, the other holding the compress gently in place. He was cold. So cold. *Shock,* I thought. His pulse beat, too fast, an erratic tattoo of movement, beneath my hands.

"I got him," I whispered into the mic. "He's alive. But I can't move him. He needs—"

From the front lawn, I heard Leo shout, "Jacques Shoffru, former Master of the City of Veracruz and Cancún, Mexico, and all hunting territories between, you are forsworn. You will meet me here, now, in Blood Challenge!" So much for the trash talk. He'd skipped it entirely and gone right for the challenge.

"He needs a vamp to heal him. Fast," I finished, in a whisper, knowing it was too late. Eli's heart pumped a single hard thump, then sped with shock. He was dying. His pupils were blown, wide and nearly black as a vamp's. Bruiser slid in behind me and started working the chains holding Eli upright, iron chains, the kind a monster truck would use to haul a cattle car. As if Eli was dangerous—

A shadow flickered in the edges of my vision. One-handed, I grabbed a knife. Threw it. With muscle memory, practice, and pure luck I hit my target. But the compression bandage slipped. I grabbed it as a blood-servant fell, my knife buried in his throat. Blood gushing. Gouting. I'd hit the carotid artery. He tried to shout, but sucked in blood with the breath. Choked. I'd hit his windpipe too. He writhed on the floor, dropping the short sword he had been holding. Trying to pull a gun. Gently, Bruiser took it away from him.

The man died. I remembered to breathe. The air ached in my chest. I blinked and saw the man's bright green eyes, as if burned into my retinas.

Bruiser checked the hallway again and returned to the chains. He loosed the bonds holding Eli upright in the chair. My partner started to slide down, boneless. The T-shirt bandages slid again and fresh blood gushed over my hands. "No! Nononono," I whispered, repositioning the bloody cloth as Bruiser caught him. The blood was so watery, like Kool-Aid, not something to sustain life. *Eli is dying.* Together we eased my partner to the floor. Instantly blood soaked into the carpet beneath him, thin and watery. Fresh and weak. Tears gathered in my eyes. "Nonononono," I murmured, over and over.

"Jane," Alex said, his voice full of fear in my earpieces. "Jane?"

"I can't— I don't know what—"

From the front yard, I heard the clash of steel. The roar of vampires in a duel. "Alex, I need two things. Fast. I need Shiloh here, in this room. And I need Molly to drain the pirate. You understand? Now. No argument. Just do it. Tell them. Or your brother is dead. *Do it!*"

I heard Alex giving orders on the makeshift coms system. I felt more than saw Bruiser leave the room. And it was just Eli and me on the floor, my hands trying desperately to hold in the blood. To hold in the life. His pulse thumped and stuttered and raced. I leaned in and hissed, "Do not die on me. Do. Not. Die." Tears ran from my eyes and snot dribbled under my nose. They dripped onto my hands as I sobbed, trying to be silent. Knowing that if I had to defend him, if someone got past Bruiser and I had to let go and take up a weapon, Eli would die. Right then. "If you die"—I snuffed up the mess on my face and wiped it on the shoulder of the fuzzy purple shirt—"I'll tell all Derek's men you weren't as tough as they are. I'll . . ."

Fuzzy purple T-shirt. I repositioned my entire body and held the blood-soaked wad of compression material over his neck with my knees as I ripped off the T-shirt. It was stupid to remove the compression bandage. "Stupid, stupid, stupid," I whispered. But I eased it slowly back. Blood had pushed past the clot that had formed from the charmed stake. I hesitated for half a second, grabbed the stake from my pocket, wiped it cleanish on my jeans, and pressed it back into the wound. Instant clotting. I wrapped the T-shirt over the wound and tied it all off with the T-shirt's arms, not tight, loose enough to let him breathe. I repositioned Eli's legs up high, a mound of pillows under them. I pulled all the linens off the bed and tucked them around his body to treat the shock. I was thinking now. At last.

A hand touched my shoulder. Bruiser leaned down to me and said, so softly it was less than a breath against my cheek, "Someone is in the hallway. Shiloh has a shot. Stay down." I saw the vamp fall before I heard the rifle shot. It didn't echo far, not on the flat land, but the echo in the midst of the houses was fast and tapping.

On the front lawn, swords clashed. I heard Leo shout, a sound of pain. I smelled vamp blood, and had been smelling it for a while, what seemed like hours, though it couldn't have been more than two minutes. From the back of the house, I heard a scream and the faint snap of a whip. Go, Bliss and Rachael. Just hope it wasn't one of ours.

"Molly says she can't draw the life from Shoffru without drawing it from Leo too," Alex said, controlled panic in his voice. "They're moving too fast and she can't figure out how to separate them in the spell. Jack is pulling through the bond he has on her, using Molly's magic against Leo. And Shiloh can't help you. She says Leo is pulling from her and her new servants, but it isn't enough. She says all of Shoffru's vamps are on the front lawn. They're closing in on Leo." His voice in the earpieces went emotionless and low. "They aren't going to honor the Blood Challenge. They're just gonna kill him."

I cursed. "Okay. Tell Evan to get up here any way he can. Tell Bliss and Gee to help him get in through the back door. Tell them all to get to Eli and save him—I don't care what it takes." I yanked the mic off me and tossed it across the room. To Bruiser, I said, "Cut the light."

"What are you doing?"

"Flying by the seat of my pants." I yanked up the chains from the blood-soaked floor. And stalked out onto the porch.

Below me, Leo and Jack Shoffru fought in a ring of vamps and humans, like a couple of homicidal kids on a playground, both bloody, scored by dozens of cuts. They were surrounded by a nimbus of magic, sparking and red. The reddish magic around Jack was a haze that glittered with black and red motes of pure power. Motes that stabbed at Leo. Burrowing into his skin. It was death magic, Molly's magic. And I knew I could survive it.

Jackie Boy wanted the blood diamond. If Shoffru ever got his hands on it, all hell would break out. Hell on earth. That could not happen. I had to find a way to destroy that thing. Somehow. Later. For now, I had to endure. And suffer Molly's death magics. Again. Deep inside, Beast growled, more vibration than sound, the reverberation echoing through my soul home like a slow-beating drum. Below me, Leo seemed to take heart from the sound and in a move so fast I couldn't follow, he cut Shoffru three times: groin, kidney, and face. Blood splattered across the lawn, black in the security lights. Leo shouted, and I felt the shout through the binding, holding me close to Leo.

I climbed up on the railing, one hand holding the chain, the stronger arm steadying me on the narrow iron barrier. And I picked out Jack's second. A lone vamp stood to one side, the circle of vamps bowing out around the ground she held. Shoffru's heir. She was tall, muscular, with a small waist and broad shoulders, her hair cut short to the scalp. She was armed to the teeth, and those teeth included fangs two inches long. She also had two long swords, one on each hip. And she had a nose ring.

In an instant, I put it together—the reason the scents had never worked for me. The reason the timeline hadn't worked for me. It wasn't Shoffru who took Molly. Who took Bliss and Rachael. Jack had used his heir, pulling strings in the background, letting his heir, Cym—Bancym M'lareil, I realized—do the dirty work. Sending a woman to host a party. To approach women. To take them away. And it was the woman who smelled of the Damours' lair, and who had been working with Adrianna, maybe for a long time. I remembered the look they had shared at Leo's party, long and full of desire. The woman had been working for and with Jack all this time. Jack hadn't been working alone, just by himself. How sexist of me was it that I had never once considered a woman as the culprit? And, for sure, she was part of the magic that was hurting Leo. Somehow she assisted it. I narrowed my eyes and focused Beast's night vision on her.

She was holding a sword in her right hand, the naked blade reflecting a streetlight. She held something else in her left hand, something small. Something shiny.

Blood Challenges are formal things. They almost always, depending on the language of the issuing challenge, required a second. They always had rules. And witnesses. I didn't know enough about them to say if using magic was against the rules. I didn't know if what I was about to do would cause me problems in the future. Or problems for Leo. And I just didn't care. Not anymore. I sought out Shoffru's second, aimed my body at her, and shouted. "Hey, Cym! You want some of this?" And I leaped.

Beast flooded me with her power. In midair I swung the chain over my head. It whirled. And wrapped around her as I landed. With a *clank-snap*, the end of the chain, tacky with Eli's drying blood, caught her. Secured her. Holding to the end of the chain, I rolled, seeing the vamps scatter around me, the ground absorbing the impact of my landing. And I pulled the chained vamp with me. End over teakettle. She dropped whatever she had been holding and I grabbed it up. And I started to burn. Three red motes scuttled through the flesh of my palm and under my skin. Into my blood.

Beast screamed. Her scream shrieked through my own throat, tearing. I tasted blood. I rolled to my feet. With my weak arm, I let go the chain and pulled a stake. Rammed it into the second's heart. She went still. Maybe true-dead, maybe not. But true-stopped. I pulled a throwing knife, my arm aching. My flesh on fire. And I threw it.

As knife throws went, it sucked. The blade flipped in midair, losing power and trajectory. And hit Shoffru in the back, just below his neck on the right side, nicking the muscle before it tumbled to the ground. Shoffru whirled to me. He was vamped-out. Fangs like tusks, eyes like the pits of hell. Terrifying. He let go of the pull on Molly's magic and whipped back his sword to take my head.

Beyond him, in the irregular circle of vamps and their dinners, Leo dropped to his knees. He was bleeding everywhere. Red motes of power scuttled like roaches under his skin. He was dying. Eli was dying. Rick was gone. Molly was as good as gone.

I laughed. It was not what Shoffru was expecting. He

hesitated. Just a moment, a fraction of a second. And from somewhere close, I felt the first touch of death magic.

Black and soft as cashmere yarn, glistening with black stars, it settled on Jack, just as the spell on the throwing knife started to work. From every cut, slice, graze, and scratch on his body, blood began to flow. Bliss' spell combining with the death magic. And as the blood welled, it blackened and fell like ashes on the night air. The two spells working together, evolving.

Shoffru's eyes went wide. He grabbed something on his neck. The lizard. It came away from his body, limbs reaching, mouth open. Throat extended. Glowing red. Pulling red motes out of the air and into his mouth.

Dang. A magic lizard. My laughter bellowed out over the yard. But from my hand, the three red motes reversed course and flew from me, into the lizard. And through its skin and into Jackie Boy. Shoffru landed on his knees, mirroring Leo's fall. His blood ran faster, graying and thickening, taking on texture and form, becoming semisolid, a gel, instead of blood. Beginning to pile on the ground at his knees. He turned to Leo, holding out the lizard, and the red motes inside Leo began to fly back, through the air, hurtling into Jack. He was trying to recall his magic, to heal himself from the spell. Trying to draw power from Cym.

The red motes pierced his skin, entered through his mouth. They zipped around inside him. And as he began to shrivel, they bunched up, in the areas of his heart and brain, spinning like tops. When he began to shift and sift into a pile of gray ash, they were still spinning. And I realized that they had to go somewhere when he died. I leaned forward and tossed the thing I had grabbed from the staked second to the grass at Shoffru's feet. And then I rolled quickly away.

Looked back. It was a gem. Not a diamond. Maybe an opal. A fire opal. Red and glowing with inner heat. The motes dove toward it. Inside it. Leaving their host. And Jack Shoffru dusted to death.

I stared at the gem. Reached over and lifted Jack's shirt out of his pile of granular ash and shook it clean. And wrapped the opal in it. From the ash, the lizard scampered across the grass and right into the hand of Gee DiMercy. Who winked at me.

I was pretty sure no one saw either of us as we confiscated Shoffru's magical implement and his familiar. All attention was on Leo, who had made a miraculous recovery. He was standing on his own feet. And he had a vamp in each hand, forcing them to their knees. "Your master is forsworn. Surrender all rights and power or die," he said. I looked at the second floor and saw Evan. He held out a thumb to me and disappeared back into the room where Eli had been dying.

My partner was alive.

We had won.

Leo was gonna feed.

Oh, goody.

In the far distance, sirens sounded. Lights were on in houses up and down the street. The neighbors had waked and called in the cops. I needed to get Leo into the house or the backyard. I thought of the bodies upstairs. The blood everywhere. This had FUBAR written all over it.

Knowing that the young vamp would hear, I called, "Shiloh. Get our people out of the tree in back, and take Molly and get out of here. Tell Alex to tell all our people to get out of here. Move it."

With a pop of air, she was at my side. "Yes, Jane," she said. "This was . . . interesting. Aunt Molly-Lolly said it would be." I had no idea what she saw on my face, but she laughed. "We're going." With another pop of displaced air, she was gone.

I looked over at Leo, with no idea of how to get him to a safer place, one where law enforcement wouldn't try to arrest him for what he was doing. Human cops wouldn't understand the dominance, neck biting, and bloodletting taking place. From the corner of my eye, I saw Derek with something over his shoulder, carrying it to Leo's car down the street. I hoped he got to it in time. Cops would arrest a brother in a heartbeat for carrying a headless body. Arrest first, convict later, ask questions never. I looked up at the window where Eli was. War Women were fairly useless when it came to saving people, but I wanted to be with him anyway.

Bruiser walked across the dark yard to my side. As if reading my mind, he said, "The healers are with Eli. They have him stabilized, but it won't last. I've called for the priestess to help heal him." The sirens I had been hearing turned in, drawing closer, the combined wails heralding at least four cruisers, maybe as many as six. We had a circus on our hands. "I'll get Leo to the back," Bruiser said.

I looked at the MOC. He currently was drinking from a male vamp, and one woman was kneeling in front of him. I did *not* want to know what she was doing. "Yeah. That might be a good idea."

He grinned, teeth gleaming in the night. "Remind me to tell you later how splendid you are. How extraordinary. And how beautiful."

"It would have been even better in the mud, dude," Derek said, jogging past. "But for chick-on-chick fighting, it wasn't bad."

At which point I looked down, to see that I'd fought the last battle in my ripped bra and a pair of bloody jeans. *Go, me.*

CHAPTER 24

Some Kind of Whammy

The hours before dawn sucked. My people got away just in time, taking with them the guns and ammo, the dead vamp and the human I had killed, and the human Shiloh had shot. Leo took his new people to the backyard. Derek tossed me a black T-shirt as he drove past, so I wasn't bare when the police arrived, though I smelled strongly of Derek for hours after.

The cops arrived with lights and sirens, a mixed bag of city cops and sheriff's deputies, which drew all the nosy neighbors out of their houses to the street, rich, older humans in their jammies, talking angrily about the peaceful neighborhood and the evil supernatural types disrupting it all. And generally getting in the way. The cops got in the way too, wanting to know where all the blood came from, and why Eli was nearly dead, and what kind of vamp ceremony was taking place in the backyard at the pool. They tried to stop the elder vamp priestess, Sabina Delgado y Agulilar, from getting to Eli, and one actually drew his service weapon. Bruiser started calling in lots of favors at NOPD headquarters and to the local sheriff to get the police to stand down. Tension was ratcheting up fast.

But the old priestess had little tolerance for human law or conventions. Instead of waiting for Bruiser to work through channels, she put some kind of whammy on the neighbors and the police, which was surely captured on the footage from the cop car cameras. There was nothing I could do about that part; Leo would just have to deal with it later. But whatever she did, the neighbors went back to bed and the cops were suddenly all smiling. They got in their cruisers and left. That wouldn't be the end of it, but I took what I could get.

Sabina got Eli fully stabilized, his throat healed over, and his blood supply reestablished, but it wasn't enough. He had lost too much blood and she was afraid that he would turn. Eli would have hated that. So I made the decision to call an ambulance and take him to a human hospital. The transport and paperwork were speedy, and the doctors efficient. Eli was pumped full of other people's blood, four bags full, in just a matter of hours. His girlfriend, Sheriff Sylvia Turpin, showed up and took over, shoving me out of the picture, which worked perfectly for me. He had a bunch of new scars that he needed to explain to Syl, and since they might technically be my fault, I wanted to be long gone. The only good part in it was that at least I wasn't having to tell her Eli had died on my watch. The Kid let me know that by ten a.m. Eli was griping about being released, which had to be a good sign.

While dealing with the cleanup at the house on the golf course, I received confirmation from Leo's lab that the poison on the weapons wielded by Clan Arceneau's jailbirds was indeed Jimsonweed. Which opened up a whole new area of concern for me. What effect the poison might have on me—on a skinwalker.

I also received final proof, way too dang late, that Shoffru had indeed hosted the coming-out party at Guilbeau's, a situation I was going to have to remedy. Part of security for the vamps and humans in the Big Easy would mean, in the future, that a social secretary would schedule everything. Not that the vamps had a social sec. That was something they would have to deal with later too. All that took way too long. I was exhausted as the clock neared noon, and was tired of the dried blood crinkling on my skin and the stink of Derek caught in his T-shirt. And just plain tired. Tired to the marrow of my bones.

When I got home, it was well after noon, but I discovered on my bed a note on a fancy card, in a fancy envelope. Vamp-fancy, which meant calligraphy and high-bond paper and even some gilt. In the note, I was given orders to appear at Katie's. "Posthaste," the little note said, which would mean my very first ever meeting with a vamp during the day. That the vamp was Katie was a bit scary. And meant no nap for me.

I took a fast shower, put on clean clothes, so no stench of blood clung to me, and my vamp hunting gear for self-protection. I texted Adelaide Mooney that I had been summoned. She called me back quickly and made some recommendations.

Politely, still digesting Del's comments, I knocked on Katie's door.

Troll, trying to look unworried, let me in and secured the door from sunlight. I was about to ask him what the summons meant, but Katie appeared at his shoulder with that little pop of air that meant she had traveled fast from her lair, and since her flesh wasn't smoking from contact with sunlight, I knew she had been in the lair that I had helped to design and build, in this house, under the stairs. She was dressed in a floor-length brown dress, her blond hair down and catching the lights. She looked human, not vamped-out. I figured that was the best I could hope for.

"Katie," I said.

"Enforcer," she said back. Which was not a fortunate start to the interview, centering on my job to protect vamps and follow orders. Which I hadn't done. "You have news about the ones who took my servants and your friends. News you did not share with me."

"Yes." And those *ones* would be Jack and Cym. I took a steadying breath and drew on Del's counsel and legalese. "I found them last night. The ones who took your girls and fed them to a newly freed scion are dead. And the girls have become blood-servants of one of Leo's newest scions, Shiloh Everhart Stone, and they are all well again from the magics that were making them ill. But you know all this. So I'm thinking you really wanted to tell me something else."

Katie said, "You have done well to find and destroy my enemies. I commend you. I shall provide the standard form of financial remuneration. I approve."

"Um. Well, actually, Leo killed one of them."

She smiled and it was a truly terrifying smile. "He did.

And he did this for you. Use caution, little cat, that you do not stalk what is mine."

She meant Leo. And *aha. This* was what she had been wanting to say. "He's all yours, Katie. Honest to God. All yours."

Katie's fangs snapped down. "Remember that. *Leo* is *mine.*" Behind me the outer door opened a crack. Katie threw up an arm against the light and I got out of there fast, through the door that Troll had opened. Sadly, that was the high point of my day.

As I swung over the back fence, the Kid and Tia and the children were heading outside to play—which was grown-up talk for getting out of the line of fire. When I entered my house, it was to walk into the middle of a huge fight between Molly and Big Evan. Evan was standing in the middle of the living room, his hands fisted at his sides, the air swirling around him, lifting his red beard, shuffling through his clothes, his magic activated, but contained, for the moment. Molly, less than a third his size, with her weight loss, was standing at the entrance to the kitchen. Her dress hung perfectly still, her hair a spill of rich color, unmoving. Her hands were relaxed and still, her magic tight against her skin, a dark shadow of potential. Of the two, Molly looked far more dangerous.

"—tell me you were on the pill? How could you not, Mol?"

"Because she was afraid the death magics would interfere with the baby's development, or with the childbirth, or with something else equally horrible. She was afraid of giving birth to a magical monster or killing the child in her womb. Right, Molly?"

My friend gave her head a tiny nod, one I might have missed had I not been living with Mr. Infinitesimal for the last few months.

"She was also afraid of hurting the children, or draining you in your sleep. She was hoping to find a way out of the problem, but when she heard about Shiloh being alive and in danger, she put her troubles behind her and came to New Orleans. It was stupid, and it was bad timing that she got taken before she could get to me for help. It was also stupid that she didn't tell us about her magic going bad and let us help her find a treatment or cure, but she wasn't cheating on you. And stupidity isn't a crime."

Molly shot me a glare. Big Evan didn't take his eyes from his wife, but his face turned even redder. "You talked to *her* about all this and you couldn't talk to *me*?"

"She didn't tell me anything, you idiot." I could have been a bit more diplomatic, but I was tired, my house was full of angry witches, and I couldn't just leave them to it and try for a nap. I might wake up with the house on fire. Or dropped on top of one of them, a pair of ruby slippers sticking out. I grinned, imagining the glittery pumps on Big Evan's humongous feet. From the look on his face, I probably shouldn't share the vision with him. "I figured it out. Molly loves you guys with all her heart. She wants her magic back. Or a way to control the death magic. And—" I stopped. It was possible that I had a way, if I could get the familiar back from Gee DiMercy. Or if—

Something launched across the kitchen at Molly. Molly whirled and lifted her arm. Evan raised both of his fists. "No!" I shouted. They both stopped. The kitten landed on Molly's shoulder. And meowed. A lot of things flitted through my mind, like Aggie's mother's prophecy and Molly's desire to be her old self, and lots of old stories about witches and cats. Puzzle pieces settling into place. "When I was a kid, in the children's home, before I understood English, I was standing somewhere, maybe in a kitchen, watching some girls put a puzzle together."

Big Evan looked at me as if I were insane. "*What?*"

"Yeah, I know. Weird, huh? Anyway, I had no idea what a puzzle was." The kitten on Molly's shoulder arched her back and walked around to her other shoulder. Molly held perfectly still. Eyes wide, fingers spread. As if she was afraid to even breathe. "I didn't understand. Not for, like, two days." I shoved my hands into my jeans pockets, talking, watching Molly and the kitten. It put its cheek to her and purred long and steadily. "But I knew it was important, it had to be because two of the girls I lived with were so totally focused on it, like, the way a mountain lion focuses on prey when she's hungry and has kits to feed. Anyway, on the end of the second day, they put the last piece together and they got up and left. They left me alone with the puzzle. So I walked over and looked at it."

Molly smiled slightly and reached up to touch the kitten. It started to purr and Molly gathered the kitten in her arms. KitKit settled against Molly's chest, and her purr ratcheted up, echoing, the rumble far too loud for her size, seeming to fill the whole room. Molly took a breath, let it go. And the black cloud of energies wrapped around her began to lighten.

"I knew there was a pattern there," I went on. "I could almost see it in the greens and reds and yellows. But I didn't understand humans or two-dimensional pictures. Or most anything at that point. But as I stood there and studied it, I realized what it was. It was a kitten, crouching among some potted flowers, hidden in the board. Trapped there. I didn't understand about pictures yet. But I did understand about traps. So I started taking the puzzle apart, trying to find a way to free the kitten."

Big Evan's eyes filled with tears as he watched his wife. The fine trembling of her fingers eased. She took more breaths. And her smile widened.

"It was the wrong thing to do, of course," I said. "I was never going to free the kitten. It wasn't really trapped. But it was all I knew to do. Culturally, educationally, emotionally, I did the only thing I could. I pulled up each piece of the puzzle and looked at the table beneath. Then at the back of the puzzle piece. There was no kitten anywhere. I sat down and studied the puzzle. And I slowly put the picture back together. I realized it was like a spell, a moment of magic captured in the paper, printed on the puzzle pieces. And I enjoyed the moment, the moment of . . . the kitten, crouching beneath the flowers."

I relaxed. "Kinda like what just happened here. This moment of magic. Her name is KitKit. An old Cherokee woman gave her to me. I gave her to Angie Baby, but I'm sure she'll share the gift with her mother."

"Familiars are rare, if not totally fictional," Big Evan said, as if trying to make sense of what we were seeing. "Witches keep animals, not for their magic, but for their love of animals."

"Yeah. Maybe. But this animal is absorbing Molly's death magic." I shook my head and grinned, picturing *Lisi's* face when I told her about her KitKit. "Somehow, some way."

"It won't be enough," Molly said, bumping her nose to

the kitten's, "not by itself. But it's enough for now. It gives me a chance to learn how to deal with it, without hurting someone by accident."

Big Evan's fists unclenched. His stormy air magic quieted. He crossed the room to his wife and gently folded her in his arms. Her head didn't even reach his chin, and he had to drop his face down to place a kiss on the top of her hair. "Okay," he said. "We'll do it your way. I won't fight you anymore."

I had no idea what they were talking about, but it sounded promising, so I let it go. Then Molly raised her face and kissed Big Evan. There was a lot of passion in the kiss, so I got the heck outta Dodge, leaving them to some privacy. In front of the house, in the heat of the day, I removed my weapons and secured them in the back of Eli's SUV, all but one throwing knife—just in case some angry blood-servant wanted to try to take me out.

And then, having nothing else to do with myself, I got in and drove.

I ended up at the little church where I had attended a few times since I got to New Orleans. The place was quiet, seemingly empty, and I checked my phone for the time and day. And discovered that it was Sunday, well after noon. I locked the SUV and went to the door, knocking before I entered. Most churches stayed locked when not in use, against vandals and thieves, but the door was open, and I pushed it wider. Inside, it was cool, and I realized how hot it was outside. But it was cool here. Boots thumping on the worn floor, I went to the little chapel. It was empty but smelled of humans and peace and acceptance.

I took a seat in the front pew and stared at the cross hanging on the wall. It was the empty cross, not the cross of the dead Jesus, and that was obscurely comforting. I had seen too much blood in the last day or two. Even redemptive blood, the kind Aggie One Feather talked about, was something I didn't want to see right now.

When I was growing up, counselors in the children's home were always talking about redemption, especially to me, because I was always in fights, stirring up trouble, though at the time I had seen my actions as protecting the helpless and the bullied, and in hindsight I'd have done nothing different. Early on, I hadn't understood why the counselors had wanted me in Christian training classes, why they talked so much about salvation. I didn't understand what I needed to be forgiven for. But even back then I had understood about peace and the lack of peace. And I had accepted the kind of redemption that brought peace, the kind that brought *me* peace, or as close to it as I ever got.

Now? I wanted that peace I had lost. I wanted to forgive myself for the lives I had taken, knowing full well that I would take more. I wondered if soldiers felt this confusion, this mixed-up, complex, complicated, crazy set of drives— for peace and for battle. For rest and for blood.

I was War Woman. I was *meant* to kill.

But . . . I was never meant to enjoy it, to take pleasure in it. My *uni lisi* hadn't taken pleasure in the deaths of the men who killed my father. It was a job, a responsibility, and she did it well. That was all. That was what she was trying to teach me when she put the knife into my hand. That lesson was my obligation—to see that I performed my job well, for good and for life, not for death. Weird as all that seemed.

I closed my eyes and sought my center, my core, the dark place in the midst of myself that was my soul home. Here I found a peace of a sorts, though it was far from the peace of the soul that the redeemer brought. It was a cavern, dark and damp, smelling of flames from a dancing fire. And the redeemer had never been here. There had never been that kind of peace here.

I opened my eyes to see the flames, to smell the burned, dried herbs, sharp and astringent. In the dream state, I was dressed in deer hide, tanned in the old way, the way of the *Tsalagi*. The leggings brushed against me as I walked, to my right, toward the shadows, my moccasins tied tightly to my feet, making my passage silent. I was carrying a blade in my right hand. A steel blade, exactly like the one *Edoda* carried in the memory of the fish gall and the lesson learned. It was oft honed, the cutting edge curved and sharp and promising death. I carried it to the niche in the wall, where the black big-cat slept.

The black cat—not truly a lion, but something else, something known only to my dream state—was not without defenses, even here, in daylight, should I try to hurt him. But I had no intention of hurting him. I only wanted to free myself from him. I could let my anger against him go. I could find that much peace.

With my left hand, I reached up and touched the mountain lion tooth that hung around my neck on a leather thong, and I entered the gray place of the change. There, in the gray, flashing energies of the skinwalker, I bent and took the silver chain that shackled me to Leo Pellissier and I cut it with the steel knife. In the way of dreams, the metal parted easily, falling into two pieces. They landed on the floor of the cavern with a clanking rattle.

Leo opened his lion eyes and stared at me. "Jane?" he said.

"Yes. You are free."

And Leo thinned into a mist and smoked away, the air of his passing smelling like sweetgrass and cedar and papyrus. The smoke rose in a spiral and touched the curved ceiling of my soul home to spread slowly on the calm air.

His passing left my soul home cleansed, like the burning of aromatic and bitter herbs.

I turned slowly, knowing what I would see behind me. Whom I would see.

Beast was on a ledge, at head height, stretched out, chin on her paws, her amber eyes watching me. "I'm not a killer only," I said to her. "And I've gotten used to you being here. Even if it makes me insane, I'd like you to stay."

"I/we should be together," she said aloud. "We are much more than Jane and *Puma concolor* alone."

It was the first time I had really heard Beast's voice. It was softer than I would have thought, and purring. Not unlike Molly's familiar. I reached out a hand to Beast and scratched her behind her ears. The purring increased in volume. "Molly is in danger still," Beast said. "KitKit is not enough to contain her death magics."

"Yeah. I know. But you are."

Beast chuffed with laughter and closed her eyes. And I woke in the church. It was still empty.

Silently, without speaking to anyone, I left the church.

Twenty-four hours after the battle on the golf course, I woke. Angie Baby was cradled against my stomach, curled as a kit might curl against Beast's pelt. Her breath was regular and even, her lips making little popping sounds with each exhale. She smelled of strawberry shampoo again and, oddly, of pancakes. EJ was curled on my pillow, his entire little body at an angle to ours, the covers rucked up over him. He snored slightly, softly, smelling of little-boy sweat, dirt, and peppermint candy. The bed was a haven of warmth and home.

I rolled over, careful to not dislodge the children. I stretched, and thought back over the fight the night before. It had been horrible. We came close to losing it all, the entire territory of New Orleans. And we still might if the European vamps got involved in local affairs. Word had come giving us a date for the arrival of the emissaries, and a list of their expectations—not demands. That would have been too crude a word, not that I could tell the difference between the two. It seemed the EVs were not happy with the American vamps, and Leo's growing in power and influence was a problem they needed to consider. Whatever. Someone would deal with the diplomatic crap. Not me, but someone. The real problem was the impression that the EVs left, that they wanted all the magical items that had come to light in recent months. And they wanted info on, and research done into, the Soul-like thing that had attacked me, the thing that nearly killed an Onorio. The impression was they wanted to capture it and take it back with them, along with all the magical mojo items. Yeah. Not gonna happen. Magical stuff and vamps were problems. Usually big problems.

The magical items in Jack Shoffru's possession were things that Leo had feared, things that Jack held over Leo. Not knowledge of crimes past, or a loved one imprisoned somewhere, but magic that Leo had figured he might not defeat without calling on the might of all the clans. And maybe even then, losing all the clans, all that power, to Shoffru in a transference as he was killed true-dead. But at the first possible opportunity, Leo had chanced it. Because Bruiser was there. And Molly. And me. And because Jack hadn't been ready for the challenge, assuming it would be a far-off, distant fight. Sneaky, that early challenge. And maybe a bit stupid.

I didn't *want* the stupid reason for the challenge to be that Leo believed in me. Or because he owed me. Because he . . . *liked* me. But maybe because he knew I had magic of my own that might counter Shoffru's? I had a feeling that was part of it. Yeah.

We had been really, really lucky back at the golf course house. Really lucky.

I had been a lot less lucky in other ways. I remembered the feel of Leo holding me as I cried, his arms stronger than a human's, but cold as death. Holding me because my former ex-boyfriend had become my once-again ex-boyfriend. Dumb. Stupid. I had been both dumb and stupid to let myself care so much about Ricky Bo.

Rick was out of my life, and I could accept that now. *I could*. And if a still, small voice, one that liked drama, continued to whisper that he might come back, I could ignore it for the dumb, stupid thing it was.

There were things I still had to deal with, like the betrayal by Reach. Or the supposed betrayal. Technically, our spy *could* have been someone else. It just wasn't very likely. And I needed to determine if Cym, hiding under a don't-see-me, don't-smell-me charm, had drunk on Tattooed Dude when he was in captivity at Leo's, and killed Hawk Head, which meant looking through hours of slo-mo security camera feed. I kinda hoped the mystery vamp was Cym, because I'd rather it be her than the alternative: Leo had enemies at HQ, but hopefully all of them had scent signatures.

I had managed to tell Katie that I had killed the kidnapper of her girls—the woman with the nose ring, Shoffru's heir and partner, not a witch like him, but a former human carrying a potent forget-me magical charm. I'd forgotten her all along, but once she was dead, I remembered every time I'd seen her. Every time she had done something that affected me—like exchanging Molly's pillows and towel in her hotel room. On my first visit, the original ones had been white. On my second visit, the used ones had been cream. Visual clues like color were things I tended to miss. I relied too heavily on scent and motion. I needed to work on that. But mostly I was just glad to have survived Katie's demands.

And we needed to clarify the timeline of the events that led Adrianna—who had her own plan in place from the day Grégoire left for Atlanta—to merge her plans and her goals with Shoffru's, because that's surely what had happened. Nothing else made sense.

All we had so far was: Jack discovered the Damours were dead. Jack wanted the blood diamond. Jack hired an investigator—likely Reach—and found the gem was in

Molly's hands. (Except it wasn't.) And the investigator discovered the identity of Shiloh E. Stone, something even Leo hadn't put together. And so Jack got Molly to come to him, then took Molly, and then took Shiloh and Katie's girls. And in there somewhere he had found Adrianna and convinced her to work with him to mutual goals. I was sure there was a lot more.

Overhead, I heard the floorboards creak and placed the sound as coming from Bruiser's room. He was up and moving early, getting ready to do whatever it was that Onorios did. Maybe saving the world. Maybe he was dressing in a cape and tights. Which—unlike seeing the Kid in such a get-up—I would pay to see. *Oh yes.*

Eli and Syl were in his room. They had been remarkably silent, for which I was grateful. The Kid had been sleeping on the couch, his tablets on his chest, moving with each breath, when I went to bed. I figured he was smart enough to still be there.

Across the hall from him, Molly and Evan slept together. They had been closeted alone there since KitKit joined them. I wasn't stupid enough to think they were sleeping the whole time. The house had thin walls and thinner floors. The rest of us had made a lot of noise several times, turning up the TV, clattering pots and pans in the kitchen, to give them privacy. I was gonna tease them unmercifully about it later. Like much later. Like tomorrow.

For now, I snuggled deeper into the linens and closed my eyes in sleep.

ABOUT THE AUTHOR

Faith Hunter was born in Louisiana and raised all over the South. She writes full-time and works full-time in a hospital lab (for the benefits), tries to keep house, and is a workaholic with a passion for travel, jewelry making, orchids, skulls, Class III white-water kayaking, and writing.

Many of the orchid pics on her Facebook fan page show skulls juxtaposed with orchid blooms; the bones are from roadkill prepared by taxidermists or a pal named Mud. In her collection are a fox skull, a cat skull, a dog skull, a goat skull (which is, unfortunately, falling apart), a cow skull, the jawbone of an ass, and a wild boar skull, complete with tusks. She would love to have the thighbone and skull of an African lion (one that died of old age, of course). Faith recently bought a mountain lion skull, and it rests on a table below the enormous painting of Beast in her living room.

She and her husband own thirteen kayaks at last count, and love to RV, as they travel with their dogs to white-water rivers all over the Southeast.